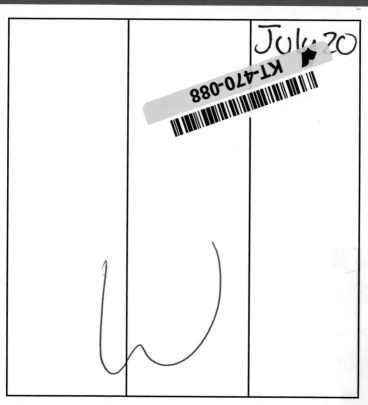

July 20

KT-470-088

This book should be returned/renewed by the latest date shown above. Overdue items incur charges which prevent self-service renewals. Please contact the library.

Wandsworth Libraries
24 hour Renewal Hotline
01159 293388
www.wandsworth.gov.uk

THE BRIGHTER BOROUGH
Wandsworth

THE TREATMENT

THE
TREATMENT

Michael Nath

riverrun

First published in Great Britain in 2020 by

riverrun

An imprint of

Quercus Editions Limited
Carmelite House
50 Victoria Embankment
London EC4Y 0DZ

An Hachette UK company

A CIP catalogue record for this book is available
from the British Library

Hardback ISBN 978 1 78747 936 4
Ebook ISBN 978 1 78747 938 8

10 9 8 7 6 5 4 3 2 1

Typeset by CC Book Production
Printed and bound in Great Britain by Clays Ltd, Elcograf S.p.A.

Papers used by Quercus Editions Ltd are from well-managed forests and other responsible sources.

To Sarah Tabrizi, Jean Nath, and Jacqueline Tabrizi (1940–2015)

Reputation of power, is Power.

Thomas Hobbes, *Leviathan*

There is usually no *ressentiment* just where a superficial view would look for it first: in the *criminal*.

Max Scheler, *Le Ressentiment*

Of all things he counteth it a mighty disgrace to have a man jostling by him in haste on a narrow causey and ask him no leave, which he never revengeth with less than a stab.

Thomas Nashe, *Pierce Penniless*

DRAMATIS PERSONAE

Carl Hyatt

a *Chronicle* journalist, and the teller of this tale

Karen Tynan

his second wife, and dark lady: a northern teacher

Lolly Morris

her friend and colleague

Goldie

Lolly's cousin

Gina

the bohemian proprietor of the Tiresias club

Lord Larry

another bohemian

Cassie Evans

and another

Angie Pole

a dynamic friend of Karen's

Mother Jago

a wise woman from Karen's childhood

Víctor Hanley

a flash and fluent lawyer

Milly Hanley

his wan wife

Esme

their daughter

Donna Juan

(aka 'DJ')

a scholar and sex worker, major-domo at Lords

Pep *and* **Albo**

his fellow workers at Lords

Roadie *and* **Atlas**

two of their chums

John Fabian Morgan

(aka 'The Cunctator')

a one-eyed stand-up humorist

Turbo

his minder

Eddie Singh *and* **Terry Ireland**

old pals of Morgan's

DI George Arnold

(aka 'Big Ears', 'Scopic' and 'Geordie')

an ex-copper

DS Charlie 'Chas' Bowler

his dark driver

Michael John Mulhall

a seasoned brigand and developer

Mandy Woods

his daunting sister

Van Spenser

a South African pimp

Raymond Vernon

an Anglican priest, and former landlord of The Bosun and Monkey

Bobby

his assistant

Sibyl Grove

a riddling woman

The Gonk

an elderly busker, and nark

Paulie Charalambous

a barber and whisky-man

Tyrus

his buff boss

Arsenal Cap

a tech guy

Gunther

a Nantucket-Red neighbour

John Waugh

a supplier of Olympic anoraks

Ellis

a fruit-and-flower stallholder and proxy journo

Andy Ravage

a rubicund newspaper editor, Carl's boss on the *Chronicle*

Mandy Ravage

his wife

Fabiana

his right-hand woman and loyal lieutenant

Colin

a photographer

Mayor Montgomery

a Tory mayor

Sandy Clinch

a council officer

Steve Barnfield

a Labour councillor

Marcia Jones

his Kiwi girlfriend

Zac Cumberbatch

a slime-o councillor

Meredith Jhaliwal *and* **Conor Gard**

licensing inspectors

William Cook

a travelcard tout, and witness to a cover-up (deceased)

Beefburger Mike

his neurologically damaged friend

Frankie

his girlfriend

Scotch Al

(aka A-No. 1)

a compassionate fellow tout

Mad Max *and* **Yardling**

his further associates

Earl Holmes

a bully tout

Gunga Baines

a tout of Brixton

Laura

Carl's absent first wife

Edward

his son by his first marriage

Nigel

his brother

Frankie Sly

an antiques man, and influence on Carl

Alison Sly

his alarming niece

Craig Norman

Carl's former boss on *The G********

Justin Fox

a young intern

Saffron

his girlfriend

Alexander Brons

a boyish editor on *The G********

Camilla First

a posh and hearty lawyer

Ellis McMahon *and* **John Dragonheart**

former colleagues on *The G********

Eldine Matthews

a murdered youth

Carson Marshall

another murdered youth

Nate Nulty

a murdered accountant

Mick de Lacey

The leader of 'L Troop'

Pete de Lacey

his brother and lieutenant

Vincent Drew *and* **Alan Roche**

the convicted murderers of Eldine Matthews

Danny Flowers

their craven associate

Julie Flowers

his wife

Robbie Woods

(aka the 'Sixth Man')

a well-connected psychopath

Jeffrey Gidney

the landlord of The White Cross

Andy Sargeant

The leader of the 'Young SS'

Tony Cass

his lieutenant

Josh Rider

a wanker

Norah Field

a trainee WPC

Claire Sykes

her former colleague, a greenhorn undercover cop

Kim Perry

her contact

Marcus

Kim's boyfriend

Gemma Cook

the owner of a hair salon

Sally Roberts

her employee, and pal

Julie Webb

their client, and Claire's spitting image

Bobby Singh

Julie's boyfriend

Lola

a Spanish restaurateur

Joe Pordio

an old Spanish bum

Magnus

a Norwegian widower

Rico Flores

a pargeter

Luna

his girlfriend

DS Chris Butler

a swearing copper

Dillinger Ismaél

a hopeless thief

Fatty Donovan

an Australian

Paloma Friendlikova

a litigious Russian

Sveta Sekshenko

a Ukrainian cleaner?

(all of them associates of Victor Hanley)

Instructor Alex

a Krav Maga trainer

Liam X. *and* **Sammy Y.**

two hypothetical Irishmen

Tony Friend *and* **Noderick**

two thoroughly useless criminals

Ady Beaumont *and* **Deano**

two separate childhood tormentors

Coroner McQuaid, Sir Horace Grinter, Jonas Kubb, *and* **The Honourable Mr Justice Aubrey Clarke**

various members of the legal profession

PART I
Murderers

CHAPTER 1

S O WE WENT TO Lola's again and ordered *al piedra*. Lola brought the gear, and came back with the meat, watching as we laid it on the stones.

The stones hissed.

Lola's hair was skillet black, outfit combat black; she wore a little apron where stains hid. '*Tienes que vivir al límite!*'

'Ha ha!'

She said so again and walked away. My Spanish stunk. On Google Trans I looked up Lola's words. 'You have to live dangerously!'

Blood formed little runnels on the flesh; as the meat cooked, they darkened and went.

In the kitchen Lola cackled with her guys.

'You should have tipped that sea-dog,' Karen told me. Late afternoon at the long beach, we were looking for a short cut. Factor 50 on her mush, slap running, that was Karen, living dead from Manchester morgue. No way was she walking up the road. There was a path through the Parador but you needed the code, so we came under the cliff, past a hut where old boys were drinking. When I asked about steps to the town, one of them took us where the beach curved. A wave soaked his plimsolls, nearly put him on his arse. I told him *muchas gracias*, he kept with us. There were the steps. How d'you say *You can go now, pal?* We mounted together. Near the top, our fella dropped back. We'd reached a terrace. By a cannon of rotting bronze, a man tensed his throat, silver head shaking as we turned to say *adios*. Fifty yards out, there was a brown slick; a girl frothed for camera on a platform rock . . .

'She wasn't a bride. That was her communion dress.'

'Ah.'

'I never had one like that.'

'You weren't pure enough.'

'Was till I met you — God, these are hot!'

Brown-aproned Lola flew past, down the step. On the terrace, she was dealing with someone. No shit. Back now grinning at favourites.

On the way to the apartment, we stopped at Charo's. I ordered Karen a Bushwacker, reminding the *camarera*. Behind the jump, she told the bearded guy, who knew us and nodded. Charo's was a snug, dark box. Could have settled there forever. You know how you miss a place already, like it harbours the spirit of the holiday? At the second taste, Karen closed her eyes, tiny pulse in the lids. Her right leg came into play. Tonight she wore a mauve-silk cheongsam. Locals and Irish were watching football: Lazio–Tottenham. They'd checked her when we entered. I told her she'd inflame 'em; we had some persiflage. She wanted another.

The barman stared at TV, shaking his head. Crowd trouble. I saw a banner: 'FREE PALESTINE'. '*Fascistas,*' said the barman. '*Putos fascistas!*' Our *camarera* brought the cocktail, and a boot of lager for your pleb. Mussolini's team were Lazio. Ultras. *Irriducibili.*

Sucking brown cream, Karen was telling me off about postcards, of which she'd sent a number, and I hadn't. Spurs cop it time and again, this kind of treatment. Foul. We could go to the caves, couldn't we? Which ones? Gas-chamber hiss when they visit West Ham. The caves Lolly recommended. She'd told me so many times! Really, really wanted to see them — so could we?

4

Sure.

We could take a picnic.

*

'MAYBE IT WAS THEM cocktails, Carlo.'

Overnight she'd been throwing up, on the half-hour, two till five-thirty. Fucking awful. An argument against God, seeing someone like that. And hearing. In my view, the Bushwackers weren't to blame. She had a fever. After a visit to the *farmacia*, we made it to Abril's.

'You can't have slept either.' She patted my hand. 'Are you feeling all right?'

'Yeah.' I ordered iced *aguas*, coffee for myself.

'*Qué tal, amiga?*' The *camarera* was a stately young woman in black dress trousers, with a wide enchanting mouth. She could have come straight from opera, big-band rehearsal.

'She was sick last night.'

'Sick? *Ay – devolver!* There is a virus. Very bad.'

'Here?'

'Yes. *Mucha gente –*' flowing gesture from the mouth – '*por aquí. Mucha gente.*' She waved at someone, shook her head. 'No omelette today?'

Give her a trumpet, let her blow, Daddio!

No omelette. Around us they were tucking in: train-wheel tortillas, saw-mill chip stacks, lager, bacon, long, complex salads. Karen swallowed. The *camarera* adjusted our parasol. I wouldn't eat either.

'I don't think I'll make the caves, Carl. I'm sorry.'

'Don't worry.'

'But today was our last chance.'

Over there, a man tapped his phone.

'We can come another time.'

5

By the cannon, wasn't he, silver-haired.

'Do you promise?'

The man tensed his throat. Today he wore a shirt of pink checks. A blonde expat came to ask about pargeters; he took his time, named a man in Calahonda; the expat went away. He tapped some more, drank of his beer; the *camarera* brought him olives. He took his time with them too; looked about like he was counting, caught my eye:

'You should take the lady to the caves.'

'We'd like to, but she's not well.'

'Where'd you eat last night?'

'Lola's. – I don't think it was the food, though.'

'Don't you?' Shaking head. 'What do you think it was, then? Something in the water?'

'The waitress said there was a virus going round.'

He sniffed. 'Ain't heard anything to that effect.'

'Well, it feels like a virus!' Karen said.

'Where's the evidence?'

'I know what I've got, pal!' Karen told him.

He watched her: 'Just said it felt like a virus. Now you're knowing.'

'Well, I've decided!' Karen told him. *So stick that up your arse, cock!* She'd row with anyone, all five-foot-two of her. Friend was giving me the hump as well, sitting there in Prada with his olives, and dry laughing way.

He tapped his phone. 'Local newsfeed. Nothing about viruses.'

'What have you got against Lola's? It's our favourite place.'

'Never suggested I got anything against Lola's. Eat there myself, once in a while.' He tensed his throat. 'Not my favourite, by any means. But I ain't reviling it.'

'I should think not!'

Under the table, I tried to find her foot.

'You were swimming yesterday?' said our friend.

'Yes.'

'Saw you coming up the steps with Joe Pordio.'

'Who?'

'The old boy you was with. – There's an outfall just off the long beach. Water ain't too clean.'

'Ugh! How disgusting! They ought to tell people!'

'Exactly,' said our friend. 'It won't do. Which is why I was advising your husband here to take you to the caves. Pure air in there, very pure. Nice and cool, too. Just the job if you been down with the gastroenteritis.'

'But the water's so lovely, like stained-glass.'

'Now that's a choice way of putting it, that is,' nodded our friend. 'Are you a poet?'

'Get on one! I'm a teacher.'

'Very good. Teachers are a necessity, whereas poets are a luxury. I put my poetry books away after school, and to be honest, I never looked at them again.'

'But poetry's important.'

'If you've got the time.'

'You could always read a poem, instead of tapping on your phone.'

I wished Karen'd cool it.

'Maybe I ain't got the inclination.' Tensing his throat.

'Well I've heard the caves are poetic!'

'Who d'you hear that from, you don't mind me asking?'

'My friend's been here a few times.'

'And she told you like?'

'Yes. She loves them.'

'What would her name be?'

'Lolly Morris.'

Our friend hummed, said the name.

'Well, you don't know everyone, do you?' laughed Karen.

'Oh no! Course not, dear.'

'Do you live here?'

'I have got a place. Yes.'

'Lolly says the caves are full of monsters – and weird shapes.'

'The caves are OK, dear. All the monsters are out here in the sun. And your weird shapes.'

'See! You could have been a poet!' cried Karen.

'I go by experience, babe.' Nodding at me. 'Don't know nothing about poetry!'

'We'd better be off now.'

'You ain't making the caves, then? You'll be sorry!'

'Next time.' I looked for the *camarera*.

'I'll get that,' said our friend. 'On me. – No. Please. Hope I didn't cause offence.'

As we stood, he said, 'Try Bales. Town end of the Calle Carreta. You'll like it there. – Hey, son! Careful! Your shoelace!'

He bent to pick up something as I tied it. We hadn't introduced ourselves.

*

WE SPENT THE AFTERNOON on the balcony. The flavour of cigs from below reminded Karen of her grampa, reading the *Bury Times*. A vigorous reader was Grampa Tynan. Better iron the evening paper when he was done, if you wanted a turn. The apartment under ours, a Norwegian called Magnus took on a long let, autumn to late spring. Magnus was a widower of ten years. I wished I'd never be one, moved the shade to keep the sun off her. It was coming as a reflex from a window opposite.

IN A BOOK I used to read my boy Edward, there was a road like the Calle Carreta. You could walk from a front door on to it, for the pavement was narrow; the road was narrow as well. Counting tiles upon the houses, their little infinite patterns, I went along . . . Say a jolly farmer on a tractor came down here, you'd be well fucked, son.

Why should I like Bales? Karen briefed me to expect a den of tarts, but it was a mixed crowd: locals, families, well-behaved kids, Brits who could speak decent Spanish, Brits taking photos of their plates; selected English papers on a table by the door; more Brits. The hanging ham whiffed like a changing room, so I went outside. Outside was too dark to read. When I came back, eyes were on me.

Déjà-vu headline, two mugshots: hazel-eyed man, Teutonic, hair receding; blue-eyed man, potato face, hair receding. Vincent Drew and Alan Roche, convicted of killing Eldine Matthews. Top left, repro box: 'SUE US IF WE'RE WRONG!' Christ, but that took bottle! Three to go. Sleeping easy now? Inside were twelve pages of reports and analysis. When we were kids at the barber's, we devoured the men's mags; so I read now, but my hot dreams were of libel . . . Karen texted: feeling lonely. Folding the paper, I drank up and left.

At the town end of the narrow road, she texted with a wish, so I hied me back to the ice-cream place, and bought her three *bolas* of yoghurt. Down the way, a taxi was idling.

There was a sound system in the apartment. I found her lolling creamily, in an emerald nightdress. She was listening to *The Firebird*. The last bit choked me up, which I didn't let her see. I wondered if Magnus could hear. On the side, the yoghurt melted. The taxi wasn't necessary.

Before we left for the airport, we went to the terrace. An old man was making nets. As if a god threw dust in handfuls, sun sparkled on the waves below.

'Half close your eyes,' Karen said, 'then it looks like dancing stars. It's so good when you're feeling better. Worth being ill for. – Promise we'll come back, Carl?'

Yeah. We took a selfie. The black-and-tan cannon was below me, out of sight. *Mr and Mrs Hyatt and their Dog.*

CHAPTER 2

LONDON. AFTER FOUR, THE rain paused. In the mews I had a word with Sibyl Grove; the cobbles shone like rows of liver. On the high street, someone called my name. By The Tavern, that was Hanley; how long since I'd seen Hanley?

'Look like one of us, *paisano*!'

I told him we'd been in Narixa. Glinting, he suggested the pub. There was something he'd been waiting to tell me. Before we were through the door, he'd begun . . .

So his man's pulled a Russian in the West End, taken her back. They've necked a bottle of Grey Goose, shared a fentanyl patch he had over from a rugby injury. His man's crashed. Russian bird's rummaging his DVDs. When he comes round, she's cheering at *Zulu*, munching ham from the packet. Through the front door they hear another Slav. This being the cleaner. Who's changed her day for a hospital appointment. Which he hasn't remembered. Russian expresses desire to leave, scowling at his *pinga* like so. Problem. He hasn't locked the door, since he hasn't left for work, so the cleaner's now locked the mortice trying to open it, and he's overlocked it from the inside. Our cleaner's howling one way through the letter box, his man's arse naked howling back, Russian's howling blue murder. It's a howling bee.

Hanley began to roll cigarettes.

Our cleaner's chagrin increases. She's on lock-out for a Russian black-leg, while Paloma Friendlikova, her understanding is he's invited a Ukrainian hooker round for a three-way shazam – and does she not like that! Gives his man the treatment, exits drainpipe left.

His man lets in our cleaner, she's putting egg-white on his injury (folk remedy) when the police arrive. The magistrate, Sir Horace Grinter, is dubious about the welter of complaints (theft, assault, false imprisonment), especially given the state of his man's left eye; the way Friendlikova sucks her teeth under cross-questioning; and the following facts: (1) a neighbour heard her shouting *Front rank, fire!* with gusto at 6 a.m. – not a peep from his man; (2) her 'stolen' Louboutin pump's been found in the moat by the janitor. Nonetheless, Horatio's requested a postponement, pending evidence from a locksmith that reasonable attempts were made to open the door once Palomakova expressed the desire to leave.

'Why's she cooking this up, though? Why bother?'

'The Russian? One of these turbulent people.'

'Didn't your cleaner testify?'

'Keeping her for the postponement.' Hanley glinted.

As I rose to get us another, he said something I didn't hear. From the bar, I considered Hanley. Moustache, short beard, gold glasses; Hackett suit and good suede brogues. Life seemed a splendid fit for this gent. I knew him from the courts. And times I was hobnobbing with the Crime Squad, he'd be spieling, drinking Kronenbourg, in the snugs and back-bars of London Bridge. The cops called him Zipmouth, Groucho, puzzling why a fast-talking brown boy's name was Hanley, not Mendes, Singh or Cruz, nor Patel, Kuldeep, Bobby Santos. Those were the days when such things counted. Someone used to call him Master Claypole.

'You still at *The G*******?*'

'No.'

He knew. In a fancy pewter case lay his new-born fags.

'How d'you know?'

'Someone was talking about it at Snaresbrook.'

With a full glass, I could hardly beat it. I asked him who was.

'There's a clerk over there called Jonas. He was telling me.' With sad devilry, Hanley glanced about.

'Jonas who?'

'Jonas Kubb – K-U-double-B.'

'Never heard of him.'

'No reason you would, *paisano*. He was giving me the broad picture.'

'What did he say?'

'That Mulhall obtained a master's injunction, and someone at *The G******** breached it.' Hanley sat there like a fixture in my gallery. This glinting busyness, had I really forgotten? So friendship makes its claim.

'He said it was me?' By now we'd come outside for a cig.

'Someone like you. – By the way, you never made it to Milly's birthday.'

Nice of him to change the subject, though this took me by surprise: I'd no memory of an invitation (none of Milly either).

'Told her all about you, boysie. She wanted to meet.'

I apologized, Hanley was gracious, and desiring to smoke in unbroken rhythm led me round the corner from the high street, gazing upwards at an ornamental oddity on the roof of The Tavern, which I'd noticed often enough in my lazy way, without benefit of such explanation as he now furnished, like a bright schoolboy showing a visitor around – though it wasn't me who was visiting.

So was he still living in the same place?

Hanley was, and of course didn't name it, since I should have known already, then helped me, since he could see I didn't. The place was World's End.

We were neighbours then – in the metro sense. Though what he was up to down here drinking pale ale invited explanation. From the Magistrates' Court he'd named to his home wasn't that far, but it wasn't this way either, unless you'd made a detour on purpose.

'I like to walk home different ways.' He saw what I'd been thinking. 'Like Dickens.'

'I've heard he was a walker.'

'He'd walk to Kent and back, he had something on his mind, *paisano!*'

'Why Kent?'

Hanley acted startled by my question: 'Kent was his turf, wasn't it!'

Oh yeah. I watched Hanley's mouth. Should have been making for harbour. He seemed to be on to Dickens's lawyers: Copperfield and Traddles, Carton, Jaggers, Tulkinghorn, Lightwood, Wrayburn . . .

'Who's Wrayburn?'

'Eugene Wrayburn, *Our Mutual Friend*,' Hanley advised me. 'Another great walker. He spends hours sporting with a stalker.'

'How does he do that?'

'By walking stalker off his feet. Then he tricks him by popping from an alley and laughing in his face.'

'Who laughs in whose face?'

'Wrayburn laughs in stalker's.'

'Does he come out on top?'

'Not immediately. Gets his head kicked in.'

While I considered this, Hanley waved with his cigarette. Where the road beside us forked, was a little cabin. 'That's changed!'

'That was Van Spenser's.'

'You're right, *paisano*! His sandwich joint. Ever sample his wares?'

'No. You?'

'Once. Once only. Years ago. Prawn-Peri-Peri-and-Pineapple sub-marine. Made me shit like a sandblaster. Had tickets for the theatre that night.'

'To see what?'

'To see nothing, boysie. Spent forty-eight lashed to the khazi, like a dungboat captain in a tropical storm.'

I wondered about Hanley's interest in Van Spenser, who'd gone up in the world . . .

'He ran hookers,' remembered Hanley. 'Had them in there making baps, travelling girls. If he caught them chucking food away, he lectured them about the townships. When they'd had enough of that and his groin pressure – you can see how narrow it is – he sorted them with kiosk cards and introductions. Which he called "promotion".'

It had a jaunty seaside air, that cabin. Nowadays, it was occupied by a hefty-handed Arab in an Arsenal cap who unlocked phones. On the roof, a gull settled. I was making with departure phrases when Hanley pointed over the main road at the Tube: 'That's changed as well!'

I agreed.

'The foyer, I mean,' Hanley expatiated. 'Twenty years ago, it was a scene, street people, drinkers, touts.'

The lurking places had been eliminated.

'Fancy another?'

'I have to get home.' Text from Karen: *Where the bloody hell . . .*

'Okey-doke.' He looked away. 'Oyster did for them.'

'For who?'

'The travelcard touts. You don't remember William Cook?'

'Can't say I do.' Following his gaze to the underground.

'William Cook. Scotch Al was A-Number One, but William was some *hombre*. Craziest tout under the sun. Poor bastard. He was a saint, a prince!' Hot-eyed, Hanley bowed his head.

I could have asked about William Cook, but here came a young man with hair in fierce braids, taking up a lot of pavement with his arms.

'Hey, Turbo! *Qué tal?*' called Hanley.

'Smooth, boss,' Turbo told him. 'Is you wanting see J. Fabian?'

'Not yet,' Hanley told him.

'Luxe,' said Turbo. 'No disrespect, but Mr Fabian, he said he got bum-ache tonight so he's cancelling; you wants to go round, the man'll make a special effort, VIP like.'

I took my chance and got out of there, leaving Hanley with Turbo on the kerb.

CHAPTER 3

CROSSING THE FLYOVER, I spied the black-haired lad, waving steam from a potato in the hypermarket café. I got lunch for myself, Andy, Fabiana. At the customer-activated terminals, you had the future: loiterers, code-men, loblolly boys. To keep her employed, I paid the check-out woman. In mulberry leg-warmers, the black-haired lad went past. The check-out woman gave him evils. Outside, he said hi. It was raining again.

We stuck the curries in the office microwave, and Fabiana turned her iPod to communal. The microwave roared.

'How about this?'

'Fab, can you turn that down. Carlo's got an idea.'

'I'm trying to!'

'Not the microwave oven! The music!'

'Stop yelling!'

'I've got a diesel in one ear, Lady Dovo in the other!'

'It's stuck!'

'Here's the idea. I hang about with a rent boy for the day.'

'Carlo!' laughed Andy. 'You aren't trying to tell us something?'

'There's a joint up the road. You must know it?'

'Where?'

'The mansions.'

'He does know,' Fabiana said. 'He's being coy. It's that man one, isn't it? The molly house at the top. Penthouse conversion.'

'Molly house?'

'Old word, Andy.'

'That's the one, Fab. It's called "Lords".'

'Coo!'

Andy, our editor, chewed a while. 'D'you know the rent boy?'

'He always says hi.'

'But what's the story, the issue?'

'Something edgy?' Fabiana wore boots like the Chevalier de Recci and a gold-foil puggaree. She looked ready for anything, except work. Who could blame her? *For once*, she meant, by 'edgy'. The nearest she got was editing Ellis's 'Shout-Out'. Ellis owned three fruit- and flower-stalls on the high street, prime spot, sponsored by Collingham, Clarke and Murrain, an estate agent near the unlocking booth that used to be Van Spenser's bap shanty. Like tents at a medieval tourney, his stalls bore the CCM standard and flag. Once a week, Ellis sent a local entrepreneur's opinions to the *Chronicle*, which Fabiana edited into a column, a task that required skilfully preserving Ellis's 'saltiness', while minimizing the range of potential offence. For this, we received a donation from CCM; and when Fabiana or I passed the south stall, Ellis, leaning from his campstool in Chelsea-blue gilet and deerstalker, handed us a punnet. He said nothing; we didn't either. On grounds of transparency, Andy refused to pass the stalls. He was editor. While he pinked for honour, and tried to explain why kickbacks were acceptable when soft fruit wasn't, we chewed bumblebee peaches. Say he was caught on someone's phone with a melon he hadn't paid for . . .

'It's community interest.'

'In what sense though?'

'Come on, Andy! You know you want some kuff stuff,' Fabiana told him. 'It's your mission.'

Like a kid saying no to sweets, Andy Ravage smiled. But he was a big lad now, and to that smile his size gave force, as it would to the day he cut loose (should that day come). He looked round where we sat. Where we sat was all we had. Rum premises (perched on a flyover). Before people started reading match reports on MSN and the Audit Bureau decided his circulation figures didn't count anyway, he'd been a decent editor on a sports supplement in the Midlands. With his severance pay, he set up the *Chronicle*. He was told he'd never draw advertising, sponsors. In fact, he reeled in enough to pay the three of us properly. There was something about him people wanted to invest in. If 'Big Society' meant much, maybe it meant something like Andy Ravage, the way he took on life; giving his all, then giving more, with a face that challenged you to laugh in it. Worrying now about business people, local politicos, Collingham, Clarke and Murrain, their interests, sensitivities. Though never a word of a promise I'd made – too big for that.

*

COMMUNITY INTEREST WAS ONE thing. I had a hunch as well, and a grudge. Late afternoon, the black-haired lad passed me in wellingtons, sack on his shoulder. He didn't say hi. I watched him enter Pom-Pom's, hung about by The Khartoum. A German came to see the window menu. As the chef skimmed the mince, I heard a little talk and the two of them were off. Bitch! I'd been blind-sided.

From the window of The Tavern, I could keep an eye on Pom-Pom's. He'd be back for the laundry. Rain on TV, people rowing over England. I fell to thinking of Mulhall. When you feel yourself doing that, Karen told me, you must breathe deeply, empty your mind, imagine nothing.

That's what you've got to do, love. Twice a week, her pupils had meditation time. She got them to imagine nothing as well, though that was a way of giving them a handle on cosmic microwaves. And Mulhall abhorred a vacuum. The TV showed England's group for the Euro. If Gerrard didn't smile, and Rooney stuck to a diet of radish, who knew how far we could go? Really was as open as that. The Spanish were tired of winning . . .

> For Mulhall was a Kentish man,
> And killeth one or three,
> But when the intern came along
> Mulhall did smile for glee . . .

It's a top twenty entry . . . The lad with black hair still hadn't come along for the laundry when Karen texted. Homebound, I passed two covered girls, discussing *Mein Kampf.*

*

IN KAREN'S 'DEDICATED' AREA was a decorated screen. Her pals at The Tiresias bought it for her wedding. They'd loved her; and though she never returned, painted with a shimmering woman 'in the manner of Moreau', the screen must have been a reminder. Maybe wished herself still there. Well, I'd promised to improve, and be truthful. Over the screen hung dresses, indigo, crimson, forest-green. The truth about things just bought online called for a particular dispensation, however – as I'd discovered. These sessions flattered judgement, in return for attention.

Here she came in the first, dark trim at collar, lace flowers below. My verdict made her happy.

The crimson made her look like a French murderess.

Bingo!

Forest-green I couldn't recommend.

Pray why not?

Why-not gravely submitted.

Straight back with that, lad!

Here she came again, in violet-blue.

Verdict expatiated.

'Really! I thought I could wear it to the Mayor's thing. You said we should go. Don't make a face!'

The Mayor rode round the borough in a big hat, gathering comments, complaints, and cakes, in the basket of his push-bike. His Town Hall Levee was obligatory, for those without money, distinction, power-pals, whose working lives depended on sponsorship, adverts, micro-grants, or an inglorious office on the flyover.

In the red alcove, we adjourned for tea.

LOLLY WAS HAVING GRIEF with two lads in Black Flag T-shirts.

Wasn't uniform compulsory?

They wore them under their shirts. In class, they were permitted to remove their blazers, but it had been that muggy, their shirts were unbuttoned, right down like this.

Did they know she was Jewish?

They'd got wind of it. They were forbidden to wear political badges or motifs, of course. She was supposed to warn them – and write to the parents if they did it again.

What age were they?

Year 10.

Were they Middle Eastern?

One of them. The other was a white lad.

Why hadn't she warned them? Lolly was an anxious strawberry blonde, with a laugh that sometimes took me by surprise.

She was collecting evidence on Tapestry. (Tapestry being a Prevent resource.)

We discussed procedure and personal dignity for a while, till I started going off on one. Karen said the fish pie was a brahma. I mentioned the proposal I'd made Andy Ravage.

'You aren't bi-curious, are you, Carlo? I wonder sometimes!'

Ho ho. 'That's what Andy said. It's a human-interest thing. People want to know what goes on up there.'

'Which one is it?'

'The one in the mansions.'

'There? Everyone knows what goes on! Where have you been, cock? You're that naïve.'

'Everyone knows, no one does either.'

'I'll tell you exactly what goes on with these boys and boogs.' Karen sat back in her chair, and did so. I could have blushed, for both of us.

'Bit of an expert, aren't you?'

'Not particularly. D'you want pudding?'

'You're probably spot on, but what about the background?'

'What d'you mean by that?'

'More to these boys than their jobs.'

'As long as it isn't going to lead you-know-where. We've had enough of that, Carl. Really we have.'

'I know, sweetheart.'

'It isn't, is it?'

It wasn't.

We watched a thing Lolly'd lent Karen about the Olympic Deliverance Committee, clever, funny, merciless, then began to talk about this and that, fashions of the past, like the post-New Romantics, when young men took to suits, and eyeliner, ladies to cocktail dresses (something like the ones she'd been modelling before tea), and they danced as if they were stoking boilers. You had to hunt in vintage shops or Oxfam for clobber like that in those days. Online hadn't been heard of.

When I was witnessing a *revolution* in style, she was confined to bedroom, park, or Arndale – or visiting a curious old woman. So she liked hearing of those times, as a child enjoys the memories of Grandad.

We sat and listened to the rain. We didn't have much space here, but were happy enough. When my first marriage went west, and Laura took wing with Edward, I downsized, but remained in the area (as if that proved anything). So Karen consented to save me – from myself, and detestable practices.

Let me be your Shunamite!

Fucking hell, babe . . .

CHAPTER 4

A YELLOW-TROUSERED MAN PISSED IN the corner. 'Poor flowers!' cried Donna Juan. We sat on someone's bench at the far end of the mews. The houses had portable gardens, in barrels, troughs, pine boxes. 'You don't want to come up with me?'

His hair was dyed goth but he was daintily tanned. Today he wore a green hat with broadish brim, white blouse, leather trousers, flip-flops.

'Can we just talk?'

'That's cool. Some guys like to talk.'

As we looked across the cobbles at the high street, he recited the names of flowers: fuchsias, hydrangeas, clematis, in a frame like Skeffington's Daughter.

'Why d'you always say hi?'

'Say hi to lots of people.'

Ah.

'But especially to you!'

'Why especially?'

'Cos you've lost your way!' He laughed, hand to mouth.

'Where are you from?'

'Punta Arenas!'

'Argentina?'

'Chile, silly! – Furthest south you can get a manicure.'

'Really?'

'Sucker! I'm from Halifax!'

'I thought you sounded like a Yorkie.'

'How can you tell?'

'My wife's from the North.'

'Your wife? What's her name?'

'Karen.'

'You have to make out you're from South America, Naples, Rome or Ivory Coast. They'll not have tykes or Geordies at Lords. Imagine!' He lit a Dunhill International, offered me the box.

'Thank you.'

'*De nada.*'

We smoked and watched traffic and shoppers pass, far end of the mews. It was a solid cinema, projector behind us.

'Me name's just John really. The boogs who come up, they don't know a word of Spanish anyway.'

'What are they like?'

'Like everyone. Including you. Some are *repugnante*. Not that you are. We get a lot of lumber. Like, "*Qué quieras, Señor?*" Don't even know what you mean. They're just, "Uh, can you diddle me, son?" Their kegs are a crime against humanity. Had a right walrus this morning. His sac were oven-baked!' Donna Juan laughed shrill.

'Are many of them straight?'

'That's what "lumber" means.'

'Ah.'

'Didn't you know that even? Grandad!'

'Not the word.' Let them teach you.

'You can tell 'em coming down the road, thirty yard off.'

I knew.

'How d'you know?'

25

'Cos they watch the distance.'

'Why d'you think they do that?' Donna Juan drew a figure 8 in the air. Smoke rolled.

'They don't know the territory. They're looking for the address. And for people they wouldn't want to bump into – a friend of the wife, that kind of thing.'

'Mr Observant!'

'I'm a journalist.'

'Oh my God! Is that why're you're talking to me? Betrayal! Just after the celebs, aren't you? *VIPs*.'

'Thought you said it was just boogs? Boogs and lumber.'

'Told you it was everyone. Need your ears de-waxed. Everyone. *Todo el mundo.*'

'I'm not bothered about everyone.'

'Who you bothered about then?'

Sibyl Grove came out like Drag-a-Chair. Turning to the sun, she lit a Superking. Over the road was Eiger Essentials. On the step, a sullen Saxon watched the distance.

'It won't do, that thing squatting there,' called Sibyl Grove. 'He's lodged now. Too late.'

'Who is he? A busker?' Sometimes he carried a guitar case. Today he had a Tyskie and car battery. The hair that fell to his collar was the colour of piss-stained pants.

'He's a bleeding gonk, that's what he is. Nasty piece of work.'

I'd happened on him once at Embankment. On the escalator he rose into sight, cursing Poles like a guild-play patriarch.

'Lives on the other side of the mansions. In that authority house. Free.' Sibyl Grove continued her complaint.

'I thought you and me were meant to be talking!' Donna Juan hissed. 'Not her!'

'What did he say?' Sibyl turned about in her chair. 'Your boy?'

'Nothing. We better get some lunch now, Mrs Grove.'

'You should do something in your paper about things like that. You should campaign!'

'Who does she mean?'

'Not you!'

'Who is she anyway? Her tan's *horroroso*. Looks like an orange.'

'She's lived here years. Knows a lot of stuff about the area.'

'Where are we going?'

'What d'you fancy for lunch?'

'Could I have a Rodeo-Burger?'

McDonald's was just round the corner on the high street. On the step, the Gonk now had a megaphone. Donna Juan returned to the question of who I was bothered about anyway, to be talking to him, so I said I'm bothered about you. Tell me about yourself, how you got into this, tell me your dreams.

'What dreams?' Wiping his mouth with his napkin.

Remembering something Karen'd said about the boys, I asked if he wanted to be a model, for example.

'Model? At my height! What a divvy question!'

'OK! D'you know where you're going?'

'Yes I do, thanks very much. Unlike you!'

'Where?'

'The Dry Valleys. That's where!'

Once upon a time, he'd been a Geography student. He was taunted about his voice, his nails, being queer. Posh whites skipped behind him like they had a rat up their arse. Faith students gave him evils. They called him 'batty kaffir'. He heard lecturers joke about him after he'd been to collect handouts (he had sharp ears). So what if he wanted to wear lace? They were cool with the other minorities.

One night he went to the bar. They were waiting for him on the three-step by the Mandela Ramp. Spat in his face and said he should be gassed, him and his kind. All giggling and snarling in his face. He smashed a bottle of Brahma neck first, striped their hospodar. Then of course they backed off. The parameds arrived in a trice, three cars of cops. He got four months at Lancaster Farms, with demmicks and micro-gangsters; the m-g's gave lectures on stabbing. When he came out he was a non-person, studies suspended. GBH with intent. The uni said he'd never been enrolled.

'You want to continue your studies?'

'Only the fieldwork!'

'Can I see you again?'

Donna Juan gave me a mean look: 'If you're honest with me.'

The Gonk was bawling –

> 'Day-O!
> Day-ay-ay-O!'

Turbo went by, sucking his teeth.

*

ON AN EVENING WHEN Karen was at the music hall with Lolly and other pals, I was hailed again by Hanley, who must have used up his stock of different ways to walk home, and was rubbing his hands, on the understanding we were bound for The Hank of Rope to eat pies, chops, or what d'you say to a mixed grill, guiding me round the corner and down the way. To make up for missing Milly's party, I went along.

The Hank of Rope was down the left of that fork where Van Spenser used to trade, on a quiet road that led to a bulwark of houses. Behind them was the Westway, over there Tyrus's place. Like there'd been no interval, Hanley continued his talk of William Cook, as we entered and found a pleasant corner . . .

William having been a tout, though not the type with a flat cap, big wad, tickets for Take That. William lived on carbohydrates, and he dealt in travelcards, hitting on passengers as they came through the barriers.

So he'd nagged for used cards?

'You remember him, *amigo*? Lanky-white fella, furrowed-face.'

Couldn't say I did. When was this?

'95, '96 – thereabouts.

Weren't there many such hustlers in those days?

Many such. But William was the paladin. If he drew blank at the barriers, he dogged you on the steps, floated at the entrance, watched for card in hand, dive-bombed, tracked and turned, aieee! The staff were on to him, but William, he was everywhere.

What was the law on touting at the time?

The pies arrived. Eating busily, Hanley went on.

Not for resale was printed on the front of a travelcard, on the back, *Purchasing tickets from a ticket tout could result in the buyer being prosecuted.* Say William got hold of a three-pound fifty Zone 1-&-2, he'd take a sheet. Nagged for two, two-fifty, but he'd take a sheet. For a 1-to-6, he'd trade higher. Then he hung by the machines, spying what passengers were minded to purchase. It was subject to Byelaw 20 if he was on station premises, as he typically was (different status outside), though for various reasons (e.g. evidence-gathering, small sums involved in individual instances) prosecutions were comparatively rare, civil or summary. For instance, it took D-Day planning between underground staff and BTP to nick a single tout, the notorious Gunga Baines, at Brixton around 2001. The general idea was to discourage touts such as William, see them off. But of course, back he came like Elastic Man.

Different if he'd been aggressive, like Earl Holmes. London Underground took an injunction to keep Earl Holmes from the foyer at this
time, on account of the way he spat, jostled, made fists, bawled for
pussy.

'That the fellow in the white scarf who stands outside Paddy Power?'

'Sounds like Earl Holmes,' nodded Hanley. 'He's still about?'

'Yeah. Saw him this evening. Eating sweetcorn and hissing.'

'Well, the injunction only stipulated twenty yards from the Tube in
either direction. Standing there, he's legit.'

'Your boy William wasn't aggressive?'

Not in any of the worst acceptations. William accosted, importuned,
got in your face; but he caused neither fear nor disgust. People chatted
to him, or advised him to fuck off. Hanley'd witnessed this. So advised,
he sprang away, as a hosepiped cat, or vampire at dawn's first light.

Hanley chewed at the last of his pie and mash. He was right. Class
fare: Steak, Red Wine, Stilton.

Other touts, drinkers, runaways – Scotch Al, Mad Max, Yardling –
they scored William, shouted points. Passers-by, idlers, locals, louts,
joined in. The staff began to dig him. Livened up their day, didn't he?
They eased off with the sweeps, the dragnet, let him have his stage.

And that was how William moved. But his vocals were something
else. Hanley glinted.

'Say he's trying to flog a One-to-Four to a tourist . . .

'"Yowsa, yowsa, yowsa! Northern Line to Hampstead Heath. Marvel
at the skyline and the tussock where Wordsworth composed his cat
poems which your dream holiday in London ain't complete without
seeing performed by humans at Shaftesbury Av. via Leicester Square,
Northern Line, only seventy sheets a ticket, but before you leave the
Heath don't forget to explore the bushes and have your jacksie twanged
for free, providing you're nice-looking, lads only – sorry, ladies! You'll

have to wait till you get to the West End, where a dapper white boy who tells you he's a banker with a big apartment and a NASA TV treats you and your mate to cocktails and when you wake your clothes are all ripped and your holiday's ruined and your life's ruined. Remember, only with your Zone One-to-Four!

'"Or take the Bakerloo, Circle, Metropolitan, Snark, Pomeranian or Jubilee lines for Madame Tussaud's where you can dally among the celebrities, twats and abusers and actually touch 'em without getting your head kicked in or shoulder dislocated by a minder with a big nickel bracelet, then head for the café and discuss how real they look over a steaming plate of gherkins and fine cheese – and don't forget, they'll be remembered forever unlike you toe-rags whose only purpose in life is to shell out a commodore to come and stare at these much-loved entertainers and dictators, so I suggest you sneak back in with a box of Swan and light 'em like candles. How? Use your fucking shoelace for a wick! Ram it in their head with your thumb, darling! They're only wax. You got trainers on, ain't you?

'"Make your way eastward on the District Line to the famous Tower of London, built by the French to commemorate their murderous adventures between here and the borders of Kent. We didn't want it in the first place and they can fucking take it back whenever. Linger over a steaming sausage bap as you marvel at the little brown chair where Joe Jacobs sat with a broken ankle when they shot him through the heart for spying. To this day, the Doncaster Tower is used for banging people up cos they think *Silent Witness* is shite and they ain't paid their TV licence. They are paraded every day at three p.m. in their rags – BST only, terms and conditions apply. On November afternoons, the ghosts of the Kray Twins may be witnessed in the Old Kent Keep, murdered by their Uncle Altab for being a pair of twats and he's never had any thanks for it, which is a national scandal. Shudder as they proceed along the stones of the Inner Hall shadow-boxing. But we would ask you, ladies and gents, not to accept cigarettes or other 'souvenirs' from this spooky duo. And remember, only with your fabulous Zone One-to-Four, for the joke price of one pound fifty from your Uncle William!

'"Change for the exciting Docklands Light Railway with its authentic tweed-lined carriages. The driver may not turn up cos he's getting pissed on sherry with his cousin in Rochester, but the trains are remote-controlled from a heritage office in Poplar-under-Shadwell where qualified personnel and youth trainees shunt 'em round by monitor, and they go so slow anyway that even if you're in a head-on, you'll get out of it with a green-stick fracture. As you move east above the city, gaze down on Canary Wharf and the Isle of Dogs where the dockers of Millwall slaked their honest thirst at the Piccaninny Arms. They was once the redoubtable supporters of one of our most colourful English eccentrics, Enoch Powell, the first cabinet minister to cross Pakistan by hot-air balloon in the particoloured sweater that became his trademark when he was treacherously sacked from the government and spent his later years on afternoon TV explaining the Greek origins of Cockney slang on *Jump-Phrase*. The dockers are long gone from these parts; they've all relocated to the marshlands of Essex to make way for the bankers who live in these smart waterside flats that were built by robbers who done the biggest bullion job in British history and they wanted to layer the swag before the cops found the bars. They done nicely out of it, the ones that ain't topped each other, and they now got lovely mansions in Kent with electric gates and bears in the garden and woe betide any sightseers or tourists that go down there for a look-see cos you might be legitimately murdered on the lawn.

'"Further east, we come to Custom House and Canning Town, where after a steaming supper of Cajun whelks and a pint of traditional Stella Artois, you may join the Bobby Moore Murder Walk to the Victoria

Dock where two West Ham fans took a ride with a Bengali taxi driver after celebrating Sir Bobby's funeral, gave him a hiding and just for jolly pushed him and his motor over the edge. The *blub-blub-blub* noise with which your guide will round off the evening is the sound of Fiaz Mirza drowning, as performed by these loveable rogues on their way home from the scene.

'"And remember, only with your Zone One-to-Four Travelcard!"'

THE GLASSES WERE EMPTY, the plates had been cleared, our corner wasn't so pleasant.

'How d'you do the voice? Come on!'

'Like Dickens,' grinned Hanley.

'Why d'you keep turning up?'

Hot-faced, he watched me.

'Fuck off back to World's End! You aren't wanted round here, pal.'

CHAPTER 5

I WALKED OUT, HANLEY CAUGHT up, in the twilight I howled at him for dogging me, he suffered the tantrum, so we were sitting on the kerb outside Tyrus's, smoking roll-ups from Hanley's case, when Paulie came from the dark shop and asked if we'd join them – they were having a drink in the cellar, heard us through the grate.

We followed Paulie Charalambous to the stairs. They had quite a lair down there. One side was a sort of laptop A&E. Under a power-lamp in headphones and Arsenal cap, the guy from the cabin was de-ionizing a motherboard. Injured computers waited in line on a workbench, and armchair. On the shelves and along the walls were canisters of hair product and plastic tubs; a thick pipe ran above them, rising flume-like to a vent. Bags of snacks, flat boxes of baklava and dumb-bells lay on another bench with a vice and tools. Paulie and Tyrus were drinking at a whisky-bar conversion. Tyrus was a strongman, shaved head, arms of oak. On a functioning laptop, they studied Arsenal–Chelsea.

When Cyprus was still a colony, Paulie trained as a barber. He arrived here before I was born. By boat and train via Venice, the journey took six days. Times I sat upstairs, he pressed whisky on me. Around his chair, bottles glowed. We chatted of London in the sixties. He and his brother walked home from Hammersmith Palais. Twelve miles to their digs in Caledonian Road. On the way they fought men who called them wog. The whisky was a sign he'd made it – that, or some sort of consolation. He disliked Tories, Lib-Dems, UKIP, royalty, though Chelsea and Turks attracted his darkest animus – they and the British Empire. Tottenham sometimes felt its edge. Indeed, the Arsenal–Tottenham loathing may have induced generalizations that sometimes supervened the exit of a Jewish client whose head he'd just been handling with affection. I'd stopped calling him out on these. He was the only person I'd heard defend Miliband as if he meant it. 'Labour Party' was a sacred phrase with Paulie. While he cut my hair and reminisced and groused, I checked other punters like a king.

He displayed his cellar bar: Aberlour cask-strength, J&B, Smoke-head, Yamazaki samples, customer poteen; and Blue Label, which he was saving.

Hanley wished to know what for.

'When Van Persie signs the new contract! What else?' Paulie Charalambous slapped his knee. He wore good dress trousers and welted black slip-ons. He'd had a triple bypass and a stent, his shoulder'd been reconstructed (common procedure among veterans in his trade), he had diabetes, neck spasms, and gut ache from his pills; he'd fought, survived, thrived; sent money back till there was no one left to spend it.

We settled for J&B, and Hanley said he thought they'd be Chelsea round these parts. Paulie swore and dry-spat, Tyrus grinned. No Chelsea ventured here.

'Cos they'll go out missing an ear!' Paulie laughed. We all laughed. 'Fucking look at this!' Replaying in slo-mo Cahill's tackle on Van Persie.

'Referee's took a bung from the KGB,' suggested Hanley, and Tyrus was, Yeah – you'd be surprised.

They got on with their analysis. It was snug down here. I felt fucking bad for blowing up on Hanley.

'Dunno what got to me back there.'

'Don't sweat it, *paisano*.'

We could have changed the subject. But Hanley had something to get off his chest. And it takes a stronger man than me, an unusual one, not to want to hear more, once he's been affected . . .

Had he represented William?

'If there was an offence of putting people off London, I would have had to,' Hanley told me. 'Say he'd been around now for example, with the Olympics, telling tourists what a khazi this place is once you lift the lid, a complaint of defamation or malicious falsehood would've been mustered against him. Someone would have had a word with the objects of his slander.

'Nearly came to it at the Diana funeral – not the funeral, the mourning. I was doing legal aid at the time. William went down to Kensington Palace with Beefburger Mike, a buddy of his who'd been diagnosed with new-variant CJD. He was an ex-Chelsea headhunter, Mike, but by this time he just shuffled and moaned. Used to hang out in the foyer with the touts; his girlfriend Frankie, she treated it as a crèche for him, once he started getting heavy symptoms. Anyway, William and Mike, they were there that Sunday afternoon and you had the crowds with the bears and flowers and whatnot, and William went off on one, standing on the bank below the path: "Where were you lot with your tears and bouquets and your infant junk when Eldine Matthews got cut down? How many of you cunts went to the bus stop next day and left a ten-quid bunch of lilies? Shall I help you if your memories are letting you down? Precisely zero, wasn't it? You had another chance at the Inquest. How many of you went to Southwark to make your feelings clear? Come on! It was only fucking February! You come along here crying your eyes out for a pom-pom with O-level needlework but you got no fucking heart for a black man!"

'And with that, Beefburger Mike starts kicking the bears. There's cops around – luckily, seeing as the crowd's in a mood to lynch the pair of them – and they get pinched for Threatening Behaviour. William calls me from the nick and I go down there and explain that Mike has a serious neurological disorder, which must have caused him to trample accidentally on soft toys on that grassy knoll in Kensington Gardens (it helped that Frankie'd stitched his ID and address on his anorak) – and William (aka "Uncle Billy") is actually his unpaid carer, which gets a bit too much for Uncle Billy at times so he lets off steam by shouting about Current Affairs. At this point, William starts fidgeting like he's going to go off on another one (Mike's been moaning to himself since I came in). Sergeant asks me to escort the two of them away, if I'd be so kind, care in the community being outside his jurisdiction.'

Paulie and Tyrus were saying something about Fabian, Hanley listening in.

Time to chip. Couldn't sit here all night cadging whisky.

'Hyatt, you should bring your lovely wife down here for a drink!'

'One day, Paulie.'

Arsenal Cap waved his heavy-dexterous hand.

*

ENTER KAREN IN MURDERESS-CRIMSON, regarding suited stranger.

'So who've you brought home now?' (Not the rent boy, surely?)

'This is Hanley.'

'Hark at you, Cholmondeley-Warner! What's his first name?'

With a kind of flourish, Hanley told her.

'What are you up to in the alcove? Is that brandy with your tea? I'll have one, with lovage.'

When I returned from the company store, Karen had confirmed Hanley's domestic arrangements (married to Milly, father to Esme) and they were yakking about the music hall.

'It's a right perishing knees-up!' Karen told him. 'Imperial Music Hall.'

Hanley was eager to know where.

East End – Cable Street.

'Ah!' cried Hanley. 'Where they saw off the Fascists!'

'That's right,' Karen said. 'Our Lolly's well up on all that. She's Jewish, is Lolly.'

'*No pasarán!*' Hanley clenched his fist.

'Are you Spanish, Victor?'

On his mother's side.

'What about your dad? Have some of this in your brandy. Makes it delish.'

Hanley paused. Dad was English. Mother'd met him at King's. He removed his spectacles, polishing them with his pocket square.

'Did you get stick at school?' Karen on to something (as ever).

Oh, he'd been called 'Paki', 'nigger', 'coon', now and then, on account of being dark-skinned – and 'Gandhi', because he wore glasses. Wasn't only him. A Portuguese lad got the treatment, and a Greek. Some of the black and Asian kids showed solidarity, others had the hump. Those words belonged to them. Not that they weren't employed with a curious lack of discrimination at times. For instance, Judge McKinnon informed a jury that he'd been called 'nigger' at school, and didn't mind in the slightest. Trial of John Kingsley Read, NF Chairman, Incitement to Racial Hatred, after Read told a BNP meeting, 'One nigger down, a million to go' – referring to the murder by stabbing of Gurdip Singh, a Sikh teenager, by a white gang.

'Jesus Christ!'

The case was widely reported. Jan '78.

Silence . . .

'Probably got twitted more for being called Víctor though,' Hanley told us bravely. 'My mother chose it. Accent on the "i". – Not to be confused with the comic!'

'Meant to be a comic on at the Imperial,' declared Karen. He hadn't turned up, or rather he had, inviting the audience to come and find him. What next! Well, they accepted, carrying their drinks backstage and even up to a gallery in search of the evasive entertainer, then down some spooky stairs to the performers' dressing rooms. The comic was called 'The Cunctator'. He'd obviously just vacated his room – you could feel he'd been in there. Someone thought she saw him trundle round a corner, and a couple of guys heard him going up the stairs to the gallery and set off hallooing in pursuit.

Had they tracked him down?

By that time, they were being called back for the next act, a bloody excellent torch-singer called Kitty Strychnine, who gave them 'Surabaya Johnny'.

'I'll have to go to the Imperial myself sometime,' vowed Hanley.

'Well, I'm going to bed,' Karen told us. 'Nice meeting you, Victor. – Don't let Carl keep you up all night talking about criminals!'

Warned.

CHAPTER 6

THE CONVICTIONS OF VINCENT Drew and Alan Roche for the murder of Eldine Matthews, wasn't that something? Hanley shook his head. Nineteen years on. Magnificent. Were the de Laceys sleeping easy in their beds? (If you could imagine them sleeping.) Danny Flowers, now he might have the wind up, being a hanger-on, a foot soldier. Always the last of L Troop to be mentioned. But Pete and Mick de Lacey, they were the captains. Could you imagine them worrying? Of course, the cops had been to see Roche; but he was fresh in his sentence, still claiming innocence. If he pressed that grass-green button in his cell which connected him directly to the detectives of Operation Flint, he was admitting. Furthermore, he'd been following the de Laceys since olden time; was he going to rat on his captains? Hanley cocked his wrist to see his watch, and I'm back at Bales.

But what about William? Smells of ham down here; eyes are on me, scanning the *Mail*.

All that time William was hanging out round this way, he was hiding. The night it happened, William was in Thamesmead – Thamesmead being his endz. I knew the reports of a sky-blue Astra driving by the scene with some youths in it, then coming back on the other side and cheering?

Yeah. They'd been associated with the crime, hadn't they?

They had been. But in point of fact, they'd driven from Thamesmead to the crime scene to confirm a kill. They were the dogs who'd murdered Carson Marshall a couple of years before, and L Troop were trailing behind them. First thing they did after killing Eldine Matthews, Mick de Lacey phones the Young SS (that's what the Thamesmead boys called themselves) and tells them it's one-all now. Come down if they want to see nigger blood on the pavement.

Those words exactly? How did he know?

'Because William told me.' Hanley swallowed.

Lowering his voice, he came from the window. William was in The Lunar Five, a pub in Thamesmead Central, when Mick de Lacey called and the landlord put him on to the Young SS. Their captain was Andy Sargeant. Keeping to himself with his Coke and crisps, William heard Sargeant tell the rest. They slammed their drinks and they were out of there, away in the Astra screaming.

Within the hour they were back. They were pumped. They named all the names, the five that everyone knows, Mick and Pete de Lacey, Alan Roche, Vincent Drew, Danny Flowers; and the sixth, which not everyone knows. William heard them; others could have heard them; they were too excited to whisper. The blood-lust, the race hate, it had them *cachondo*. One of them'd jerked off in the back of the Astra.

Jesus Christ. Was there anything worse? Jesus!

Yeah. The wanker was called Josh Rider.

As to the sixth?

The sixth? Hanley checked his watch again.

The sixth name. Sure I'd heard something of this.

Likely I had, Hanley glinted. Matter of record. Five faces had stuck in the public mind; but the cops thought there may have been a sixth. A fair-haired youth with a distinctive nose. Certain witness statements had referred to such a figure.

41

That was it.

Operation Dex was dedicated to him.

Dex?

Yeah. For some years. A micro-op. Run down now. Officially at least.

And what about William?

The YSS told him to sling his hook, but he kept his head down. He was frightened staying, frightened to leave. He thought of going to the cops, but no one went to the cops round there. Besides, he was known locally as an odd fellow. Kids listened to him spiel, till their mums called them away. He wouldn't cut it as a witness. What's more, if he went to the cops, the Young SS would hear about it. Then they'd do him, and no one would think of going to the cops: William knew he wouldn't be missed.

Poor bastard.

Yeah. Poor bastard. Then the Astra went off again. William, he left The Lunar Five and he went to stand across the road in a little park, barely a park, more a green afterthought for mothers to get their kids off the road on the way home from school. There was a swing frame from which a junior gang had taken the chains, and a black slide that looked like a gibbet, which the Young SS had used for petrol-bomb practice before they obtained a car to drive round in. He felt it was his duty to stay here as a witness (also, he hated going home to watch videos with his dad). He had to be a witness.

When the sky-blue Astra came back, there was Andy Sargeant, his lieutenant Tony Cass, and two figures who hadn't left in it but had been brought back carrying bin bags. This was Pete and Mick de Lacey, and this was the clothing.

So they brought it here?

They brought it here. They were going to torch it on the slide, but they took it in The Lunar Five, and they came back out some time later without it. Someone else picked them up, and drove them off.

Drove them where?

Shooter's Hill.

For definite?

It seems very probable. For there was a pub called The White Cross in Shooter's Hill which was George Arnold's surgery. Here sat good George on seasonal evenings with his pipe, his crossword and personal tankard, dispensing advice to parishioners, the poor, those who had erred from the straight and narrow through poverty and ill luck, businessmen betrayed by their accountants, herbalists whose trade had been rendered illegal by crushing laws and customs and excise officers, importers of recherché books and films oppressed by an illiberal culture, proponents of free speech, free assembly and the national interest oppressed by Judaeo-liberal culture, some bearing hams and simnel cake, some with envelopes, and some with information. So on this night five Kentish youths, elated by the hunt, foreseeing arrest . . .

Letting Hanley go on like this because it sounded better – embroidering filthy material. But what's a report without brass tacks? We have to get it straight . . .

So, he meant someone brought the de Laceys to George Arnold to be briefed about how to respond to police questioning?

Yeah. This was now pretty much accepted as what happened.

How did two become five?

Someone picked up the other three as well, from their turf – between Thamesmead and Shooter's Hill. (The sixth was already fading from the scene.)

Who was 'someone'?

Hanley shook his head.

Though George Arnold was a copper from the Circus?

43

So I'd run up against him?

Not to my memory. Used to meet with Crime Squad boys in a pub on the Jamaica Road. A merry bunch in holiday shirts and deck-shoes. Laid their G17s on the table in the snug, as they played the golf machine.

Ever mention 'Big Ears' or 'Scopic'?

Maybe. I got an echo: foul-mouthed, wise-cracking. Spoke their own language, that bunch.

Arnold's nicknames, on account of his informants.

You couldn't keep up with the nicknames.

His sergeant's name was Bowler.

Bowler?

Chas Bowler. A dark horse was Bowler, ex-FRU.

Wasn't that the Ulster hit squad?

Not technically. That was the MRF. An outfit that no one seemed to have authorized when the inquiries started and lawyers and journalists were asking about those troopers in flares and bomber jackets carrying Thompson submachine guns as they drove round the Ardoyne and Falls Road in a pale-bronze Cortina. The Army had no knowledge of the MRF, and neither did the MOD. Hey, pass! SRU, NITAT, Int and Sy, Captain Snooty and his Pals, 14 Intelligence Co., 14 Int, 4 Field Survey Troop! Names change, killers fly back to regimental nests, retire with the Military Cross, buy farms in Australia, become mercenaries, security consultants, Waitrose managers, PE teachers. Prosecutions: zero.

Hanley was not finished.

Come the eighties, out with the Noddy hairstyles and drive-by shootings, in with the FRU. The Force Research Unit (aka 'The Manor', aka 'Your Love is King') used intelligence, which is to say, rather than using troopers to give the treatment, it got the Loyalists to do it.

Tell how, Víctor.

By burying agents in Loyalist groups, to recommend who might be popped today, the idea being this would eliminate mistakes, like blowing down the whole queue outside a chip shop on the hunch there might be a Provo lurking among 'em, since your UVF chopper would likely know faces in a way troopers didn't, conducing to operational accuracy. But the Force Research Unit also ran informants in Republican groups, which could lead to confusion if an agent in a Loyalist group hadn't been cross-briefed, or he'd forgotten that Liam X. was actually working for the Army, when he recommended that Sammy Y. took the bastard out, whereupon the FRU'd have to decide on a substitute pronto and look down its list for a name, Sammy having left the The Rex twenty minutes ago with the hard glint in his eye. And now and then, agents or informants got turned or rumbled; at which time, the Force Research Unit had to decide whether to pull them out for a deep cleanse or identity transformation, have them hit by a fast-moving vehicle, or, in one instance at least, merely forget about them. Dark world, dark decisions.

Yeah.

So following accelerated discharge from the FRU, some personnel found their way into the Met, bringing with them their professional skills. And DI Arnold's sergeant was one such agent of darkness.

(And what about you, Hanley, with that moustache and little beard?) So William – how long did he stay put, stand his ground?

Two days after the murder, William came west.

He just upped and left without a word?

There was a squat in Notting Hill, of which William had heard on CB, or a pirate frequency. There he made his way, thinking he'd be at home. The other squatters didn't take to him. His class was one problem, though they might have borne that if it hadn't been for the fact that his voice drove them up the wall, like *loco*. He was trying to keep down what he knew, but it churned and issued forth in low-pitched muttering;

sometimes, if he'd really striven to censor himself, the output was intolerably foul. They gave him diazepam, they gave him Browne's Mixture that they'd fractioned, they gave him hash and opium. He dumped the lot down the khazi. They made a Beltane fire of packing and green twigs in the back garden, with a cup of white spirit to get it going. As it smoked and spat, they danced about it on mushrooms and microtabs. William didn't dance. He's stood back by the wall: 'You lot seen Baal yet? He's over here! I seen him! He's got a face like a frog and a fucking big knife!' Which was the last straw. When he was out getting chips, they changed the locks.

Early May, he was sleeping rough in Hyde Park, hiding from Baal when that gentleman appeared in the long grass, hustling for bread rolls on Queensway. At Bayswater, he was pulled into the ticket hall by a Scotsman, who said the cops would pinch him for begging. Did William want to know how to make a few bob honestly? William did. Did he have anywhere to kip? William did not. So Scotch Al brought him to a hostel round this way after furnishing him with false docs, GP, DSS and so forth, and here William rested a day or two from his excitement and his terror, and ate soup and fishfinger batter, and he saw through his fingers how the good men, the brooding men, the roadmen and madmen who'd landed in this place – saw how they passed his bed and shook their heads. Then Scotch Al took him round to the foyer, where he was A-No. 1, and showed him how to do the cards.

At this point, Karen phoned me from bed to say it might be news to us, but it was 3.15 a.m., and Hanley was away into the night.

CHAPTER 7

WHY I LOST IT with Hanley in The Hank of Rope was a kind of professional jealousy, the feeling he had something to add to my knowledge of a screw-up in the past that was mine alone, which I guarded like a dog on a shit-pile – not wanting a flash bastard with a pocket handkerchief doing voices, and other tricks, that dogs can't hack. I knew he hadn't levelled with me yet, but I could sense its coming in a future reminiscence-bout, as a certain kind of smoke foretells a blaze. So I'll get my levelling in first.

Well, some time ago, I mentioned a hunch, and grudge, as reason for getting to know Donna Juan, and this takes us back to my final days at *The G********, when I had an intern called Justin. It was a week after the election of Barack Obama that Craig Norman and I interviewed Justin Fox in Farringdon; his eyes shone. Justin's credo was already, *Yes we can!* On the wall, a 'STOP BUSH' poster had been framed, advertising a Dublin rally. Justin grinned. He'd actually been there, after first-year exams at Wadham. The interview being informal, Craig Norman clapped and whooped.

A Friday afternoon the following January, Justin asked if I fancied a drink so I logged off and took him to a place on Back Hill. There'd been snow that week; an easterly turned the air to spearheads. He wore a cord jacket, drainpipes, trapper's cap. In The Red Hand, they still had a jukebox, which I thought he'd find quaint. He was only twenty-two, and downloaded or streamed or otherwise magicked his sounds, though he'd told me and Craig with shining eyes that he loved live music and was mad for festivals; and of course he dug the jukebox (a challenge indeed to find something he didn't like – apart from the obvious). The place hadn't filled with office folk yet, so we had full use, and listened to a string of ancient hits, 'Come Back and Finish What You Started', 'The Night', 'Take Me Bak 'Ome', 'Sylvia'. For the last he had an immediate passion. Bored behind the jump, the Polish barmaid came out to bus the tables in a dainty red apron; Justin got her moving.

I looked on. The barmaid giggled, and just when the chords revert, like everything's going to turn out all right, she led him in a bouncing whirl: her national dance.

Justin put the track in his phone, finished his ale, tasting every hop, then told me his news: 'Mulhall likes boys! I've been finding out. My round!' As he dashed to the bar, I thought of my boy Edward, now growing tall, and given to strong silences (when I called, at any rate).

So how had he come upon this information?

He'd been in Soho last night with friends. Had a late one, and he was buzzing when the rest went home – still wanting to talk. So he found a bar, through a crack in a wall (Archer Street). The bouncer asked if he was sure he wanted in. Of course he did. It was a scene in there, guys with their shirts off, a lot of coming and going up some stairs at the back, and a big red-haired woman in an officer's cap who was watching Justin like a hawk as she chatted to Calpol Gains.

Calpol Gains was in a joint like that?

Justin knew it was him, since CG was scruffier than everyone else, hadn't shaved, but looked like he was trying to imitate Mr Gains like someone who wasn't actually him.

Well, the woman in the cap was probably his minder. Justin hadn't published this in any form, had he?

Course not. He knew the rule. Well, two Roman guys, they'd bought Justin a beer, and he stood them a slammer, then they all three went off on a *puttanesca* hunt and ended up in some sort of kitchen in an alley. They told him the only jobs in Italy nowadays were down south on the farms, though the brother of Pep had found work as a witch (expenses only). So to London they came, where they were earning money to set up their own recording studio with the help of a guy called Roadie who dug the sound of their funk trumpet and bazooka.

Bazooka?

Trombone they meant. Roadie gave them drugs, he gave them sausage and chips, he played them wild stuff from when they weren't born. One night, Atlas, a friend of Roadie, he took them round to see sights in his jeep. They came west along the river, the sky was blazing with a storm, the London Eye was a torture wheel from the Colosseum, like the peoples in the pods were burning as they turned (they were out of their heads on speed and spice). So they come to a boat, a big boat, and Pep, he wanted to go on in the jeep, but Albo, shit, he wanted to sail, so Atlas let them out and said back in one hour – Atlas was a good guy. Except, on the boat, which wasn't going nowhere, it was a party boat, an older guy, snake-slim, in black denim, he bought them sambucas and little snacks and then, next, in the Gentlemen's, he stood by Albo and said, Hey, you pissed on my trousers, watching Albo's *cacchio*. You *finocchio*, huh? Excellent. We have another drink and go for a ride.

So this guy, he had a driver, and they all went west past the Queen's palace up Holland Park and Notting Hill and round and round and up and down, just looking at the fucking money, till they come to mansions on a square, and Snake says here's best money! Then up to a long penthouse on the top, and a *finocchio* with sparkling face and a big brush, major-domo, he told them welcome to Lords and they go down the corridor past other boys watching satellite and playing with their consoles, drinking protein shakes and Muscle Monster, and into Boss Cabin for a chat.

The Romans got plenty work at Lords. Snake, he was a *fica*, a *faccio a culo*, but he was cool with Pep and Albo. On a fair night, they could make two-fifty each. Much of the clients was boogs and *antiquaratios*, but there was men who was locally known, and a parliament man that had his chauffeur park up on a little road by the garages, and two or three television men that everyone knew since they'd seen them on panel shows or weather or Freeview – though major-domo told them not to gossip outside Lords.

Cap tilted back, Justin paused for a sip. He'd caught the voices of these Roman fellas. No word of acting on his excellent CV.

But there was one name the boys mustn't even say aloud, even to themselves, like in an open field with no one else around, or up a mountain, or under the pillow when they were alone in their bed at night, or even in a small boat at Santa Marinella and speaking to the wind, or whispering to their mother when they call her. Like any boy said this name, he suffered.

'So what was the name?'

'The name was Mulhall.' Justin bounced in his chair.

'So if no one ever said it, how did these Roman boys know it?'

'Cos the Snake said it, then looked over his shoulder to see who'd heard and made a gun of his fingers.'

'So your Pep and Albo, they serviced Mulhall?'

'Could have!' Justin's eyes shone.

'You mean they wouldn't know if they had or hadn't?'

Justin nodded. Off fell his cap. The barmaid skipped out and saved it.

'But what would bring him to West London? All the way from Kent for cock fun? Mulhall? Come on!'

Our interest in Mulhall had recently been piqued by his interest in an area of green land. If you'd gone down to Bostall Woods any day in the last six months, you wouldn't have been surprised to see Mulhall or one of his adjutants undertaking an arboreal quota, gazing with concern at the oaks, elms and beeches, sampling soil, or giving a fair impression of being engaged in some kind of measurements, often in the company of someone giving a fair impression of enjoying ecological authority, and two or three others giving no impression of bearing harmful intent towards you if you hung around for a while asking uninvited questions. That's how it was.

For Mulhall had moved to purchase the woods from the borough – from the borough, and from the co-op. Not for development of an indoor ski slope, health club and spa, outlet shopping village, or mul-tiple-screen recreation hub, with Cajun barbecue, tapas belt, hologram fountain, supervised arcade, and other appurtenances of the good life by which businessmen share with us the proceeds of their honest endeav-ours. In fact, Mulhall wanted to keep the woods exactly as they were. It was the borough council that had been eyeing those green acres since the Olympic bid, and, envious of its shabby neighbour's award of the Games, devising plans for their development into an 'Olympic Vale/ Grove/Soul Garden/Omnispace' (the title being a subject of agreeable tussling at the council's Impact Lunches), with meditation copses, anti-colonial rockery, humanist cabin, juice-bar tree houses, and poly-ethnic snacking meadow. A winning picture.

'Sustainability', however, is a powerful word in our time, and when the MP for a certain SE London constituency was lobbied by a coalition of green activists and an ecologically minded businessman with a big house on the Kent–London border with a gold-star garden in which rare plants ran wild, as did bloody large dogs and small compact dogs that could take a dinosaur out – when that MP was lobbied to lodge an intervention against the 'Olympic Grove Development Initiative [Bostall Wood]' at the European Parliament, the councillors tore their hair and gnashed their teeth-o. For the European Commission was just then accepting the first progress report, complemented by a detailed staff working paper, on the Sustainable Development Strategy, and with detailed enthusiasm discovering its determination to 'reverse the loss of biodiversity'. Accordingly, the Development Initiative was blocked to the extent that the Commission recommended a conservation order on the woodland to be funded by the European Union in collaboration with any private interest or organization that demonstrated a persuasive concern for biodiversity in combination with financial competence and probity. Which was why Mulhall was to be found down there with his gardeners, tree people, cordon fasteners, trowel wielders, and six-foot ball-head hardcases who came on like Monty Don for reporters.

Now obviously, the first response of those who make a living from reporting on the ways of our kingdom and its adventurers, speculators and ne'er-do-wells, was Oh-ho! He's got something buried there. Mulhall, art a dunderhead! You'll have the Murder Squad and forensic bods in those woods with their thermal swizzle sticks before you can whistle two bars of 'Yuss, We Have No Bananas'. We recalled the names of persons who might have been rendered missing by Mulhall, because they'd pissed him off, either seriously or just in the common way of things; or because of a certain long row about who owed who and wasn't sharing; or because someone had gone to Mulhall and said, 'Would you consider attending to a certain nuisance for, say, £5,000, Mr M.?' And this response of ours made some sense, since the police had not forgotten the time when an undercover man got very nastily bitten in the wild garden of that gentleman, and would strongly incline towards the association of Mulhall and green land with further serious violence.

But the sense was shallow.

For why should a seasoned brigand like Mulhall draw attention to himself with such tricks? His actions shouted, 'I have something buried here!' We surmised, therefore, that he hadn't got anything at all buried there – which wasn't very deep either, since we were no nearer working out what he was up to.

So we asked ourselves, Could it be possible that he was doing a legit thing, and not only legit, but conscientious – as if he repented of his crimes, and would now save some planet?

Yes, but not probable.

> *Got a two-ton hammer,*
> *Got meat by the pound . . .*

WHICH WAS WHY IT now seemed a brainwave, radiating from what Justin had been telling me as Beefheart and Ry Cooder thudded on the box, that Mulhall's interest in the woods was what we know as a 'Reverse McGuffin'. In other words, Mulhall wasn't up to anything: the woods just seemed important to the investigative eye. His conservation activities were a diversion from what he was up to somewhere else. Bingo! No wonder, then, that he'd been appearing on the other side of London, playing away. And we remembered that in olden time, Mulhall had been a member of Lodge No. 97, down by the river as it meanders in its western course. Does Lodge membership ever lapse, or exist in perpetuity? Well if he was back networking at 97, maybe he popped up to Lords when business was done.

We hummed, we had another and went on speculating, me and my intern. Hey! Maybe Mulhall was trying to get people to think that he wasn't up to anything in the woods, by seeming to be up to something in the woods when he was indeed up to something in the woods. Savvy? For seeming can create a fair smoke around something that is, as well as something that isn't.

This boys thing though, what to make of that? So to say, was he long-term undercover, a recent dabbler, curious (in the way of blokes his age), or buffing his tyrant status, you know, like a bad emperor? The taste for Roman lads . . . but we had no proof he'd been with Roman lads. What we had, all we had, was some idea of the power of his name at this funhouse – which was a gift horse that no newsman could look in the mouth, really, as I now allowed Justin to persuade me. Since the horse was pulling a cartload of secrets, concerning either Mulhall's eastern or western activities, or even his imperial ambitions . . . And when was he most likely to give away those secrets? When he was excited, that's when!

Well . . .

Yes, then.

So that January evening in The Red Hand, eyes shining, Justin said he'd go up there. Go up and get something out of Mulhall.

I said don't even dream of it, Foxy, and what did he mean anyway?

He meant he'd do a shift at Lords, see if Mulhall turned up.

And if, as was highly probable, Mulhall didn't turn up that day?

Then he'd do another shift, and another, and if necessary another still, until Mulhall did.

Fair and square, I told him I couldn't allow him to do that. Put my empty glass on the table. So.

He shone like he'd found God. Something else he'd learned from the Romans. The Boss Cabin doubled as a VIP Lounge. Sometimes, the Snake had the major-domo brush it down and spray it with cologne, cos someone big would be along this evening.

Had they seen anyone big in there?

No. Cos the door was always shut. But they'd heard voices.

I told him it wasn't happening. Wouldn't want my Edward volunteering as a manwhore when he reached Justin's age. His experience of flogging his arse (which I couldn't recall seeing any reference to on his CV), I didn't ask. – And if you want to know why I didn't, it was because his confidence closed me down.

I asked him what Saffron was going to think. She'd been his girlfriend since Oxford. D'you know what he said to that?

Oh, they'd been planning to take a sabbatical and go to Kosovo to protest at Camp Bondsteel anyway, so this was, like, nothing by comparison.

Well I said, Over my dead body, young man! – or something to that effect – and rose from the table. He came with. On Ray Street, new snow had fallen, pleasant to walk in; as we came down Farringdon Road, chatting about the weekend, I hoped he'd got this mad plan out of his system. At the Tube, he shook my hand and was off over Cowcross Street into Smithfield. When I saw him next his eyes had lost their shine.

CHAPTER 8

I WROTE A FEATURE SUBTITLED 'The Greening of Mulhall', and it contained nothing that we hadn't known or speculated at the time of our cosy drink in The Red Hand. In fact, I had misgivings and would have withheld publication, but I'd do anything to get the shine back in the eyes of Justin, who nagged me to go ahead (and was willing for more undercover action – which had to be forestalled). On an early spring Saturday it was published, and someone down the line added certain emphases to what I'd written about Mulhall's background, alleging, for instance, implication in the death of Nate Nulty (discovered hanging without trousers in a Premier Inn off the M20), though I can't blame an editor for flamming up a story that should never have seen daylight, and wouldn't have, if I'd been aware that Mulhall had obtained an injunction against public reporting of his woodland activities. How he'd contrived the judgement from Master Aubrey Clarke, I don't know. Maybe Master Clarke, sitting in an obscure and ancient chamber of the Royal Courts of Justice, was a member of Lodge No. 97. Maybe he loved English woodland and did not love the various institutions of a liberal democracy, such as *The G********. That's by the by. The following week, Mulhall's lawyers issued a heavy writ.

In the 'STOP BUSH' salon, I was summoned to a meeting with my boss Craig Norman, Alexander Brons and Camilla First. Brons was a boyish editor and big union man, First a lawyer with a thrilling accent. We were high in the building. Wind banged the glass. From the poster, Bush Jr came at you like a troll. In his left hand the flag, dollar sign in the canton; blood dripped from his right. They wondered why I hadn't brought my own rep, or wingman. This was perversity on my part, though I declared that if they wanted to discipline me, I'd take it by myself (Karen was in tears when I told her that). Brons stared and stared. It bothered him I'd waived representation. He had your radical socialist's regard for procedure, enjoying it because patricians and liberals didn't. Craig was wearing a suit jacket and jeans, hearty, slightly mad, like a *Top Gear* presenter. Brons wouldn't look at him. Craig was trying to formulate something about a written apology, or a scout's promise not to libel gangsters anymore, perhaps. But Brons wanted the discipline to be formal, without wanting it very much at all. Camilla First said it was scarcely a 'patibulary' hearing anyway; her blonde face grinned. Craig was trying to get in with the lawyer, but she took pleasure only in her own gags. Something about the master, jurisdiction without appeal, wiliness of the plaintiff. Was she speaking to herself? Invisible clerks, plummy silks? Grinning now over 'the punies'. Did she mean us? Brons hated her; she was nearly as posh as him, of which it was agony to be reminded, though probably quite a bit posher than Craig Norman, whose public-school bills had been paid by a 'self-made' grandmother from Cork who'd fallen out with the rest of the family, as a way of burning up their inheritance (a tale of scorched earth that Craig spiced for the radical ear with dark references to Grandma's Republicanism). They were all of them posher than me, which made Craig and Brons uneasy. I think this was why, when they asked me if I'd perhaps leave them *in camera*, ha ha, for a few minutes, I said take your time, walked out of there, into the lift and up Farringdon Road, where I stopped for lagers at The Red Hand.

The Polish barmaid checked me, like, Where's your friend? Their dancing days were over.

When I got home, Craig phoned panicking about where the hell I'd got to, or if something had happened. Before he could announce their verdict, I told him my resignation was in the post (a detail never brought to Karen's attention). Which was how I ended up at the *Chronicle*, career terminal.

Bringing us to my reasons for getting to know a rent boy, which this account may seem to have lost sight of; but as pilots know, and captains, if the wind's blowing strongly against you, then you have to 'crab' or tack, to get where you want. And I'm nearly there now.

One day, I searched for the establishment that Justin told of, and it was such a surprise to find it was virtually on my doorstep, midway between the flat and the *Chronicle*'s shabby office, I experienced something like the jerk which affects sleepers. From the other side of the road, I looked up at the penthouse, expecting a boy in the window, or a face or a sign. Nothing. Unless you knew. I watched a man in a tweed jacket come along the street looking at his hand. Avoiding my eyes, he passed me, came back and buzzed. As he entered, out came a grampus, blowing on his phone. If you didn't know he'd just been milked, he might have been a resident of the block. Neither of these punters was Mulhall.

Something Justin told me was that the snake who'd brought Pep and Albo here was called Van Spenser. Small world. Van Spenser of the poisonous cabin, who'd once recruited hookers from his sandwich makers, according to Hanley. He was nicely set up now, with a choice town house and regular takings. As for Justin himself, well he'd gone travelling after the libel fuck-up, and changed his phone number. I didn't know whether Saffron was at his side. Would he have been ashamed? In my worst moments, I wondered if he'd led me into a trap. My head was full of scorpions for a while, mind stinking like a blocked U-bend. I feared that Mulhall had turned Justin, as if gangsters had given up on laundering and extortion, and found a new vocation in taking journalists down. But when I thought of how his eyes had lost their shine, my boy Justin, the shame was mine.

Have you noticed how failures can't let go? Talk to anyone who's cocked up – marriage, exam, sporting contest – they'll produce explanations by the yard: they're re-living what went wrong, but imagining they're getting it right this time – if there were a second chance. Well, this failure had learned something about the defect of pride, or *vainglory*, though not enough about the defect of perseverance. So I brooded about Mulhall and that penthouse, till I hooked up with Donna Juan.

CHAPTER 9

Ο N HER CHAIR TWIRLS Fabiana Longboots, but Andy stands at the pup desk, watching for storms.

'Yeah, I've spoken to him.'

'About a Day in the Life, Life in a Day, kind of thing?'

'Still getting to know him. I'll work round to that.'

'So you've made contact?' Nature's master had issued Andy Ravage a cinabrese complexion, comic jaw, strong flaxen hair. On Wednesdays and Sundays, he turned out for Putney Diabolics, going in hard on the tackle. Opposing sides had lodged complaints. We'd been round for dinner. He grew his own chillies, egging me on to crunch one raw. As I waved for emergency tracheotomy, he showed how it was done. Afterwards, we had quizzes. Andy quizzed as if trying to defuse a bomb. His life depended on it; everyone's did. I thought he'd pierce his face with his fingertips. Sons appeared at the door, asking him to cool it. They were playing Call of Duty. He was still trying to impress his own father – so his wife confided to us.

'Did he disclose much about the clients, Carlo?'

'They get everyone up there.'

'They can't!'

'What he said. *Todo el mundo!*'

'Well, no need to dwell on the clients anyway – is there?'

'No. But you need the basic terminology.'

As one recovering from a neck injury, Andy moved his pale-straw-berry head.

'You've got two categories, right? Boogs are one, and lumber's the other.'

'Boogs and lumber?' Behind him, Fabiana made satiric signs. 'How do they differ? Do they want different stuff?'

'I dunno.' Trying not to grin at Fabiana's dumb show. 'I'm just getting acquainted. Never spoke to a rent boy before.'

'Sure. But professionally, how do they sort? Like boogs are private sector, businessmen and so forth, and lumber's public . . . ?'

'Don't fret now, Andy,' I told him. 'These are just terms. We aren't talking reputations.' Mulhall excepted, and him I'd libelled already.

'Cos it's the Mayor's Levee Saturday. You can go, can't you, Carl?'

'Sure I'm going. Karen's bought a new dress.'

Andy rubbed his hands.

'How exciting!' called the Chevalier Fabiana. 'I'd love to go as well, to the Lev-*ee*!'

'You could come with me, Fab!' suggested Andy.

'Can I get a new outfit on expenses?'

On the flyover, traffic faded.

*

SIBYL GROVE WAS OUT sky-scanning, so I volunteered for an errand. Where the cobbles met the street, Earl Holmes scowled. Old bastard didn't care for me, chanting as I passed:

> 'Engine a run
> W' fire an' coal,
> Look 'pon the gal
> With the big nose hole –'

. . . straight in at number 5! Turbo passed on the other side, brisk-limbed. I picked up a Warburton's Toastie, some stuff for home, free *Standard*s.

Waiting in a transparent mac with her purse, Sibyl Grove squared me up for the loaf, and asked why I never brought a *Chronicle*.

Because there was no news in it.

She shook her head: 'You're no hack. Know about you!'

Not from me she didn't. 'What d'you know?'

'How you got the heave-ho! Caused 'em trouble in Farringdon, didn't you, dear?' Crackling laughter.

'That's not fair! I resigned. My decision.'

'Bonaroo!' croaked Sibyl Grove. 'Here comes the sun!' She went to a cupboard by her front door; I saw long brushes, fishing net, deck-chairs . . .

'Kids come in and make it higgledy-piggledy! Little bastards! Lost my key and they tangle my things. Come in the dark, that's what they do. I'll set a trap for them, one of those poacher's things! Give me a hand!'

I helped; she asked me to sit a while.

Under Mary Quant hair, she was leathered like Keith Richard; but the brown eyes were handsome, face fine-boned. Hot days, she lay in a bikini, smoking long cigs, not giving a damn. Once, I didn't see her all summer. Maybe gone to the country – Riviera, Marrakesh (such a world I imagined behind her). And I never knocked her door. Could have been in there dying. When I caught her tending ferns in her big cobalt pots, I was glad. She'd cut her leg on a nail; cellulitis, sepsis, supervened; ward-bound for months.

She drowsed a while, brown force relaxing . . . 'Why d'you bring that hyacinth down here the other day? He's a one. Poncing round in that floppy hat like Sophia Loren. What you up to with him? You're no bumboy, Carl, not to my mind.'

'I'm doing a story on him.'

'Said I looked like an old orange. I heard.'

Jesus.

'Never mind. You're not his daddy.'

'No.'

She lit a Superking. Behind her a man in Nantucket Reds watered plants with a tiny can. 'There's Gunther,' murmured Sibyl. 'Bugger all to do. Raining all fucking day, now he's watering.' She stared my way as if losing light. 'That one there, look in it! What can you see?'

'Nothing.' The cobalt pot was empty. Turbo passed again and clocked me.

'Not what I see. Think I'm meshuga, don't you? I am too!'

I laughed.

'We'll have our day.'

Who will?

'Seen you with that C-U-N-T.' Sibyl Grove pursed her lips. 'One with the suits and golden face. Legal eagle.'

'Hanley?'

'You'll listen to him.'

'Why? Why will I?'

'Because!'

'Because what?'

'Ha ha! Look at you!'

I rose and walked away.

'He's your man!'

ADMIRING THE ORNAMENTS ON the roof, Hanley waited by The Tavern in a trilby. I told him I couldn't have a pint – the wife was expecting her tea. Hanley understood. In his pocket bloomed a square:

dark pink, paisley swirls — like he was dressed to the nines to enjoy life's last hours. I felt for the moustache and warm eyes. They deserved the full span. The news would have hurt him that he'd just been called a cunt. Well, he'd been delighted to meet Karen the other night, though feared he'd overstayed his welcome (in truth, he'd been shy of bumping into me since that evening); though maybe we could all go along to the Imperial one of these days? Why not, said I, trying to see my watch, and Hanley, whose shyness evidently wasn't chronic, admitted he'd booked four tickets online for Saturday, with the idea of inviting us.

Saturday might be tricky, owing to the Mayor's Levee.

Hanley hummed, looked sad, recovered.

Making to leave, I asked something to be friendly.

That time he'd had the arse trouble from Van Spenser's Kut-Lunch Kabin that he'd told me about — when he'd eaten the Peri-Peri-Prawn-and-Pineapple bap — what was the play he'd had the tickets for, the one he had to miss?

Removing his trilby, Hanley cooled his thick hair: 'Jesus, *paisano*! How d'you remember that?'

It had made me laugh.

'I'll have to think,' Hanley said. 'Really will. It was years ago — you should be off. Look after the lady!' Making with his hands like a pigeon fancier. Behind me he shouted, '*Paisano!* It was *Doctor Faustus*! *The Tragical History of Dr Faustus*, Christopher Marlowe! *Adios, amigo!*'

He was your man.

'HAVE YOU JUST BEEN seeing Victor?' Karen looked up from her phone. 'I've lost me umbrella again. It's so annoying. You haven't seen it, have you?'

'No, I haven't. Sorry.'

'You have been seeing him, you lying get. I passed you on the 94, outside The Tavern.'

I bent to kiss her. I hadn't seen her brolly was what I meant – which was why I said sorry, obviously. Why would I be sorry for seeing Hanley? Wasn't even on first-name terms with him.

'What d'you mean by that?' Karen bent to look in the carrier.

'Víctor to you, Hanley to me.'

'Mint! A banquet! You don't have to be on first-name terms with someone to be up to something.' Rummaging in the freezer.

I had an impulse to discuss Sibyl Grove's words with her. Karen had an appetite for old witches. In Bury, there'd been a Mother Jago, whom she stopped to chat to as a teenager on her way to park or shops. Ma Jago seemed to have been quite attached to Karen. Kids sang rhymes outside her house, threw rubbish in her garden. I imagined Karen challenging them with her green look. It was a toughish neighbourhood. Catholic dads settled issues with a fist-fight. Catholic lasses scrapped as well, on the top decks of buses, behind the bowling green. Mother Jago had her in for tea and fairy cakes, told her things about boys, and her fortune. From a cage of black brass, a mynah bird shouted, 'Docherty!'

Tactical sense overruling impulse, I spoke instead of Hanley's offer of tickets.

'You what?'

'I said he's got tickets for the music hall, Hanley has.' Ramsden's peas hit the pan in a sliding column.

'Who for?'

'For us. He's bought four tickets. Wants to take us.'

'Why does he want to do that?' Karen had a habit of hard-bargaining when her interest was aroused.

'Must be your influence!' Going at the column with a venerable spoon.

'You're up to something, you and him, aren't you? Don't deny it!'
I laughed at her in her little suede slippers.

With her right foot, she made like a dancer. 'Is he a swapster?'
Remember the persiflage in Charo's, this one flashing her leg?

'Do you fantasize about swinging?' I put it to her. 'Or just like
talking about it?'

'Both.'

'Ha! So you want to try it?' I delved at the peas. 'Thought as much,
you little tramp!'

'No, actually. What I said was I fantasize about it —' hands on hips —
'like everyone does if they're not being hypocrites. And I also *just* like
talking about it. Like a lot of folk. That's as far as it goes. In between,
you've got the people who try it, and they're dead close they are, like
you!' She opened the soft-roaring oven to turn the crumb-crisp and the
chips. We called the cod 'crumb-crisp' after a recording of Orson Welles
losing his temper with some ad-men.

'Well, Hanley's no swapster,' I declared. 'He's got more on his mind
than orgies. A lot more.'

'Yes, and that's what worries me. That's exactly it, Carl.'

Damn her! Damn her hazel eyes and cat-black hair! The swinger
talk had been a dummy, a decoy, to get me telling the truth. Should
have been a bloody lawyer herself.

'Why have you started knocking round with him?' Pointing the
fish-slice at me. 'You knew him before, didn't you? Before you knew
me, or I'd have heard of him. And he's popped up again. I can see that.
You haven't gone looking for him. He's come for you. About something
in the past. Something in the past, or something you want . . .' Jabbing
air. 'He's a lawyer, so he'll likely know of the trouble you've had; but
you go further back than that.'

'Never knew him as anything but an acquaintance.' Tapping

pea-slime off the spoon, I made at her. 'He's a criminal lawyer; doesn't have anything to do with defamation. Years ago, I used to bump into him drinking with cops. And in court now and then. Nothing suspicious about that I hope.' Which was nothing but the truth.

As we sat to eat, Karen changed the subject to Lolly's students and their summer-term history project (a GCSE taster). So you had to evaluate an event or person. Guess who both the lads had chosen?

The pair that'd been bothering her?

That pair.

Who?

Imad Mughniyah, that's who. To 'decadize' the alcove, Karen had painted it dark red and fitted wall lamps which emitted a dusky gold light, like the bureau of an odalisque. We sprinkled our chips and peas in the Sarson's ritual, scent rising in sour billow. A Hezbollah super-ter-rorist was obviously provocative, but Lolly could hardly ask them to pick a different topic without throwing fat on the fire.

Was she logging it on Tapestry?

She was. But logging it didn't help when your feelings were hurt, did it?

I concurred with this, earnestly . . . But wasn't he in hiding, rather than history? Must have been a student, when the barracks was blown up in Beirut. Cheering in the union, as Reagan spoke of casualties; Mitterrand passing through the hole in the wire, on towards the coffins.

Karen ate her fish like a dreamy cat, relating Lolly's dossier. Imad had his head blown off in 2008. He was leaving a do at the Iranian Embassy in Damascus. Mossad agents planted a bomb in his car seat. Other of his big hits were the Israeli Embassy and a Museum in Argen-tina. 114 Jews were killed.

Plenty to evaluate there. Wasn't the Israeli invasion behind it though?

Where of?

Lebanon. Early '80s.

With her last chip, Karen wiped a streak from her plate. Well, that made it all the harder for Lolly, who was extremely fair-minded. But the lads who'd chosen Brother Imad weren't likely to have fair argument as a priority, were they? Bigging him up, that's what they were doing. And the school was letting it happen, because it didn't have the balls to say no. That's what we'd come to. Just as well let them spray 'Gas the Yids' on her front wall!

Clearing the table, Karen scratched her thigh; in the movement of her dress I saw the Lazio banner.

CHAPTER 10

KAREN COULD WAIT TILL she got inside, so I set off down the ramp alone. On the way we'd stopped for drinks, and felt a touch of holiday madness; I hoped she'd suggest we tarried, maybe she hoped I would – then retire to the flat and hit the hay, sit and laugh at the box, run away to the river. Things might have turned out better if we had, but duty called; and she'd spent time getting ready.

At the bottom were the Gents. Hard by the entrance lay the supervisor's den. Pale central light, desk, kettle, hot plate; *Metro* open at the puzzle page; for company, a radio. A sign asked you not to loiter. Discharging Pilsner in the hard-scented air, I saw us hitting the hay; three down, a man with woollen cap and short beard, sprung from nowhere. I hurried out; Karen hadn't clocked him coming down.

By the Town Hall steps was a sculpture: room, staircase, mineshaft, resting on a thick four-sided stand, the whole about the height of a medium man, cast in bronze. The room appeared to be imploding; so it sucked you down the stairs, into the shaft.

'Heyday!' cried Karen. 'A Vorticist!' Behind it, with sad clowning air, stood Hanley; beside him a little plume of smoke. Today's rig was a grey suit with caramel pocket square, brogues of chocolate suede, a chocolate broad-brimmed trilby, which he tipped at Karen, as the Mayor arrived by pushbike in trademark dingy Stetson. I nudged Colin, who took photos for the *Chronicle*.

Hanley, completing apologies to Karen for overstaying his welcome the other night, now explained that he was shopping with Milly. Remembering the Levee, he'd taken the opportunity to try and catch us, on the off-chance we might be up for the Imperial tonight. Because he could easily dispose of the tickets, if we were otherwise . . .

Distracted by Hanley, Colin asked if the Mayor could arrive again for photos. Monty rode off, returned, and left his bike against a post, ascending with a slogan: 'No rust on trust!' Colin snapped him, snapped the lock that wasn't there.

'Don't be daft! We'd love to come,' Karen was saying. 'Carl told me you'd invited us. We're all togged up for it!'

'Your inspiration!' glinted Hanley. 'We'll wait for you at The Horseshoe.' Tipping his hat, he hurried away.

'Looks like a chewing nut with his accessories!' observed our Karen as we entered Town Hall. 'Why've you got a face on, Carlo? Bet you called him anyway, you crafty get!' She disappeared into the Ladies. I hadn't called Hanley, he hadn't called me either. And if you lived at World's End, why not use King's Road for shopping, rather than traipsing up here? Another fishy appearance.

The Parminter Room had a barn roof with skylights; portraits of former mayors hung upon the walls. I hushed Karen, who would giggle at these dull or devious worthies. The Mayor was now entering, in his robe of scarlet and ermine, with a tricorn where his Stetson had been. The Officer of the Council entreated us to stand. A young man began to work the console, as the Mayor begged us to sit.

'As some of you know, I have little patience with ceremony!' Mayor Montgomery wore the beard of an outdoor man, and was missing his bike and Stetson. Given the chance, he'd have made his speech from the saddle. 'But with the Council Elections imminent, it's time to rehearse some of the achievements of the last year and talk to you frankly about the challenges we are dedicated to overcoming. Sandy Clinch, our Information Officer, has devised a presentation – haven't you, Sandy? Which I will now run through. There will be time for questions – followed by a catch-as-catch-can reception!'

Laughter. Mayor Montgomery rubbed his hands. Sandy drew his notice to the rugged-font Powerpoint:

STREETLIGHTING

SOCIAL SERVICES

POLICING

STATUES

OLYMPICS

LICENSING

BUSINESS GRANTS AND EARNESTS

KAREN WAS BITING HER knuckles. She wore the indigo dress, a beret, and a Chanel handbag which I was to say was from eBay, if anyone asked. Her leg was against mine and I felt we were pals, and I wanted her terribly to myself, like a teenager wants his girl, and not to traipse along to the bloody music hall; but I supposed we would. For that seemed a kind of duty as well . . .

'Now, as to the securing of Olympic events for the borough,' Monty was saying, 'we've given this a super-colossal crack.' Laughter (to my left, near-hysterical). 'And it is no small achievement considering our geography and the allocation strategy (let no one utter the word "bias"), that we have been allocated . . . Beach Volleyball! "Hurrah for Beach Volleyball," I hear you cry! Oh that it had been Cycling! But we can all play our part, and we have recruited to date over three hundred

Orientation Ancillaries, Helpers and Guides who will assist visitors in finding their way about the capital to events for which the visitors possess tickets, and who will issue free Day Travelcards to self-same visitors on presentation of legitimate event tickets. The Ancillaries will be recognizable by their distinctive purple anoraks in this borough, which have been generously donated by John Waugh of Eiger Essentials. Could you raise your hand, John? Thank you, sir! If the rain continues, we shall have the snuggest and most battle-ready Ancs of any borough. An army may march on its stomach (take that as an invitation to bring food from shop or home to our Ancs), but it serves in its anorak – or cardigan.' Laughter. From one of the skylights, a figure with a squeegee peered down at us. I hoped Karen wouldn't clock him. 'Sandy, where are we?'

In Master Clinch's bony face, passion and high competence had made a match. Slenderly suited in green corduroy (Agnès B., according to my friend on the left), he could have spent the morning in a thicket conceiving a poem, on leave, say, from governing a province of Iraq. *Con calore*, he clicked on LICENSING. Up came a photo-collage of people eating and drinking at outside tables, and inside tables, laughing in groups, waving to others who must have been just down the street, laughing and dancing, dancing and chatting in multiracial pairs, drinking and laughing in mixed multiracial groups; and here at the end a young white woman vomiting kerbside. Sandy terminated; in his features I saw steel. If someone had tried to spike the show, someone would be paying.

'No one will gainsay, we are an hospitable borough!' The Mayor now named the premises that had been granted extended licences, or temporary or first-time licences, to enhance visitor-experience at this momentous time, and improve the 'Ovaltine reputation' of West and Central London for late-night drinking amenities. As he went through this bingers' charter, naming places and street numbers, Karen whispered something about the penthouse. In my pocket rolled the 853 (Olympus). I could play the whole thing back. Monty was on to business grants, subventions, earnests, handsels, the deserts of unassisted trundlers, 'our' *Chronicle*. Karen nudged me.

Questions were invited.

So a Labour member asked if the Mayor would refute allegations that the Olympic Ancillaries had been recruited from an Offenders' Hostel in Challenger Road, Housing Trust tenants in his own ward, the Community Psychiatric flats in the Albemarle Ward, sex workers (male and female) who'd had Community Service orders commuted, kerb-crawlers ditto, street-drinkers ditto, and football fans who'd had banning orders from Loftus Road and Craven Cottage repealed in exchange for Olympic service.

'No one ever got banned from Fulham!' called a wag. I turned. It was Andy Ravage, who'd come in late, but from the glow on him must have heard the reference to our handsel (to be explained in full hereafter). Monty let us settle.

'I will neither "refute" nor *deny* allegations produced by the member. I suspect that he meant "deny". One *refutes* charges or arguments, not "allegations" – particularly mischievous ones. Let us be straight. If Ancillaries are to be recruited solely from that band of dedicated volunteers who give their all for the borough, year in, year out, we will hear complaints from the member's side about a "Middle-Class Olympics", "Class Apartheid", and so forth. So we give everyone a chance to participate, regardless of background, wealth, reputation, and we are faced with allegations that – that what exactly? What is it we have failed to do, half done or overdone with our Ancillaries? Don't cavil, Mr Barnfield! Out with it!'

Sandy Clinch tried to have a word in his chief's ear. The Mayor's

Levee wasn't meant to go off like the council chamber. We twisted our necks to see Councillor Barnfield (Labour). Principled and cocky, he had a big brazen face like a sportsman from down under.

'C'mon, pal! There's serious exploitation going on with these recruits. They need a decent wage, not an anorak! Don't come it with the Big Soc bollocks!'

'I'd advise you to mind your language, Mr Barnfield!'

'And there's a bigger issue, isn't there, Monty? All very well joshing about the allocation strategy, but some of us have questions about how many times application was blocked for the flyover site, and who's interested in keeping three and a half acres of prime wasteland exactly as it is.'

'That has been debated and minuted, Mr Barnfield! All on record!'

'Oh, I've read the minutes, Monty.'

Among subsequent questions there were no grenades, though when Monty answered one relating to licensing and the police, I turned to catch sight of Mr Van Spenser who'd shown interest in the matter; the faces would not give him up. Waiting staff began to appear at the back of the Parminter Room. The reception was ready.

We lifted a glass of champagne each to celebrate with Andy Ravage and his missus and Colin; we lifted several more. The waiters were good and near. Mayor Monty didn't stint on his Levee. Head lowered, Andy asked what I made of Barnfield's performance – Andy being one of the Mayor's best boys. In the corner, Barnfield drank a bottle of Becks. Mandy Ravage and Karen were discussing Fabiana, with that murderous suavity of women. Cold-shouldered, Barnfield made a point of chatting to the waiters. Did I think he'd been referring to the 'molly house'? No idea. That hadn't sounded like his major beef anyway. I wanted to catch sight of Van Spenser after all these years; I also fancied a word with the Labour man, though it wouldn't be tactful with Monty hovering. I could call him in the week, but as a token of goodwill should acknowledge him now – we'd got our handsel anyway. So I made off for a chat with Brother Barnfield, but Andy set his jaw, and closed me down; then Karen returned from the buffet with salmon, cold beef, game pie, remoulade, tansy salad, Flan Cameron, Celeriac Clegg, and we were trying to gorge ourselves standing . . .

'I see the lady's got her appetite back!'

'Oh, it's you!' cried Karen, polite enough though not greatly pleased. At first I didn't know him. The room was full of silver-haired men in lounge suits; then his image kind of fanned, and it was our 'friend' from Abril's, who told us about the water and the caves, doing that thing with his chin.

'Yeah,' the man said, 'it's me!' and he laughed like he was used to people knowing him and liking him, for it was the form of the world to know him and like him when you were face to face, the ceremony of recognition, though people had been saying in private what a bastard he was for years now if he didn't get his way in a restaurant or back-stage; and people had been whispering for years about some rotten habits and likings of his. And for his part, he'd got beyond troubling whether people really knew and liked him, either because he knew that power lies in appearances, or because he'd persuaded himself that how things seem is of the essence, especially when proof to the contrary is merely private, or whispered. But he wasn't a celebrity, since no one knew his name; wasn't a forgotten seventies comic, MP, retired foot-baller, actor, newsreader, DJ, star of British films – or any of the other things by means of which celebrity is conferred. And I felt he liked it like that, as well; so to say, it wasn't celebrity he had, but a more powerful thing: reputation. 'We didn't introduce ourselves that other time.'

We did now, for it wouldn't have been easy not to; then he told us his name was George Arnold, and he asked how I'd liked Bales.

CHAPTER 11

O N THE STAIRS, A man with close-cropped hair and short beard stood aside as Karen complained. She'd been enjoying herself. I hadn't said goodbye to Andy properly. What was Mandy going to think? I could bloody well text Andy and tell him it certainly wasn't Karen's idea leaving like this.

Leaving like what? How long did she want to hang around freeloading? We hurried up a lane past a Bentley showroom.

'Why d'you react like that to that fella from Spain?'

'Wasn't to him.' With Karen, I'd become an exponent of tactical denial, which is your not telling it straight until the full story may be favourably presented. Marriage No. 1 never called for this. Laura's rational personality . . .

'Think I were born yesterday?' Karen was saying. It's "three times enemy action" isn't it?'

'How d'you mean?'

'He was standing by that cannon when we came up the cliff. He was sitting at the next table when I was too ill for lunch. Now he's here hobnobbing with the Mayor. What d'you know about him? Someone's told you something since our holidays. Either that, or you've been bloody digging!'

'Don't know what you're on about, darling! We're late for Víctor!'

'He said he'd wait for us.' Hurrying along beside me, horsey click to her heels.

'Can't wait forever, can he?'

Obviously, Hanley's tale of George Arnold and his Shooter's Hill surgery wasn't to be spoken of, yet. For one thing, our silver-haired friend 'might' not be the same bad cop. Meanwhile, digging was my instinct; we knew that. As well command a dog not to. She meant digging in a certain corner of the woods. And between George Arnold and Mulhall, there was no demonstrable association, from anything Hanley had told me to date. Was there?

At The Horseshoe, I went in for drinks, while Karen perched among the flowers. Through the window, I saw Hanley arrive, and Karen get up nicely, offering her cheek. She'd be at him now with her habitual open cunning. Well, let him use his lawyer's skill. Fudge her, *amigo*! As the barman did his stuff, I checked 192.com. There were many George Arnolds.

When I joined them, Hanley'd been introducing his company. A tallish woman with a peaked cap, front-laced boots, dark cape, was like a northern immigrant from another time. In dark-blue Oxfords with tractor grips, style jeans, and blazer opened to reveal crimson braces, Turbo stood to rear, examining his phone.

'Here he is!' Karen flashed her teeth. 'Probably been skulking one in at bar, knowing him! Well you can go straight back and fetch Victor and Milly a drink – and Turbo while you're at it.'

Turbo backed off, making signs.

'Oh come on, mate!' called Karen. 'What's up with him?'

'Low profile,' murmured Hanley.

'Why's he doing tic-tac then?'

In the distance, Turbo gave us 4/1, 9/2, 11/8.

'Keeping himself flexible.'

'Oh, aye.'

'Maybe he'll have an orange juice,' Hanley decided. 'Small one. We haven't that much time. Small one to sip perhaps. Small one, Turbo?'

Turbo pressed air. 100/1.

'What will you have, Milly?'

The pale lady smiled as if happiness were dangerous. Maybe it would come at the end, but you must never grab, lest the gods were watching with their knives.

'She'll have a small white wine,' Hanley was saying. 'Set you up, sweetheart.'

Milly didn't demur. Why waste energy on a scene? That birthday I'd apparently snubbed, say they'd made the list together, then she never sent the invitations. No one came. And she'd have liked that; not for self-pity, but conservation. Hanley must keep her going, from his own reserves. But what burns bright burns quickly. So she might outlast him, might wish to. As I fetched more drinks, I pictured his wake.

*

JUST AFTER SEVEN, WE made tracks. Pausing by a row of vintage-clothing shops on a sloping lane, Hanley disappeared. The windows were crowded with blazers and brogues, bats and tweeds, cufflinks, satchels, cricket boots, bears . . .

Karen was made up: 'Suits you, Carlo!' A fucking silly shepherd's smock had taken her fancy: 'What d'you reckon, Milly?'

Milly smiled like she was seeing ghosts.

Out came Hanley with a chocolate trilby much like the one he was wearing – though this was of rabbit-fur felt. The distinction was appreciated by Karen, which increased Hanley's delight, and as he modelled the hat, I was envious, hating how his toffee-eyed joy was spreading – even Turbo seemed affected; then hating myself. He'd bought the hat earlier, but left it for stretching. So that was what he was doing over here. Something cleared up. We passed a church where the PM prayed, and took the Tube.

Opposite with the ladies, Turbo showed tricks on his phone. Rascal had snapped me and Hanley strolling; now we were blown up by ASM; swept away as a dam collapsed; pursued by a tarantula. Turbo turned the screen to show us. The spider was the size of a cow. Delighting in this murderous app, Karen devised torments, nagging Master Turbo for quicksand as Hanley grinned beside me. Like a kid who's just found friends, Milly looked on. Her cape was fastened with a little chain that tightened as she breathed. She wore a white blouse beneath, and necklace of small pink-purple stones. How often did they, she and Hanley? That look of hers, patient, self-conserving, did it give way when they were coiled? Behind her, I saw my other in the glass.

At South Ken, we took a load from the museums. Satisfied with the distraction, Hanley said he ought to finish telling me; and, announced without urgency, this made his tale seem graver, not anecdotal but a thing ordained. The elegance of his outfit, chocolate hat honestly canted, framed the impression, yet made play of it – as if the ordination weren't written in stone, but whispered from offstage. He didn't much lower his voice; it kept the others from tuning in.

'As you must have gathered, *amigo*, when we were talking at The Hank of Rope and afterwards at your place, I'd started spending time with William. What I was picking up from him when he ranted at tourists – that's what got me interested, though I was just passing by at that time. And I'll tell you why it got me interested: when you start, you wouldn't believe the bullshit, bad memory, self-deception, rank denial, the capacity for fantasy, you get in the majority of defendants. It's funny – for a while it is – something to amuse your friends in the pub; then it's routine; in the end, it's exhausting. "Just tell the truth –"

This is how you coach them. "Just tell the truth, and with a fair magistrate, fair judge, reasonable jury – you'll get the best deal. If you lie, they'll have you. Nothing people like less than being lied to. In the Bible, the Devil's called the father of lies (my mother made me read the verses). Montaigne said lying is the worst vice because speech is all we have to hold us together, and it's in speech where lying goes on. The Koran has it that—"'

'Were they impressed by your sources?' We slid into Victoria. Karen like a para, black beret, arms folded, Milly and Turbo either side.

Hanley laughed, Karen's eye on him. Like that caramel pocket square, his script was artfully tousled. Should have been on guard, but I was falling for it. Was a story ever told straight anyway? At Hastings, they taught us shorthand, libel law, press freedom; and how to 'cone out' – from a few known facts; nothing straight about that, expansion the principle. And people who tell it straight, aren't they just in a hurry for results? Let him wind about. No truth as the crow flies.

'A guy of mine called Ismaél,' Hanley glinted, 'years ago. Robbed a 7/11 in Acton. They had a dummy till; gave him coloured paper he couldn't spend. The woman chased him down Bollo Bridge Road with a ceremonial sword – she was a Sikh. Went over and twisted his ankle. When I meet him at Hammersmith, he wishes to see my law books. By chance I had *Doctor Faustus* in the case. He wants to know the story. I tell him the story. So Ismaél wants a go.'

'What at?'

'At conjuring the Devil, *paisano* – or his lieutenant anyway. He's very persistent – wants to draw a magic circle. I explain it isn't a law book; he calls me shyster, "brief-bwoy". I had to advise him Mephistophiles was a bullshitter and he'd get Dillinger Ismaél into the same trouble as Faustus, but my guy, he wants a big car, money, bling, he wants big friends and mighty weapons; wants to play tricks on the magistrate, like Faustus and the Pope. Won't see the difference between law book and play book. And so many of them are like this – fare-dodgers, shoplifters, robbers, thugs: they've got severe reality issues, see no further than what they want. Round the edge of their desire, it's all a blur. But William, all he could see was what he didn't want: black reality. His whole *raison d'être* was the truth; but he trusted no one to listen.

'Those rants of his, something'd happened to inspire them; I wanted to find out what it was, though I have to say, I felt I knew already. I got my chance that time he and Beefburger Mike were pulled in when Diana died and William "truthed" the crowd. After that, William was willing to chat with me. We went for strolls, I took him for breakfast at Benjys – that wasn't so easy; he couldn't sit still; words like "Full English" and "Builder's" wound him up; the knives and the munching – like sticking needles in him. A fella came in I happened to know, Fatty Donovan (used to chat with him about cricket); liked his tuck. William's in his face: "Hoy, Bombo, you lot repealed the White Australia Act yet? Nuffa you cunts stuffing your faces with sausage in our manor! Don't these darks put you off your food?" I paid up and took him out. There was a place he was more comfortable.

'He knew a hole in the fence at the bottom of the flyover. Took me in through there, and he had a little shack he used to go to, a place for the track engineers that wasn't used anymore. William and Beefburger Mike, they'd knocked the lock off with a Slug Devil to use it as their den. Well, there we sat with a bag of cakes and plain rolls and a big bottle of Tizer, silver tubes rolling past, and William said, "Ain't no one can hear us down here or see where we are, Mr Hanley. I got something to tell you, and I'm telling as a white man to a brown man, because I ain't had no one to tell before now, and I'm telling as a witness to a lawman, cos I ain't had any law to speak to."

'Then he told me what I told you at your place about the killing of Eldine Matthews, told me all that; and he told me about the Sixth Man – he'd heard the name dropped that April night in The Lunar Five, before he came west. And he asked me what he should do.'

Monument. Changing now for the Docklands, five of us in our finery. When my wife asked me what 'Victor' had been telling me, as she would before the night was out – she could sit on a question like some people a full bladder – was I going to tell her the truth, relying on her strong sense of justice? Yes. If he came to a conclusion. And was that likely, before the night was out? In a pig's eye – with Hanley's sense of narrative drive. Moreover, the appearance of George Arnold (who probably was the one who'd coached the five youths in Shooter's Hill, unpleasant as this was to face) no doubt signalled matter to come that was yet unscripted. How could I answer for that?

'Had a strong persuasion at the time – being young and more *campaigning* then, if you know what I mean, or to put it another way, a believer in legislation, statutory reform – that race crimes were a form of terrorism, political violence,' Hanley was explaining.

Oh, wandering one!

'Attended a seminar with the Met's Intelligence Director, late '93, and I raised this point; he agreed with me. We had a chat after about the BNP bookshop in Welling. Gerry Gable joined us. That part of Kent was a hotspot for racist murders: Carson Marshall, Eldine Matthews . . . May have been only teenagers who'd committed the crimes, but their hatred was indoctrinated; and not only by fathers and families. It had an idea-base. The idea may have been stupid, but stupid ideas aren't less persuasive than good ones, from racism to sub-prime mortgages. No less effective either. The de Laceys boasted about their idea – you must have seen the secret film of them? The cops didn't boast about it; the cops denied they thought that way at all. But their conduct of the immediate investigation suggested infection – and the Inquiry confirmed the suggestion.

'Nowadays, we're highly sensitive to terrorism – barely talk about anything else – but then, we weren't inclined to see a race crime as a political matter. Maybe because it wasn't whites who were getting done. We thought we'd had our terror with the IRA, a seventies thing. Whereas drowning Bengali cab drivers, "doing a black", shit through the letter box, swastika graffiti, phone-box and bus-stop stabbings – what was that all about? Simple thuggery. Delinquency. Imbecility. "Mindless violence and hooliganism". But to me, it was systematic.'

'Where's the idea now?' We proceeded down Cable Street from Shadwell, Karen in rear, rallying the others, Hanley checked by my question. 'Let me ask you something else – and say if I'm out of order. You told how you were called names at school, that night you were at our place.' Hanley nodded. 'Anyone ever call you "kaffir"?'

Hanley's face worked unhappily. A Rhodesian had told him all kaffirs should be gassed . . .

With minutes for drinks, and interval orders, we'd arrived at the music hall. Turbo disappeared on an errand. I could tell him later why I'd asked, murmured Hanley as the lights went down and we took our seats between barley-twist columns.

Should I, though? The idea to which he was dedicated had changed its ground; the kaffir weren't the same now – so my latest sources gave me to believe – but we journalists lack respect for what's old and still vigorous. Besides, Hanley was better at telling.

CHAPTER 12

BACKSTAGE, SOMEONE CLEARED HIS throat the way my father's Marina sounded on winter mornings, when me and Nigel had to push-start the bastard. In German sidecap and plus fours, our compère Johnny Slot spun about like he'd been goosed. Announcing the tragic death by helicopter of Pygmy Striptease Artiste, Mrs Bernadette Plantagenet (as she flew in from a private performance at Sting's), Johnny raised hand to ear (that sound again). As consolation we had fabulous Naomi Gilray with her Shadowplay. Play with us, Naomi!

Here came teacher. She wore a kind of *Little Women* rig, hair piled up, but the skirt was split so you could see her boots rise arsewards and her mouth was sweetshop red. Lights dimmed as Miss Gilray made hand shapes on a board and easel: rabbit, snake, vase, mole, grasshopper; kissing crows, kissing couple – what next? Falling knives? There'd be a hidden projector, for the images grew to scenes, and the scenes were elaborate with forms, human, animal, till she had a five-way going on, turning to us wide-eyed, like *Look what I've gone and done now!* More of them, and more. Humping like the children of Baal, sinuous blacks, horned and long-eared beasts, fuckasmagoria . . . We were glad our faces were dark.

Remember the talk about swapping the other night? Well in our fantasy fiefdom, how often's our beloved alongside, or on the other bed? Don't care to imagine them enjoying themselves astride a bearded truck driver or nifty French short-arse, or a glinting swarthy man for that matter, with a dick the size of your lower arm and the stamina of Zeus. Of course, we're at it as well with a big German redhead in an officer's cap, that pierced blonde from Ilford, or the lawyer's wan wife; but we don't care to imagine the beloved observing our enjoyment either. Lord, let it stay dark – know what I mean?

As if one of Naomi's animals had entered his plus fours, Johnny returned with awkward steps. Introducing now the Cunctator himself, our elusive humorist, Mr John Fabian Morgan!

The curtain rose on no one.

'Round by here, Jack!' Large figure stage left. He wore a yachtsman's cap, good dark suit, something I saw at first as the shepherd's smock we laughed at earlier, which was in fact a toga, as on a Republican joining a bunch of old frat pals for a carouse. Stage right in a bendy walk, clearing his throat like a diesel, Johnny jumping for fright. The toga back bore a spray-can legend I couldn't make out. Watching from a distance, he sat a while on a director's chair drinking from a bottle as Johnny hovered, then downstage to look us over. Was he staring straight at me? Maybe we all thought so. One eye had a strange way of fixing. On a chain he'd withdrawn from a fob pocket, Johnny checked a watch. Time without words . . .

'Forget the trousers. Forget the time. I'm Fabius Maximus Verrucosus, and here's your ancient history. *Togatus sum*. Ever heard of the Second Punic War, sir? Much like your latest marriage? Come backstage later. We'll compare warts. *Contra Hannibalem* . . . Don't hold your breath, lady – remarkable as they are! I'll be centuries. Backstage if you like. We'll check the pressure. I've got a big bock – B-O-C, madam (British Oxygen Company) – got a big BOC gauge, vintage brass, calibrated. Hannibal . . .'

'This is the one I was meant to see with Lolly,' whispered Karen. 'His timing's bobbins.'

'. . . at Lake Trasimene, he broke our army, when Flaminius ignored the omens . . . Stop fiddling with that, sir! The wife's watching. Wait for the history! . . . Avoiding the head-on, I dogged him wood and vale. Hit his supply lines, disorganized his foraging.'

[*Hectic gestures. Pause.*]

'They called me "Cunctator", F.M.V. Cunctator . . . It means "delayer". What did you think, madam? Rome grew impatient with the Cunctator – Hannibal doing what the fuck he fancied, "ravaging Campania unchecked" – ever been ravaged unchecked, sir? I know a Dutchman who can change that for you. While he ravaged Campania, I dogged him without haste. While he ravaged Campania, I dogged him without rest. After me: I dog, you dog, he, she, it dogs; we dog, you dog, they dog. Conjugate!'

He waited till we did so, grudging every person.

'They divided my command with Marcus Minucius, "Master of Horse". This Master of Horse had the brains of a horse . . . Commodious to your consuls – thoughts vanishing at speed!

'What say a tear-up at Cannae, Cunc? And he's off! Mother of all hidings. Hannibal's cavalry ride in blood; our boys blow bubbles in the Aufidus. Cunctator reinstated in full command. Practical wisdom generally acknowledged.'

Inceding with waist lowered: strophe, anti-strophe. His moves had some distinction, like quagmire king, or lord of denser planet. I suppose we could have laughed; he wasn't that funny, though we'd have rewarded worse. Did he care anyway? Now that would be funny, though not laughing-funny, for laughter wouldn't recognize the attitude. At last he spoke in passing: 'I can do this for twenty years! Cunctator on tour –' and some of us broke out. It was easier.

'Check out the Delayer!' Coming to a stand. 'Since the Greeks built beacons, Troy to Argos – speed-of-light news (plus kindling time) – we've gone mad with making things quicker, shortening the gap, de-severance. Trans-Atlantic jet lag, Jonty? Try it the old way, bub! When you get to Baltimore, build a coracle! Forget the vessel . . . de-evolve. Turn to cod and head for Cornwall! What's the fucking rush?

'How now, madam – yes, you with the villainous grin! Still anointing his pick-axe with Bullock Butter? I've heard you lamenting his celerity! You aren't lost to the art of delay. Nor you, sir! Still practising with the truckle? Yes, the one with the lignocaine bore-hole! Does she know how you gained those extra minutes? Something for you here –' from his toga withdrawing small packet – 'Slowhand Condoms, three monotonous flavours: "M25 Gridlock"; "Gondwanaland"; "Neurotic Poltroon".

'Slow fuck, slow book. Never read a novel that couldn't be three times as long? Make three five! Fifty-five! State Express! Life's too short, sir? You have no more life than a galvanized toad: twitch, flicker, check display. You're just a spasm at the monitor. How many pages to your day, lady? Yes, you with the spiritual pout! Half a page? I'll give you half! Your day's a book without end, yet I smell urgency on you – *an* hectic perfume! Bet you can't wait for the interval! Check your phone – just in case you've missed nothing. You're moving through nothing, destination nothing, you, Minucius, the Futurists . . . Angry? Let hate give you pause. . . . F.M.V. Cunctator delights in a slow hater.

'Revenge Olympics!' He slow-punched and dodged assailants of air. '*Festina lente!* Kill devils all the parish over!' Beside me, Hanley moved. Exit Cunctator, chanting 'Delay!' In the chant was a name, if you listened.

Short interval.

On our way to the bar, I asked Hanley if he'd known the Cunctator would be performing. Oh, he was advertised, said Hanley, as if the matter were incidental. This smacked of dissembling, since the name 'Fabian' had surely come up recently, in circs Hanley seemed to have an interest in, though they weren't easily sifted from what Karen'd told us about the hue and cry for the Cunctator the time she'd come with Lolly . . .

I'd ordered a round but they seemed to have multiplied about the paper with my name on, so I necked the first and as the gin flared, I felt this gathering was significant, like it wouldn't be the same again, one way or the other, if we willed it, or failed to – then confused myself. At a distance I followed discussion of the Cunctator . . .

'He ain't no stand-up comedian,' Turbo was explaining, thumbs in blazer pockets, remaining fingers gunslinger free, 'and he does not make out to be one on his spec. That ain't his declared profession, Mr Fabian.' I remembered now when I'd heard the name. Outside The Tavern, Turbo telling Hanley Mr Fabian had bum-ache but he'd see him as a favour. That was it. Hugger-mugger . . . 'A humorist, aight, he ain't like a laugh machine. That ain't the way he's chosen.'

Hanley tilted his trilby. Karen watched him swank.

'So what's a humorist then?' she asked Turbo. 'You're just insuring him in case he isn't funny enough!'

'Pooh! Tonight, he was if anything too funny, Mr Fabian – aight? Believe me, lady, I seen Mr Fabian come in drier than that; seen him come in low, seen him swag, seen him strafing; seen him shoot up ground forces. Trust me.'

'What the heck are "ground forces"?'

'Hostile parties.'

'Where?' Karen persisting, as with class bluffer.

'With my own eyes, lady, seen him take out whole place with his humour.'

'Where, though?'

'Greenwich.'

'Did he just trudge up and down till they died of old age?'

It was crushed in the bar; we were forced into a ring of five, drinks held high like an eternal toast.

'No, ma'am.' Turbo sipped orange juice. 'No trudging that night. Half the clients was shanked up. It was open mic. They'd heard a lot of stuff they liked. Mr Fabian turned the tables. Told 'em what they didn't care to hear. He truthed those punks. In their faces. Lady, he merked 'em. They were making this —' Turbo drew his hand before his throat. 'They was up for beef. Like, "You won't make it out the car park, mono!" Mr Fabian, he jived 'em down as if they no more than beetles. He cast his spells, like things no man can understand. He can spit bars like a sorcerer, Mr Fabian. Ah, lady, these badmen and their captains, they just crept away, they hung their heads like little kids, when Mr Fabian was done. His satires is bangin'!'

Hanley was listening greedily; Milly with that expression of only just belonging.

'Have you got it on your phone?' demanded Karen.

Turbo shook his head. No way. I hoped Karen wasn't going to start ragging him about making it all up, but the bell was going for us to return to our seats. As we began to move through the crush, I spotted a face from the past; from the way he re-addressed himself to the woman with him, he'd been talking about me.

So what had Milly made of it so far?

She didn't know. Ever so briefly, her eyes sought approval in mine, irises swirling with tiny sandy patches, like pelted sea. Karen took her arm.

CHAPTER 13

WE'D BEEN OFFERED A drive home with Mr Fabian, which
we seemed to have accepted. Maybe we didn't want the night
to end; or wondered how long it could take; or didn't want to get home
at all. Looking back, it was around this point, I fancy, that I at least was
starting to slip, subject to a gathering will.

As Turbo led us down Cable Street past kebab joints, tech shops,
photographers, Hanley and Karen made fists: *No pasarán!* I listened for
hooves and cries. Nothing. We turned left on to an empty street, passed
a school; on the kerb, a shopping trolley tilted. Red carriages slipped
west across the sky. In an alley stood a long, boxy Mark II Granada.
With us four seated, Karen on my lap, Turbo cruised back for his guvnor.

As he got in, he looked at us, and his face appearing between the
seats was alarming now close, because his right eye was brown and
matey, but his left was a little narrow – and dead. He had a glass bead
in there.

'That's Hanley, that is!' He spoke with a peculiar delight, as if there'd
been doubt in circulation over Hanley's identity, or whether he'd ever
come to sit in Fabian's car. His dead eye was on us, as he considered
the lawyer; we were next, but half his gaze was here already. So he
watched the future. 'And who's this?' He put out his hand, Karen took
it, and Hanley said, 'This is Karen, and this is Carl. Friends of mine.'

'Did you like my show, Karen?'

'No. I thought it were crap!' Karen told him.

Merrily his right eye homed on her, while the left stared cold as Pluto. Like a ventriloquist, I pinched her arse for good manners, which of course didn't work, Karen twisting to dig her nails in, as he noticed: 'Is she speaking for you, Carl?'

'Not exactly.'

Right eye continuing to enjoy the rascal on my knee, he held me in frozen examination. 'Delaying cully, are you? Drive, Turbs!'

'You ain't strapped in, Mr Fabian.'

'Don't fuss, young man. Let's go!'

'Could be,' I told him.

'He could be, he could be. – And this lady?'

'I'm Milly.'

'My wife,' Hanley added.

'Oh, I'm pleased to meet you, dear.'

I was glad he didn't ask her what she thought. Settling, he murmured to his driver. Red carriages came with us in the sky. At the Tower, he wondered if the ladies wished for snacks.

'We had snacks at the Levee,' Karen told him, forgetting Milly.

'Is it a restaurant?'

'No. The Mayor's Levee.'

'Hoity-toity!' cried Fabian Morgan. 'Been glad-handing with the Mayor, have we? We have had our snacks, thank you. Not another crumb. We are replete. We will not dine with the Cunctator!'

'Who said owt about dining?' Karen asked him. 'Thought you meant stopping for chips.' On my knee she was a lively weight. She knew how to perch, this one.

'Chops I was thinking of,' Fabian told her from the front. 'One vowel out. What say we pick up a tray of Chops Hyderabadi from the

LKH? Turbs, would you take a right up there, down Goodman's Stile and back on to Commercial Street? I'll guide you in to the chop joint.'

'Do you want chops, Milly?' asked Karen.

'I'm OK.'

'What about you, Mr Hanley?' enquired Fabian. 'You're quiet back there. Something on your mind, or just quietly enjoying yourself, as is your right?'

'Few chops wouldn't come amiss!' Hanley rubbed his hands.

'Well, I'm not eating chops in a car!' Karen expostulated. 'We've got our best threads on and we'll get messed. Ugh!'

'Wasn't proposing we eat them forthwith. We can go back to my place and consume them in limited luxury. With a cup of claret.'

'I like chops, boss,' Turbo reminded him.

'I know you bloody well like 'em. Sell your soul for a chop, you would, Turbentino – if you haven't already!' The young man enjoyed this, dropping his shoulders at the wheel, as Karen appealed to Milly, in that way of women resisting male plans, or checking the other's wishes. It needed persistence: what *did* she want? Like, ever? Must have wanted Hanley once. But she'd let the marriage go out, unless he kept stoking; for in the higher scheme, nothing mattered, except the final test; then the soulful proved themselves. Saint Milly. Maybe she needed winding up . . . *Hey, Milly! That birthday of yours? We answered in a bottle – unstamped!* As we rolled up Goodman's Stile, Karen kept on at her nicely, as a carer might check an ancient's fancy, in the corner of a day-room.

J. Fabian Morgan crossed Commercial Road, pausing drivers, out of sight. Back with a long box, bandy-legged, in his own time, traffic-heedless . . .

'"Wibbly Wobbly Walk", centenary performance. Original recording, Fred Sheridan, November 1912. Aka "They All Walk the Wibbly

Wobbly Walk", regarded by cultural historians as the missing link between Northern Soul and punk rock.' He sang in different voices as Turbo made for the river, sweat-fume of mutton filling the Granada.

'Hey! Why didn't you turn up the other week?' Karen interrupting the mad din from the front.

'Have a chop and I'll tell you!'

After negotiation we stopped on the Embankment, where we ate chops watching the river and a moored party vessel. Led by a bright, bare-shouldered girl, a group of young men skirted us. Chewing, half listening, I thought of Justin's Romans. Morgan was explaining that he had, as a matter of fact, turned up the other week, but decided not to restrict his performance to the stage, and when Karen suggested that that was an excellent way to carry on when punters had paid fifteen quid to see him, he began to toss chop bones (which he'd been lining up on the parapet) into the Thames, crying, 'There and gone! There and gone! . . . Now you see him – so you think!' till the bones were gone.

We returned to the Granada, and cruised for a bit enjoying the golden lights on the bridges while our humorist chanted something about grim wars and the Thames foaming with blood, then a song Karen knew (since she corrected him), till we hit Chelsea at warp speed, landing by the hospital on Fulham Road. 'Give us five, Turbs!' shouted Morgan. 'Keep the crate running! C'mon, everyone!'

At the big revolving door, he paused to make sure we were all five in the same sector, then shoved the glass wall so hard we had to skip to avoid getting it in the rear. Momentum compelled another circuit, then another, for the humorist was now accelerating the device. Porters, patients who'd gone out for a late smoke, flowerless visitors, quick-dressed for fatal business, passed us like time travellers.

When we'd slowed and entered the hospital, Morgan, pausing by a gel dispenser, invited Karen and Milly to use it.

'Who are we visiting?'

'No one. Thought you wanted to get the food off your hands.'

'Well there were no call for all this palaver! Honestly – what are you on? Making us whizz round in that thing just so we could have a squirt!' Behind Karen, Milly was doing hers like a child setting an example.

'Smells nice though!' explained Morgan. 'Like those gins you made free with between the acts. Often come in for a quality handwash.' This was followed by some business with Hanley, during which Karen mouthed, *We aren't going home with him!*

'Why not?'

'Cos he's up to something with Victor, and I don't want you getting involved. All this messing around's a bloody front. Anyone can see that.'

'Hold on! He's a professional comic. You went to see him first.'

'Don't change the subject. You're coming home with me!' Behind her were signs for the clinics and wards, a sculpted man with a belly of cash. Midnight. This great house of concern still teemed with people: medics, muffin-men, volunteers, traders. It was also a kind of fair.

Clearing my throat, I announced that we were off.

'Oh!' Morgan made a curious movement of the hand. 'In a rush?'

Like cousins on an outing, the Hanleys watched us go.

CHAPTER 14

S UN PATCH ON THE blind, birds rejoicing . . .
'What are you thinking of, Carlo?' Hands behind head, our
Karen, right leg crooked outside the quilt. Against her native energy
and lively ways, this woman was also a great loller, and could while
away a weekend or holiday morning on her back, reading, chatting,
with a plate of red fruit; sometimes waiting her moment: 'You've been
quiet for ages. What was Victor on about last night? Don't pretend
you're dropping off!'

Are you the cunning type? Then you'll have noticed that free answers
in the present foster expectation of free answers in the future, when a
matter may have become less safe to speak of freely. So stinginess in
explanation with respect to merely incomplete truth right now is the
recourse of the 'tactician', against that future time when the truth may
be dangerously incomplete. Or to come to the point, telling her much
at all about William was imprudent. On the other hand, free discourse
of a matter might be resorted to as distraction from another matter that
is 'in the air', and known to be dangerously related to the first (though
knowledge of that relation be still incomplete). So telling her plenty
about William was a means of putting off talk of George Arnold. Yet
you must seem at first disinclined to 'tell plenty', in order to pique the
interest of your lolling interrogator, and then to be discoursing freely

only on account of her tricks of persuasion. Though if this tangle makes no sense to you, you're probably free from deceit and its practices. May your honesty thrive!

So I told her stingily, then more plentifully, of William, excluding the murder theme, amusing her at my expense by trying to do his voice like Hanley, until she hummed that for all my effort to make it funny, I'd looked mighty serious when Hanley was talking to me. And so we turned to other matters.

Incidentally, I'd not been thinking of Hanley at all when she commenced interrogation, but comparing her leg with Laura's, askance, so the whole discourse was a distraction anyway. Laura's leg – *legs* (I hadn't married pirates) – were gold and athletic (she'd run at school and university); they were long, as well. Karen's were white (though the whiteness had decadent severity), and, shall we say, *not* the legs of a racer; but greatly superior as aphrodisiac; and this was due to their various comportments as she lay, glowing like coconut milk. Indeed, the lolling habit itself, around which time voluptuously oozed, was in contrast with Laura's way of rising briskly, always before me, which set in not so long after we'd met, and well before Edward's appearance, turning her back on my brooding recumbency. With positive Laura there'd been no need of tactics. At university, she'd read Earth Sciences, accepting me as any natural form, herself as well. The obscurity of persons wasn't interesting. Marriage was a kind of field-trip.

Now the wife down here, her active interest in the obscurity of her husband arose from a certain luxuriousness of soul that disdained the normal economy of marriage – it pleased her to indulge curiosity. And this I fancy was the artist in her, or aristocrat, whose attention decorates a dull world, makes the pleb feel splendid. Laura was a posh girl, Karen wasn't; her class was rarer. I suppose her interest was due as well to our difference in age, having something of the passion of the antique collector. But it was probably due above all to her belief that I was a liar.

'Have yer finished, cock?'

Rising she went firmly to the door where her platinum kimono hung, donning it like a boxer, tying wristily, humming. Furtive white plebeian, I followed the music, her showband of pots, jars, tubes. In the shower she made queenly quarter-rotations.

'Don't want it again, do you!'

She passed me in her bath cap and towel, northern odalisque.

'That's what Fabian was singing,' I told her, behind the painted screen.

'When?'

'When we came up through Pimlico.'

'So what?'

I stood at the window. Making for a fair afternoon, dry yellow light. There was a text from Hanley, to see if we were OK. Karen and I chatted a while about the head-of-school programme and her upcoming interview (deputy). She'd be a good boss. I bucked her up about her age and experience and background, as we drank strong tea, let her know how proud I was.

But it wasn't just about her, was it?

'I've not to be compromisable.' Inflating her chest. 'Know what I mean, Carlo?'

'Of course, darling.'

'Of course, says he. Cos a whiff of impropriety or owt dodgy where my other half's concerned, dealings with bent folk, law trouble, and it'll be a scandal for me. I stuck by you before. You owe it me.'

'I know.'

'I don't like that grey-haired dibble.'

'Which one?' By God, how she worked round to things!

'Don't "which one" me, Carl! George Arnold.'

'How d'you know he's a copper?'

'I can sniff 'em a mile off. We all can where I was brought up. It's a Catholic thing.'

She made quite a lot of religion in the way of self-explanation, considering she didn't attend mass – or any services, to my knowledge. But with her, it was social-economic, a matter of attitude: anti-authority; sensitive to persecution – sensitive to patrols, and grinning desk sergeants, whose attention was hateful to her community, their pale, quick-fisted sons and defiant daughters.

'He was glad to see you had your appetite back!'

'None of his business! Bloody impertinent coming out with that, like one of the family. – La! Here's Lolly!'

He'd have had dealings with Mulhall. Breathed the same air. Cars parked at woods' edge. Country clubs. Lodges. Nights by the pool. Hardmen, flunkies, WAGs . . .

Isn't too late, son. Keep your head down, support her, grow old. Turn to with Andy like you mean it. Filipino festival, film reviews, treasures of the borough, pollution triangle, happy high-rise, centenarian interviewed: *Dilys Carew remembers her brother coming home early 1919. 'Oh he didn't say much! We went to the ABC tea-rooms.'* – Restaurant of the week: *Noodle fans will be suitably impressed by the choices on offer at Ramen Daddi. My guest got a shred of pork stuck under her crown and was up half the night poking at it with a cocktail stick, but is demanding I take her again!* – Football in the borough: *Old Oak Freebooters are unlikely to forget the visit of Putney Diabolics on the 15th, Andy Ravage, Diabolics' centre back, defending his goal with such determination that the Freebooters' subs' bench was like a 'war zone', according to coach Howard Cant.* – Mayor Montgomery's 'Olympic Night-Ride': *All borough cyclists welcome – bring whistles, trumpets, cow bells!* – Bake-off-Gate: *Mr Piper later revealed*

to have bugged kitchen of crack French pastryman – prize defaulted to Giddy
Kemp . . . This sort of stuff. Is it to be scorned? What is it drives some
of us to darkness?

WHICH OF THESE FOODS *is the essential you?* (d) A lump of undigested
chips – if we remember the days when they were wrapped in newspaper,
with half a gill of vinegar.

As a Politics student, I was a flippant, brooding fellow, though much
attracted already by the idea of investigating corruption, smashing
cover-ups, taking on the powerful (for power equalled evil). My parents
were inclined to the right, so I was reacting against them, after a period
of irritation. The students were committed to the left; I reacted against
them, too, because their slogans annoyed me; and they clarified my
sensation of not being middle-class. My flippancy developed as a way
of impressing, and annoying, them; it extended to my attitude to study.
On the philosophy side, I was flippant about Plato, Machiavelli, Rous-
seau, Hegel, Marx, but particularly about Hobbes, that prudent old fart
with his doctrines of peace, felicity, fear, self-interest. Which didn't
leave me with much in the way of ideas. I took to journalism, where
my flippancy was indulged, and I found expression in irony (or sarcasm),
making some success on the student paper, when it appeared that the
flippancy was only a pose, as I found objects for investigation, powers
to take on. As my enthusiasm grew for truth and justice, so did my
popularity. Evidently, I'd found my calling.

By the time I got to *The G*******, the enthusiasm had fermented
bitterly. That any institution or individual (aside from the typical exemp-
tions of the left) could act without self-interest, or manipulative purpose,
I couldn't conceive. My reaction to a development was to suspect its
motivation. Everything seemed falsehood. My brooding extended to

colleagues, social life, marriage. In company, I poured acid like prosecco. I demanded Laura's loyalty. (What a wanker!) She tried, came out with the denunciations when solicited, browbeaten by my mask of grievance. This was the tension between us, or to be just, the tension I produced. Between the open sea and three walls lay the harbour of her being: the walls were named Prudence, Peace, Felicity. For us, small Edward, and her own career, she planned sensibly, with reasonable expectation of little gains, deserved success. Why did there have to be a fight about anything? If people sat down and talked rationally, listened to each other instead of taking offence if others didn't agree immediately, and left their 'principles' at the door, no more violence – though testosterone was admittedly a biological obstacle. Just look at my face when she said that!

I had to be winning rather than listening. So the tension grew, until it was like a lodger we hadn't invited but now could by no means be rid of, since he was an expert in tenants' rights, as well as an implacable foe of bourgeois couples. Falsehood was everywhere. On this I subjected her to a protracted monologue. I turned on our friends: their voices, their policies in child-rearing and education, their tastes in film, music, food. Ah, the middle classes and their food babble, their long tables, their bread . . . *Do you make your own baba ganoush? Yes. I siphon it from my arse!* So I gnawed at the vitals of a class which I seemed to have joined, I gnawed at my wife, and gnawed at myself – an accumulating lump of undigested chips.

In the end, Laura, who had of course her own will, a quiet and rather effective one, left me to work in the Met Office in Devon, taking Edward with her. Didn't want him falling under my vengeful influence; he had a sunny nature like hers, steady temper and strong arm. He was representing the county at youth cricket. I would have taught him how to sledge.

I suppose around this time, my insistence that the fair is false gave way decisively to the belief that the foul has a truth of its own – though that belief had been forming since my first days on papers. And it was this that drove me to darkness. But more of these matters further on . . .

———————

'LOLLY'S AT THE MELANCHOLY Minstrel. She wants us to join her for lunch. D'you fancy that, Carl? It'll be a hoot! Say yes, and stop looking mardy.'

'I'm not mardy. I'm just thinking.' I wanted to go over to her in the settee corner. I was feeling well lucky to have her, I can tell you. If we stuck together, it'd be all right. Bugger Hanley and his texts. 'Why've you been nattering to her for quarter of an hour if we're going to see her?'

'Cos I didn't know if you'd say yes. Besides, we were just burning off the top gas.'

'Hey?'

'Like they do in blast furnaces. You know nowt about industry, you!'

At my direction, we went to join Lolly and her cousin by the main road north, passing the hostels, and eluding Hanley.

CHAPTER 15

MONDAY MORNING, I SUBORNED Fabiana, who'd had her hair finger-waved, to obtain councillors' numbers, and tried to ring Barnfield. I left a message at his office (he was a finance man for Unite), a message on his mobile. Around eleven, I had another shot, piqued he might be giving me the swerve. I made the first calls in the toilet, the second out on the flyover when I went to fetch coffee, so Andy didn't hear.

Just before lunch, I had a call from a woman called Marcia Jones on Barnfield's mobile, asking quietly who I was. I told her who, said I wanted to speak to Barnfield on council business. Well, I'd have to wait, because he wasn't conscious. Had he been taken ill? No. Steve'd been hit by a car and was in hospital. She wasn't at all keen to identify the hospital, but when I made out I was a friend (which the councillor was in no condition to confirm at that moment), she named it as the place where we'd gone to clean our hands the night before last with J. Fabian Morgan. Before she rang off, she told me the car hadn't stopped; she had trouble keeping her voice down when she said that.

Standing at the window, rear of the office, I watched District Line carriages emerge from the slot beneath the flyover, curving west. Among the bushes, rubbish, and trackside sheds, must have been where Hanley talked with William. Three and a half acres of prime wasteland down there. Barnfield risked his neck saying so.

Andy had something to say. After we'd departed from the Levee, the fella called Arnold took him aside, asking about the paper, who I was, etc., so Andy told him, thinking that this may be an entrepreneur, developer, or some sort of money man we could benefit from knowing, and the fella went like this with his chin and was sure my name rang a bell, at which point Andy asked Mr Arnold his interest, whereupon that silver-haired gentleman laughed again and said, when he'd had lunch with me and my wife in Spain, he'd been meaning to ask if we hadn't crossed paths, or some such, a while ago, but with one thing and another we'd never got round to the past. Lovely woman, my wife, by the way, knew her mind and wasn't afraid to speak it either. Oh, she'd given George Arnold the *no jodas!* and no mistake when he pulled her leg about a stomach upset and asked if her old man had slipped a Mickey in her cocktail the night before . . .

What was '*no jodas*'?

Andy wasn't sure.

Meant, 'Don't fuck with me!' If Fabiana'd been pale, silvery, she'd have passed as a twenties screen siren with that finger wave.

So was that it?

There was more. Friend Arnold had been pushing it a bit, to Andy's mind, about my career, like he was after something but waiting for Andy to supply it, rather than coming at it direct, then he was going to click his fingers like, That was it! So Andy, not liking the feeling he was being played, and not liking something else either that he couldn't quite put his finger on – Andy told it to Mr Arnold straight. I'd been a *G******* man, which had George Arnold shaking his silver head in a kind of wonder. And now working on a community paper? Struck him as noble, very noble indeed, as fine an example of what they now called 'downsizing' as you could hope for. Bravo! And no doubt there'd been some problem where I was before, personality clash, honourable resignation, or some such – or one of these spots of bother like Lord Leveson was presently looking into? With the report due in November, must be a good many press people losing sleep just now . . .

So Andy Ravage, he told Mr Arnold, Sorry, but he didn't discuss his staff, and Mr Arnold nodded; for that was a wise policy, in his experience, and no doubt it was all on record anyway for nosy parkers to have their fill – and good luck to them; but nothing worse than intruding into another fella's professional mishaps, misjudgements, and so forth – and he fancied I had more lives than a cat anyway; then up comes a character with shaved head and short beard who looked like he was ex-services, and Mr Arnold said, 'What's been keeping you, Bowls?' Bowls told him they were ready now, skip, whereupon George Arnold shook Andy's hand, proposed that life was full of failures who give up five minutes too soon, and before Andy could ask who he meant, took his leave.

'Did I tell him something I shouldn't?' Andy watching my face. 'What is it, Carlo?'

'He going to vom!' called Fabiana. 'Get him something! Don't just stand there, Andy! God's sake, you men!' Emptying the waste bin by her desk.

Stinking black mass of suffocating bubbles. Double aspect, treble aspect, overload. It cannot be processed. You fucking try – you've been following this shit. You try, bub, you, sister! The alreadiness of Mr Arnold – process if you will . . .

I rallied as I had to, before Andy twigged I was still preoccupied with Mulhall, making out it was Arnold's way with Karen had upset me. But here if ever was a warning. Well, there was still time to bail out, draw the horns in – wasn't there?

Gathering papers and cartons, Fabiana filled the bin.

*

HERE CAME DONNA JUAN, sack on shoulder, below a paper sky. He wore a yellow T-shirt, big brown beads, leather jeans, Uggs.

'Why are you looking so mardy?'

'My wife calls me that.'

'Your wife calls you what?' T-shirt decorated with butcher's diagram: *REAL MEN EAT MEAT!*

'"Mardy".'

'Do I remind you, Carol?' He was wearing black eyeliner.

'You still up for the article?' Half hoping he wasn't.

'Not on your nelly!'

'How come? Has somebody had a word?'

He checked parked cars.

'Well,' I told him, 'better not say anything to me. Can't trust me any more than any of them. Best get along with your sack, kiddo!' I pointed to the top of a gold-brick apartment. Corinthian columns formed the entrance.

'But I haven't got anyone!' he hissed. 'Not a soul to talk to. Not now. How d'you think that is? You don't know you're born, Carolo! Just step on and leave me! Yellow-bellied rat! What a skank!' He'd become shrill. 'You said we were mates! Where've you bastard been, hey? I hate you! Hate your skanky eyes! Out of my bastard way or I'll strike you down, I swear!'

I made to let him pass. Could have let him go forever. Wouldn't that have been prudent? Very. But there are times when more than vainglory drives us, even dogs like me – something resembling a virtue.

At six and twelve o'clock, we stood facing each other. I bent to him: 'Why've you got no one now?'

'What?'

'You said you had no one to talk to now. So you had someone before. What happened?'

'They took him away.'

'Who?'

'Pep.'

'He was your mate up there?'

'Suppose so. He weren't bad for a *mignotta*.'

'Hey?'

'A *bagascia*! Don't you know owt?'

'Ah. He was Italian, Pep?'

'He was Roman!' Donna Juan scolded me, like I could get nothing right. 'Him and Albo. But me and Pep got on better. He taught me good words when Albo didn't come in. We had a laugh. Told me all about his city and the river. I could name the seven hills. My subject, that is. *Was*.' In passion of bitterness, his face hardened, then relaxed. He was a trouper, this lad.

I'd thought of him yesterday with Karen and Lolly, in the narrow, walled garden of The Melancholy Minstrel. We had talk of the classroom problem, Lolly filling in Cousin Goldie. The lads tormenting her with the Imad project, students who'd called him 'batty kaffir' and told him he should be gassed – weren't they the new face of Hanley's past tormentors? Like the state can't eradicate hatred, since its correction among one group tends to pass it to another, blowing the seeds where they're fertilized, by the spirit of entitled revenge. Seen the footage of the Nation of Islam, ramming the Matthews Inquiry? Got the measure of 'institutional racism'? Call Al-Muhajiroun the new NF, and think you've worked it out.

Except that one of Lolly's tormentors was white. What quality of hatred was this? What degree of conversion, when the white anti-Semite joins the Black Flag? When I was done with Mulhall . . .

'Wake up!'

'No one else is on your side. Your sack's heavy, you're on your own.'

'Where are you off to anyway?' He was stalling.

'Hospital.'

'Are you having a scan or summat?'

'The man who took Pep, he had silver hair, didn't he?'

'No. It were a guy with a beard, and a beanie. He were getting on, he was fit though.'

'Bet you didn't see what he was driving. He took your mate and you didn't even clock his vehicle.'

'That's what you think, Carolo! I were up in the belvedere peeping. Red hatchback.'

'Who else was in it?'

'Another man was on the pavement.'

'Did he have silver hair?'

'Could have.'

'Where was Albo? – D'you want to drop that sack off? We could have a burger.'

'It's OK. I'll bring with.'

'OK, droog. Let's go.'

In the mews, Sibyl Grove sat wrong-way on, back to the solid cinema.

'He's been staring down here since quarter to eleven! I'm not having it!'

'Who has?'

'Had a megaphone the other day. The coppers don't do a thing. Or these community lilies. He sees 'em off. They're frightened of him.'

Where the solid cinema rolled, her bugbear sat upon a folding chair, guitar case at his side.

'He's a nark, that's what he is,' decreed Sibyl. 'I've got his fucking number.'

'You called him the Gonk the other day,' remembered Donna Juan.

'Who asked you, poppet?' In unrequired shades, Sibyl Grove turned her head.

'Just showing I listen.'

'He's that as well, dear.' She seemed to have thawed towards DJ. 'He'll cop it one of these days. I've seen it in the stones.'

'Which stones?'

'These.' Waving at the cobbles. She lit a cigarette, offered DJ the pack. 'Where are you two off to anyway?'

'Just for a bit of lunch.'

'Is he still there?'

'Yeah. He's supping from a silver tankard.'

'That's his loyalty present.'

'How d'you know he's a nark?'

DJ gave me a look as if everyone knew.

'Well he doesn't make his wad from strumming that fucking lute, does he, Carlo? He's in the bookies often enough, he has plenty for beer; and as I said, the fuzz leave him be. What's your abduction, cupcake? He's on the payroll. – *Bon appétit*, boys!'

'Bye, Sibyl!'

'Say a prayer for me, poppet!'

In the burger palace, Donna Juan told me that Albo hadn't been showing up lately – not regularly. Might have been frightened. That, or he'd been ratting on Pep.

'Who'd he have been frightened of, Donna?'

'Don't call me that, for Christ's sake! Just call me John! You don't want business.'

Good to have that settled. 'Did they use force when they took Pep, John?'

'No.' Donna Juan chewed neatly at his Rodeo. 'The bearded guy, he just asked for him and told him someone wants to see you.'

'It was only Saturday they took him. He might be back.'

'How d'you know that?' On the couch where we sat, Donna Juan drew away. 'I never told you it was Saturday. Oh my God! Who are you? I'm out of here!' He'd begun to shriek; we were being watched. 'Are you a pig or summat? Don't touch me! Take your bastard hands off! I'll stripe you!'

'What with? A gherkin? Now listen to me, Yorkie!'

He ran outside, leaving his sack. Returning, he'd lost face. Back in the mews we lodged down this end, by a planter crowded with shrubs.

'I know it was Saturday – stop looking that way, I'm levelling with you! I know it was Saturday because before they came for Pep, they took out a councillor who'd been asking questions, knocked him down in that red hatchback.'

'How d'you know that?' Orange flowers hung above him on a trellis.

'Cos I'm a bloody journalist. I find things out. He's in Intensive Care now, the councillor. That's where I was going when I bumped into you. They'd have meant to finish him. I was you, I'd get out of that place pronto and fuck off home to Halifax.'

'I can't.'

'Why can't you?'

'Van Spenser put me passport in the Phoenix this morning.'

'The what?'

'The Phoenix Fortress. The safe.'

'What on earth for? You're a British citizen, for Christ's sake!'

'I have to pretend to be Latin or I'll not get work!'

'You mean Van Spenser actually thinks you're Spanish?'

'Colombian.'

'Does it look like a Colombian passport?'

'He never checked it.'

'Fucking hell! How stupid is he? Can't he tell accents?'

'Oh, he's South African. He's got no education. I tek it round with me anyway.'

'Why?'

'So I can go exploring anytime I fancy! That's me goal. The Dry Valleys.' Like, *Try and stop me!*

'You better get back with that laundry,' picturing my Edward in beads, fur, leather. Strictly fancy dress. 'You'll be trying Van Spenser's patience.'

'Oh, he won't be there. Just comes in to nose or cash up.'

'So who's the boss – the day boss?'

'Me.'

'You?'

'I've made Major-Domo.'

Attaboy!

We agreed he should take the laundry back and accompany me to the hospital – he seemed set on this; so I went to chat to Sibyl while he nipped up to Lords with his sack. The southern sky was bright-stained, she drowsed beneath an oozing sun, but on a sudden rose and turned her chair. Watch! On the screen of the solid cinema, Turbo in leather hoodie and joggers, Gonk squatting. Turbo giving him the come-on, wafting air like a man refreshing himself, doing him twice with rapid dainty kicks . . .

'Hee hee!' Sibyl Grove was well satisfied. 'Serves the bastard right! Called him coon the other day. I heard. Had the bloody megaphone with him. Chanting through all morning, strumming his ukulele, lilies giving him wide-o, then the spade, he walked past and he's, "Hey, coon! Banana boat's leaving. Get back to where you once belonged!" Well he's had his today. Look at him! Oh, spume blood, Daddio! Jet it, baby! Your boat's well and truly fucked!'

The old hate was still vigorous.

CHAPTER 16

O<small>N THE WALK TO</small> the hospital, we had Cornettos, then stopped
for a gin and ginger; Donna Juan had something to tell me.

One time he'd been chatting with Pep – they were playing Angry
Birds – and Pep, he told Donna Juan that Albo excepted, who was like
his brother, and Donna Juan excepted also, who was like his sister, the
only other English guy he'd cared for, his name was Justin. But Justin
wasn't really no *mignotta*. Pep and Albo met him one time in the West
End and they all three went to eat some whore food cos they thought
he was a fun guy. So they chat about this and that, and he told them he
interned for a big *capo* in a newspaper, a cool newsman, *uomo da ris-
pettare*, and this *tipo*, he was going to give Justin a good money job if
Justin helped him take down a big don who ran a lot of shit, and he'd
whacked out three people at least, maybe five, so it was dangerous work,
but Justin, he was up for it, cos his passion was justice. So they ask
Justin the name of the don, and he told them and they're both like,
cazzo! cazzo! porca puttana! The manager told them they got to leave
his place if they didn't cool it. Well they couldn't eat no more anyway,
not after Justin said them the name, so they went round and round the
three of them *chiacchierando*, by Soho Square.

Cos this don, he came to Lords. He didn't like contact with the boys,
didn't want that. Told Pep he couldn't touch him – if he did was a risk.

What he liked, for all anyone knew, was talk with the boy he selected. Sometimes he talked about his family: didn't have a boy of his own, *Sistamandi* did. How you test a kid when he's *nipote del capo*? Prove him? Bastard's always had it his own way, spoilt, protected, *sotto l'ombrello*. What kind of man is he? Who grows without effort, *vale la pena*? These boys here made effort all right, they were soldiers, shit they put up with: three, four times a day, they engaged the enemy. Maybe the last guys who raised themselves from the bottom, old-school like himself. It was foul graft but they aspired for something better. Respect. On and on like this. *Bla bla* . . .

They wondered if he was *capo genuino*. His suits weren't cool, shirts too dark. It was only Van Spenser who kissed his ass, gave him Boss Cabin, sent out for shawarmas and prosecco if he wanted a snack; and told the boys, no one mention his name, not even to themself *sotto voce* or under pillow, or to their mother . . . Mr Mulhall did not like publicity, Mr Mulhall this, Mr Mulhall that. All Van Spenser talked about. Why didn't the guy give himself a false name, he so damn particular about anyone saying his proper one? Putting on Van Spenser he was big-shot *capo*?

But now *Gesù Cristo*, Justin telling them this, they're gonna watch their mouth!

When Justin came, pretend *mignotta*, Mulhall talked to him *doppia tariffa*. Pep and Albo, they could see it – Boss Cab had closed circuit – Mulhall wasn't even bothered to tell Van Spenser to switch it off. Like *Grande Fratello*. Talking to him, on and on and on. But when he'd gone, Pep and Albo, they asked Justin if he was coming up town with them. He wasn't coming with. OK. He wanted they go for sushi down the road? He didn't want sushi. Didn't want nothing. His face was changed. They asked him, What is it? He speak bad to you? *Dillo, amico!*

So he told them. Mulhall asked him what kind of man he was. Was he like the other boys at Lords? His own man? *Uomo singulare?* What d'you say to that? What's the good answer? He asked Justin if he believed in heaven. Justin said he didn't believe in heaven, didn't believe in God. So Mulhall, he asked him, You got a better idea, then? Must have! What's your better idea? I got one! But you've got to have your own. But Justin couldn't tell him. And he's, Well, maybe you want to come down to the woods? Or is it possible you just want to run off and see your guvnor, put your report in? Cos if you ain't your own man, you have to put in a report, account for your time. That's how it is, that's how the world clicks. What you frightened of? Coming to the woods? Ha ha! You ain't got no more bollocks than a *scoiattolo*, you're frightened of coming to the woods. I'll warrant it's all you been thinking of, these last weeks, what goes on in Bostall Woods. But when I invite you to take a look, you shy away. Now it strikes me there's two reasons why that could be so, Justin. One: you're frightened of dying, which suggests you been playing with the idea there's something *cattivo* going on down there. Two: you're frightened of nothing, and that does tend to suggest that when you've finished playing with the idea there's something crooked going on under the trees, you will face the fact you can't come up with anything, you ain't got any evidence, gossip, rumours, information, you just got a hole. And your budding career, it's getting sucked into it like spaghetti in a fat man.

Cos a third thing you are frightened of is your guvnor. You come away from this penthouse with nothing, how's it going to stand between you and him? Either he persuaded you to come up here, and he'll know he can't rely on you for the goods. Or, you tried to show some initiative – maybe he was none too willing – and you're going to look like a hothead, a berk, a fool. Whatever, he'll be looking for a new boy pronto. That's how it will be. Cos that also is how the world clicks.

So my advice to you, Justin, you want to avoid death or disgrace, is to cross the seas. Never come back. Not until the rest of us has finished with each other. Maybe not even then.

A HUNCH CONFIRMED IS a glory. Even when it shows you've been right royally played, it caps that. Now check your sources!

'How've you got all that, John – I mean exactly like that?'

'Exactly like what?'

Entering the hospital, we were separated by the segments of the door with which the Cunctator'd had his sport, and by the time we'd rendezvoused, I let it drop. Doing voices was on-trend. We passed the sculpted man with his belly case of glass, sterling meal within, looked for directions to Intensive Care, took an escalator to a bank of lifts. Here we waited with a gently tutting crowd.

'They should paint angels up there.' DJ pointing at the bright glass roof. 'And the Devil as well.' I wished he'd cool it. 'Like *Nuestra Señora de Putas*.'

An old lady asked him what that was.

'It's a big church in Bogota!' glimmered DJ. 'You could be an angel, Carolo.'

The lift revealed a trolley, patient in bliss. We parted like the Red Sea.

'You'd be a darling angel with big white wings like an albatross, all by yourself on the southern oceans!'

Fucking hell.

'But albatrosses are unlucky!' the old lady remembered.

'Exactly,' Donna Juan told her. 'That's why he must keep to himself, south of the 55th Parallel!'

'Where does that go, dear?'

'From the Land of Fire to the South Sandwich Islands, and then open sea, for thousands and thousands and thousands of miles!'

'How do you know all these things?'

'I'm studying Geography.'

'How wonderful! My grandson's a BSc. Your dad must be so proud!'
She went away with her hessian bag.

'Come along, Daddy!' Taking my sleeve.

'Why d'you spout all this bollocks at the top of your voice?'

'You are so mardy, Carolo, it's untrue. Look at face on you!'

At ITU reception, we had a palaver. They wanted to know who we were and hadn't heard of Barnfield. I persuaded them to search for admissions because I was his brother. Behind us, people murmured in the family room. A white kid with close-cut hair came out in a 'Terry 26' T-shirt and stared at Donna Juan's bull diagram. DJ made a face and the kid ran back. An Irish nurse with her hair up told us Mr Barnfield was off the ventilator; OK for friends to visit. As we passed the family room, where people held hands or stared at free papers, John Terry pointed at us and his mum said, 'Him?' Then we cleansed our paws in that fabulous gel, squirting extra shots till we were almost high; Donna Juan touched my forefinger.

We entered by a desk of monitors. A nurse smiled; behind him, a redhead bent to Barnfield, who lay among wires, vessels, screens, mumpish and grey. He stared like a fish. Was he seeing the scene where they drove him down, striving for the faces in the red hatchback?

The redhead was now stroking his face, eyes wishing us away, if we were there at all – Joe Buck and Ratso Rizzo in reverse. This must be Marcia Jones. She took off her shoes and lay beside him, like a gawky schoolgirl with her pet. We hadn't even brought fruit or flowers, or whatever you bring a Labour man who once blacked a Tory's eye and wouldn't take a taxi on council expenses.

'Take a pew, Hyatt!' he called. 'You and your friend. Brought any beer?'

I sat in a chair beside a ventilator, Donna Juan perching on the window sill.

'He's only just come off that thing.' The ventilator looked like a Carthusian nun.

'How's it going?'

'He's punctured a lung, dislocated his shoulder, broken two ribs, fractured his cheekbone, and he's been severely concussed,' Marcia Jones told the world. Wouldn't look me in the face.

'I'm alive,' Barnfield told me. 'Which wasn't the plan, I'll warrant.'

'You can bloody bet it wasn't!' said Marcia Jones. She was an Australian, or Kiwi.

'Have the police been up?'

'Oh they're in no hurry.' Marcia held his wrist above the inserts. Donna Juan stared at *Grazia*, shamanic glamour boy. Barnfield did something with his head, wired to an EEG. 'He wants to know who your friend is.'

'I'm a whore.'

'A sex worker?' said Marcia Jones.

'Please yourself,' Donna Juan told her. 'I'm also a geographer.'

'What's your specialism?'

'Well, I was doing a project on ventifacts – before I interrupted my studies.'

'This is John,' I told them. A Filipina appeared at Barnfield's side with a little plastic tube for him to drink. Donna Juan watched him closely, caught my eye, sniffed.

'You a Yorkshireman, John?'

'Yes I am, actually.'

'Where's home?' Barnfield rallying from the morphine.

'Halifax.'

'You've got the original guillotine, haven't you?'

'Ayuh! We call it the Gibbet. It's only a model there now though. Have you seen it?'

'Yes. Did some auditing at Calderdale Council. It's a horrible bloody thing.'

'They'd lop your top off for stealing owt in those days,' explained Donna Juan. 'Like the Saudis do now.'

Marcia said something about Amnesty.

'Who decides the punishment?' Barnfield a little high.

'It were Mayor of Wakefield,' Donna Juan told him. 'Every school-kid knows that. We used to doss on it when we were teenagers. Take turns to lie under the block.'

'The Mayor!' Barnfield grinned among his wires.

'Went back to the Lord of the Manor.'

'Lord of the Manor, Star Chamber, Parliament, the courts: our punishment officers . . .' Barnfield faded, concentrated. Staff murmured at a table of monitors. Round another bed, curtains were drawn. 'And anyone else with connections, clout.'

'You're thinking of what's just happened to you?' I said.

'Bastards gave him the treatment! Don't laugh, honey! Just take it easy.'

'They were a Millwall mob!' Barnfield was amused. '"The Treatment". Used to wear surgical masks. Looked more like fucking nuns. Came to the Lane once. You had to laugh!'

'To my mind,' said Marcia Jones, 'it's a complete bloody racket, football in this country.'

We groused about football a while, and I was thinking we should leave this battered Tottenham fan in peace, or get to the point, when he starts on Donna Juan about Van Spenser, and how was life with that old fox these days. DJ demurred at first, like he didn't know where the good councillor was coming from, but I noticed he was going easy on the insolence, Barnfield being in the condition in which we'd found him, suggesting now that he'd give Van Spenser a right braying if he had his way, but a job was a job, and a working girl, tee hee hee, couldn't be fussy in time of austerity. So Barnfield wondered why a student should be expected to interrupt his studies and enter exploitative employment on the say-so of a Tory Chancellor? Cunning councillor (my little whoreson on the window sill caring for no one's 'say-so', even if the interruption of his studies wasn't actually down to the government) suggesting now that a deal of trade at Lords was composed of Tory faces, from his info.

Oh everyone knew *that*. Those boogs were in and out as casual as if they were popping into Pret. It was the big fish Van Spenser kept 'Incognito Order No. 1' for.

So what happened if you broke that? Barnfield closing his eyes.

Well, you had your passport destroyed, you never saw your mother again, you got drugged, stripped, dumped – in the middle of Northamptonshire; force-fed rotten chicken or poisoned oysters; sodomized with a Hansson flare; your Twitter account hacked with paedo images; you just got taken away.

Barnfield asked if he was serious. Well what did he think? So Barnfield expressed the opinion that John may be making light of it, and understandably, given his working conditions, whereupon DJ began to droop on the sill, either because Barnfield had got him right, or because the councillor had no sense of irony.

Then Barnfield lay back in pain, Marcia Jones giving me the hard look, though she knew this was necessary even if it was killing her man, for our councillor was wondering now whether Incognito Order No. 1 might not be helping a certain criminal, who was in the business of destroying the community to line his own pockets. Donna Juan sneered. What concern of his was it if the community was destroyed, seeing as he had no part in it, and people spat and said things whenever he went out to take the laundry? But Marcia said, 'Look around you, John! This ward you're sitting in, these nurses and docs, Hyatt there and me and Steve, we're your community!' So DJ asked how Mulhall was going to destroy any of this, and my stomach tightened like a chopping board.

Quietly, Barnfield asked if he should have said that name, and Donna Juan, like fuck it, all the totty up there, every *mignotta*, said the name, and you might get taken away, or arse-raped *terminado*, and you might not either, because as even an idiot knew, it screwed up the economy to kill or disappear the workers. You had to be a right lemon to think it was run like that.

Here I had to interrupt, regarding the fate of Pep just two days ago, and DJ sniffed. *That* was nothing to do with Mulhall. And as I worked back over our talk on the way here, he drops a bombshell. Pep had been talking to a lawyer lately. Not in the penthouse; lawyer took him to The Hank of Rope, and when Pep came back for the afternoon, he was saying what a *pranzo* he just had with a beautiful golden guy in a trim suit and funny voices he was doing him, and not letting Pep pay for a thing, and they'd had pie and greens, several Belgian beers and brandy to finish, and Pep slightly pissed and not watching his tongue – but why should he really? – when Van Spenser pops out from the Boss Cabin where he's been installing faster broadband, and smiling in Pep's face like, Oh, who was this then? So Pep says, Oh, just a friend. So Van Spenser's like, Well why not bring your friend up here so he can enjoy himself proper? You weren't doing him up in The Hank by any chance, like in the Gents – and pocketing the whole fee? And Pep's like, Absolutely not. Man didn't want business. Just wanted to chat. So Van Spenser's asking what they chatted about, and Pep, he isn't so good at hiding things, being a truthful guy, so he's like, Oh this and that, and trying to make something up, and it's obvious there's something else he's not saying to Van Spenser, though he thinks Van Spenser didn't hear him say the golden guy was a lawyer – luckily. Well, Van Spenser, he grins, like *Ag fok dit!* Let the matter drop! Just so long as Pep takes care who he lets buy him lunch, and make sure you tell Van who you been with, baby – OK? *Geen probs!*

We were all ears, as DJ continued.

But Van Spenser, he kept his spies round the area, and by evening, he got wind that who Pep had been for lunch with was Lawyer Hanley, which Donna Juan knew to be the case since he was just coming on reception after his break when Van Spenser went to the front door. The person Mrs Grove called the Gonk was out there (and the boys were mighty glad that fright wasn't coming in for a tickle, cos he was out of any known category). Van Spenser wouldn't let him in either (even he had some sense of hygiene), but Donna Juan could see who it was, and though he didn't know who Lawyer Hanley might be, the information was obviously interesting cos Van Spenser gave the Gonk extra and said to keep it coming, for if he didn't, Van Spenser would be having a word with the housing association about the guy's place and stuff he got up to in there and brought home that were grounds for eviction.

'So what's Van Spenser's interest in Lawyer Hanley?' Marcia Jones wanted to know. None of them could tell. It was a black bubble that I fancied that Hanley's unfinished story would process (keeping this to myself). We had some talk of the latter, who was known to Barnfield and Marcia Jones as a bonzer brief, heart in the right place. By another bed, a bright-eyed nurse checked readings. Once, she turned her head and listened – and Marcia Jones gave DJ a look.

Barnfield tried to speak, controlling pain, so Marcia Jones's face became hard against his enemies and she took over. From what they'd heard, there was a visitor to Lords who was interested in the flyover site, all three and a half acres of it, and no doubt that visitor (who we could all name if we were under oath, but why take risks when we were sitting in ITU precisely on account of that visitor's influence, it may well be?) – no doubt that visitor took advantage of the presence of local politicos to advance his interest by means that ordinary men and women would consider totally bloody corrupt. For instance, proposed developments of those acres as an Olympic venue had been blocked three years running at least.

Fucking right, said Barnfield, coming in from pain. The visitor in question was a dab hand in managing ecos and Tories, so as to keep prime land on ice. And obviously, eyeing me, the impact on the community was going to be felt pronto in the disappearance of worthwhile concerns like the *Chronicle*. When your visitor's POPGS application was granted with three cheers, after phantom consultation, our premises'd be flattened.

'What's "POPGS"?'

'Privately owned public green space, John.'

I felt the pressure of this, of course, as I was feeling the pressure of several persuasive tongues these days. A decision was being called for, and the promises I'd made to Karen about not getting involved in any more dark shit, would not be honoured – already weren't being . . . But a big-thighed consultant and his team were along to look at Steve Barnfield, and DJ and I really ought to sling our hook, though we'd had no talk with the brave councillor about what I'd come with a mind to discuss directly – namely, the attempt on his life: another of those recent issues that seemed shy of complete representation.

On the way out, after the long weight for the lift, Donna Juan said something that did, I suppose, bring one of them to an uncomfortable terminus: 'You were his guvnor, weren't you, Carlo?' Justin he meant.

So glory, or its shadow, drives us on.

PART II
Predy; or,
The Treatment

CHAPTER 17

THOUGH I DIDN'T THINK Donna Juan should go back to Lords, I wasn't kind or mad enough to invite him home, where Karen informed me that Hanley and the Cunctator'd been to call – and why'd my phone been off for much of the afternoon? This being why they'd 'popped round' in person, apparently. She'd only just got in herself, and there she was, trying to meditate, when they'd turned up, fresh from the pub (fat chance of concealing that), Hanley coming on all suave and holding his hat, Mr Etiquette, J. Fabian Morgan practising jokes, asking her for daft names, trundling into the living room without being invited. Really, it was just too much . . .

Hold on! Had she felt threatened?

Not as such.

Had foul language been used?

No.

So far, this had been a mobile complaint, voice following, receding. By the red alcove, she confronted me, still in her dress of butterflies, with the cakey scent she somehow picked up from a day among kids.

'Why was your phone off, Carl? It's not like you.'

I switched on the wall lamps. It had been off because of the hospital visit. Explaining which was not likely to take the following course . . .

Oh, Councillor Barnfield was the victim of a murder attempt on Saturday, sweetheart.

No! By whom?

Why, I strongly suspect our silver-haired friend from Abril's and the Levee, and an ex-member of the notorious 'Force Research Unit'.

Goodness me, Carl! Can you be sure?

Well, it certainly fits in with certain things that are coming to light, which I've yet to connect into a story that will persuade the authorities.

Oh, darling, but you must pursue this to the end, for justice's sake!

The lamps emitted their harem light.

So I told her I'd been with the tyke from Lords, the one I'd mentioned. I'd taken him to see an occupational therapist called Marcia Jones, a Kiwi, who was talking him through his options of returning to study (on account he'd interrupted his degree after a problem with radicalized students) and then resuming his life on a normal basis.

Karen hummed: 'Because it distracts me when you have your phone off, and I've my interview and mock to get ready for.' In their startling way, the school had brought the deputy-head interview forward to Friday, and she was having a dry run Thursday. 'Angie Pole's going to put me through it.' A dynamic person, Angie Pole was her chum at an all-girls' school in Ravenscourt Park, where the pupils learned mindfulness and Chinese ideograms in Reception; by the time they hit Level 4, they could recite *A Midsummer Night's Dream*, the Declaration of Independence, and the 'Periodic Table Song'; and defend themselves against knife attacks . . .

To make up for the Hanley-Morgan invasion – I took my wife for tea at the Lebanese. If I wasn't going to come clean now – when? Yesterday morning's reflections on a quiet life at the *Chronicle* were a coward's reckoning. I was being called on – by community, it now seemed. The Andalusian waitress brought paradise salads, grilled cheese, broad beans, lamb, chicken, shatta, glossy toum – a Monday-banquet. As one recovering from outrage, Karen feigned small appetite. Through a window, two guys packed cushions of bread from a belt. I mean, what's community but the voices you most hear, how they border your experience, have their part in it?

'You need them like you need me!' Green soul-searchers working deep (if you had depths). 'Don't you? That's the thing, Carlo.' Tearing bread neatly, Karen wiped her plate. 'Mother Jago told me I'd end up with someone like you.'

End up? 'Ah? – Lamb's very good today, isn't it? Massive helping! Have a bit more, sweetheart? Can't finish this.'

'Yes, it was an autumn afternoon just after clocks went back. We were having tea and slices, and she said she'd been looking at my cards again, and he would be tall, deceitful and dogged.'

'Was that it?'

'No it wasn't, Carl. She said he'd never be finished, the man I married. Which we know one meaning of; and I fancy another is you can't be yourself by yourself: you need others for your meaning, your sense of what you're about – or you think you do; because even when you've got your team together, what you do with them won't be the thing that completes you, tells you what you are by what you've achieved – or satisfies you.'

She was laughing with the waitress as I paid the bill.

On the high street, Turbo appeared from the glass of Frango Oporto like Harry Worth, and smiled as we came on, bowing slightly to Karen. Mr Hanley and John Fabian Morgan were waiting, if I'd be kind enough to come up. Karen made an 'Off you go, then!' face, and though I'd just been forming a resolution, the sensation of slipping I'd had before we accepted the lift home on Saturday was strong again.

She was proposing to take Turbo for an ice cream while I was with my chums – from a certain dilation of the nostrils and movement of the chest, I saw she'd enjoyed being bowed to by the young man. Turbo looked uneasy. Was he shy about an older lady, this ruthless gallant who'd broken a man's face earlier in the afternoon, on the solid-cinema screen? For the evening, he'd changed into smart pants, shirt with braces; brown brogues glistening. Maybe had a date . . . Announcing now he didn't eat sugary foods. Well, they could go to The Tavern for a drink, then, just the two of them, and wait for me to come back. Turbo could have an orange juice, or a bottle of Fentimans delish cordial – how about that? Left thumb in braces, Turbo declared Mr Hanley and J. Fabian Morgan had invited the lady to attend the summit. Oh had they now? Well, she'd had enough of that pair of jokers already this evening. Here, Turbo raised his hand as if on oath, or to halt the progress of error. His boss used his jokes to get his work done, nothing more, nothing less than that. Well that was pretty obvious, Karen pointed out, seeing as he was a stand-up comic. Didn't make him funny.

In the event, I went up alone, Turbo accompanying Karen to The Tavern to justify the ways of his boss. The passage between Frango Oporto and the charity shop next door was narrow and not clean; upstairs, the landing was poorly lit. Was this the permanent residence of the Cunctator, a pied-à-terre, a 'gone to the mattresses' set-up? He let me in with a heartiness offset by his fixed eye: 'Upsy, Calderoni! Missed you earlier!'; and we passed through a front room looking on to the street where there was an unusually long brown-leather sofa, L-shaped, and not much else apart from plastic packing tubs, and a turntable. The kitchen was narrow, cleanish; on a surface, I saw power drinks and tubs of protein powder, as J. Fabian Morgan led me out on to a black iron balcony that overlooked a patch of garden and the Tube tracks. From a kidney-shaped occasional table, Hanley rose to kiss me.

'So here we are at last!' cried Morgan, producing a chair and pouring red wine. 'Good to take your time about these things. That's cunctation, know what I mean?'

Below us clacked a tube: *Not in Service*. Carriages old stock, unpainted aluminium.

CHAPTER 18

Camply, MORGAN SAGGED AGAINST the wall: 'What am I now?'

What was he now?

'"Third Mystery of the Annunciation is named Angelic Colloquy, comprising five Laudable Conditions of the Blessed Virgin. Number One: *Conturbatio*, or Disquiet" (Fra Roberto). Any warmer?'

'You're the Blessed Virgin?' Hanley said.

Thank God Karen wasn't along for this nonsense.

'You're a quick bastard, Mr Hanley!' Morgan told him. 'And why have I just affected *Conturbatio*, or Disquiet?'

Why had he?

'Because you've appeared,' Morgan explained, 'like the Angel of the Annunciation!'

I'd been asked to come up – and didn't have anything to announce, either.

'Oh, you will have,' said Morgan, coming from the wall to join us. Pulling out a little silver tube, he cast red shapes this way and that.

'Use this on people who are fucking about or looking smug in the audience.' Morgan turned the laser to white, shone it at his dead eye. 'How d'you think this got the way it is, Mr Hyatt?'

'Your eye?'

'Spot on! My eye, sir! What's wrong with it?'

'Well, I suppose it's prosthetic.'

'Suppose it's prosthetic. And d'you suppose it's a Horace Cockles style-statement?'

'No.' Whatever that was.

'What happened then?'

'You had cancer – a melanoma, say?'

'Oh no I didn't!' He wore a good suit. Hanley too.

'OK,' I said, 'you had an accident.'

'No accident.' J. Fabian Morgan shone his laser away. 'Someone sucked it out.'

'Fuck's sake!'

'How many men in London d'you think are capable of sucking an eye out, Mr Hyatt?'

I was in no condition to offer an estimate. Too concerned with trying to keep lamb, salad and haloumi from spurting over my knees. Hanley handed me something, held it to my mouth. After a slug, after another, I got my interest together.

'When was it?'

'Some twenty years ago. Bosun and Monkey, Bostall Highway. In those days, Mr Hyatt, I hadn't taken to the stage. I was a kind of scholar in the history of movement, an anti-fascist, anti-Trot, researcher at Congress House, rhetoric consultant . . .'

'Who to?'

Morgan pointed white light on my face: 'The Right Hon. Neil Kinnock, MP.'

'Really?' I didn't regard this as plausible; on the other hand, would it have been a thing to make up?

'Now, on the night in question, I've gone to see a couple of union boys who live down that way, Eddie Singh, Terry Ireland. All tidy, till a group of youths come in, five in number. They are trouble. The landlord isn't having any. Won't serve them. So they take over the pool table, and he faces them down about that as well, turns the lights off, so they're banging with cues, making like spear-throwers. And now we may hear them hooting, across the years: for another youth's come in, fair-haired, with a little sharp nose like a bullfinch, and he's straight in the landlord's face: "Where's the lights? Let 'em play, Raymond! Let 'em fucking play!" And Raymond does put the lights back on, and the music: "Justified and Ancient". Which I can hear now.

'Well one of 'em, he's looking our way, and he clocks Eddie thus: "Hoy! Kuldeep! What's your problem?"

'Eddie says, "That ain't my name, son, and I haven't got a problem."

'"Oh yes you have, mate!" says the youth. "You got a problem in the middle of your face."

'"Tell me about it, son," says Eddie. "Tell me the fucking problem with my face!"

'"Tell him, Pete! He fucking wants to know."

'"Pete" comes over, Pete spits, Pete says to Eddie, "You got a Paki nose in the middle of it, mate — that's the problem. And I ain't your fucking son. Ain't no Paki in my blood."

'So Eddie gets up and he kicks him in the bollocks. Dark-haired Pete — wearing shades, indoors, on a February night — down he goes, then they're all on us, waving their bloody cues like Athos and Aramis. We're mobbed but hold our own. Someone hits me with a stool. Black out. When I come round, a girl's screaming, "What's he doing? Oh my God, what's he doing?" When I come round, I'm being humped by a pig. Someone laughs, "You can't do that!" Someone calls, "Nice one, Woody! Popped his cork, mate!"

'He'd sucked my eye out, he'd bitten it off.'

'Which one had?'

'The fair-haired lad with the finch nose. Sophie B. Hawkins was playing. "Damn I Wish I Was Your Lover". Memory suggests I found it soothing. Then the whole place is swarming with cops, parameds; but the youths have disappeared pronto.'

'Did they pinch them?'

'They were all known round there. And the boy who supped on my eye, was called Woods. He was arrested the next day. But the witnesses, well they got variously visited, bunged, you know the routine, Mr Hyatt. Mr Hanley certainly does. The investigation was undertaken with formidable negative energy.'

He could have sought a review. His gaze discouraged the question, so I said, How have you got over it? I'd never heard such a thing. Not as a matter of direct experience. Crime reporting had brought nastiness aplenty, but that was black matter for professional conversion, leaving soul unstained (one affair excepted). This, however, was initiation into a level or region of depravity that commanded attention as the general unconverted real. How could you overestimate it – or turn your back? From Hanley's offered case, we took cigarettes, Morgan glowing in the lighter flame:

'How have *you* got over it?' He wasn't mocking.

'Over what?'

'Your dealings with Mulhall, old boy. You have had dealings, I'm told.'

'I told him, *amigo*,' said Hanley.

'You lost your job, maybe your name. I lost my eye.'

Mulhall being my soul-stain. Why'd Hanley told him? I should collect Karen, be off, out of London, before their gravity got me entirely. But it was strong; and there was no other planet. There were questions to ask. How can we turn our back on the questions?

'What's the connection?'

'Robert Woods is his nephew.'

'Mulhall?' An incoming tube rolled beneath us, iron wheeled, 630-volt traction. Over my heart. 'He's the uncle of Robert Woods?' I could hardly breathe. Blackest bubble yet.

'That's right, Mr Hyatt. A proper uncle. Boons bestowed without stint upon this happy young man, a regular avalanche of topping treats: buns, burgers, Charlton Number Ten shirt (signed), pool table, pool room, quad bike, etc. And when wee Robbie's sucked an eye out – "Boys will be boys, after all!" – Uncle Mulhall makes it cushty with anyone who's got upset, or chatty. To you, Victor!'

'Well, I've been making my way round to this recently, and Carl's been a good listener. Maybe I can complete it now, though it still needs time.'

'No rush,' decreed the humorist. 'Except he may be wanting to get back to his wife. I'm conscious of the timetables of others, believe it or not.'

'Go on,' I told Hanley, wondering at the fussiness of their manners. I could take another twenty minutes. Morgan poured more wine. Under the window stood empties.

'Those times I was talking to William in the engineers' shed, and he told me about the night Eldine Matthews was murdered, then he asked me what he should do – well, I made a suggestion. More than that, I persuaded him.'

'To do what?'

'The Inquiry was in the offing. I persuaded him to present evidence, testify – what he'd seen and heard, everything. He was willing. With these things, it's a written statement, producing which wasn't straightforward, as you can imagine – the document he gave me was like one of his rants. I told him, you can't submit a statement like that, William. It's a Public Inquiry. Let's work on it together. He gets the hump: "You are one of them, Mr Hanley! Shoulda known better than tell you about

134

The Lunar Five. You wanna take it from me, make it your way. You're gonna leave me to the dogs, when you got what you want. Gonna let Baal have me, ain't you! See him in the corner? Cunt with five grins. Waiting for me! My way, or no way. That's how it is!" It was a job to calm him down; and I mean, there was some risk in this – more than some. But like I told you, I was campaigning in those days. So I persisted with him, wore him down, talked him round. He didn't have anyone else. Then I showed him the version I'd written, and he told me, "OK. Fuck it! As you want, Mr Hanley. But one thing I ask you. Don't forget me when it's done." Seen. We shook on it.

'Went to Peter Jones to buy him clobber. For love or money, he couldn't dress smart. Somewhere on earth there must have been threads to suit him. Not in West London. He'd have broken the will of a make-over expert. When we'd chosen something, finally, the jacket was halfway up his back: 36 chest – they only had short; the trousers ended here. He looked like a bullfighter. In his street clothes, he was natural – relatively; but you couldn't turn up at an Inquiry dressed like that. Even the suspects had been to Top Man, after they got their no-show appeal turned down by the Divisional. Waistcoats, the lot. Should have bought aprons, the amount of eggs chucked at 'em.'

Supposing Hanley must have paid for William's rig from his own wallet, like kitting out a son for big school, I felt a great slipping sadness, like a cliff was collapsing, into sea that would always have its way. This big agitated kid, his fate was close at hand now . . .

Hanley lit another roll-up. 'Should have escorted him. Spain went out to Paraguay the night before. Drank a bottle of brandy and surfaced late. We'd arranged to meet at the Tube here, but he'd gone by the time I appeared, made his own way. Scotch Al passed on William's message: he'd meet me at Elephant. Told me I'd made something of William. The crew were proud to see him in his best bib. At last, the boy was sprucing up! So I went alone to Sidon House, June twentieth, 1998. There I waited for him. William never made it.

'He must have got off the Tube early to walk the last half-mile, practise his words. You may know Alaska Road, how narrow it is? This was where he was found. A vehicle had mounted the kerb, crushed him against a warehouse wall. He was taken to IT at St Thomas's. Sat there with him best part of a week. No one else came, and William said nothing else. He was done with shouting.'

We were silent.

'I say no one else,' added Hanley. 'A couple of CID turned up once or twice, waiting for him to come round; they vanished. I saw them late one afternoon in the canteen, chatting to a man with a circle beard. Who could have been anyone.'

'It's on your hands, this, Mr Hanley,' said J. Fabian Morgan. Round the table, he was playing the red point of his laser. 'That your way of thinking about it?' Not only this either, thought I. He did for William, and so he has for Pep – unless that young Roman returns from the darkness. Would he finish us all? But the evil in the world wasn't caused by him, nor the cars that crushed or took people away.

'Yes,' Hanley said. 'That is my way. There's a question, though. How was it known that William would be there? The hit was planned, exactly, rapidly. Who gave the word? Here's who.' Offering cigarettes.

John Fabian Morgan decided he'd have a pipe; in the kitchen I heard throat-clearing, drawers, cupboards opened, slow show of searching. So much for twenty minutes. How long would Karen's patience last? Unless these dawdling panders were setting her up with that young man . . .

Morgan gently tamping a Peterson, Hanley continued:

'William couldn't help but broadcast what he was up to with the other touts. They were his spars. He was proud of himself. Here was justice, wanting to listen. Gave him a boost like he'd never had, and for Christ's sake he deserved it; and if I'd been with him, drunk less brandy, maybe I wouldn't have advised him to cool it in that foyer; let him have his day; there was no calming him once he'd started anyway, and he had his new threads; he was made up. But someone else was listening as well. And when he starts blowing the gaff about the Sixth Man, someone else makes a call *rapidamente*.'

'Who was it, Vic?'

'Tell us, son.'

'Took me a while to identify. You remember Detective Sergeant Butler, *paisano*?'

'Had a way with words, didn't he?'

'Putting it mildly. Must have said "cunt" at least a hundred times per day. Probably starting when he drew the curtains and saw the sun. Any rate, I bumped into him in Snaresbrook, two or three years after William died, this would have been. And he said to me, How's tricks with Lodge 97, *amigo*? Down your way, isn't it?

'Yeah, says I – more or less. What of it? Well, says Butler, it's a fucking shit-bed. More slags in there than Four Floors of Whores (which is in Hamburg, apparently). Come over from Kent like *Wacky Races*, Tuesday nights. They've twinned with lodges in Málaga and Mallorca. Down your way, they've got their eye on town houses and arcades. One of 'em's in consultancy with the council on trench technology. I asked what he meant by that, and Butler told me that this slag in particular'd obtained a cable contract for a laying outfit no one ever heard of, for which outfit one of his younger family members drove a JCB. I asked who it was, this particular slag, and Chris Butler, he winked at me. Made me guess; and when I got it, he told me to keep it to myself because his activities were under investigation. I said I trusted they were, too, and Butler says yeah, so long as the investigation doesn't end up in a trench, or landfill, or under a high building, or whatever. Not that the slag I'd just named – it was Michael John Mulhall by the way, as you two will have guessed – was being particularly careful about his enterprises. For instance, one of his properties was now functioning as a gay-sex penthouse. But of course, these slags could never help drawing attention to what they were doing. Did I remember McAvoy's babe? Called her bear cubs 'Brinks' and 'Mat' – big gold signs hanging from their chokers. For inside every slag and his people, no matter how shrewd they were at breaking the law and deviant activity, there was a highballing cunt in a dunce's hat the size of the Grand Wizard of Alabama. These people, they had the maturity of four-year-olds. What they wanted, they wanted now, and they smeared their fucking chops with it like Kinder Egg.

'Anyway, to get to the point, Butler told me there was a South African up there running the place. Some kind of street pimp and bap businessman who'd been hustling the area like a thoroughly useless cunt for many a moon, after exiting the Orange Free State in a hurry. Why he should be honoured by the man whose name I'd guessed accurately was a nice question, though the fella was a 54-carat sneak, and the subject of a number of complaints by these travelling girls and backpacking Jennies who never stayed around long enough for the evidence to settle. So he must have done a favour at one time, this fetid Boer, and the prudent conclusion was a big one, too, for him to have been called away from his shanty, his tubs, and underground lair, to a place in the sky. Indeed, it wasn't certain that the penthouse's particular constitution wasn't Van Spenser's own initiative, since he knew the area, its niches, requirements, punter base, probably better than the Kentish man would have. But at any rate, he must for sure have done the latter a big service. Thus, DS Butler.

'And of course I sussed eventually,' Hanley told us now, 'that Van Spenser'd been lurking in the foyer, trying to pick up strays, that afternoon when William came through for the last time. He'd known to make a call when he heard William spouting about the Sixth Man, though I can't find that it was Mulhall himself he phoned to say there's a homeless boy from the underground, coming down to the Inquiry to talk about your nephew, boss. There's no evidence he already had the contact with the big man. It was afterwards he was gifted Lords, for services rendered. Accordingly, it's been my supposition that there was an intermediary, someone already acting for Mulhall that Van Spenser was in the habit of nattering to. Yes?'

Thus Hanley's tale made its way about the past. Someone told me once that where the river begins is the future, not the sea it joins. Which I couldn't see the sense of, until now.

So when you thought of all we knew so far, all they'd spoken of, while I listened, you had to conceive of a sea of which only a vast part swelled, broke and sounded, while more, still, moved below sight, and in this was much submerged or dissolving matter – this side of the horizon; while on the other lay a greater vastness still, moving and acting in a similar way, but invisible to us. Why then should we now know, have a right to a possibility of knowing, who it was that Van Spenser called that day? He, or maybe she, might now be buried or gone beyond the horizon, carried out by time into the blue reaches. So many crucial bit players are lost, from all events and history; they have to be, since there's no universal recording. Leaving us with our inferences, probabilities, and will. And a fink with no name.

As best I could, I put this into words, and John Fabian Morgan suddenly rose and fell back into his pose called *conturbatio*. 'That's what you have to tell us, Mr Hyatt? Damn! Knew it when I laid eyes on you, you've come here to spread daylight! What d'you say, Mr Hanley?'

'That isn't an interpretation I'd have been capable of,' Hanley replied quietly, reaching for my shoulder like a gassed infantryman. 'Thanks, *amigo.*'

What was all this? If a complaint were to be made to the police, the evidence could scarcely stand on speculation such as I'd just entertained this pair with.

'Have we got enough?' Hanley was asking.

'For what?'

'To proceed.'

'You're the lawyer. You tell us!'

'Law won't work, *paisano*,' Hanley said softly. 'Isn't that what we've been speaking about, these last weeks?'

'Why?' I said. 'Two of them have gone down. Come on, Vic! We've spoken of that as well. What is it you're after?'

'What about me, Mr Hyatt?' said Morgan. 'Asked me how I got over it, didn't you? What's my answer?'

'What is your answer?'

'An eye for an eye! That's my answer.'

'You've had long enough!' I told him. 'And stop pointing that red thing. You're like a bloody kid with it!'

'I'm the Cunctator!' roared Morgan. 'I take my fucking time! That's what I'm about! God help me if I don't strike you down!' Anxious movement from Hanley to my right. Spoiling the show, was I? Good. *Someone hurt me, therefore I am interesting*: the cult of our time. Here was a prime specimen, rising now and vanishing from the balcony, this one-eyed loser who'd turned himself into an unfunny stand-up comic (sorry, 'humorist'), not from any desire to entertain or bring mirth to the world, but because he'd been violently dealt with in a racist row. Which was his chronic way of exacting revenge, a prolonged goal diversion, but now he also wanted the thing itself, like lying in wait was a way of accumulating dignity, respect, rather than becoming one of life's spiders.

Remind you of anyone?

CHAPTER 19

S TABBING AIR OVERARM, MORGAN came from the kitchen, shadow cast large upon the garden below. He brought cheeses, water-biscuits, bottles, slate, a knife with heart-shape holes. As we fell to (appreciative murmurings from Hanley), the humorist told me I was good under fire. He didn't know my wife. When I got back from this session, she'd hit me with the works, high-explosive, armour-piercing, ball-shot, those chain-things for bringing masts down, depth charges . . .

'Good words!' cried Morgan with his mouth full. 'Very good, sir! Try some of this Baobab Chutney! Sourced by Turbo. An education to me diet-wise, that nipper. He'll make vice admiral, or I'm no more historian than Dame Paola di Canio. So we come closer. More wine, Mr Hanley? Never say no. Depth charges are the lads. I'm reminded of Roosevelt and the *Greer*.

'Now, FDR wished to mix it with Adolf Hitler, but this was not the will of the American people. 1940, into '41. "Isolation" was their watch-word. Sit around the ring and watch Britain take a battering. The Kennedys were some of the worst, which we seem to have forgotten. Chicago was non-involvement HQ. If JFK's old man'd been in the White House, we'd never have been born free, you, me, Mr Hanley. Remember that. As for FDR, his motto was "make haste slowly", or *festina lente*, which I'm also an advocate of (you know all about that).

He kept his eye on the North Atlantic, waiting his chance. This man was a master of slowpolitik. He'd been supplying us with killing power under Lend-Lease since 1940, without participation. How did he persuade the people to consent? Summoned the journalists, and spoke thus: "If a man's house is on fire, you don't offer to sell him your hose. You lend him the fucking thing and when he's finished firefighting and had a breather, you ask for it back, or for payment in kind." Ever heard one of our politicians speak like that, Mr Hyatt?'

I hadn't.

'No. They speak like they learned English this morning. Speak without salt or flavour. Speak without courage. Of the colours of rhetoric, they know fuck all. Can they write a letter even? Note the power of Churchill's letter-writing in persuading FDR. Where were we?'

'North Atlantic,' remembered Hanley.

'You're like an elephant, Mr Hanley. Sitting there in a posh suit remembering everything. We'll make Babar of you yet. Never mind Babar, you can be Hannibal, crushing your foes beneath broad feet, remembering every howling face as it goes under! How about that? Now the USS *Greer*, a destroyer delivering mail to Iceland, got word from a British bomber that a German submarine was prowling. American vessels were still understood to be neutral; but the *Greer* tracked U-652 on sonar and took bearings, which she radioed to the bomber, and along it came and dropped depth charges (five Mark VIIs, amatol-primed). These failed to damage the sub, but early afternoon, another bomber joined the hunt, since the *Greer* was still tracking, and so it went on till *das Skipper* became concerned about his batteries and fired two torpedoes in irritation, whereupon the *Greer* responded with eight charges, shaking things up below, without decisive effect. Around teatime, a British destroyer appears, drops a depth charge, hangs around a while, makes off, and now the *Greer* really starts throwing the kitchen sink at 652, before resuming passage to Iceland with the post.'

'What happened to the submarine?'

'U-652 slipped away, pretty much unscathed. Killing these subs was no easy business. You had to get a blast within twenty foot of the hull, ideally on either side – which was why they dropped the charges in multiples – for the first shock wave to pop the lungs of the crew, and the second to crack the hull. And note that you had two destroyers and a pair of bombers collaborating in this incident, that's a quartet of killing machines, crews highly trained, and they couldn't bring it off – with four hundred pounds of high explosive in every charge they dropped. *Greer* alone fired nineteen charges. The will to destroy an enemy isn't enough, even when you have more than adequate means – get me? You have got to introduce his moves to the calculus, also his will not to get killed – and to come back and do you when he gets the chance, because he won't forget.'

'Yeah.'

'That's a tactical parable. My broad point is that America wasn't at war at this time, though the *Greer* warmed to her combat role in this incident, from signalling to the British, to energetic retaliation. But when Roosevelt got his report of the incident, he knew he could make hay.' In the person of a satisfied president, John Fabian Morgan rubbed his hands. 'So, he has one of his fireside chats with the people, and he tells them, when you've got a rattlesnake in your yard, you don't wait for it to bite you. No, sir. You strike first, rip his fucking head off, ram his rattle up his arse and douse him in paraffin. Can't remember his exact words – that's the gist of it. So from now on, we step up our armed presence in the Atlantic and if these bastards so much as spit, we give 'em a taste they won't forget.

'Which was his way of getting aggressive escorting of convoys through Congress, turned to law, and it depended on FDR's holding something back, namely, the *Greer* was harassing U-652 until she provoked an action against which she could retaliate – and then hanging around in the area retaliating lavishly, until she turned back to the mail run. See how a little dissembling was cardinal in gaining legitimacy for the big, honourable plan? Yes? Whereas if you go by the book, what is it you end up with?

'Before we answer, note the president's handling of time: slow, sure, lethal!' In the course of this instruction, J. Fabian Morgan rose and arranged himself in another Laudable Condition, at which we marvelled.

SO KILLING WAS NOW on our horizon? You may be incredulous, but you've not begun to slip, or felt the pull; though how often on the Saturn rings about the heart have you not wished death? For the rings are many: hatred, irritation, anger, indignation, envy, boredom, prejudice, impatience. Am I wrong? You've been there, pal – and you, lady. The wish is yours, and mine, and it grows beyond exemption. No one inadmissible, single or group, who is *not you*.

It is a war of all against all, till we make a state and laws, obtaining relief from violence of our will; so we hand it to a bigger, longer-lasting man. In nature, we would kill and kill; in civil society, that right's abstracted; converted to dreams, higher forms, entertainments. Count the posters with guns (. . . and wonder where the knives are).

Yet still we kill and are killed; or either way, we die – something sees to that. Meanwhile we wait on our felicity, gnash teeth, bite our lips; till someone says, How about a killing? And there may be even freedom in the thought. Freedom from the great coil of consideration, self-deceit, the burden of the question why. Why have we given our wills to the state? For fear of death? For fear of violent death. But there are worse things. Shameful life, coward life, life without fulfilment. Yet the criminal hasn't come to this accommodation. His will's his own. A sensation that we cannot stop reporting. What else do we make news of? Violent men, celebrities, perverts, politicians. Creatures of will; while the rest of us look on from inside the cage. Tamed, resentful, ruminant. Look what they are doing out there! Keep us locked, but grant us our felicity; and Lord, if you love us a little, please you punish the wilful! For they make us small.

So our way out's to kill back?

I TOLD THEM THAT Pep had been abducted, and I suspected it was by the same party whacked William out last millennium.

How did I know? When was this? Why hadn't I said something? Hanley's questions came like a siren.

I told them about my boy Donna Juan – and more to the point, why'd Hanley been taking Pep for pub lunches? What was that about?

Because they were closing in, said Hanley, who looked ill. That was why. Since the trial of Roche and Drew, and the convictions, the other murderers and their protectors were mobilizing, visiting potential witnesses who may have had their memories and good intentions encouraged. But they were closing in on themselves as well, that was his feeling, checking each other out, watching for signs of readiness to turn evidence, inform, bargain . . . Which was why he'd been talking to Pep. Van Spenser being, to his mind, a minor devil in this affair, but one who knew too much, with a patron who might be thinking it was high time the South African was tidied away. And at least he'd been justified there, had Hanley, since Pep advised him that the patron was a regular guest at Lords, where he was obviously keeping tabs on the manager of the establishment.

He likes boys as well, I now advised them; though recalling Donna Juan's words on the way to the hospital, I wondered if Mulhall's voluble 'hobby' wasn't indeed a cover for the business of checking on the man who'd sent the information to protect his bad nephew. Well, if anyone knew the ins and outs of Mulhall, Hanley said bravely, it was me, which had Morgan relighting his pipe with a shrewd air, while Hanley sparked a half-smoked roll-up. Did he have a second death on his hands? Poor bastard. Only trying to do what was right.

Did Pep go back and tell Van Spenser he'd been talking to him?

No. It was a snitch.

Who would that be?

The old busker on the steps of Eiger Essentials – aka 'the Gonk'. By the way, I'd witnessed Turbo tuning him up earlier today. (Bloody long one it was turning into, as well.)

Did he fuck him up good?

Kicked his face in.

'A foretaste!' cried the Cunctator. 'You want to blow, Mr Hyatt? See you around!'

With time, I could have told them about Barnfield.

CHAPTER 20

I PLUCKED *NATURE* FROM HER breast where she napped on the settee. Winds from black-hole accretion discs . . . 'Powerful winds driven by active galactic nuclei are often thought to affect the evolution of both supermassive black holes and their host galaxies, quenching star formation and explaining the close relationship between black holes and galaxies.' *Quenching* – like a chip pan? 'Mass of central supermassive black hole in IRAS F11119+3257 estimated to be MBH~1.6X107M@, where M@ is the solar mass.' Figures, symbols, curious shapes, tiny house, belvedere, fan-tail creature, 4.11, superscript positive, subscript negative, ergs to the minus 1cm. Line dance of dreadful power. I got that; but she could understand it: ionization, outflow velocity, forces rationalized. Had these mighty winds blown her troubles away? I could do with some big science. You had to know at least 90 per cent more than you taught your class: her motto. At Keele, she studied Maths and French. After lectures, she rambled in the woods, smoking kif with her pals. Down the hill lay the last colliery. When it closed, she marched with miners' wives.

'Now then, Carlo! Did you think you could sneak by?'

'No, ma'am!' That cotton thing with green flowers was new on me. Shunamatic . . .

*

'IF YOU'RE A CATHOLIC, what's the deal with these science articles?' A private suspicion was she'd gone down the maths route because of Laura, like to outdo her. So if Laura hadn't been a geographer, Karen would have stuck to French, *la vie bohème*.

Could I not pipe down for five minutes?

In the alcove, she'd put flowers, snapdragons, lilies, tulips . . . 'Can you tell me now?'

She'd explained before. Maths and Physics people were often godly; it was the Biologists who weren't.

'Why aren't they?'

Because they were dealing with something smaller than themselves – cells, genes, what have you – and that made them feel big enough not to bother with God. Also, they cheated about purpose.

'In which way?' I liked hearing this.

Because they played push-me/pull-me with it.

'How?'

'You know already, you fool! If I had you in a class of mine, you'd be under scrutiny. Listen. I'll not tell you again. They say successful procreation, gene propagation, survival, is what drives behaviour – at whatever level, from a bacteria smudge to the Roman Empire. Then they say that whatever has survived, whatever *is*, rather than isn't, has confirmed that that was its purpose all along – savvy? From hunting wasps to differential calculus – or Shakespeare. They're having it both sides of the bridge.' She shook her head; I was thick when it came to such things. I wanted to ask, but daren't, if that meant there'd been better things – better than the ones we know – that hadn't survived. Sad thought . . .

'Those flowers are nice.'

She'd done them specially.

'Snapdragons.'

No they weren't.

'And what's the religious word for love?'

Eros, in a recent manifestation.

Say I had Turbo to thank for that. So the world clicks. One man works his fellow's benefit. How's that for community!

'What are the others, though?'

'What d'you want to know for? You're always bloody delving, Carlo!'

'Just tell me, sweetheart.'

'*Agape* is another; that's the highest form.' As she bent back from me, I thought of those poses J. F. Morgan pulled. 'Christ's love for man is *agape*. And there's *philia*.'

'Now what's that?'

'The love of fellowship, love between friends.'

That was the one.

'Satisfied now?'

I made like I might or mightn't be.

'I'll bet you are, cock! What were you gassing about with them ne'er-do-wells? Tell Mummy!' And if I'd been a boy again, I might have admitted, *Oh, the time J. F. Morgan had his eye sucked out by Mulhall's nephew. And how 'Victor' got a witness murdered* . . . Instead I said we'd been talking of history and literature, fussed about the time, gathered her up. She'd better get some kip.

'Who was on about history – Fabian?'

'Yes. And Hanley was talking about *Doctor Faustus*.'

'What was he saying? Have you done your teeth?'

That second question gave me the chance to answer indistinctly above the sound of running water, from the en suite. Luckily, I'd been reading Marlowe's play lately (the end anyway). Emerging mintily, I found her sitting back against the headboard like a truck driver.

'What did you have to contribute?'

'Oh – not much.'

'Did you feel like a dunce beside them?'

'Why should I?'

'Not having a specialist subject like?'

'I'm a journalist,' I said. 'We're just dabblers. Like novelists are.'

'What d'you know about novelists?'

'Nothing really.'

'You're no dabbler. You're not a specialist either.'

Could have asked what I was, but she was settling herself . . .

SO WHAT ARE YOU? Are you enough? When the lights are out, and the rain comes back. Oh for that steady power! Not to be a chattering, furtive man, will and rhythm lacking, fighting with half-hours. What counts is the whole picture. The greats don't see the picture; framed already; you must look for yourself. Did the painter bother? That one in the corner, upstaged by the event, that you? Well he's there at least forever . . . Poor you just come and go; don't stick or hold. Where's your force, your image, your distinction? . . . To be a painted individual, lose an eye, get your witness killed, would be enough – so you did, were done to . . . Haven't done enough, haven't suffered.

As mics picking up another section of the crowd, rain loses sound. She sleeps; you lie. Aren't I who I am? That's not enough, she can sling her hook . . . *Need them like you need me . . . need others for your meaning . . . Can't be yourself by yourself* . . . So who the fuck can? Show me such a hero, I'll crawl to them; I'll shut myself away with the spiders. What's wrong with community, brotherhood, socialism, *philia*? No modern woman wants a stand-alone. Check the celebrities. Hey, George! Re-tuck 'em with your own needle and thread? Sportsmen, singers,

South Pole sponsored walkers – support systems like D-Day. Jesus Christ said come unto me, not fuck off and leave me alone. It's all about gathering: we gather from our fear (Hobbes).

You're fudging, son. Ain't the issue. Dredge . . .

He'd never be finished, the man I married. Like always striving? No, son: like always being incomplete! An individual's complete, isn't he? I aren't and never shall be. How now! Not complete? Out my bed, and get you gone! To the kitchen and dwell in straw, hamster! Ssh, Carlo! Sleeping; she's complete – know that, don't you? Belly full of dinner, you, hard science, future general-charted. She has force, she speaks her mind – take lunchtime at Abril's: *I know what I've got, pal!* That's an individual. One who speaks what she feels without hedging, leftovers, policy, fear – speaks with effect; then she's noticed . . .

ON A NIGHT WHEN the millennium was young, Craig Norman, then my boss at *The G********, took me to The Tiresias. It was Craig's birthday and Craig was amply furnished with cocaine – which he wouldn't lay out till we'd been to stare at strippers in Commercial Street and put pounds in the pot, then come west to the Red Fort, and later, heavy-stomached, up some stairs in an alley to this club that was the threadbare side of seedy, even church-hall side of seedy, lacking in anything but functional comfort, with tables that rocked and ungrateful chairs. And this was the time when the capital's celebrities of the kind you'll remember for their brilliance, beauty, wit, élan, and tendency to be exculpably involved in the deaths of others who'd been chatting to them only half an hour ago by the open window, wouldn't have been permitted to be seen dead in such a place by their agents, minders, or PR units. Thus, The Tiresias.

Craig signed us all in, me, righteous Ellis McMahon, a buffoon called

Dragonheart. Laura and I were now separated, on grounds of blandness and anti-spontaneity (my complaint) and irritation and fake spontaneity (hers), and she was living in Devon; along with a miserable sense of vandalism, I had a gap to fill. By the bar, a blonde in a peculiar hat and a husky woman in unclean plimsolls and leather trousers were grouped before a high-backed bench of dark wood, when a voice said, 'Yer look like Charles Bovary in that cap, our Cassie,' and they parted to reveal the speaker, who had in her lap a little dog. A hazel-eyed young lady it was, with dark hair and lipstick like a 'This Way for Sin' sign, who asked me what I was staring at, and the church hall became a sort of coven. I was about to apologize or back off, but her eyes were merry, so I asked her who was Charles Bovary, and she cried, 'Sling this one out! Meant to be a literary salon in here. Doesn't know first thing about books!' Craig Norman suggested I knew a lot of other things, and she said, 'Well, tell us summat!'

I was saved by John Dragonheart, who found it difficult not to be the most *heard* person in any gathering, and began flyting with the dark lady about her accent while I swayed in her eye-magic. Some time after, she came and sat by me at a rickety table like she had the freedom of the place and asked what I'd eaten for tea. Pickled chicken and vindaloo puffs. She thought as much. Then Craig Norman made signs and we two and Dragonheart went down to a shithouse where the smell of piss was like strong condiment, and the light didn't work. We snorted powder off a pocket-size listings mag, reascending to the coven in good fettle, where the dark lady reappeared at my side to advise there was a nice clean lav upstairs, for future reference. I was about to deal with the little witch, when she disappeared. Dragonheart kept me occupied; the bracket lamps made anchors in his eyes.

At work, I had a mind to ask Craig about her, but couldn't catch him in time, and something suggested keeping it to myself, so a couple of nights later I walked from Farringdon to Soho, with a sense of adventure that I should have been too old for, and which therefore felt kind of fake and ripe for humiliation, muttering, *This is it then!*, *Tonight your fate is settled!*, *You can do it, son!*, and other naff encouragement. As I cut through Leather Lane on to High Holborn, a long monochrome advert showed the sombre head of Beckham: 'Cometh the Hour'. Ominous. But beyond the pomp, delusion, sense of folly, like the breeze that blew air-kisses this May evening, there was something that was nature's own, unstained by what men do and always do.

I had to buzz from the street so I said I was Tara Palmer-Tomkinson and they let me up from curiosity. The dark lady was on the pew again in a plum-coloured dress and fishnet tights, playing with the little dog, and looking at a sheet of paper. Oh it was me. Was I still pissed? She offered to sign me in. Her signature was Karen Tynan. I was her guest.

I bought us a drink and asked what she was reading. It was her column. We both sat on the pew and she told me about it, though her eyes, a way she had of grinning, the closeness and swell of her in that purple dress, distracted me. We were kids on a bench considering homework; I fancied her fanatically. I gathered that Gina (of the dirty plimsolls), who was the hostess and founder of Tiresias, and the owner, who was a lord, ran a monthly mag called *The Dedicated Vagrant*. As it happened, I'd seen it in the newsagents at Chancery Lane, a medley of scandalous confessions, sarcastic reviews (restaurants, videos, shows), execrations of fashion phenomena, blessings of fashion phenomena; an effigy of the month; absinthe recipes; dangerous alleys; decadent doggerel; gnostic sex positions; notes on phrases such as 'turn the cat in the pan' drawn from actual or imagined experience; nice pictures to look at; grimoires; advice on addressing dukes, bishops, gangsters, or taking a whore for a picnic – by this time, she'd produced from a drawer beneath the pew the last issue for me to inspect. Karen Tynan had her very own column, inspired by Flaubert's Dictionary of Daft Ideas, composed in French, which might have made a man feel a clodhopper, if he'd forgotten his O-level French, and hadn't heard of Flaubert's dictionary.

So what was this month's daft idea? Tapping her sheet like there were no flies on me. She looked a bit shy – though she could have been putting it on (I suspected her capable of all sorts of tricks) – and offered me it to read for myself. Oh-ho! says I, coming the Pub Landlord. Anglo-Saxon only, miss! None of this Gallic flim-flam! Oh, she doesn't know if it's any good in English. Well I'm sorry to hear that, no fan of affectation, plain journalist – and woe to a ponce parlance that anyone with a little cunning can use to bamboozle honest souls. She gives me a green look, translates in good Lancastrian.

And excellent it was; she had a gift for phrasing, and identifying bullshit, which made me sit away in envy, or respect. Then we talked of my paper. I supposed she was angling for an opportunity, since we had such columns at the time, in the weekend section, though they were sarky and laboured compared to hers, composed by young Oxbridge graduates (who often turned out to be uncannily attached to the senior staff of an organ famed for its canons of independence and dislike of 'tradition'). But all she said was it used to be called the *Manchester G********, and how did someone like you get to be working there?

Now what did she mean by that? Thought I was common, didn't she – or *lower-middle-class*? The pits.

My old man had been an RAF engineer and I was brought up near Bury St Edmunds. Oh, she was from Bury herself, Greater Manchester. We compared our towns. Cops and pogroms. My mother was a clerk on the base. When my old man retired, he started his own bathroom-fitting business. My mother was company secretary and director. So far, so *lower-middle*, what? Forgotten majority. And did I take after my mum, or dad? Well she was a good dancer, did a lot of sport, ran road races, and so on – which I didn't take after. And my dad – he hadn't been sporty; waited near the finishing line eating hot dogs. So I took after him? Well, we never agreed on much. The waiting in the cold and hot dogs did for him, by the way – he'd been dead a couple of years. She crossed herself. (Was she taking the piss?) But he'd been a man of competence; good with his hands, knew how things worked – Vulcans, VHS recorders, boilers, businesses, councils, quangos – more than I could say for myself. Did I visit my mum? She visited hers, every third weekend. Lively description of her sisters followed; I told her of Nigel, my solid brother at PwC; how we went to football or cricket together once in a while, sank a few pints . . .

While we were at it, she might as well hear about my education.

Well as a schoolboy, I'd been an idler, prat, show-off (had I, actually?), though competent in English, History, Economics, and so, to UEA, where I pretended to study Politics and International Relations. In the student paper, I did bar reviews, club reviews, pieces on CND and apartheid. She wanted to know about CND (how young she was!). My views weren't popular with the union activists – since I was genned up by the RAF background (not strictly the truth). Weren't popular with my old man either, who suspected I was being turned commie at the campus. I had it from both sides (exaggeration). She watched me. I'd also done interviews with musicians who performed at the university or locally. Such as? Oh, Paul Young, Mari Wilson, Billy Bragg, Bananarama, Jaz Coleman, Mark E. Smith . . . (adding names till someone registered).

And what did I do then? In this rickety coven, her eyes glowed hazard green. A girl at the bar was trying mouse ears.

Applied for a press apprenticeship in Hastings. Mornings were shorthand and libel lectures; after lunch we went out for vox pops. A name that came up was the Sly Crew, who were the local mafia, though they didn't go much beyond shoplifting, and hooliganism at Brighton's home games. I got to know the daddy, Frank Sly; the crew were sons, nephews, and a mad niece called Alison, who put the wind up a lot of folk. Frank had the face of a happy pig, zest for life unballasted by conscience. He went about the south coast on the knock, ripping people off. Fantastic patter-man. I could hear him now, marching by his stall . . .

'Player's No. 6?
One and nine a thousand!'

. . . he'd just been offered a cheapskate fag. 'Write what you like, son!' he told me. 'Ain't got nothing to hide. Come on the knock. Frankie'll bring you back alive – handles intact!' I didn't take him up, but he had his effect. There were seventies paperbacks on a wire tray. *Run Down: The World of Alan Brett*, by Robert Garrett, caught my eye. Two sharp-suited hardcases fighting. One had a cut-throat, the other gripped a rubber bulb.

Why was he trying to spray perfume on him?

'Wet behind the ears, ain't you!' roared Frankie Sly. 'That's ammonia he's got in there, you plum!' A sea breeze whipped his stall. He gave me the book as a present. Outside McDonald's, Alison stood gurning.

'Wouldn't think she set her own cat on fire, would you? Maybe you would.'

What did I see in Frankie Sly, Karen Tynan wanted to know?

He was very upfront for a crook – more upfront than straight folk. And happier. He gave me time.

What about all the old ladies he chiselled, taking Georgian dressers for a tenner?

Encovened in a place like this with her spellendrical eyes, she could be testing how wicked I was.

I tried to meet her honestly. Frankie Sly had been my introduction. When I got my first reporting job, I was soon hooked on crime-world manners and degrees. Reporting pub and club and warehouse incidents, Braintree, Billericay, Grays, Southend, punch-ups, glassings, and so forth, I found certain names recurred, and in time, I moved up a level, to the relatives and associates of those names, who were seldom involved in pub incidents, and didn't appear in clubs, or warehouse parties, or violent burglaries, because they were running things, supplying pills and sniff, and when they weren't doing that, they were working out in power gyms, driving about in Range Rovers because they were too mighty in bicep and thigh for standard saloons, entertaining other musclemen and their families at barbecues where T-bones that had slipped under the BSE ban smouldered on grills where you could have martyred a saint, and the WAGs had spent more on nails, belts, hair, tans, Cartier, Gucci and holidays, than the daughters of dukes.

But when you'd discovered that level, you still weren't at the top. At the summit were guys who weren't flash anymore – but they were behind a great deal that went on; for example, shazaming money from pill shipments undertaken by the bicep fellas – and if it came to their notice that things were going on they hadn't authorized, then they punished the bright spark, freelancer or independent soul who'd been foolish enough to think he was operating in an unprotected market and that up on the summit, a certain unflash individual was lost in the clouds. For instance, freelancer might end up getting *N* for 'naughty' cut in his face in a pub car park, in an unspontaneous incident – first offence. If he'd been at it a while, things got heavier: then a dog-walker came across the body, where a copse abutted on a muddy lane. The system was dedicated to its own authority, and integrity.

I knew what she was thinking. *Integrity?* These were just a bunch of psychopathics, with no more integrity than a shithouse rat. Which might or might not be the case; but the big point was that this mountain of shit held together – like straight society did. So I thought. And it affected me, this thought, as something they'd forgotten to tell us in the days of my degree. It held together, but with something extra. Did she want to hear more?

Oh, she was all ears.

Well, it was that the criminal was happier, complained less, did more of what he wanted, than the common subject; he'd kept more of his natural will. The common subject, in his contract with the state, gives up a lot of what he'd like to do, so the state will protect him – in civil society, that's the deal; but the criminal doesn't ask the same of the state, because he's prepared to use the kind of violence that the state sanctions to itself, in order to get what he wants; and at the same time, he's prepared to receive extreme violence, or at least he knows he runs the risk of it. But where the straight gives authority to an abstract man (which is the giant called Leviathan), the criminal recognizes the authority of a real man, who's no less concrete or actual for the fact that he lives on a different level of activity, and is often out of sight or self-obscured by shadow. It was this greater reality that fascinated me, with respect to will on one side, and authority on the other. And there was something else. The Political Science I'd paid most attention to said that, above all, men feared death, but especially violent death; and this is why they give up their will and natural rights to an abstract man called the state, so that they'll be protected from violence. So here, I thought, I was coming across an area of society where people simply had more native courage than the straight subject: so to say, they reckoned with the likelihood of violent death, took it in their stride. Which had to be looked into.

I wasn't stopping till I reached the top!

'What d'you reckon to that, our Cassie?' said Karen Tynan. Cassie laughed. So she'd been listening in? The Tiresias had filled while I was going on. A woman posed, exhibiting tattoos; I could almost see her arse. The girl with mouse ears had an audience. From the door, we were watched.

'Come over, Larry, we won't bite!' Karen told him.

Through the mobbing air, he made his way in tartan jacket, with peculiar swerves, and choo-choo rotations, blond hair unevenly massed. Karen introduced us. This was in fact the lord, probably the youngest of his line and conflicted about his status, judging by his comportment. When Karen announced I worked for *The G********, he moaned 'Oh, God!', and gave a pleading look, as if I'd have him taken outside and shot. Karen handed him her column and, producing gold-framed glasses, he read a little and said, 'Brilliant, isn't she! I dunno, Karen – you're a one-off! Could I buy you both a drink?'

———————

YES, SHE WAS AN individual, with a lord's ratification; she was, I wasn't. Hadn't I admitted it that night, that I had to know people who were more concrete and less scared of violent death than I was? And by then, of course, my cowardice had turned into the rancour regarding straight soc and its manners which poisoned my first marriage.

Let's have a list. So, Karen's an individual, and Councillor Barnfield and Marcia Jones, cast-iron; Andy Ravage too, funnily enough, and Fabiana, for all you know; Donna Juan, Sibyl Grove, for certain, and Paulie Charalambous; Goodman Turbo, in the making; the Cunctator – not half; and you'd have to include Hanley; maybe Lolly isn't, and Carl most definitely isn't, though Millie Hanley so isn't, she almost is; and Mayor Montgomery is, even as a joke, but Van Spenser isn't; and William – what was William? A very perfect tout. And Mr Arnold – what d'you say? And Mulhall – oh, Mulhall was a Kentish man, and killeth one or three . . .

CHAPTER 21

IN A MOLLY PARKIN turban and suit of charcoal linen, Sibyl came out with her breakfast. She seemed a little cock-eyed.

'My lounger, Carling! Unfold, would you?'

'Here you go.' As she reclined among her ferns, I stood away by a coned box bush. Gunther and a neighbour had their heads together.

'Don't lurk over there, poppet!' called Sibyl. 'Look like a leprechaun.' Her toast was streaked with brown paste. 'Gentleman's Relish.' Eyeing me, she licked it. 'Tastes like a whore's thong! – What's up with you?'

'Nothing.'

Gunther made a shape in air, neighbour nodding.

'"Nothing," says he. Nothing'll get you nowhere, cupcake! You look out of sorts. Where's hyacinth? See in there?' Her vacant cauldron. 'Voles. Two of 'em. Mating. They love to gnaw box. Well they can gorge themselves on Gunther's, to their hearts' content! Hee hee!'

'What have you got against him?'

'Hey? Speak up! Don't mumble!'

She'd definitely had a couple. I went nearer and repeated myself. He could hear everything.

'He's waiting for me to die so he can put in a rapido bid for my cottage. I don't have rellies and he knows it. Always asking why I'm not visited, what a shame it is. Two-faced bastard. Never trust a cunt in Nantucket Reds. Wants to turn it into a weekend place with a barmkin for the daughter and her whining kids.' Whining imitated. 'Ooh, there's Earl! Coooee! Hello, big boy!' In cricket trousers, dinner jacket, white airman's scarf, Earl Holmes, who was having a smoke, disappeared pronto from the cinema screen. 'Thinks I'm after his dong! Maybe I am too! He's a real man, Earl!'

'What d'you see in the stones?'

'Mind your own business!'

'You saw the Gonk was going to get a hiding. Which he did.'

'When?'

Jesus. 'Yesterday.'

She lay back in her man's suit and turban, shut her eyes a while.

'Come on! What else d'you see?'

'Blood. And hawks. Pell-mell.'

Bullshit. Sinister . . .

'When you warned me about Hanley the other day, what did you mean?'

'Wasn't a warning.'

She lit a menthol cig, smoke mingling cleanly with the smell of ferns. Like an ancient trick, her ash grew; when it toppled, I'd catch its dying heat.

*

'MY FEELING IS THIS, Carlo,' Andy was saying. 'What happened at the Levee, that belongs to your old life. Now and then, the past comes back to bite us – happens to every man in the course of things . . .'

'Why not to women too?' Fabiana rotating our way.

'Fab, I'm speaking generally. Has Ellis sent his shout?'

'No.'

'Why don't you finish the reviews?'

'I have. And they're crap. We need experts, not these punters. All they care about is their portion size and if their wives liked the pudding enough to put out when they got home.'

Andy flushed. 'All you have to do is pass on, mate. The past's chained up. Can't hurt you if you keep out the yard.'

'Ah.' This was well put; unfortunately, it was bullshit.

'You're with us now. We're your community. This is your ship.' Hand on my shoulder. Strong. 'Fab, dump those reviews. Carlo can take Karen for dinner. Get a proper writer on the job. How about that, Carlo?'

Ah, lovely Andy. Thus you comfort frightened children. You're a good man, so you are. But the world runs rings around good men, till their eyes are tired and their throats dry; then it cuts them down.

'OK; but I have to see this rent-boy thing through.'

'Why?' Removing his hand, he remained above.

'It's a point of honour, Andy.' (Was it, actually?) 'I've got to know this kid. We've had conversations.'

'It's not the kind of news we want, Carlo. Whatever you've been talking about with him.'

'That's what you think.'

Fabiana slid into view. Looked a million dollars with that finger wave. What was she doing in this dump?

'What happened to Barnfield?'

It had clouded over; the door blew open and banged.

'What did you hear, Andy?'

'He had an accident, when he was beered up.'

'He had an accident when someone drove a red hatchback into him, and didn't stop to say, "Sorry, old boy! We'll drive with lights next time, and keep well within the limit. Now how's about an ambulance?"'

'That stinking door!' Andy yelled. 'Why can't we have a proper one?' Backing off, he watched us redly. Fabiana and I must have discovered as one his likeness to a boss ape, for we cackled. You could say he didn't have a proper anything: furniture, microwave, office, staff – or newspaper. He had himself, though, that was something decent; and his family; and Fabiana, she really was a loyal lieutenant; yeah, it was the door was the problem, and me. But I was going to let him have it, share it all with him. Whether this was because it was useful for him to know, or necessary; or because I was a newsman, and I couldn't hold down what I'd discovered; or because I wanted to teach him a lesson in world-wickedness, because we all have to grow up sometime, and I thought in my conceit that I had – well, you decide.

'Me and Donna Juan, that's the boy, we went down to ITU to have a talk with him.'

'What on earth d'you take him for?'

'Well if you listen, I'll explain.'

'I'll put the kettle on!' Fabiana opened the drawer where she kept treats. 'We'll all have tea!'

I'd taken Donna Juan to the hospital because Lords had been visited by the two men who'd been at the Levee: Mr George Arnold; and his driver with the shaved head and dark beard, who Andy'd been right in identifying as ex-services. They'd abducted another boy – his name was Pep – and it was their car that whacked Barnfield. Andy asked the evidence for that, and I said Barnfield's missus, Marcia Jones, had told me. Had she made a statement? No. They were waiting for the police to come and speak to Steve. Oh, 'Steve' now is it, Andy said. I told him not to be petty, the poor bastard was lying half dead in IT still, and Fabiana said, Yeah, Andy, don't be a sourpuss, ain't your style, handing round a bag of Cadbury's Eclairs as Andy sulked and rallied.

So what was Steve Barnfield going to expose, Andy asked, as they do on TV and box-sets, where the murk is dispersible by the industry and charisma of the lead lady or man. That thing about sex workers and Olympic volunteers, presumably.

Barnfield was just stirring there. The boys at Lords wouldn't be seen dead in John Waugh's purple anoraks anyway. Had more ambition than that. Besides, the legal status of the place was kosher, apparently. Barnfield, he'd said something else in public that had alerted someone at the Levee, who'd got to thinking, Here's this local politico with a big mush prodding at what ought to be left quiet. Who knows what could come of him prodding and mentioning? Best take him out pronto, by the tried and trusted 'Silly bastard forgot his Green Cross Code' technique.

As to who it was who'd pricked up their ears at Barnfield's intervention, well that was the silver-haired gent who Andy'd so helpfully identified me to, George Arnold. Andy grinned, well out of his depth. Did I mean that Arnold tried to kill Barnfield? Yeah, I did – Arnold and his driver, Chas Bowler, who served in an army dirty-tricks unit in Northern Ireland, before his Met days. That's how they operated, this pair; and they were veterans.

But, Andy now coming over, why was Mr Arnold so interested in me?

Must have intuited I had some concern with the Eldine Matthews murder.

But you never did, Andy protested.

No, not professionally. But in recent times, I had, thanks to a lawyer called Hanley; and what was bloody strange was when I encountered Arnold in Narixa, he'd recommended a bar, where I went for a beer, and ended up reading about the two convictions (of Drew and Roche) – like he was managing my interest.

I don't get it, Andy said. Sorry, Carlo. Sounds like hocus-pocus to me.

Yes, might well do. Specially as I hadn't spoken to Hanley in years at that point. But here was something to consider. It was George Arnold who coached the boys who committed the murder, before they were questioned. They went straight to him in Shooter's Hill, to a pub he used as his HQ, and they got well advised what not to say in a police interview — and what to dispose of and how (if they hadn't already). He was a rotten cop, Mr Arnold.

Andy pinked for loathing.

How did they know to go to him, asked Fabiana, why would he help them out?

The uncle of one of the boys sent them. The uncle being professionally acquainted with George Arnold, in the course of a career in importation, integration, forestry, liquidation, the more illustrious for the fact that he seldom got convicted, since when he did end up in court, it was like a plague of Alzheimer's had erased the memories of everyone the prosecution mustered. That boy, incidentally, was the mysterious 'Sixth Man' referred to by witnesses, who themselves became selectively forgetful in the days following the murder.

But who was this uncle, who carried so much influence, Andy wanted to know? So I let him have it, the name that'd already caused me so much trouble, and of the kind he'd been praying I wouldn't bring his way.

It was Michael Mulhall.

'Right.' Andy nodded brightly. 'Right.' Like I'd just told him I'd been shagging his wife, for quite a long time; in fact, I did her most nights, while he was asleep, just over there.

'Mulhall. Right.' Andy looking at me, past me, into the void. 'So Arnold, he was asking about you because he's still hand-in-glove with Mulhall, and he fancies you're still on his case, in spite of your disastrous efforts in your quality-press days? But you aren't on his case, Carlo, are you — because you promised me, you gave me your word, that you were done with all that. And I accepted your promise, because I respected you, and thought we could be pals. I believed you.'

'Yes, you told him that, dude!' cried Fabiana. 'And now you've skanked him! For shame! I never knew you!' Turning her back.

Lord, was I abashed . . . Nothing like a dressing-down from the righteous, is there? One feels their justice, and disappointment, as the wrinkled sheet the hot iron. I'd joined this little paper to keep on Mulhall's trail, that was the truth of it, the mean truth.

'It's not much but it's something,' Andy said now, with gestures at the office. He'd started acting.

'Yes,' said I. 'And I want to help you keep it.'

'We can't afford libel probs, Carlo; we really can't.'

'I said I want to help you keep it!'

'So how the hell are you doing that?' Himself again.

'Well what d'you think I am doing, squire? Got any idea what I'm up to?'

'I don't want to know, Carl. Something to do with Lords, obviously. More than that, I just don't need.'

'Mulhall goes there.'

'What?' Andy's voice rose to a shriek. 'Christ! What d'you mean? What for?'

'You're so straight, Andy,' declared Fabiana, now re-entering conversation after renouncing me forever. This excellent woman bore no grudges, I was beginning to see.

'But why didn't they knock you over instead?'

'They probably will before this is over.' Andy flushed watermelon. 'As a minimum. Time being, they're trying to work out what I know – I think that's how it is. They're already disappearing boys from down there. Barnfield had shown his colours.'

'What do you know?' asked Andy.

Here we go. 'Mulhall's after this land.'

'What, here?'

'Yes. That's how I want to help you, Andy, you and the *Chronicle* – and Fabiana.'

'Last but not least!' Patting her waves.

'When the site was turned down as an Olympic venue, it was Mulhall doing the persuading against.'

'But they said we could keep this if it went Olympic, we had a Land Charges indemnity, an undertaking.'

'Yes, and no doubt an honourable one, Andy. But if Mulhall gets his hands on the land, you won't be getting an undertaking. You'll be getting a "Fuck-off-pronto" notice.'

'Shit to that!' Andy kicked the bin across the room. 'We have mortmain!'

'There's no mortmain with Mulhall, bub. He eats away at all rights and perpetuities. He's like universal acid. Don't forget, he bought a bunch of woods the other side of London on a sustainability bid. He has private security patrolling, ex-army, Charlton hooligans with banning orders, unfriendly dogs, and a falconer who trains sparrowhawks and hobbies to strafe uninivited visitors. What he's doing in there, nobody knows. There's talk of a gated green community. Mulhall's in no hurry to build though . . .

'Community!' yelled Andy, who'd gone to fetch the bin, but now kicked it back our way.

'Andy, for Christ's sake cool it!' called Fabiana. 'You've got a testosterone leak! Look at the colour on you! Carl, stop winding him up! He'll have a heart attack. His cholesterol's 6.5.'

'What I'm telling Andy is the truth, Fab,' I said calmly.

'I'll fucking show him community!'

'Andy, Andy,' Fabiana told him, 'an office is an office. We can get another one.'

'Can?'

'Could, I meant – we could always get another. What matters is we're together, as a team, the three of us – which we won't be if you don't leave that bin alone. Sit down immediately!'

Andy sat.

Me and Karen were reading something the other day about 'work wives'. They don't sleep with you, just perform the other wifely stuff, like *Have you taken your statins?* and *How many times you eaten red meat this week?* Get me?

'We're staying put,' Andy said. There and then, I wouldn't have liked to differ with him – he was king of his decision; though when he asked himself what Mulhall was up to, his words seemed like mine.

CHAPTER 22

DOUBLE-DEALING PARDONED, JUSTIFIED, whatever, I told him and Fabiana what I knew, what I'd heard, on the walk to the hospital with Donna Juan, by Barnfield's bed. In its frame, the door juddered.

So Mulhall just talked at these boys?

'It's called "dictating", Andy,' Fabiana said. 'They have to jerk off while he's talking.' Andy flushed.

'Well my source didn't say anything about that, Fab.'

'And this intern of yours – Justin – that's all he did to him: talk?'

'And fucked his mind over good and proper. Mind and soul. He can break people with his voice. That's how he gets his way. Break, turn, sweeten, suborn. He's got a range.' Improvising. 'Not but that he hasn't whacked a few in his time – three murders he's strongly associated with. Never charged, but no one doubts it. He's moved on from that though, on and up. Higher you get, smaller the effort required; in the end, he'll need to do no more than blink or scratch his arse, for effect. For the time being, he's still in the talking business.'

Then Andy wanted to know more about the Town Hall connection. We might as well have it. I told him certain guys in suits turned up for service at Lords. Local politicos among them. Common knowledge

'And Mulhall's blackmailing them, or just talking? Which is it?'

'What I'm trying to tell you – what I'm suggesting – is that Mulhall talks and gets his way. Simple as that. There's no straight coercion, extortion, blackmail. His will's the thing.'

'So he says to Councillor Treachman, "I'd like to bid for that land, Treach. You know how I'll go on if you don't listen!" And bingo, he has it without a murmur from Planning?' In Andy, there was a strain of competitive scepticism.

'We don't know he has the land yet, Andy.'

'So what in God's name are we fussing about?'

I suggested he visit Councillor Barnfield and ask him about Mulhall's POPGS application for the flyover site. Barnfield had our back on this.

He ignored me: Barnfield had disrespected the Mayor.

'What he's doing is forestalling,' Fabiana said.

'What?'

'Forestalling.'

'Who is?'

'Mulhall.'

We looked at her.

'So what were you intending to do about it, Carl – when you started scouting the boy brothel? What was your plan?'

'I'll tell you what it was, pal!' He was getting on my tits. 'It was exactly what I've been telling you so far: to complete my picture of this hump, his connections, what he's up to. That's one thing. And here's another. The more I've found out, the more I feel in the fucking dark; but I'll tell you something for sure, you get mixed up with him, it's going to get dark for you too, very dark indeed, my man.' How about that?

'And the more in the dark you felt, Carlo – well how were you going to play it then?'

'That's where we are now,' I told him. 'That's where we've got to.

What more can I say?' As a matter of fact, I could have said more, about J. F. Morgan, Uncle Mulhall and his nephew, or Hanley, Van Spenser, and the de Laceys; but that was pretty dark as well, wasn't it? Compelling, but dark, and with no plans to speak of . . . *Oh, we're going to kill the lot of 'em!* That wasn't a plan; it was a wish, a kind of vengeful dreaming, that a one-eyed comic with history, and a lawyer with a mortal fuck-up on his plate, had made their hobby-horse . . .

'So you're going to do nothing?' Andy said. 'That it?'

'You don't take a fight where it can't be won.'

'He's right, Andy,' said Fabiana. 'We've got our "Trundlers' Handsel". We should be grateful.'

'Pathetic!' Andy grinned hard (Bomb-Defuser at Work). 'This is a community paper and it stays exactly where it is – in this community, in this office, on this bloody flyover.'

Fabiana and I checked one another; better not giggle. He was having his moment, finest hour, whatever; you don't take that from a man, if you care about him. Besides, if he was serious, it wasn't funny.

'Fab's right though,' I said sensibly. 'There's the Enterprise Award to think of as well' (for operations such as ours). 'You start kicking off, you—'

'When I kick off, they'll know it!'

Now, quite as much as other parts of this tale, you may dislike what you're hearing, since I'll seem to have infected Andy . . . *Just as you wanted, pleb! Bring a good man from the daylight, to that filthy cave you brood in, and persuade him this is how the world is, this the essence . . .* I swear I haven't wanted that – not in those terms. But we must always be wanting the other to recognize our truth, our reality – musn't we? Not to infect, but to influence; for influence is glory . . .

Andy was asking now about this lawyer I'd mentioned, and if I could arrange a meet. See what he had in mind? That's right: a campaign.

And the elements? An ex-cop who knocked down councillors who asked about a fuck-house where a talkative gangster held court, and threatened the very heartbeat of the community, your *Chronicle*, with a development plan, which gangster and ex-cop were intimately involved with the corruption of the case against the murderers of Eldine Matthews. An investigative sensation. Oh dear.

How to advise him that if he barked up that tree, he was going to get covered in shit from big birds he couldn't reach, and when he was blinded with filth, have his eyes pecked out? He wasn't advisable. His competitiveness was no joke. I've mentioned his success, against advice, in the matter of obtaining advertising. As a matter of fact, he wore business people down as he harried centre forwards, in the spirit of sport. Many people work as if they'd rather be at leisure, or play; but with Andy, play was whatever he undertook, in the office, in the kitchen, on the pitch; he played for his life. He should have been a monomaniac professional, artist, sportsman, soldier, hunter or backbencher, occupation so filled his attention, and heart. That journalism was a chiselling, two-faced, ironic, second-order activity to so many of its exponents, he did not understand; to him, everything was the game, pursued with rosy passion, chin canted like a champion.

———————

NOW THIS OFFICE OF ours had once belonged to a hippy who'd used up his inheritance on a conscience café where no green, vegan or campaigner would go, the flyover being demonstrably rich in nitrogen and particulate emissions of a kind hateful to these activists. If only he'd checked the website for hotspots! There he sat, alas, with holy eyes, over his verge-plant soups and salads, carob briquettes and pulse blancmange (from an ancient recipe of Egypt), his rack of magazines, spiritual pamphlets and leaflets for energy bracelets; in winter, he donned a woolly hat, warming his hands at the samovar. No one came, but Japanese and South Koreans in pollution masks who'd got lost trying to find the Tube, made quizzical noises and bought nothing; and hoodies who rode their bikes round the room, looked in his till, spat at him and left. The unhappy fellow having become bankrupt (and, it was said, homeless), the property'd reverted to the borough, whereupon Andy secured it at auction under the long-lease referred to in his 'mortmain' outburst (above).

Fabiana, bored managing subscriptions for the mag of a 'major' retailer that he'd nagged about advertising, admired his chutzpah and came with. In those early days (she'd told me this) Mayor Montgomery visited the office of the fledgling *Chronicle* on his bike to 'jaw' with Andy, who badgered him about a grant. The Mayor made a drawbridge with his hand. An elected body should not be seen to fund in any wise a paper that may then report on it. Andy kept on at him about *sport*, *team*, *community*, with enough force to drive him out the door on suddenly remembered business, and Fabiana said now look what you've done! But in a day or so Mayor Monty was back, still doing the drawbridge thing though obviously well disposed towards Andy in some way, and waiting for Andy to say something he himself couldn't, while murmuring cakily of handsels, earnests, donations, until Andy hoofed the issue of the council into the stands, editorially speaking. Well on those terms (Monty letting the bridge down), wasn't beyond the bounds of propriety that a token handsel might be found, there surely being precedents (benign) his adjutant could dust off. Which Andy the Bold immediately turned down, exacting promise of something bigger, if he kept the thing going for two years, without any aid whatsoever, except what he'd gained by his own sweat, tears, toil, or bigger still if he managed three years.

'By Gad, sir! You know how to drive a bargain!' cried Mayor

Montgomery, cycling from the room and on to the flyover. Oh, Monty! Last of the Informals. You and your 'Trundlers' Handsel'! In fact, as I'd learned when I joined the little team and we chatted over the traffic on Friday afternoons, there was something particular in Andy's comportment that had endeared him to the Mayor: he was a soldier's son.

His old man had been a major in a battalion of the Parachute Regiment never called on to participate in Britain's violent excitements in Ulster, South Atlantic or Sierra Leone, which spent its time training to remarkable levels, tumbling from the sky over Salisbury Plain, and kicking its superfit heels in Warwickshire. For a few years, it was attached to the BAOR and Andy did some form of O-levels at a barracks school in Westphalia, while his father trained even more, discussed Intelligence reports, lost his temper with his wife and took part in wargames, against the day Third Russian Shock Army crossed the Rhine. They returned to the Midlands. Midlands, Minden, Midlands.

His son had much to bear with this irritable moving about and waiting for apocalypse. Major Ravage's frustration at (a) being a permanent reservist, and (b) the Soviet Union's headachy quiescence in Western Europe while it wallowed in the Bear Trap, he took out in hard expectations of discipline, neatness, excellence, in the boy. After making his bed and tidying his tidy room, Andrew awaited inspection. At the Blondie poster, the tucking and folding of sheets and blankets, the soldier shook his head. Bed like that'd be a disgrace in a dosshouse, never mind the home of a 4 Para officer. Yanking the poster down.

By the touchlines of Warwickshire schools and clubs, while Andy played rugby or football, he appeared after kick-off in moss-green hunting jacket, keeping apart from other parents, leaving before the end. From the corner of his eye, Andy caught the upright figure as he put in his tackles, waiting for him to score.

Mayor Montgomery, a military-history buff with no army connections (believe it or not), rather gloried in Andy. With Coalition talk of the 'Big Society', the Mayor saw the *Chronicle*, now publishing community news weekly from the flyover with a rosy soldier's boy of unshakeable integrity, formidable energy, etc., at the helm, as the epitome of that good and very flexible vision. Which being the case, the borough having made a nugatory profit from the sale of the property, this might be returned, handy-dandy, *manus manum lavandum*, times two, or three, say, as handsel for an enterprise that did not deserve less than others who asked for more, in recognition of what too often lay hidden under a bushel, namely, the light of our yeoman trundlers – to convey something of the Mayor's accountant-baffling oratory. Fabiana thought he might be queer for Andy. That's the history.

———————

ANDY WAS NOW DECLARING that if the cop's driver was an ex-services man, esp. one who'd no doubt been in Belfast around the time the Parachute Regiment was the most prominent British presence in the province, then he wouldn't rest till he'd got to the bottom of this.

Ah.

Wouldn't. Couldn't. It was the one thing he could do for the old man, who was still around and straight-backed, collecting for veterans in a red beret in November, and years ending with a '4' for Arnhem: root out a dirty soldier . . .

'Your dad's not even lucid,' Fabiana said. 'His short-term memory's gone ping.'

All the more reason for Andy to defend the reputation of the regiment, and in his book, that meant weeding out and shaming rotten elements.

But this driver, Bowler was the name, wasn't a Para anyway, according to my source, and here I named the unit referred to by Hanley, which Andy bent over Fabiana to google . . .

Ha! Men were seconded to the unit from other regiments (as if that proved the point). Whatever, he had the bit between his teeth now, and he'd become more obstinate the more I cavilled, so I sat back while he marched about. But how he could feel such loyalty to a father who'd made his early life a misery?

Maybe there'd been a big bust-up at some point, Andy'd held his ground; more than that, he'd actually got one over the dad, humiliated him, won. So I imagined the scene. And then, perhaps not at once, sooner or later, he'd have felt the sorrow that comes from destroying a big thing, like a demolition man or hunter, when tower or great beast has fallen, and he looks upon his work.

Or he'd have come to know that the father's disappointment was no matter for irony, but the mark of his soul. And what are we to do when we learn this of another: that there's nothing we can do to console them or make amends for what the world's welshed them of; that they've compounded disappointment by searching for themselves in us, when we can't make a bed or score at sport? Mock them with salutes? Ah, is there anywhere a cure for disappointment? Can you live or thrive by not doing well?

Then will's the issue? Has the will existed that – not enjoys disappointment, for that's perversity, and again a kind of fruition; but that's able not to wish, plan, look forward, imagine better? From Karen's meditation apps, I'd got wind of such an ideal; but first you had to succeed in breathing in an ancient way, and you had to really want tranquillity bordering on nothing: plenty willing going on there still. So what's the deal?

Check these two. This showboating of his – it's not to impress Fabiana, not directly. It's a way of raising the desire he feels for her, into something fine; so he campaigns for his community, instead of her love-box. And she, she'll stick closer to him through all this, and wherever it leads (God help him), than ever she would in a common-or-garden affair. For why? Because they admire a man who can hold off, with a big conscientious plan. That's a man: he'll go without to get the job done. They're so used to us pestering, like dogs, it seems a kind of magic. And so she is enchanted . . .

'Now, Carlo,' Andy was saying, 'the thing is, stick with this rent boy – Donna Juan – and see what – but you know the m.o., better than I do by a long way! He's our—'

'He's a source,' I said, 'but his occupation is about as unreliable as it gets in the opinion of the public. He also has a conviction for GBH.'

'So what *are* you doing with him?'

'As I told you earlier, I've been finding out how dark this thing is, and let me tell you, darkness is the diametric opposite of journalism . . .'

'Because *jour* means day,' said Fabiana.

'But I'm paying you to be a journalist!' grinned Andy. 'Aren't I? Not the opposite – whatever that is!'

'Listen. What else I'm doing is getting to know him, *his* story. And believe it or not, I've been getting interested in that, very, because one thing it has is clarity, right? And another is a bloody strong quality of injustice. And for thirds, it's contemporary. The politics he's been up against are topical, extremely. A new hate-form. So I will stick with him.'

'The lawyer, though,' said Andy, who'd been waiting for me to finish, 'what about him? Can I have his number?'

'Not yet.'

'Why not?'

'Because you haven't thought this through. Go and play football tonight, or take the kids to Pizza Express. And have a think. Or maybe stop thinking. Tomorrow, you'll be fresh.'

Fabiana signed for me to go.

CHAPTER 23

I NEEDED TO EXAMINE THE conscience with which I'd taken my
leave of these two, but here comes Donna Juan, treading softly.
Slippers of black suede, black polo neck, skinny denims, chain of office.

'*Buen día*, Carlito.'

'Where you off to, John?'

'Why? You desire cock play?'

'Of course I don't.'

'*Un pocito?*'

'No!' Definitely not.

'Sibyl said you were out of sorts.'

'Did she?' On an elm beside the gates of the garden square, a crow
was revving.

'Yeah. We're pals now. Like that!' Fingers twined.

The crow took off.

'Just after lunch –' hand on hip – 'can you imagine who came up?'
Donna Juan began to walk with me.

'Tell.'

'D'you really want to know?'

'I quite do.'

'Well I won't then. But they're ex-C-List.'

'Really?'

As we moved along, he told a tale of massive ejaculation. Had to wash his hair after. I looked up at Lords. Did the Incognito Order operate for celebs?

'Hey?'

'Incognito Order Number 1?'

'What you on about, Carlo?'

'What you were talking about in the hospital yesterday. Come on, John! You know!'

'Never said any such thing, you wally!'

'You bloody well did, John!' He stared and there I was, tiny in his pupil. Backwards up the road I went, he following, like dancers.

'Look at face on you!' he cried as we slid along. 'Did you there! Believed me, didn't you!'

How should I know when not to? Experience, that's how. I knew something of liars. Donna Juan was different.

I took him for coffee and muffins. In the window of Café Charybdis, we sat planning our day out. Thursday was cool. I'd write up the profile, he could see a draft. That was cool. And what about Lords – could he get time off?

Oh, he was quitting soon anyway. A Russian had asked him to be his housekeeper, £500 a week. Holland Park. Once he'd got his passport from the Phoenix, he was out of Lords. The profile could be his swansong. We chewed our muffins. By the end of the week, I'd be finished with him.

What was I doing now? Did I fancy a bevvy?

I checked my phone. Had to get back to my wife.

Did she know about us two?

I'd mentioned him. What of it?

Oh as long as she'd been all right about it.

About what?

That I talked to him, took him for Rodeos and muffins. Not to mention our outing! Wouldn't want me to get into trouble.

It was cool. Brooding on the Russian: gated driveway; Hyatt waving; heavy moves me on . . .

What did she do?

My wife? She was a science teacher. Maths and Physics.

You needed those subjects for Geography; only a half-arse geographer would get by without 'em.

I mentioned the article in *Nature* about black holes, accretion-discs, their mighty winds.

Well, Geography and Astronomy were like cousins: we wanted to know the universe as well as we knew our earth-home – same kind of knowledge; whether it was cosmic winds or katabatic ones.

I asked what they were, and he shook his head, finger to lips, eyes bright.

Well, they couldn't be that strong if they were just down here.

Don't bet on it, Carlo. You haven't faced one. Yet!

Did it put things in perspective, Geography? Was that his experience?

Meaning?

I meant like when people say looking at the stars puts things in perspective.

Oh let's doke Thursday. He'd become listless, pressing crumbs on his plate.

Over the road, an elderly copper. Donna Juan nudged me.

The copper passed along and back. Either his beat was pretty short, or he was specifically tasked, looking for something close at hand. From his helmet poked a coarse white pigtail; at his belt, a compact baton, radio, cuffs. An ancient fuzz all right. Fucking Nora! Caught any jack boys, Grandad? Radio out. Who's he looking for? Check Fancy Smith!

DJ and I had the giggles, pair of us. Then he turned to the window of Charybdis, gave us the Saxon stare . . .

'It's him!' hissed Donna Juan.

'Jesus! They've made him Special Constable!' The Gonk was bruise-free, Turbo's work of yesterday invisible. Maybe his nose didn't crack like normal.

'Is he looking at us?'

'Yes.'

'Shall I go and twat him, Carlo?'

'What?'

'You look dead frightened!'

'You never hit a copper, right? You've already got a record. They'll bury you for that!'

'OK. Just asking.' And there he sat, rattling his chain. By God, he was a soldier, this one!

At home I 'pestered' the wife; not because I wanted it (any more than normal), but to make it seem as if I had nothing but normal on my mind. She told me to go away and make dinner; she was meditating. What was she doing after? Preparing for her interview.

Wasn't the sulk of a man who's not getting any that I fell into in the kitchen, but a *brown* study. So much to reflect on, so little in the way of reflective, rational, power – if I say so myself. But this latest development (powers of arrest conferred upon the Gonk) suggested general mobilization. All I could think of was running away.

CHAPTER 24

'THERE'S SOMEONE WAITING DOWN there!' At the window, Karen whisked her dressing gown.

'Where?'

'By the railings. He keeps looking up.'

'Ah!' I stepped over, withdrew. Couldn't she get ready for work, instead of chewing nectarine crescents? Not more coffee! Skates on, lady! Away from the window with that tiny cup! Damn her. Any attempt to persuade would provoke her, so I hummed, checked my phone. Damn him as well, hanging about down there like we were schoolboys on the mitch.

'What did you wave for, Carlo?'

'When?'

'Just now, you waved quickly at that trollop!'

'The one outside?'

'Yes. The one outside. The one in shades with the gold satchel. That one.'

'We're doing an interview. He's much too early.'

'Don't tell me that's him!' She looked down again.

'Who?'

'The one you mentioned the other week.'

'Yes it is, actually.'

'He's wearing bloody hotpants!'

She belted her dressing gown. Acting. Like this was all we had: our marriage, sunny room, red alcove, goodly fruits in fridge and bowl, posh coffee maker – not much maybe, but something, unstained to date by the presence of a rent boy. Scratching her thigh, preparing a line.

Get you to your chamber, lady! Prepare a self that will be entire; not this double being, both here and somehow beside herself, outraged and curious, unwilling to miss out.

'What'll the bloody neighbours think?' That was her mam or gran speaking. She itched her thigh again. Like a favoured person who slips off at a party, her will had gone.

'Aren't you going to be late, sweetheart?'

'It's an Inset day. I'm seeing Angie.'

'Ah, about your interview? Of course.'

'Is he coming up?'

'Who?'

'The lad down there.'

'No. We've planned a day out. You don't want him up here, do you? You're not dressed properly.' She was coy enough about the delivery men who climbed the stairs (with things *she'd* ordered).

'So where are you going?'

'Dunno yet. It's his choice.'

'Why can't you interview him up here?'

'Wouldn't be regular, would it? Never interview anyone at home. Why him?'

'So there's a chaperone.'

Meaning that – or the opposite? She was imagining a 'scene'? Come on! Pure fantasy. What would he do? Not that he wasn't an expert. Within the annals of envy (mine), she'd had her times as well . . .

AROUND THE TIRESIAS PHASE, she was into some louche stuff, a kind of decadent dabbling, such as a young woman arriving in London for the first time with her eye on the experience-dial and a notion of glamour would allow herself, and of which she was evidently in excellent control. *The Dedicated Vagrant* contained a 'Gnostic Sex' column, which fuelled this fancy. What was 'gnostic sex'? That's what I wanted to know. Also, was I getting any? In a column by-lined 'Carpocratina', the writer described an orgy on a hired bark, where she managed four cocks. *Managed?* Buffeted by commuters at the Chancery Lane newsstall, I brooded on this. Was it her? In The Cittie of Yorke, I had a couple of pints, phoned Tiresias and asked for Carpocratina. They put on Karen, who was very deadpan. I could pick her up at the club if I fancied. Then I could take her out. And then?! I did as suggested, but there was no managing that night; or other nights. In fact, not until I'd asked her to marry me. She was a Catholic, after all. If it had been her on the bark, I never asked. She didn't want to know me the way she had other men, was something she suggested. In which I managed to find a compliment.

———

STILL WAVERING. SOONER OR later, you may come to notice a partner in life is making a critical readjustment, and unless you've just attained a condition of steady or temporary glory, such as offering your life for another, or making a lot of money, it's generally downwards (you'll know the signs for what they are). Apparently, she couldn't effect the readjustment. I went towards her . . .

'Oh, Carl!' Burned sweet from fruit and macchiato, a breath-jet caught me in the eye. 'What are you doing?'

*

I'D KEPT HIM WAITING down there, and he'd shown manners not to call or text. Satchel-dazzled, I covered my eyes.

'What you got in there, John?'

'Nowt so far – except condoms.' With the hotpants noticed by Karen, he'd matched a black toreador blouse and espadrilles that tied at the ankle. No wonder she'd been 'ambivalent'. I'd given no thought to the planning of our day. Drift and doke, let it happen.

'What d'you want to do?'

He sniffed. 'Go shoplifting.' Patting his shining satchel. 'Called a "Hermes", this – know why?'

'No. Bit early for shoplifting, isn't it?'

'Don't know much, do you?' Pleasant sneer. 'Thought you were meant to be a crime bod. Early's best for nicking. Everyone in Boots is half asleep still. More you stand out, less they bother about you. Trust me!'

'When did you start shoplifting?' Might as well get the interview rolling. We moved off. At the high street, I directed us south, away from the retailers. Red hatchback passing, other side.

'When I were nine years old! With lasses. They're better at nicking.'

'What did you used to pinch?'

'CDs, batteries, pets, knives, eyeliner . . .'

'What d'you take pets for?'

'Dad wouldn't let me have one. Wanted a hawk, like in that film. You know, where that scrawny kid gets a hawk?'

'Oh, *Kes*? Bit young for that, aren't you?' Two red hatchbacks; not them.

'Showed us it at secondary.'

'So you stole a bird of prey?'

'Yeah. From Crossley Pets.'

He was making this up, or I was a Dutchman. Who ever heard of a hawk in a pet shop? 'What d'you do with it?'

'What d'you mean? Trained the bastard, that's what. Up on Beacon Hill. Had all the right kit, I did. Then set it on a twat that wronged me.'

'Who was that?'

'Ady Beaumont. Him and his mates were mocking me dancing at the Zoo.'

'The zoo?'

'It were a club. All mincing around me they were.'

'Right.' I adjusted the picture: thickset Yorkies in a bunch, this fella with his fey moves . . .

'So I waited in my garden, right, and when I saw Beaumont coming down, I shouted, "Set, Adbeel (that were hawk's name). Sink deep. Peck bastard's eyes out!"'

'Did it?' Fourth red hatchback, school-run.

'Aye. Fucking went for him, Carlo!'

'Didn't *blind* him though, did it?'

Gaily Donna Juan swung his satchel. 'No. Dive-bombed him though. Frightened living daylights out of him. Never mocked me after that. Where are we going? To the hospital again?'

'No. D'you want some breakfast?'

'Can I have a Bloody Mary?'

'OK.'

'Nish!'

I led him to The Melancholy Minstrel, where he checked the posters for ancient gigs, this month's poetry readings, open-mic nights, the black-and-white photos, scrimshaw and 'objets d'art' that gave the Minstrel its much-loved 'Don't-change-a-thing!' distinction. Slowly spooning porridge and prunes, young women tapped on tablets; in a sideroom, a man worked his way through 'What Doesn't Kill Me Makes Me Stronger', the Minstrel's renowned fry-up, turning pages of *The*

Guardian. I thought of Hanley taking William for those breakfasts: sound of cutlery setting him off . . .

'God this place is grannypits! Where shall we go?' I indicated somewhere, away from a young woman who seemed to have overheard something he'd just said about a Cleveland Steamer – and known what he meant. Hitching satchel, DJ bent to sniff the seat, made eyes at me, and clapped his hands for joy at a witticism I hadn't uttered, like a two-grand courtesan. The day wouldn't be without its challenges; I ordered his Bloody Mary, myself a coffee.

'Did you really have a hawk?'

Sucking thick red bevvy through a black straw: 'No. Could you tell?'

'Yes. I could actually.'

'How like?' Playing the fluid round his mouth.

'I don't think you're much of a liar, John.'

'Could be.' His eyes had a liquorice shine.

'You aren't, though. Isn't in your bones. Who ever heard of a lying geographer?'

'Known many?'

'Yeah. My first wife was a geographer.'

'Oh my God! You're not serious!'

'Yeah. And I have you down as a truthful guy.'

'Well I wouldn't trust me too far, I was you.'

'Why not?'

'Cos I can turn, that's why.'

'You can turn violent, but not untruthful. That thing you told me about the students picking on you at university, now that wasn't made up, was it?'

'Obviously not.'

I knew it wasn't, because I'd checked the *Yorkshire Evening Post* crime archive. His name was John David Kippax, and he'd been convicted of GBH with Intent, April 2010. A spokesperson stated that his university was energetically committed to diversity and that its compliance, training and reporting procedures anticipated the Equality Act (commencing October that year). The university's 'Firewall Policy' had proved extremely successful in prohibiting hate speech while protecting free expression . . . *You and your kind, you should all be gassed. Sssss!* . . . In no circumstances could violence be condoned on campus . . . *Striped their hospodar with a bottle of Brahma* . . . In court, his lawyer'd suggested that the bottle had been broken in a scuffle as the complainant tried to confiscate the defendant's alcoholic drink, whereupon the defendant raised his hand to defend himself against three assailants chanting homophobic-racial slogans, causing a deep facial wound by accident. Kippax waived defence: he'd 'bottled' the complainant on purpose because he was sick of being taunted. Six months.

I brought this up now, wondering if he'd get hyper that I'd been checking on him. He looked a little surprised, even impressed. That was right. How it had been. He'd told the truth. What else was there to do?

How to get the measure of this one? Geographer, soldier, headcase, queer, tyke, imitation-Colombian . . .

'We were going to talk about Geography and Astronomy.'

'Were we?'

'Yes. Remember when we were having muffins? We flagged it.'

'Oh yeah.' He yawned, flashed his eyes. 'Go on then, Carlton! Remind!'

'I said I was looking at Karen's science mag, about the cosmic winds. We were talking about perspective. You said they were like cousins, Astronomy and Geography. The stars give you a sense of perspective, that's what they say. Does Geography do the same thing?'

'If you like.'

'What's that mean?'

'*Nada.*'

'Hey?'

'Possibly. If you like.' He yawned. 'Can I have a ciggy?'

Patiently, I took him into the garden. Away from other munchers, we sat at a table of unvarnished wood, under a Japanese tree.

He lit up. Wanted another Bloody Mary. 'All nature, isn't it? Whether you're looking at really old rocks, or sitting at telescope with your pee-pee in your hand.'

'What's the better perspective to take though? Universe or earth-home – that's what you talked about.' He seemed amused by this. I didn't mind too much. 'Which one should you go for?'

'You're such a kiddy, Carl! I swear.'

'Why?'

The waiter came with his drink, and an ashtray. He had a bright blond face; it smacked you in the eyes like a snow field. As he walked away down the narrow path, DJ checked his arse.

'Cos you think –' he touched me nicely on the arm – 'that it's all in the facts. You're like, "Which are the best facts to get things in perspective?" That's so dumb, so standard. No wonder you're a journo.'

'Sorry. That's my life, John.'

'It's like staring at famine people, starving Africans, to make yourself feel well off, when you're having a shit time. "Always someone worse off than you!" That kind of bollocks. And it is bollocks, mate, I'm telling thee.'

'Why is it?' I wasn't too pissed off about being dumb, or standard.

'Cos it's just quantities. We have more water, fresh fruit, hospitals, and better roads and drains, and all our brothers or sisters have survived till they're fifteen year old or whatever. But you can't weight it like that.' He spoke fast, low, decisive; no eye tricks. He'd evidently thought this through.

Go on.

'You weight it like that, then it's always the big picture's where the truth is: big misery, big stars. Have you heard of Immanuel Kant?'

'Yeah. What did he say?'

'*The starry heavens above me, the moral law within!*'

'What's it mean, John?'

He checked my face.

'What it means is that the universe might be big, but only man has reason; only man knows what's right and wrong, regardless how much awe we're meant to feel about enormous things.'

'So why're you into Geography? Can't get any more truth from that than Astronomy, can you?'

He twitched. 'Cos we can see the world with our eyes, we can touch it. We can cross the seas to look at things. We can dig and chip. We've shaped the world, Carlo. It's like us now. We can see ourselves in it. People say. "Oh, but we're made from stars, you know! All our vital elements and that!" Well, so what if I've got some fucking star iron or carbon in me. Isn't interesting or vital, it's just a bastard fact. Geography's living, it's a mirror.'

Bloody clever . . . Was he bitching on my marriages?

'Must have been hard for you, John, not to finish your studies: real disappointment.'

'Read enough for three degrees while I were there anyway. No one bothered me in the library. – Can we chip?'

'OK, droog. Let's go.'

CHAPTER 25

THERE ARE THREE WAYS through the cemetery. Mothers and cyclists take the central road, workers sit along it with their lunch. For the curious, a gravel path to the right passes monuments, angels, crypts. Here ravens gather on the headstones.

A dumpy mausoleum made us shudder. DJ giggled, held my arm. The door was mightily padlocked. Over the wall rolled the District Line. From an arcade of creamy stone, an outlaw signalled.

'He was offering e-t-c,' Donna Juan told me. Don't look back! Never do that, Carlito!'

The outlaw wore a tight vest, chains.

'Why not?'

'It's uncool!'

'What's "etcetera"?'

'You what?'

'That thing you just said!'

'It's not "etcetera", you fool! It's E-T-C — *entre tres chicos*. Three-way.'

A bare-chested man pissed against a yew. By the wall, a boog looked on. A Parks Police van passed. We read the headstones: down here they were small and regular, set off with a little railing. The men died at Neuve Chapelle, 1915. Many were younger than DJ. At the end of the path, we sat on a bench. He looked up Neuve Chapelle on his phone. Brits fired that many shells, they ran out for the rest of the year.

Did they win?

Looked like they would, then they got bogged down. The phones broke, so they couldn't co-ordinate; the infantry went in the wrong field, artillery wasted all their ammo. The Prime Minister had to resign because of the 'Shell Crisis'. Wouldn't get that now, would you? They'd lost shame.

Fucking wouldn't get that. Look at Blair. Flying about with his shit-eating grin, lecturing on peace at 50K a pop. Who was it turned Iraq to a khazi, where the rats were gathering?

DJ went back to his phone, liking knowledge. There'd been a bunch of Indians fighting with the Brits, from Meerut and Lahore.

Meerut?

One of the oldest cities on earth, Meerut.

Really?

It were about 3,000 year old now.

He knew a lot.

Yeah. Compared to me. Took 4,000 casualties at Neuve Chappelle, the Indians.

We got up and went to look over the little railings for Indian names. There weren't any. On the way back to our bench, DJ twisted up his black hair. Over the way was an Egyptian-style tomb. DJ checked the cemetery website. By steampunks, it was known as the 'Time Machine'.

A young woman came from nowhere with a skipping rope. In vest and pastel shorts, she whisked and snapped, plimsolls flashing.

'Who d'you think sent her?'

'Who? That lass over there?'

'Yes.'

Her rope formed an arch, which was always there.

'Why should anyone send? D'you want to bite her peach?'

'Shut up! She's half my age.'

'There you are then!'

I sat feeling the mystery of it, hoping he wouldn't be a jerk. Through the arch I saw a world.

He flashed his leg to tighten an espadrille: 'Introducing Protagoras!'

Who?

Protagoras.

What did he say?

That man was the measure of all things.

'Hey?'

'*Man is the measure of all things.*'

'He said that?'

Donna Juan hummed.

'What's it mean? Like that "starry heavens" thing?'

'Not really.' He lit a Dunhill International. I wafted smoke away from the skipper.

'What is it then?'

'Ooh! It's questions, questions with you, Carlo. Why don't you know anything for yourself?'

I sat and sulked. He looked thoroughly disrespectful anyway, tart's cut-offs, Latin blouse and lady's shoes, smoking near young athletes and graves. If the van came by, I had a good mind to shop him – for soliciting, nastiness, an irritating northern accent like my wife's, being over-educated, indecency, parasitism, tax evasion . . .

He touched my thigh: 'Sorry! I were off on one.' In his mirror shades I saw a hologram pest.

On another bench, the young woman sunned herself. She came to us now, to buy a cigarette. DJ produced a Dunhill with his finger tips.

He wouldn't take her money. They nattered a bit in youth-speak; she went away to skip and smoke.

No, *Look at me!* No effort or showboating. Light, careless, arched, exact. I watched her like a peasant, this dancing spirit who'd appeared from herself – not cloud, pentagram, or apartheid of angels. Wonderful, yet in our range . . .

'I know what it means.'

'What?'

'Man is the measure of all things.'

'What's it mean then?'

'D'you know yourself?' We rose and strolled.

'To tell you the truth, I think I do. But –' smiling sweetly – 'I can't explain.'

The central road was wide and bright, raised colonnades to east and west. Young men waited on the steps, patient as sailors. At the end was a chapel, squat and heavy with half-apple roof; I checked it on my phone: St Peter's Basilica in Rome the model. Looked like it could take a nuclear blast. A dog-collared man stood smiling.

With DJ, who was not at ease but also (I thought) trying not to giggle, he shook hands, watching me. 'And who d'you have with you here, John?'

'This is Carl.'

The churchman was Ray Vernon. I asked if the chapel was his place of work.

'Oh, nothing so grand, Carl! My HQ's down the road.' He named a church that provided drop-in sessions for the homeless, and free hot lunches. On the colonnade, two good-looking young men kissed each other deeply. Brown-eyed Father Raymond had a broad face, good head of hair, and a laughing way of saying, 'Penny for your thoughts, Carl?'

'Carl's been puzzling about philosophy.'

194

'Oh-ho!' laughed Father Raymond, rubbing his hands. 'Philosophical excursion, is it? Great idea! Room for one more?'

'Come with!' cried DJ. 'That's all right, isn't it?' So I was boss.

'Which way are you gents headed? Isn't it marvellous to see the sun again?'

'We're just rambling,' DJ told him. 'We might pop into the hospital. Mightn't we, Carl?'

'Yes.'

'Ah,' said the priest as we walked along. 'Visiting family?' I mentioned Barnfield and, glancing at me, the priest said, 'Nasty accident, that. Very nasty indeed. Decent chap, that Barnfield. Comes into our Wednesday Mind-Games. Time for everyone. Very popular man.'

'Tell Carl about Mind-Games!'

We came out on to the main road, heading south.

'Oh, we play chess, draughts, mah-jong, backgammon (buttons-only gambling!), sudoko. We have a tough quiz as well. Four till six.'

Down here was The Jennings, where I suggested a drink. Father Raymond said he'd join us for a shandy, but might we stick to the garden? Hadn't been in a pub for twenty years. When I asked why that might be, he said, oh, he'd vowed he wouldn't, so waiting at the bar, I wondered if he might be a problem drinker who'd taken holy orders; this didn't satisfy me. Returning with the drinks, I asked about his church career. Raymond shook his head and smiled. The church was a vocation. Certainly, he'd had a career in 'hospitality', which was a fancy way of saying that he'd run a couple of pubs; but that was a long time ago. Then this landlord-priest changed the subject by asking what DJ and I had been philosophizing about.

'Well, we started with Kant!' said DJ brightly, sipping gin and ginger through a sky-blue straw. 'And I was telling Carl that the moral law was more important than the stars.'

'And what did Carl say to that?' beamed Father Raymond.

'I saw his point,' I said. 'I'd been looking at my wife's science magazine, about cosmic winds. Which I found very impressive, though I know nothing about science. But John told me that what matters is down here, not the universe.'

'Perhaps John is forgetting that Kant, as well as being "a real piss-ant" (to quote the Pythons) was also an astronomer. What d'you say, John?' A car scrunched on the gravel, and a couple got out checking their phones. Blonde in mini-dress of chocolate suede, sunglasses, mark on left leg that showed through the tan; ruddy man in cargo shorts. Why do churchmen beam? Playing happy.

'Never knew he were an astronomer,' DJ said.

'Indeed he was, John. Something everyone forgets is Kant wrote a book called *General History of Nature and Theory of the Heavens* in 1755, in which he proposed that God was still getting the universe right, setting the galaxies in order, reducing chaos. If you like, it was evolving the way our species world is. A Geordie called Thomas Wright put him on to the idea. Gravity was God's ordering tool!'

'How can you believe in God if you believe in evolution?'

'It's called "Process Theology", John!' explained the churchman in his laughing way. 'He's perfecting things, is God.'

'That means he were crap in first place! Like when you go shopping in Sainsbury's and they've got a poster saying, "We've stopped adding junk to our ready meals!" Doesn't say owt about that in Bible, does it?'

Father Raymond beamed. I fell to wondering about these two. How long you known *him*? What you told him you haven't told *me*? Such questions began their drone.

'Well that's a droll comparison, John,' the priest was saying. 'I may pinch it if you don't mind. But the theology of process does admit that if God is getting better, He mightn't have been perfect in the first place.

What's more, the New Testament shows God in a very different light from the Old, so there's an admission that the divine image has been in need of reform. But the broad idea is we're all part of something much bigger: life doesn't stop at the earth, and soul most certainly doesn't!'

This churchman had two voices. The one up front was like Mayor Montgomery, or a certain comic treasure of TV, panel game, etc., who'll be known to you; the other was the sound of where he came from. Can't help tracking class, can we? Till we discover a source. So we judge the finished man, or man in process, against his original pollution, and compare our own.

Better say something . . .

'*Man is the measure of all things.*'

'You believe that, Carl?'

'I don't know. We were talking about Protagoras, John and I.'

'Man may be in measure with all things, Carl. Then we have harmony, fraternity, community. Then, too, we have the sense of what is holy. But when he measures things against himself, we have bitterness, if man feels himself lacking, or pride, if he reckons he's doing rather well thank you. These are forms of vanity.'

'Can he measure things against himself without vanity? I mean, can he genuinely do well by himself, for himself?'

'But who would decide that he had, Carl?' Father Raymond rolled his glass between his hands. 'Who can say, hand on heart, I've done all this on my own? Without encouragement, support, the faith of others? Without parents, siblings, loved ones, friends?'

'I couldn't,' I said. 'Wouldn't dream of it. But what about the individuals, Ray, the people who stand out?'

'For achievement?'

'Maybe. Or for going it alone, against the current. Doing it their way, if you like.'

'Have you met anyone like that, Carl?'

'The other night, I was thinking that a lot of the people I know do it their way.'

'But not you, Carl?'

'No. Not me.'

'But you, Carl, are the measure of them. Savvy? From where you stand, you see and judge them, and if I dare say so, you love them, for doing it their way, their individuality, personality, what have you.' He was earnest now, this churchman, wanting me to see.

'I suppose I do.' Checking DJ.

'So their distinctiveness, it depends on you, sir. Could they keep it up without you?'

'I'm sure they could,' I said, thinking this was all very kind, but really a sort of white lie, and this priest must be feeling mighty sorry for me.

'No, Carl. Without your place in the circle, everything changes, changes beyond measure; and the same goes for everyone else as well; at least from our human point of view, which is very murky even on a bright afternoon like this, when we look about us and think we know exactly what we are seeing, and who we are looking at!' Which seemed to be a challenge, though maybe a general one, rather than a suggestion that the garden of The Jennings was deceptive or illusory, or that the blonde and her ruddy pal over there behind the priest were other than they seemed. 'But God sees steady, Carl. He's always at the circle's centre. Or if you like, the centre which so many people nowadays feel they have lost, so that it's so easy to go down into despair – that centre is merely God!' I was thinking this was a cop-out, when he said, 'But what's your line, Carl?'

When I told him I worked for the *Chronicle*, he recognized my name, and rejoiced.

Was he honest, this churchman? The permanent good humour, enthusiasm, insistent small-timeness – how could you manage that sincerely, manage it and mean it with an exact fit, so the performance wasn't three or five times the length of the feeling, wrapped around the heart like a yard of butcher's doily? I couldn't.

I ventured to ask how he and DJ were acquainted, and DJ said, 'Because I go to St Aubrey's!' like I was ever so slow, and Father Raymond beamed and told he'd once come upon John sitting on the wall outside smoking and invited him into evening service, whereupon John said something rather 'pungent' and walked off. Well, this pricked F. Raymond's curiosity, on the Luke 12:6 principle, and he went to the wall the same time next evening, and there was John again, facing this way, so F. Raymond reminded him of Christ's words about the sparrows, and John said he wasn't bothered about sparrows – it was hawks he was into; so F. Raymond asked why that might be, and John said because hawks went for your enemies' eyes, whereas no one had ever heard of using a sparrow to force the issue, concluding with another pungent utterance. Then F. Raymond asked what issue that might be, and John said, 'Revenge, obviously,' and Father Raymond was taken aback, for who could the young man possibly want revenge upon?

CHAPTER 26

G AVE ENOUGH PEOPLE THIS hawk palaver, didn't he? Well I could compare versions. Told him I'm recording. In my pocket rolls the 853.

So it was revenge against the religious, DJ wanted, as the priest now explained. That second evening on the church wall, F. Raymond'd heard the story about the bullying at John's uni, and how that had ended up with the conviction of our young friend for a serious offence. So F. Raymond advised him that he'd surely had his revenge already, and ought to have learned a hard lesson against taking the law into his own hands as a consequence. But John'd been pretty defiant about all that, insisting that if he'd had a hawk, he could have taken revenge at a distance, and had the student's eye out without witnesses or getting pinched for it. Well, practicality aside (organizing hawk strikes in Leeds city centre, and so forth), F. Raymond was saddened to hear this. Surely John felt a little contrition for what he'd done to his tormentor? No. John didn't feel any. Sure? Yes. None whatsoever. In fact, he was (pungent term) glad he'd slashed the bastard's face open. Totally *£%*#^" glad he'd done the *&%^! But he'd turned the other way to say this, so F. Raymond went round to him. Now could he repeat what he'd just said, while looking F. Raymond in the eye. Whereupon young John began to weep and use many pungent phrases to the churchman. Who, without wanting to sound all happy-clappy about it, rejoiced that this young man knew he'd done a violent, unloving thing to the other student, and offered him a thick wad of tissues to wipe his eyes and clean up his mascara. Then took him into the church, not without foot-dragging and more pungency from friend John, for a cuppa – and a proper chat.

So they'd talked about Christianity, and Islam, their common prophets, and being gay, and homophobia, and drink and drugs and cigarettes, and revenge, the law, geography, education, taking responsibility, north and south; and then they had talked of love. F. Raymond showed John something he'd know from the Bible, even if he'd never read a page of scripture, where it said, 'For I say unto you, Love your enemies, bless them that curse you, do good to them that hate you, and pray for them which despitefully use you, and persecute you; That ye may be the children of your Father which is in heaven; for he maketh his sun to rise on the evil and on the good, and sendeth rain on the just and on the unjust' (Matthew 5: 44–5). And of course, so many people thought this was utterly weedy, and the worst thing about the Christian faith (or the second worst), expecting people who'd been the victims of hate to turn the other cheek, as if it were a fine thing to simper while you were getting your head kicked in, and *then* call out, 'Mmm, loving it!' Like there was nothing more *uncool* than 'Blessed are the meek', etc. And no doubt, young John thought something like that himself, which John confirmed by sneers and cold laughter, there in Father Raymond's kitchen. So the churchman sat out the sneers (smiling the way he was now, at a guess), till John, who liked ideas after all, asked how you justified praying for them that despitefully used you, instead of paying them back? Was it just a matter of waiting for them all to go to hell when they died? Like, where was the satisfaction in that?

So F. Raymond told him that some of the fathers of the Church, after Christ's time, they pictured exactly that: the souls of the saved looking over the edge of heaven down into hell, where they saw the damned being spit-roasted, and took pleasure in the sight (and sound of their screams). But they interpreted very literally, did these Church fathers, the things Christ said about the optical distance between hell and heaven (e.g. Luke 16: 20–6), and they had no feeling for the problem that if you looked down from heaven and saw an old friend, or even your grandmother, rolling in fire, satisfaction that justice was done, let alone pleasure, would be horrible things and alien to the creed of love. For which reason, what Christ meant about praying for those who used you despitefully was probably that wicked, cruel or deceitful people were in hell already – hell being a *life*-state, not an after-life *place*.

No. You justified loving your enemies not on grounds of weakness or abjection, or smallness, but for the opposite reason: it was the *biggest* thing to do, and most powerful. Which was why Christ compared such love to the sun and rain that God sends equally to the just and the unjust. The sun and rain are never used up: they shine and fall, shine and fall. Whereas hatred and revenge-desire wear out the heart that harbours them like broken glass in a paper bag. But it was also the biggest challenge, to love your enemies. Indeed, if all of human affairs had an Olympics, and not just the running and leaping department (excellent though that was), then the greatest event of all would be the Love-Your-Enemy Mega-Marathon, in which we'd been running only a couple of thousand years, with a great distance left before an end that just sometimes seemed to be getting further from all us athletes than it was at one time; though the marvellous thing about the finish line was that it could suddenly come much closer; and what we meant by faith was no more than the possibility that the finish line could suddenly be just behind us in an instant, 'Everyone a winner!' And how? By recognizing and following the example of Christ's love for man. Let all just love each other, we were over the line!

Around this point, I came in, asking DJ what'd he made of this conversation in the kitchen of St Aubrey's. Well to be honest, he'd thought it were crap (pure delight-beam from F. Raymond), starry-eyed crap, that only a retard could believe in. Like all the world knew, you loved where you were loved, you did favours to those who did you them, you scratch my back, blah blah blah. But then Father Ray, he asked John who he loved, in that case, and who he did favours for. And John said to tell the truth, he'd had to hang his head, cos he didn't love anyone nowadays, with the possible exception of his gran, and he did favours for boogs who paid tariff rate – and that was that, really.

So Father Ray, he'd shown John the Bible again, and it was another verse on from that first bit, where it said, 'For if ye love them which love you, what reward have ye? Do not even the publicans the same? And if ye salute your brethren only, what do ye more than others? Do not even the publicans so?' (Matthew 5: 46–7). Which had John thinking for a bit, and he asked about the publicans. So Father Ray told him that in the New Testament, a 'publican' sometimes meant a tax gatherer, and of course, the taxman was always full of smiles for those who'd paid up (especially in those days, when some publicans paid a premium to keep the taxes they gathered). But 'publican' also meant what it still means (which is probably what Jesus had in mind) – a pub landlord, in other words. And we all knew how landlords made a fuss of their locals, just so long as they had money in their pocket or purse, didn't we?

So I come in again. Been one himself, hadn't he? Indeed he had, before he took orders. There was an implication of 'the bad old days' in this, and it might have been prudent not to press on, for his smile had changed, but we had to. I asked if he'd loved his customers. It was worse than that. He'd kept in with them, that was the problem, the thing he regretted. How had he? Oh, he'd laughed at their jokes, and imitations, regardless of whether they were funny – or kind; bigged them up by starting to pour their drinks as they came in through the door before they'd made their order; agreed with things said and opinions, sometimes, or often, of a nasty or prejudiced quality – and as bad as agreeing, kept silent or seemed to agree when things plain vicious were uttered across the jump. He'd overlooked girls and women customers being pestered or chatted up when they clearly had no interest in the pursuit; he'd overheard accounts of nasty sexual exploits among men at the bar, sometimes of an obviously criminal kind, making no attempt to inform the local police. He'd noticed clearly stolen goods being fenced, ditto the local police. He'd seen black and Asian customers getting the treatment and not stepped in or asked the clientele to refrain. I asked if he meant physical assaults by this, but it was verbal abuse, silly noises, sniffing the air, jokes about takeaways, riots, banana boats, *in* the pub at least – what went on in the car park, or main road, well, that had been none of his business anyway. Then it all changed . . .

Here came another black bubble. I went to fetch more drinks, cursing the cemetery walk that led us to this churchman. When I returned, they were silent, not as if they'd been murmuring, then hushed, but like waiting for me alone, your painted priest and whore; and though this suggested honest dealing, or as we now say, 'transparency', I was frightened.

'There was a particular group of youths who showed up now and then. I was glad it wasn't more often, because they alarmed me. The pub was off their territory, but a mate of theirs lived close by. They were all of them underage. Once I asked for ID. They showed me ID: it was faked, obviously, and they found that funny. I made no objection, because I was frightened they'd start a tear-up. You have to understand that they were fighting or on the verge of it virtually every waking hour: they'd tussle with each other and gang up, four or five on one, in the car park, as they left; in the pub, they'd shout a mate's name, throw a punch, just avoiding contact; bottle tops and crisps and treble-folded beer mats, they could find ways of turning into nasty weapons – yes, even crisps! You can slice someone's cheek with one, if you employ a certain flicking motion, you can scratch an eyeball. Oh, they were devilishly ingenious at finding ways of hurting each other that weren't obviously illegal; and of course, what was also obvious was the knife or truncheon handle poking up from their belt, and the stitch marks in odd places where their mums had mended their jeans and shirts. What sort of violence they'd committed so far, I didn't know, and didn't want to; they were on their way to something bad, you could see this as surely as you can see genius in a child, for music, chess, languages. And as you can do nothing with genius but admire it, so with these boys, there was nothing to do but fear them (and I've some-times wondered if that isn't a kind of negative admiration). Fear, smile and comply. But sooner or later, I suppose, many blokes get a touch of the *High Noon*s. We can't keep complying, can we?

'At the time, I had a girlfriend and she didn't like what went on in the place. She used to come in with one of her friends when we were first together; after a while, she made excuses; then the rows started. If I didn't start putting my foot down with some of these yobs, that was it between us. I said, What are you telling me to do – speak to the cops? You know what they think of grasses round these parts! Well why didn't I start with the teenage trash? It was pathetic, the way I gave a bunch of sixteen-year-olds the run of the place when they shouldn't be allowed over the bloody door! For that, she couldn't respect me. What made her come out with this wasn't so much "being correct" about sexism, racism, and so forth, in the sense that we're so familiar with nowadays (though of course, there was plenty of that at the time we're speaking about, and I'd venture to say that folk were more individually committed then, whereas now, the correct attitudes are becoming social norms). With Sally, it was more an old-school matter of doing the right thing. You protected old ladies, you chased thieves, you confronted youths who were smashing the bus stop; you paid your way, didn't dream of collecting benefits. Traditional working-class values, these.'

'What did Sally do for a living?'

'Oh, she was a hairdresser. A good woman in the making. Of course, I didn't see it that way at the time. Nothing annoys us more than being reminded that our conscience isn't functioning as it should – is that true? Or is it being considered a coward? She didn't call me that; made me feel it though.'

'Can you separate them?'

'Perhaps not, Carl. Anyhow, it was on my mind that I wasn't doing the right thing; as it had been for some time, but I made excuses to myself, as I had to make a living. Where would we be without excuses? They're like shelves that support our world – except they're badly made ones, and sooner or later, everything tumbles anyway. On a February night, Sally came in with Gemma, the lady who owned the salon. Between us, things had been fractious for quite a while, but along with being annoyed, I was in love with her. Gemma'd bought drinks from the barmaid, and I could see them over the way, discussing me. It was clear that this was a sort of ultimatum. I needed to impress. Somehow, I had to make Sally proud of me. I got my chance.

'The two women hadn't been in more than fifteen minutes when the youths I've been telling you about crashed the place looking for their friend. There were five of them, but it seemed a lot more: a mob, that's what they were, a crowd that was more than its parts. There was this awful fidgetiness about them, like they were playing tag in a very small room; and they were wired: they'd been drinking already, smoking strong draw. So I refused to serve them. One of them said, "No, we ain't drunk, mate! Don't be refusing!" And they're all there at once, like the beast with five heads. And I looked at the eyes of the one who'd spoken, and I wondered what it was like in there. He hadn't much height, but he was broad-shouldered and his face wasn't a boy's. If you go back in time, a sixteen- or seventeen-year-old was long past being a boy: this one made me think of a medieval archer or pikeman, recruited from the peasantry. He was their leader, him and another boy, green-eyed, scrawny, fidgety, already converted to hate; his hair was the colour of cornflakes. The first boy had a younger brother, taller, dark-haired; his hair was well cut too, and when he lifted his shades, he had fine eyes – or would have, if he'd ever smiled; but he was like a celebrity who's notorious for kicking off when people recognize him in public, though isn't averse to provoking recognition – very unstable, this boy, but at the same time, cold, the coldest of them all, I felt, and confident about proving himself. There were two others: a big bluff fellow who was the nearest to being the comedian, and might have been class clown at school, but who'd now been poisoned so that you felt his jokes were censored and approved by the others; and a sullen chap with moist eyes who I thought was out of his depth with this lot, weak-willed, but growing in spite. I turned the music off and wouldn't serve them. If Sally'd noticed, I couldn't make out.

'They went over to the pool table and badgered a couple who were on it so they could play next, stacking fifty-pences on the edge. Well I wouldn't have that either. I was getting the taste for it, doing what a man has to, and so on. Switched the lights off above the pool table, and I went over and started gathering the cues, but wasn't quick enough, because they already had a couple, though they were refraining from mobbing me, so I put fifties in, released the balls and bagged them, and I don't know if this didn't impress them a bit since the bagged balls looked like coshes, and other punters were starting to take notice. Among the five boys there was much bluff and egging on; it was as if none of them could do something without the mass of the group deciding, yet when one acted, then another, the group seemed to swell, and they were no longer tagging in a small room, but like a football crowd, or riot. Now the two who'd kept hold of the cues were hefting them like javelins, practising to throw, and the rest were hooting, and I was wondering how far it would go, who'd back down, them or me – it was balanced like that. But their friend had appeared, and he was shouting, "Where's the lights?"

'This was the boy they came over to visit. I very much disliked the fellow, since he was so cocksure; and though this obviously wasn't his fault, there was something about his nose that upset me. We often glimpse the animal in others, don't we? Well this boy reminded me of a bird that pecks at seeds and nuts in a hurrying way, a finch of some kind. The beak's evolved over thousands of years; the creature's being is now concentrated there. To come to the point, I felt that beak of his might have the better of me as he shouted about the lights and told me to let them play. He used my name, too, and swore, as if he was twice his age, and I was just a servant, very used to getting his way and not to be crossed – or like the pub was his room, and I was spoiling things for his chums, shouldn't even be there; but everywhere was his space, this particular boy, because he was said to be connected, and though there was no firm evidence for that, no one seemed inclined to challenge the rumour – his confidence was proof enough. Robert Woods was his name.

'So I put the lights back on. Because he'd told me to – or because I wanted Sally to see that I was taking a stand? I don't know. It'd not be honest to maintain I wasn't pressurized by him; but by that time, I knew I'd gone a long way, and quite likely couldn't turn back, so that this was something that needed to be generally witnessed. I'd always been obedient, too obedient, but felt I was maybe beginning to obey something else (the verb "obey" originally means to *direct one's hearing*). Was my own sense of honour finally taking its seat, calling me to attention? But that idea's so caught up with the presence of the woman I wanted to impress, that I fear it's false, a kind of vanity. For a long time, I've told myself it was God calling me at last, to put the lights back on, so that what happened should be witnessed: that's Who I was obeying. But my behaviour afterwards doesn't convince me that I was being guided on my way, as opposed to yielding to cowardice, and trying to hide. – Sorry. I'm getting ahead of myself here.'

Ah, how do we audit the will? Is it ever really ours at the outset? Or acknowledged only when we succeed?

'One thing I feel surer of, I also put the music back on, and loud, because I didn't like the way one of the youths was calling out to a group of customers who'd been watching all this closely, and without the grins of some of the regulars. Perhaps I wanted to drown his noise. In this group were two white men, and a Sikh. Terence Ireland and Eddie Singh were locals, came in now and then – I think they were union people, refreshing after meetings; decent types, respectful. The other man I hadn't seen before: he stood out rather, had to be noticed; not that he was showing off, but he seemed – how shall I say it? – more talented than many of the clientele; he'd had plenty to say to the other two, without appearing to boss them. It could have been his presence that caused the trouble that followed – just because he stood out; though the flashpoint was Eddie Singh.

'The dark-haired boy, the brother, he'd come out in front of the others, and started asking Eddie Singh the problem. Eddie said he had no problem, but the youth insisted he had, in the middle of his face. So Eddie invited him to tell him about it, which was pretty brave, because all the other boys were now gathering just behind the dark-haired youth, like the wind was blowing them the same way, egging him on to tell Eddie the problem with his face. Then the dark-haired boy, he spat at Eddie and insulted him vilely, about his nose and his race, and the Sikh rose from his chair where he'd been sitting with a composure I found remarkable, and he kicked the dark-haired boy between the legs. He got two kicks in, very quick – looked like martial arts to me – then the rest of the gang rushed in waving pool cues like a bunch of bloody morris-men (if you'll excuse my language) and the two other men started mixing it with them; they had the advantage, too, since they were throwing jabs – and connecting – while the youths were swishing and rattling cues and hooting like animals in a great show of violence and not much else. . .'

A crow picked at the gravel. I'd forgotten the blonde and her buddy. The priest's voice filled the garden. Were they listening? Heads lowered, hands tented, phones set aside. They'd see he was a churchman. What came next, they shouldn't hear. Finishing my drink, I signalled to DJ and Father Raymond. The priest wasn't very willing to get up, but could hardly stay on his own with an empty glass. Holding his jacket in front he rose. There was a hot sour gardeny smell off him, dampness on his bench. Poor bastard had wet himself.

CHAPTER 27

FATHER RAYMOND WAS ASHAMED. I put my arm around him.
Don't sweat it, Father. DJ wanted to clean him up. I was proud of
DJ. We had to get him back to the rectory. There was the 94, but he
was embarrassed he'd bump into parishioners, and wouldn't get in a
black cab, so we walked back the way we'd come, this time looping
round the cemetery. Red hatchback southbound. DJ clocking it.

Raymond was wanting to get the whole thing out, to its terrible
climax, which I forestalled by asking if it was because of that night in
The Bosun and Monkey that he took orders. He hadn't named the place
in his account, so he sussed I knew already. We walked in silence.

He thought so – when he was able to steady himself after what he'd
seen, and been part of; and that had taken time. For a while, he'd been
in counselling. It hadn't helped. The counsellor he saw, then a therapist,
they'd been intent on absolving him. Which wouldn't do. He'd known
full well that he'd loved as a publican does (though he couldn't yet put
it in Christ's words). He wanted to accept his guilt, not be extenuated.
When the counsellor told him he only did what anyone would have
done, perhaps more, quite possibly more in fact (and had been absolutely
correct to call the police immediately), this did nothing to explain his
encounter. I asked him what he meant by this. He meant the encounter
with evil, with hooting cruelty and its executive will. He also meant his

discovery of his own cowardice; which he'd long suspected – but now here it was: cowardice that makes you compliant and nullifies anything you imagined you would be able to do in a critical situation that had been in the offing for long enough; that makes you turn the lights back on when a snarling youth tells you to. I reminded him it wasn't necessarily cowardice that made him turn the lights on (but the shame of pissing his trousers told a truth that couldn't be improved). Anyway, the therapist had let him talk and talk in this way, with the occasional question. She let his guilt out; but there was no way of showing it the door: it just swirled and collected. By that time (almost a year on now) Eldine Matthews had been murdered. For which Raymond also felt responsible. I asked why. Because he hadn't been an adequate witness. This was mumbled; I had to ask twice.

But what had he told the police about the incident in The Bosun and Monkey? He'd told them everything, identified the youths, named Robert Woods, who was arrested the day after.

And a day or two after that, Raymond was called to in the car park after he'd cashed up by a friendly man who had something for him in an envelope. Raymond didn't want the envelope, but the man said he should take it, it was no more than he deserved. Deserved for what? Oh, for having to get involved in the nastiness the other night, between the local boys and older men who were trying to sell drugs. Which was no doubt why things had got so badly out of hand, in a way to be thoroughly regretted all round – but Mr Vernon, he surely knew how the local lads were in the habit of looking after themselves when predators showed up on their patch? For sure, the uniform police wouldn't raise a finger to help working-class lads nowadays, which is why these youngsters tended to train hard to defend themselves in the local gyms – and hated the drug scene.

Well that wasn't how Raymond had seen what happened, and he

was afraid he couldn't take the envelope that the friendly man in the buck jacket, who'd now stepped out of his car, was pointing at him. Pity, said the man. It was an upsetting affair all round, what with pushers homing in on lads playing an honest game of pool and lads playing an honest game of pool getting hot-headed about it. Still, he respected Raymond's position. Very much, in fact. As he respected the fact that Raymond hadn't even looked in the envelope (which he was still pointing). Indeed, he seemed disappointed, as if Raymond were turning down an invitation because he had better things to do, or more important friends, and he stiffened his chin like he was being brave about some bad news. Then he shook his head, and apologized for taking Raymond's time, and could he offer him a lift home, by way of making up to him? Thanks, but Raymond had his own car.

And of course it didn't end there. Next evening, just after opening, into The Bosun and Monkey came the friendly man, and with him a man with a neat dark beard. They ordered a drink and tried to stand Raymond one, then began to look around, and the bearded man said, So where were they sitting, Cap? And the friendly man pointed exactly where Eddie Singh, Tel Ireland and the other man had been sitting, which puzzled Raymond because they certainly hadn't been in before, these two. Then the bearded man turned and asked Raymond, as if he were estimating something, whether he served nonces in The Bosun and Monkey. Raymond said of course he didn't, but the bearded man, who was now looking over at the space beyond the pool table, said, Well he'd served those three! Raymond asked what he meant by that, and the bearded man, he set his drink down, put both hands on the bar, and asked Raymond if he was unaware that the three men involved in the incident the other night were in the area to hire boys below the age of consent for sex, bribing them with drugs and pool money. Two of them being known to the police for their hobbies, small-time admittedly, but disgusting still, the third a big-time nonce come trawling an area he must have heard was promising – and getting found out pronto by the local youth, who didn't take kindly to perv attention. Raymond said that was bullshit, and could the two gentlemen finish their drinks and leave? Whereupon the bearded man shook his head, and said the force didn't leave when it was asked. Not a bit of it. No. The force left when it had done its work. Wasn't that right, Cap? And the friendly man, he stiffened his chin and said to Raymond he was sorry, but that was the way of things at the end of the day. Which made Raymond uneasy, not because he believed any of this in the slightest, but because he could see that these two men had the power to lie, so that saying 'bullshit', or just disagreeing politely (which would have been wiser), was likely to provoke them, and then you'd encounter a bit more power. Then the bearded man said, Where was three could be many, in his experience – how about that, Cap? And the friendly man said yeah, that'd generally been his experience – particularly when the obvious candidates were skilful about concealing their motives, as seemed to have been the case here. All too often, they snuck in under the radar of good-natured men like Raymond, and no wonder, seeing as it oftentimes took filth to detect filth, and the other man hummed at that and drew his finger across his beard, as if that was a code, and to his dismay, Raymond knew what he was signalling by this, which was, *They seek each other out, though*, while not wanting to disagree with his captain there at the bar. Then the friendly man took out the envelope and showed by his fingers it was thicker than last night, and said, For your trouble, while the bearded man turned away to look at the crime spot, then went and squatted where it had happened. And where the boards had now been cleaned, he placed his hand flat just above the wood, as if gauging a temperature or vibration. Then the friendly man called over to him, 'What you got there, Bowls?' and the bearded man said, 'Lot of nothing, Cap. Can't see what the guards were on to.' Like the whole thing had never happened anyway, then the both of them looking at him as if he wasn't to be trusted, and he felt the dark power of the power to lie. It made you doubt yourself, your accuracy, your honesty, and in the end, your sanity. Which was what the people of totalitarian states had to endure as the normal way of things – he suddenly had a dreadful glimpse of what it must be like . . .

We'd arrived at the 'rectory', which was just a flat along the road from St Aubrey's. Inviting us in, Father Raymond departed to clean himself up, change his trousers. A trim, tidy place it was, stocked with books, classical CDs, modest-size TV, but there was something sad about it – that was my fancy. I asked DJ if he'd been in before, keeping my back to him.

'Why d'you want to know, Carlo?'

'Just wondering.'

'Why've you got your back to me?' he trilled. 'Hold on!' He appeared at my left, liquorice-eyed. 'Are you jealous, Carlo?'

'No!' It was desire for honesty that was moving me. If DJ'd been round here providing fun for Father Raymond, paid or on the house, then the churchman was someone else not to trust: having befriended the young man with earnest intentions, it'd be some kind of breach to be enjoying yourself with him. Since it'd suggest the intentions weren't earnest but devious, and then the whole bloody story corrupts itself backwards, till we get to the SERCS men who visited him twenty years ago (known to us, my friends, as the popular double act Arnold and Bowler), with their sinister equivocations about nonce syndrome. Could they have induced his inner predator?

'You think he's queer, don't you?'

'I dunno. It's not that anyway, not precisely.'

'Well he's married!' DJ scolded me, hands on hips. 'Just like you are, actually. So there!'

This was a surprise. 'Have you met his wife?' The room reconstituted itself. Carnations in a vase, a couple of photos, sea scenes, elegantly framed and mounted, one of those forty-quid candles, pretty cushions on the settee, a varnished box, so forth. Still not over-swanky, but impressed by a woman's presence. News of Raymond's wife changed the filter on my vision, itself deformed by Arnold and Bowler's attempt to corrupt him.

'Yes. At St Aubrey's. Not here. He never asked me in before.'

I was wondering if it could be Sally (and reckoning with a confirmation of Hanley's story in Bowler's claim about the 'guards' – Irish slang for uniform cops), when, clean and embarrassed, Father Raymond entered, bearing a tea tray. Might be time to change the subject. But we had to get to the end of this, didn't we? The envelope, for instance.

Which I bet he hadn't accepted? He shook his head. That was something to be proud of, I told him. Enough people had been bought off over that way. Smiling, he said something about temptation, the Devil and temptation – as if the whole thing was far deeper and more poisoned than an envelope of fifties, like that was just the crust.

At any rate, after he'd finished trying to get his head sorted by counsellors and therapists – without wanting to sound as if he was complaining about professionals who were highly skilled, and a great help to many unhappy folk – while all the time the problem was in his soul, he'd heard a voice telling him to begin again. I asked about the voice. He handed us more digestives, and there was a look on him so shy and happy, like a youth who's just fallen in love for the first time, that close to welling up myself, I had to stiffen my chin.

So the voice had come to him in the kitchen one morning – he'd moved over this way and rented a flat with severance pay from the pubco. Unemployed, in therapy, waiting for the kettle to boil, he heard the voice. It was at his ear, almost his own, yet it didn't sound as beaten, fearful, as his. Of course, he ignored it. A sign the cracks were lengthening, to hear your own voice! For a while it left him, then came back. In the bathroom, at the shops, while he was sitting in the park by a miniature waterfall, watching fish that flitted and glowed. Wasn't maddening him, that he found – also that it didn't mind being ignored. No spite to it. Mighty patient was this voice, telling him to begin again. But how should he begin? One day as he was mooching, waiting for the voice (he looked forward to it now, rather than fearing it – which showed perhaps how lonely he'd become!), he passed the church on Hugo Street. Outside were gathered people who'd attended a communion service, and although intellectuals and cynics jeered at churchgoers for not thinking for themselves, for being like children, and generally pathetic, Raymond felt strongly that the people he'd served for years were certainly no more independent, grown-up, or dignified than these folk. The eyes of the drinkers shone with enthusiasm and fever, but their feelings were often selfish, vicious, while their sense of community was overheated, and liable to become stormy. Indeed, there wasn't much shining among the faces of this congregation; their eyes were calm. They seemed to be in conversation, taking turns to speak, rather than waiting on the words of the noisiest person, or paying court to the bullying wit (how much of that he'd witnessed!). Smiling, an old lady took something from her bag, handed it to a small boy who'd had his hair brushed neatly and shirt tucked in. He had to begin again. When he asked how, the voice told him, *The long way, Ray!*

Hallelujah! I'd be a Christian, too. Karen and me at St Aubrey's, old lady tipping a kid of ours; Andy there as well, strong churchman; all our team there. And Mulhall? Nowhere near. What was he going to do, take out the congregation in a drive-by? Ah, these pictures of community . . . One thing remained: how Ray learned to love his enemies. Could he be sincere about this?

I put it to him, DJ listening up. Somewhere in the flat, a landline rang. Such love, he told us now, wasn't a solid, directed feeling, like love for family and friends, or physical love for a partner. Rather, it was on the way to Christ's love for humanity.

'*Agape!*' I said cleverly, as instructed by my wife the other night – after a solid bout of *eros*.

'Indeed, Carl! *Agape*'s the one! But you are only ever on the way as an ordinary person (the saints do better – they aren't tied to the faith either). Often, it feels like a progress through the negatives, the getting-rid-ofs. The desire for revenge, which is very natural, and may seem entirely justified – that has to be thrown overboard. And that's hard to achieve without willing forgiveness, which itself is hard, because we are a sort of creditors to those who wrong us, and in the general way of things, we can fairly expect debts to be paid. In forgiveness, we have to waive the debt. But we also have to waive our pride, our own status as creditors, and understand it as a very relative and dependent thing, and not rock solid at all. So we have to give ourselves up as well. And even then we are only on the way, because we can suddenly feel weightless, and without the strength to make progress. Then the danger is that we mistake the progress we have made for weakness, or for cowardice. As if we're dodging the issue of justice, rather than learning to love where we are wronged.'

'So we shouldn't take any action at all against the wicked?' I asked, excitement rising.

'We have laws to do that for us.'

'What happens when the law's been corrupted? Just sit back and let the wicked thrive?'

'What are the options?'

'We sort them ourselves.'

He smoothed his brow with his palm, forked his thick hair. 'Best not to, Carl. You've no authority, for one thing. Will, perhaps. But will doesn't justify – even, I'm afraid, the righteous will – in a society like ours. Which may be for the best. Otherwise, aren't the terrorists justified?'

'They don't pick their targets the same way. They aren't avenging specific crimes either.'

'Oh, they believe they are! Just that the crimes are very big, historic ones, to the terrorist mind, which is why they feel justified in indiscriminate killing.' The phone rang again, but Father Raymond was in this conversation. 'The spirit of revenge is the driver in either case. And with revenge there's no forgiveness, and maybe no justice either.'

'Surely that's exactly the aim of revenge – justice?' We ruminated, and it was cool, for I'd no urge to win the argument.

'It's wild justice,' advised DJ, waiting his turn on the arm of the settee. Hey?

'*Wild justice* – that's the definition of revenge!'

I forbore from 'How do you know?' Sooner or later, we have to own that people half our age may know more than we do; not just because we've forgotten, either; no – because they've put their energies to better use: book-learning, for example – as distinct from hustling for info, in that way that misses the tradition, and big picture. Forget the encyclopedia, call a friend! That's been my m.o. for a long time. Meanwhile, encyclopedias themselves have become queer, suspicious – enough to bring the vigilantes to your door with their anti-nonce banners. Knowledge as deviance . . . No wonder his nibs was into it. I wanted to adopt him, that's what I was beginning to realize . . .

'Whose definition?'

'Francis Bacon,' glimmered DJ. 'Because it puts the law out of office – that's why it's "wild justice". But he's still saying it's justice, isn't he?'

'Where does this occur, John?' asked our solemn priest.

'In the essay, "Of Revenge"!' Like we were both too silly for words.

The landline rang for a third time, and Father Raymond excused himself. In another room, he spoke earnestly. When he returned, I suggested it was time we took our leave; he very much hoped we could continue our talk, though made no move to detain us.

CHAPTER 28

D J POPPED INTO GLOBAL PINOY for cigarettes. It was nearly
five. What I'd have liked was go home to Karen; but the day'd
mis-climaxed with a priest's tale, and we'd ended up close to where we
started. As an outing, it felt incomplete. Though I'd learned plenty,
much of it surprising, about this young man's character, it was too
original for a decent profile; I couldn't do it justice. He needed a biog-
rapher, or a novelist, not a two-page spread in the free paper he was
carrying with him from the general store.

'Look at this, Carlo!' He pointed at the front page, which led with
the story, *GANGSTER IN OUR MIDST*.

'Ah, Jesus shit! He hasn't, has he?' Snatching, I went through the
pages. Andy'd paraphrased familiar Mulhalliana from the dailies and
weekend broadsheets, introducing so far unrevealed allegations about
Mulhall's major role in a development scam in the borough, these
adapted pretty literally from the conversation with him and Fabiana the
other afternoon. Had he mentioned my name? In fever of cowardice,
I scanned.

'What are we doing now, Carlo?'

'Come on!' I pulled his wrist. We raced along like Tony and Maria,
satchel flashing . . .

'Don't run, you muffin! I'm smoking. Looks naff.'

. . . crossed the main road north, and into the Tube the back way. In the news-nook, *The Guardian* said Syria was now in a state of civil war, UN-decreed. Just beyond the barriers stood the day's thought:

THE WORLD SUFFERS A LOT. NOT BECAUSE OF THE
VIOLENCE OF THE BAD PEOPLE. BUT BECAUSE OF THE
SILENCE OF THE GOOD.
NAPOLEON

SO IF THE GOOD speak up, the gangsters'll cool it? . . . *I say, old boy, that's not yours, you know!* . . . Sounded like 24-carat French bullshit to me. The world suffered because short-arses and psychos didn't give a fuck about anyone else's opinion, and wanted land that wasn't theirs. Furthermore, I was suffering plenty from the non-silence of 'the good' nowadays, so why didn't we all keep bloody quiet about certain SE London faces on both sides of the law, and do nothing till kingdom come? Stick that on your whiteboard.

A Barking train rolled in. We found a two-seater. DJ studying the *Chronicle*, I picked up a discarded West End Final, read about a raid on a jeweller's in Ilford. As four men in helmets weighed in with machetes and axe handles, 'terrified customers fled, passers-by cowered in terror'. Always! You can rely on the passer-by to cower in terror or flee in panic, even when it's gangs fighting in Walworth Road with buckets, spades and hobby-horses, hoisted from Poundland . . . or Dillinger Ismaél fleeing through Acton, lady grocer on his tail with ceremonial sword.

The Political Science I'd dabbled with approved the general cowardice; built a system on it; but at the end of the day, can you bear it, to be an *individual* coward?

*

BOARDED ON THE *County Clare*, we headed for the bar on the upper deck. The boat cast off and came about, upriver under Hungerford Bridge to drop off passengers for the Eye. Krauts and scallies raised their phones, *abuelas* cried *Mira!* Their London was a drop-scene, from the web and travel supplements. We put about now for Greenwich. DJ and I went starboard with bottles of Cusqueña. The *County Clare* made its way between stations, picking up, dropping off. A line of mustard containers marked 'CORY' passed upriver, on rusty barges. DJ made a joke. 'Hear that, la?' called a scally. The *Clare* put in to drop off tourists for the Globe. We had another beer.

Know what DJ'd been thinking to himself while I chatted with the priest in the rectory? Well, the oldest religions had their brewing gods, and goddesses. I grinned down at my boy. Siddhuri for example. So who was Siddhuri? Siddhuri was the Sumerian goddess of brewing, and twine. About to tell him he should have been on *University Challenge*, I bit my tongue. So what was Sumerian? That was the culture of ancient Mesopotamia – which we now knew as Iraq. To them, religion and boozing were like this. He interlaced his fingers. Alcohol was sacred. Caused the states where you felt the gods were in you. Or brought you out of yourself so you were on the one with everything. Which was where we got 'ecstasy' from. Our priest reckoned alcohol was evil, soul poison. But 3,000 year ago, it were more like soul fuel. As for Islamists, they were dead heavy about boozing. DJ tapped the neck of his bottle on the gunwale. Why? Centuries before their prophet showed up, Arabs were using drink for sacred purposes. Why didn't they admit that, respect it? It were a bloody sham, going by the Bible, the Koran, the jurists, when there was a much older way of sacred practice. Well, he could have meant this and he could have meant that, interpreting Christ and Mohammed's words the way that suited them best and increased their power, and all of them fucking blokes. Whereas Siddhuri, she was a woman god. At the beginning, before Mohammed, before Jesus Christ, you had a working woman as your god. I asked what he meant by this. She was a fucking brewer, that's what he meant. Wind flicked his black hair. A brewer and twine maker. Weren't sitting idle on Mount Olympus letting Zeus fiddle her twat. She was down in the desert, with the heat and flies, making ale, rope, cords. Put in a good shift, did Siddhuri. These vicars and imams knew sod all about the past. Found their way by sat-nav.

But he was cool with Father Raymond, wasn't he? DJ watched the water. I didn't push the question. In the west, I had a blood son. Had this bright-satchelled lad appeared to take his place?

Buoys bobbed to starboard, hefty yellow barrels. You could live in one of them, said DJ, like them pods the Japanese have, if they've had a heavy night in Tokyo, and they have to clock in at 6 a.m. They sleep in pods rather than going home. I texted Karen: expect me home by nine. How was Angie Pole? In my other pocket rolled the 853.

SOME TIME INTO THOSE months when I was courting her, hanging out at The Tiresias with the *Dedicated Vagrant* crew, brooding on gnostic sex, I asked if she fancied a day out. She jumped at it.

I met her at Embankment. A Saturday afternoon near the end of August. She wore plimsolls and a little straw hat and looked very busty and girlish. I was all for a dock of white port, to set us up. That wouldn't do. Gordon's was like a catacomb. So we sat drinking pop on a low wall by the gardens, at her feet a basket of dainties, which she wouldn't let me see, slapping my hand when I tried to poke. Was this daytime self the real Karen? As we made our way to the river, she took my arm. Up to now, she'd allowed herself to be kissed at The Tiresias after we'd sloped off to the toilet upstairs with a gift of cocaine from Lord Larry in a dainty wrap of pale violet. Her nose was manly, large-nostrilled. Then that time after I called her from The Cittie of Yorke, we'd had cocktails in Greek Street before visiting the gardens in Soho Square. Here we chatted till a late hour, she asking about my work and telling of a recent visit of Craig Norman, I trying to find out if she wrote the Gnostic Sex column. She sat on my knee for a minute after watching my face in that way certain women have that men like to think is a sign of unadmitted love, then said, 'You don't deserve this!' and ran away on to Greek Street. That Saturday afternoon as we waited for the boat, I decided the emphasis might have been not on 'You', but on 'this', though not 'this' in the sense of her body, but in the sense of her in that form, a creature of the night. Savvy?

Whoo-ee, baby! On the top deck of the *Marco*, she stood beside me. She'd taken off the straw hat in case the wind snatched it, and her black hair flipped and curled. God she seemed young, hearty, unbroken by life, full of appetite for what was simply going by! I didn't speak, my heart was full. Did I deserve *this*? Her plims were spotless (putting Gina's to shame). I felt blessed, somewhat soiled. Could I be good enough for her? As the boat picked up speed, she whooped and flashed her eyes. The sense of her I'd had at the beginning rose, and swirled, and faced me, like painted smoke. That nocturnal self, which seemed so proficient, so outstanding, I'd been wondering how long before it moved on to some other exercise – that wasn't an act. But how she was today, nor was that put on, a mere playing at enjoying an outing. She belonged exactly where she was: this I was beginning to admire, as she raised one foot on the railing and above her ankle I caught a bold though dainty tattoo. Now, belonging exactly where you are, that might be the sign of a person skilful at adapting, a good actor – with all the implication of insincerity, or never being yourself, that goes with the business of role-playing. And having experience of criminals, I was familiar with another form of this faculty, which is known as fraudulence. But I fancied that hazel-eyed Karen belonged wherever she was because she was what she was: ready for life's gallery.

We bore down on Blackfriars. Carved birds on the piers; over there God's Banker dangled, bricks in his trousers and fifteen grand. Strung up from a boat, fake suicide. '97, Rome: Licio Gelli, Lodge Master, P2, cleared. Crime unsolved; everyone knows who. Under the arch.

Passing Brandrams' Wharf, she pointed at the sand. If only the boat would put us down, we could have a beach picnic. She let me see what she had in her bag: rolls she'd filled herself; iced buns; apples; cherries, KitKats, Irn-Bru; serviettes to clean our hands. Neatly stowed at the side was something wrapped in tissue. The *Marco* sped on and I took her to the prow, where the river widened. I felt my soul billow like a shirt on a line; at that moment I could have done anything, if there wasn't one question I had to ask. Canary Wharf to port now, slimeside starboard. She looked at me and giggled. I went over our ages again, thinking there were plenty of fellows and girls where the difference was twice the size. Though the difference as it was already suggested a more successful man. So I was about to ask what I had to, but out came, 'What d'you see in me?'

Not because I suspected she was a gold-digger: with her quality she could have snaffled men with real jack (furthermore, I'd let her know about the property shrink, post-Laura). So it would have been a means of finding out something about myself I hadn't yet discovered. I trusted the judgement of those green-hazel glances, and I'd have been hazarding that, in her northern way, she would come straight out with it. Say it was complimentary, then I could trust that, like a character medal. And if it wasn't, then that'd confirm something about her honesty, or her consistency – so to say, at a lovely moment, she'd still put truth first, and in that I could set my trust. Besides, I was curious, in fact compelled, to hear rotten or unflattering truths – that was the journalist in me. But I might also have asked her what she saw in me because I needed to see if she was fooling herself. If the answer'd suggested she were, I could set her right before I asked the other question; or maybe, I'd enjoy the fact I was fooling her, and let it run into our future, giving myself time to be the thing I was not . . .

Ah, we really should *not* 'go on' about ourselves, nor hanker for opinions from young women; but the truth of that time was that I was adrift, dilapidated, quite defeated, as a consequence of the divorce. Partly because Laura'd dealt with things too generously: accepting more blame than was due; exercising a thoroughly muted attitude towards maintenance (her old man, who'd liked chatting to me about cricket and rugby, had something to do with this); comporting herself pleasantly over access, and doing nothing to 'turn' Edward. A fight, or real show of bitterness: that gives you a way of asserting yourself (as a nation shows its character when it goes to war); but generous dealing, even as you admire how easy it's making things, causes a leak in its beneficiary. So, say the cynics, it too is a tactic; but I recognize magnanimity, and my ex-wife displayed it in a quantity that didn't quite surprise me: I'd spotted it below the surface, like golden sand where you're on guard against rocks, broken glass, medusas, as you first step into the water. So as I entered the dissolution of our marriage, here it was, all the time. And if I'd been less irritable, I might not have driven it under, either . . . So I acquired an awful sense of my own sour, negative, spoiling nature, and of the quiet nobility I'd forfeited. No wonder I took no pride in myself.

I was also adrift, diffident, inclining towards self-loathing because though here was an opportunity for adventure, a new beginning, as some would take it – and I, with my poses of spontaneity against Laura's providence, should have found myself among them – I was beginning to discover that there was less spontaneity in me than I'd imagined. Given, then, that I was sour, negative, spoiling, irritable, unspontaneous, was there any room left for something admirable – nice, even?

A black barge with orange gunwale and deckhouse passed upriver carrying aggregate as Karen said with her spectacular grin, 'Nothing!'

'You what?'

'Nothing, Carl Hyatt. I see nowt in you, lad!'

The black craft diminished. I watched it, heavy-hearted. Fierce glee cooling to a kind of tenderness, she cried, 'Serves you right for asking, you fool!'

'Doesn't sound too fine,' I told her thickly.

'And what d'you see in me, hey? Tell me that!' Hands on hips.

Round Surrey Quays we sped like a roulette ball. Rotherhithe. How much of the missing gold was converted in this great bulge? Smelters, fake assay numbers, Channel Island accounts; LDDC, late '83: Odessa Wharf, £35 per square foot. Yuppies coming this way from the City. It was about this time I was beginning to hear the name Mulhall from cops and lawyers I talked to. He'd stayed above the law, who were still busily enquiring about the bullion, and the gangsters who were still busily shooting each other about it, nearly twenty years on. Early the year before, the police'd been down at 'Ore', near Hastings, digging in a timber yard with a J. C. Bamford, pickaxes, RD1000 ground-radar, thinking to find the last ton. Ah, you might be thinking, silly police! Whoever tipped them off was pulling their leg something rotten. *Ore!* Come on! Means 'gold', in French, as any fule kno. But as someone was saying the other day, that robber's moll who called her rotties Brinks and Mat was typical of the way these people highballed, dropped clues, and laughed up their sleeves – till their secrets popped and oozed. Ore was plausible, though the police found nothing. Then autumn the year before, the bagman for the gold (who, incidentally, was the bright spark who first thought of converting it into swank offices and yuppie flats from those warehouses on the wharfs where only rats played), he was shot in the head three times outside his minicab office in Peckham as he arrived with his breakfast McMuffin (reported by C. Hyatt in *The G********). *Mmm. Not lovin' it!* But as for Mulhall, it seemed to be a very high peak he sat on, unfazed by all this running around, enquiring, whacking out. Which was beginning to intrigue me.

Rallying, I asked her, 'What's the opposite of nothing?'

'You tell me!'

'Something. – Or everything. Yeah, that's what I see in you.'

'Something, or everything?'

'Something to everyone. Everything to me!' I told her. What a chevalier, hey! She ran at me and put her arms round my neck, legs round my torso. Nearly had me overboard. With that energy, I thought, I could get infected, renewed. Like a panther cub, she kissed me and bullied my face, and messed my hair. Yes, with a dose or steady current of that, I might even manage the trail to Mount Mulhall! So I asked her to marry me, she was setting me on course again. She said definitely. Didn't she want to think about it? She already had, for God's sake. When we landed at Greenwich, we tried the picnic in the grounds of the Naval College. But we were both overexcited and I had an awful, grand feeling of burned bridges, while she was tearful and brilliant and girly, so we went and got sloshed and were ticked off for eating the buns in The Old Placentia, until we told them we just got engaged. She rang a few friends, her mum and dad, while I sat with my arm around her.

What she really saw in me was fate. As we left, I was assessing this when a dark-haired man in mirror shades passed me in the corridor of The Placentia between the two bars. We were unsteady, so it may have been my fault that he jostled me – or rather, didn't avoid contact; but his right elbow knocked mine with a speed and accuracy that made my face buzz. He marched on without pausing (as if we hadn't been there at all) and into the bar on the left. All the way to Mudchute on the DLR, I had a dead arm . . . 2002, that was.

RECALLING IT ALL NOW as we passed Mudchute, and Donna Juan, wind flicking his hair, said that'd be a good name for certain requests he generally refused to comply with, tapping his Cusqueña bottle like this on the gunwale, my face buzzed again like a frozen clock. That would have been the youth Eddie Singh rumbled with in The Bosun and Monkey. 'Pete', Fabian Morgan called him; Father Raymond said he was the coldest; brother of the youth who led them. Still at large. Touched by him, Karen beside me. Did she feel him?

River cops sped west, keel high, water foaming. Mudchute was meant to be named 'Millwall Park', since that's exactly where the fucker was; but London Transport thought the name would have passengers of driverless trains *cowering*, in case big fat men with eyes like slits who could trace their line to Harry the Dog boarded here, screaming –

> 'We're here, we're there
> We're every fucking where
> Millwall, Millwall!
> We're here, we're there
> We're every fucking where
> Millwall, Millwall!
> Treatment! Treatment!'

WHAT WAS MORE, TOURISM could have suffered since, when big men with shaven heads and eyes like slits, from Galatasary, Ferencvaros,

Spartak Moscow or Lazio, arrived here looking for a tear-up with the men who could trace their line to Harry the Dog, they'd only be the wrong side of the bloody river. Which they'd have to ford on pontoons or oxen, or come trundling through the foot tunnel, in search of 'The Millwall', who they'd finally discover not *in* Millwall at all, but all the way over there in Surrey, tucking into steaming plates of whelks and jeering at these euro-hardcases who'd certainly taken their time getting round London, and were now looking pretty depressed. Hence 'Mudchute', where we set a couple of people down. There was an obelisk-shaped chimney, and the front of a building just beyond reminded me of a photograph I'd seen of Auschwitz.

So the *Clare* made to starboard for our destination. The Royal Naval College glowed like heaven. A pair of busy spirits waited on the side, lit by western sun.

CHAPTER 29

'SURPRISE, SURPRISE!' LEATHER SPORTS coat swaying, Morgan did the moonwalk; Hanley glinted.

'How's tricks, *paisano*?' He was looking over my shoulder. Just behind us on the gangplank was the excellent Turbo, who must have been on the boat all along, and tailed us from the Tube (if not for longer). Braids hidden under a stingy-brim trilby, he wore a narrow indigo suit and shades; over his arm was a Jaeger mac, and he had a hard-shell briefcase.

'Didn't see you.'

'Lower deck, boss.'

'Why didn't you come up and say hello? Must have known we were there.'

'Thought you was engaged in private discussion, Mr Hyatt.' He watched me and DJ discreetly, which was more than you could say for his guvnor, who was making faces at DJ, like a pirate finding a nipper in the hold.

So we weren't escaping after all.

'What you got in the case, Turbs?' called JFM.

'Nothing, Mr Fabian,' Turbo told him, rapping on it with silver-bolt rings.

'Attaboy, Turbs! Proper briefcase that is,' J. F. Morgan advised DJ.

'So what?' said my boy, now smoking with a venomous air. His satchel flashed like god-kit.

'I'll "so what" you!' Morgan told him. 'Is he sound, this one, Mr Hyatt?'

'Yeah. Solid.' Like I knew what we were about. Say I beat it now, home by nine.

'What's your name, young man?'

'John.'

'Let's go then. We're parked behind the *Cutty*.' We'd not moved many yards when the Cunctator paused, pointing at the Naval College: 'Once called Placentia Palace, that was. Significant. Who can tell me why?'

No one could.

'I'll tell you why, then. And you'll see, it's of a piece with that talk we had the other night. August ninth to twelfth, 1941, Churchill and Roosevelt met on two ships, the *Augusta* and the *Prince of Wales*, at Placentia Bay, off the silver mines of Newfoundland. With him, Churchill had Harry Hopkins, FDR's main man; no modern politician had a higher pain threshold than Harry Hopkins, by the way. Anyone know why?'

DJ bristled.

'I'll tell you why, then. One thing: he had about fifteen per cent of his stomach left – the rest had been devoured by cancer. But he sailed to Britain for talks with Churchill, and Churchill showed him round Britain, north and south, to demonstrate morale, then up to Scapa Flow goes Harry wearing Churchill's hat cos he'd lost his own, no doubt in the course of a *session*, since they got on like a house on fire these two, then he has to fly to Archangel by the Arctic route, and from there to Moscow. Three weeks before, the Nazis had opened their Eastern Front, taking the Russians by surprise.'

We'd come to the Granada.

'Turbs, would you drive? I'm talking.'

'Ten-four, boss.'

Morgan dropped his voice, raising Turbo's trilby to murmur directions, as the rest of us sat in the back.

'In Moscow,' continued JFM, 'he got on like a house on fire with Stalin as well. Everyone thinks Stalin was a close, shifty, bugger, not to mention a sadist, and quite possibly a psychopath; but with Hopkins he loosened up – opened his heart. Told him how long they could hold out against the Germans, regarding which, Churchill and FDR were desperate for reassurance. And he told him politely what he'd like from the US: aluminium for planes; anti-aircraft guns and large-calibre machine guns, for defence of the cities; one million rifles. *One million.* You'd have enough trouble obtaining *three* nowadays, what? That right, Turbo? The scale's diminished. Uncle Joe, he even told Harry, Listen, tell your bossovitch, he wants to station American troops in Russia under American command, that's cool too! Ever heard of such co-operation? Roosevelt, Churchill, Stalin – they all dug Mr Harry Hopkins. What was it about this fella, to make him so welcome, trusted, effective? Has the type run out? Were there ever many of 'em? Nowadays, no one's even heard of him, educated people included.' DJ crossed his legs harder, heel of his espadrille cracking me in the ankle. 'And here's the second thing about his threshold. In the course of a vodka session with Comrade Koba, Hopkins forgot his cancer drugs, morphine phials, everything he needed against the pain. Lost his hat with Churchill, forgot his gear with Stalin. Without painkillers, he flew from Moscow to Archangel, from Archangel to Scapa Flow, whereupon he boarded the *Prince of Wales* with Churchill. All the time, his guts were like a sock of broken glass. They headed for Placentia Bay.

'And you, Mr Hyatt, boarded a boat for Placentia Palace this afternoon, with John there. What d'you make of that?'

What was I meant to make of it? I was absorbed in comparing the pain of cancer without analgesia with the pain of having your eye sucked out and bitten off. Were they comparable? Both bloody horrible anyway. You had to concede, the man in the front knew something about pain, unusual pain.

'Spooky!' said DJ.

'That's right. Spooky. Quite possibly more than. You like patterns, John?'

'Suppose so.'

'You suppose so. Without the patterns, we're nowhere, nothing. – Victor, are we here now? Can you navigate?'

'Could you take her up to Sayes Court, Turbo, then back to the Creek via Evelyn Street, and back again?'

'Deptford Creek, Mr Hanley?'

'That's the one, *amigo*. It was in here somewhere. According to the reckoning.'

We drove west to Sayes Court, back in a tight loop to the inlet, back again; the traffic wasn't heavy, but we cruised. My guess was we were trying to spot one of the other side, a murderer who'd taken an address down this way. Hanley put me right. We were searching for where Marlowe died.

I asked what Marlowe died of.

'He was stabbed, *paisano*. In the eye.'

'Round here?'

'In this sector. The names have changed. It was a house on Deptford Strand, a victualling house.'

'How are you going to find it?'

'Fabian's got radar!' glinted Hanley.

'My eye,' Morgan told us. 'It'll twitch.' In the mirror, I could see Morgan and Turbo, faces charged, cinematic, till the former cried, 'Feeling it, Victor! Turbs, park up here, sir!'

We got out of the Granada, and stood in front of Café Aquitaine, which was closed for the day. Breakfast permutations on laminated posters, sun-faded, adorned the windows. 'I fancy this is it,' said J. Fabian Morgan. So his live eye knew no more than present space, but the prosthetic was a probe of time. Heads bowed slightly, he and Hanley stood like pilgrims at a shrine. On the pavement a black kid on a Viking folding bike, and two white babes with dyed hair and cigarettes, came our way; the kid wore a big-peak rapper's cap. They moved off the kerb for us, then back on to the pavement where they paused just out of earshot, looking back and making signs. The kid kissed his teeth at DJ, but Turbo shook his head, and the kid and his girls moved off ever so slow, with backward glances. We stood around the Granada smoking.

'In there,' said Hanley, 'Marlowe died. Four hundred years to the month, Eldine Matthews was knifed to death. In either case, everyone knew who did it, but the bad boys didn't come to justice. In these things, you can either acquiesce, or you can try and turn the tide.'

'It's not a choice, Mr Hanley,' Fabian said. 'Not if you care about dignity. Modern way, it is, not to get involved; for the new man, and so forth, that's all very respectable. Partly owing to our pain thresholds, which really aren't what they were. We may be the first generations in history that made bottling out socially acceptable. Blokes don't ruck the way they used to. Women have made everything more middle-class.' He beckoned, and as we got back in the Granada, continued, 'The feeling, "I should be getting home now," isn't congruous with heroism (with the exception of Odysseus).' This must be aimed at me. We headed south, on to Shooter's Hill Road. 'Not that the overall increase in civility isn't a thing to be applauded – and we do have women to thank for it. I speak as someone who's been on the surgical end of incivility, the gnawing end – so I've got practical experience of all this. Obviously, I'd rather have had a discussion or argument on the night in question (which I'd have won) than have my eye bitten out (trust I'm not alarming you, John – I fancy you know about ultraviolence). But civility doesn't spread to everyone, as love doesn't, sisterhood, brotherhood neither: there are people it won't touch. What's to be done with them?'

'Love them anyway?' I said, thinking of Father Raymond, who tried to teach us to love your enemies, even if it made you feel weak and weightless.

'They'll show you no quarter for loving them,' Morgan said. 'Tantamount to surrender, that is. To love the uncivil is to give up; it's saying, "You can have what you want, have the world! We'll just get ready to die." Which you may think is all right if you believe in the soul, when there's something better beyond the world anyway; but the soul looks back on what it's left behind, doesn't it? And it looks back on the manner of its leaving it; and if it can't see dignity in that, it's a soul that suffers for eternity, isn't it? I put these questions as one who hasn't practised religion, so maybe you can set me right, Mr Hyatt. But I'm not for leaving my table when I've reserved it, and I'm enjoying the meal and the company, just because someone's giving me uncivil looks. They'll just have to wait and acquire some manners – and patience. And if they persist in looking at me like that, as if they deserve the table pronto, and fidgeting in a way that puts me and my pals off our food, then I'm inviting them outside to discuss it. What d'you say?'

He'd been a speechwriter (or 'rhetoric adviser') to a Labour leader, hadn't he? I wished I'd paid more attention to Political Science. I wished I was devout. I saw pretty clearly how his argument was working, aimed at me, not the others.

'You make the uncivil sound a much bigger party than they are,' I told him. In the mirror, his dead eye was unpersuadable. 'Civil society doesn't need to bother with them: they live by will, violence, the search for satisfaction without regard to society, and for that reason, they eat each other, wipe themselves out – because each uncivil will is in conflict with all others for satisfaction, and it can't go to law for mediation. Look at Brink's-Mat. Whoever touched the gold got dead, or jailed – and they're still at each other's throats, knocking each other off. The corpses from that crime need a pit twelve times the size of the one the rest of the bullion's buried in. They've punished themselves more decisively than law managed.'

'Seen!' Hanley was glinting with a lawyer's joy in argument. 'But you forget the relationship of the individual and civil society; indeed, *paisano*, you're overlooking the nature of the individual *totalmente*. You represent civil society as a sheep enclosure; the wolves are on the hill but the dry-stone walls are solid, and the wolves get so hungry, they rip each other's throats out. *Todos se comen!*' (At the Spanish, DJ twitched.) 'As for the sheep, they know nothing of this . . .'

'Yes!' cried DJ, impatient to shine. 'They're like mass man. Where's the individual in there? They're secure without dignity. Just huddle, chew and shit pellets, that's all they do.'

'Good words, John!'

'*Muy bien!*'

I was being got at by these bastards. One sheep versus three 'wolves'. Nor was Turbo likely to be on my side.

'Now what's your line on this, John? I get the impression you're a bit of a philosopher,' observed Morgan, seeming to watch me with his dead eye, while he flattered the young man. 'I like to learn about these things.'

'The individual originated in Italy in the later thirteenth century, as the *uomo singulare*,' explained my boy in mocking sing-song. 'And the *uomo singulare* followed his own path and pursued his own desires. He knew his will, did the *uomo singulare*. Then you have your *uomo unico*, which means the unique or singular man. And he's the one who can create his own fate.' Mockery evaporated; he was leading the class. 'Which is the spirit of the Renaissance, because it gets round Christian faith by going back to the pagans, then jumping over it. The *uomo unico* has his fate in his own hands, not God's.'

'Ah-ha!' called J. Fabian Morgan. 'So you've got the individual who does his own thing, and the individual who's a law to himself and, we might say, a fatal character, *singulare* and *unico* respectively? I'm liking this. As a classicist, it's up my street. More please, young man! Turbs, pray keep an eye out for the sign.'

'Well,' said DJ, 'over time, the idea of the individual acquired its shadow; the shadow wants to make its own choices and stand alone, but it can't. Basically, it hasn't got the bollocks or the talent. These shadows end up hating the genuine individuals and they make themselves believe that they prefer equality – everyone has to be on the same level, if the poor little shadow can't be champion. OK? Eventually, the shadow gives up any hope of being brilliant and turns into mass man. This is where you get the idea of representative democracy, where every free twat has their say, no matter how dumb or mean they are. But along with that, they want to be led – led and managed. Being governed's not enough; they want leaders who remind them of what they can't do for themselves. Death to initiative.'

Snort from J. F. Morgan. 'Sounds like eighties cant, Thatchero-liberalism.'

'So?'

'I'll "so" you! Time was, I'd have chucked Tory-lady-boys from my car, young man!'

'Would you now?'

'Yes I bloody well would – and don't act snide when you're speaking to me!'

'All good!' cried DJ. Note how he accepted discipline from Fabian, who'd turned in his seat to give him the hard eye. 'Are you a Labour person?'

'Was. With time, my politics has developed. And grown.'

'Well I was only explaining a point of view anyway,' DJ said. 'Didn't mean I believed it.'

Fabian Morgan hummed. 'There's something in it, if we suspend the cant. And as to violent action, where does the individual stand?'

'Like we've said, he's responsible to himself. Not the state, or the law – or Health and Safety. He's willing to risk it, in other words.'

'Willing to risk. Yes.'

'Anyway –' DJ wasn't finished – 'there's Marxists who think National Socialism isn't really a return to barbarism, which is what people always come out with, but a suppression of individuality. So they're onside with the Tory–Liberal view which you just got so fierce about, because the problem for them both is the managerial state, which is organized on rationalist principles – and rationalism irons out all the differences and particulars among people . . .'

'You should be fucking Mayor!' yelled Fabian Morgan. 'I'm not joking, cherub! Got a good mind to campaign for you! Turbs'll put out some tweets before this day is over. That's a promise! Carry on.'

'Well, if you were a Nazi Party member, you were equal with all the other members. A mass person, or mass monster, basically.' Here, I thought of Father Raymond's description of the five youths, the crowd that was more than its parts, beast with five heads, fidgeting violently. 'Which isn't a perversion or barbarous distortion of rational enlightenment,' sang DJ, 'but its destiny. Levelling. Individual wipe-out.'

'Yes yes yes,' said Fabian. 'This squares with Hitler's "table talk". (Cunt sat up till four a.m. every morning boring the whole company. They couldn't drink or smoke, or answer back, or go to bed.) In

Christianity, the individual is infinitely precious; under National Socialism, the individual has value only as part of the Nazi state.'

'John told us Christianity didn't promote the individual,' I said. 'About five minutes ago.'

Red hatchback passing, westbound.

'We're having a conversation, Mr Hyatt. Not one of those "Five Things You Need to Know" efforts for the middle classes who only read the Booker Prize and *The Guardian*. We'll go where it takes us, thank you.' We turned off Shooter's Hill Road and down a lane that gave on to a dirt track, where we halted. In the distance, water shone. Which had the effect of taking Morgan back to the North Atlantic, *Prince of Wales* proceeding west under heavy escort.

'So they approach Placentia Bay, Churchill and Harry Hopkins, and there at anchor is the *Augusta*, carrying Franklin Delano Roosevelt. On the deck of the *Prince of Wales* with plentiful gin and tobacco, Churchill in sailor's cap, they discuss the European crisis, the German invasion of the Soviet Union, Japanese sabre-rattling in the Pacific, the oil embargo, the refusal to withdraw troops from China, aggressive escorting of British merchant ships as far as Iceland (which amounted to the "beginning of undeclared hostilities with Germany", in the words of Admiral Stark); and they discuss a possible invasion of the United States by Germany. Geography quiz: How would this have been possible? Oh, not you again, young man!'

'At a guess,' said DJ, posh northern lady, 'from the Bulge of Africa, via the Iberian Peninsula.'

'To where?'

'To Brazil, then north to the US.'

'Pukka gen!' cried J. Fabian Morgan. 'You're right. FDR was worried that if Gibraltar fell, the Krauts'd have access to the South Atlantic.

Churchill bucked him up about that, and they agreed the Yanks'd occupy the Azores if the Germans tried to come through Spain.'

Christ, what was all this . . . *conversation* in aid of? Still trying to get me on board? That night we sat above the Tube with the laser, they were all over me . . .

Check the stage name. Say the voice in the front's even better at delaying. Say it's actually his goal. Delay without end. So the tension grows and grows – till tension itself turns mouldy, and we three white-haired, confused about Eldine and Mulhall and William and Van Spenser and the de Laceys and Robbie Woods, and which eye was which, while the young men, Donna Juan, Turbo, wheel us round ponds and lawns, down gravel paths, their own hairlines receding, murmuring legends of ultraviolence: *You want the one about The Lunar Five, Pops? OK. Well there was once a pub down Thamesmead way . . .*

But you'll be wanting some real violence soon, after all this cud, clairvoyance, speculation, *history*; your patience is well-nigh exhausted, friends. Though J. Fabian Morgan, Cunctator, is speaking now of FDR and Winston at prayer, and the church service on the quarterdeck of the *Prince of Wales*, while sailors of both navies sing hymns, and the United States are still not at war; for Roosevelt's a cunctator too, if we understand the levels, and the cycles and returns – but here came a text from Karen. An *old dibble*'d been round at the flat.

Heart flash-froze. Mulhall had kicked off pronto. Sent Mr Arnold to have a word . . . But Andy's bloody front page was well beyond having-a-word gravity. It was a gold-medal blunder, declaration of war. I knew how Raymond must have felt in the garden of The Jennings. Exiting the car to piss in a hedge and call her, I barely got it out in time and soaked my phone; nettles dripped. Morgan dropped the window for a wisecrack. I wiped the phone dry on a dock leaf. DJ giggled. He'd come with a threat, or ultimatum (certainly no envelope). What was more, he'd have the hump about Abril's. Store up an attitude like Karen's for a long time, till the opportunity came to remind her how she'd behaved under that parasol with her tummy ache: not a very nice young lady, to be asking favours now. Too late to beg. Bowler'd be with him. Or downstairs in the hatchback. Couldn't call her. Ah, darling! Shorted it with piss. Wouldn't ring. Rang and cut out . . . 'an old dibble'. *An* not 'the'. She'd met Arnold twice and talked about him. He was *the*, not 'an' . . . Jesus Christ, the Gonk! In that copper's rig. Invested as a Special Constable. Full police powers, including arrest. Arnold must have worked it. What in God's name was he doing at the flat? Looking for Turbo? Assault on an officer, retroactive charge. Why at our flat looking for Turbo? Ah, my head was a snakepit! Had to get back to her. Standing in a lane by Shooter's Hill, piss on your hands, thirteen miles from home. What in fuck's name you up to, son?

'Predy!' Turbo revved, Hanley called, '*Venga, paisano!*' over the roof, and they were off down the track.

I followed the Granada as it accelerated; Morgan and Turbo must have souped it up. It was past fifty already. Further down, a figure was approaching, black bin bag over shoulder. He'd appeared from the dip to the left, where water shone. On towards the car he came, head lowered slightly. They were just putting on the frighteners. He knew they'd swerve. He carried as well a long, thin pouch. Was there a shotgun in there? He'd no time to get it out but must know they'd swerve. So it was a chicken run. On he came like he'd ram it; or it wasn't there. If they swerved, they'd lost the game. If they swerved, then on to me, with shining bag and pouch; squat, strong, broad-shouldered. Who was he? Morgan and Hanley must know. They'd come here with a purpose. He'd be one of them. Must be. The image of a peasant seized me, as he trudged with bag and pouch. Turbo was taking the Granada into the hedgerow and undergrowth on the left so they couldn't swerve, had to hit. No chicken run. This was terminal. He had no space. I saw in a flash Alaska Road, William caught between kerb and wall, nowhere to go. They were going to do him. Does 'joint enterprise' count if you aren't in the car? Something appeared in the air, and Turbo braked viciously, and the figure leaped and rolled. Shit. It happened so quick, I thought the first flying mass was the figure bouncing off the bonnet; but he seemed to be moving fast at a crouch through the undergrowth and was gone through a gap in the hedge where sunflowers and hogweed grew, while Turbo backed on to the field, then headed for the gap. The Granada stopped, and Morgan and Hanley were out of there; they all were. Those two ran to the hedge and through while Turbo stood on the driving seat above the door with a pair of binoculars. As I got closer, I heard him cry, 'Other side of the pits now, Mr Fabian. He's took someone's bike.' Morgan and Hanley came back through the hedge; Hanley, breathing heavily, appeared to be steaming. Morgan shook his head and spat, watching with his hard eye as I drew near. On the bonnet of the Granada, the bin bag had burst. Like brass mascots or cowlings, three tench lay there; others had fallen to the grass, where one of them twitched slightly. In black lace blouse, tight shorts and espadrilles, Donna Juan crouched beside, eyelashes flickering.

CHAPTER 30

'GONE FISHING . . .' SANG Morgan, walking past me with his knees out, while Hanley smoked a roll-up. 'Toe-rag'll head for The White Cross now. Yeah –' swinging back into the Granada like a hefty acrobat – 'when he's been fishing, he goes to his local. Let's be there before him. Crank it, Turbs! If we pass him on the road, we'll show him something he didn't learn in the Cycling Proficiency Scheme. You coming in, Mr Hyatt?'

'No. I've got to get back.'

'What?'

'My wife's in trouble. I have to get back.'

Morgan stared. 'We'll sort this, then we'll go. *Delenda est de Lacey!*'

So it was him. The older brother. 'I need to get back now,' I told him. 'Don't want to hold you up. I'll call a taxi.'

'Are yer yitten?' asked DJ, head at the window as Turbo revved.

'What?'

'Scared!'

'Fuck off!'

I was of course comprehensively scared. I was scared for my wife. I was scared what'd happen when we got to The White Cross, which was Mr Arnold's lair, as well as being Mick de Lacey's local (and what sort of mood was he going to be in, after a big silver car with a cool black dude at the wheel had sent him arse-first into a hedgerow?). I was also scared that some sort of digression or history class would supervene, becalming us for hours while Morgan indicated parallels between our situation and the rest of time, and DJ showed off his learning.

'Better to come with us,' called Morgan. 'You're on your own down here. It's bandit country. He might come back with a squad.'

I occupied myself with my phone.

'Come on, *amigo*!' Hanley'd now appeared by the boot. 'We're stronger together. We've started this, we should see it through. Strategically makes no sense to go back yet.'

'They haven't got your missus, have they?' The motherboard was fucked.

'How d'you know they've got Karen?'

Zero reception. 'That old cop's been round the flat.' Making for the Granada, as I had to.

'George Arnold?' Hanley was alarmed now. He handed me his phone. I couldn't speak to her in front of them – don't ask why.

'No.' We drove off fast down the track. 'It's that Gonk, the snitch. The one with the megaphone.'

'I equalized that dawg,' Turbo said, turning east on to Shooter's Hill Road.

'I know. We were watching. Saw him bleed. But his face wasn't marked. And he's been invested as Special Constable.'

'Shit! Nothing, Mr Hyatt? But he's so ugly, maybe you couldn't tell?'

'Maybe. At any rate, he's been up to our flat bothering my wife, and he's got powers of search, charge and arrest.'

'But you don't know he's taken her?' Hanley said.

'Well he wasn't dropping by for a cup of tea.'

'Nice cup of tea your wife does make, by the way,' said Morgan with high irrelevance. 'Two for the pot she puts in. That's the way! You'll not get one lady in fifty preparing it so choice and robust.'

She'd said nothing about making tea when he and Hanley came by. Just complained that Morgan was asking for daft names. I looked past DJ at Hanley, who seemed to be examining a leisure centre over the way.

'Victor's right about strategy,' decided J. F. Morgan. 'And I'll tell you why. When we strike a blow, they realize our strength, whereupon they retreat for the time being and leave off these tricks. Show you're soft or panicking, they'll lay it on, think they can do anything. Your wife's the safer for our acting decisively. She's a redoubtable woman, by the way. I can't see her taking any shite from this javel.'

'Yeah, boss, that lady be predy!' declared Turbo.

Taken him for cordials as well, hadn't she?

'We're here, Fabian!' said Hanley. We pulled into the car park of The White Cross, sat a while.

'Come on then!' cried Donna Juan. 'Are we going to fucking rumble, or what?'

'By Jove, your boy there's got some spunk!' said Morgan. I took it they'd been filling him in on the whole thing while I was outside the car with my phone. He couldn't have been more than a tot when the de Laceys and L Troop first achieved bad fame. Meanwhile, what did I have? No practice was what. Crime was my profession, for Christ's sake, and violent men my fascination; but I had no practice. I knew the world, but as for mixing it, that was beyond my experience. I hadn't hit anyone since I was about seven; now we were proposing to go mob-handed into a pub where a dirty copper held clinics and an uncatchable murderer drank with his pals, who were unlikely to be *Guardian* readers, or awfully keen on strangers, especially when one of them was black, another brown with Asiatic overtones, and a third – well, what sort of reaction was Donna Juan going to cause when he crossed the threshold? 'Unkind,' you might say. But none of this was of the essence anyway; which was that we'd just tried to run down their top boy. Now we were sitting in the car park of *his* pub like it was a rag-week prank. Over the way was a bus stop. I could run over, and out of here. Yes. Why not? It made sense. It was rational. Out of this insane scene, home to my wife, and lock the bleeding door. Hobbes would've approved. What do men fear most? That's right, son! Death. Especially violent death. And they'll do anything to avoid it. *Anything*. All I was proposing was to catch the 161 or 244. Turbo was putting on leather gloves, tapping the wheel. As I touched the interior handle, Donna Juan put his left hand on my knee and smiled up at me. Not like he was coming on, but in a 'This is it, then' manner. I wondered at this young man. Talk about 'A Day in the Life'! What had I led him into? I was responsible for this. Shamefully. Yet he was buzzing. I was buzzing too – with a para- lysing panic. So you learn you are a coward. I moved my hand away from the door. And if you don't run for the 89 (now passing), is it because you've found courage? Or you're frightened to lose face before the men beside you – who've been managing your fear by flattering your wife?

'Now, who's good at fighting?' enquired J. F. Morgan. O wise Cunc- tator! Keep asking, talking. Let's have a chat, then see the better of it.

'I'm not,' I told them.

'Yes, well we surmised that,' Morgan said. 'Didn't assume any dif- ferent.'

'Oh.'

'And how did they surmise it, you'll be thinking? With a man, you can tell if he's ever given anyone a slap. Not as readily as you can if he's in the habit of it, but you can tell nevertheless. A fighting man has a way of standing – and I'm not talking about bullies, but men who are willing to get physical if necessary, and unwilling to back down if they're threatened or insulted. He has a stance, and he has a current flowing through him; it flows perpetually – call it will, if you like. And when he needs to fight, he doesn't have to look for the switch. Which is the point with your non-fighting men; it's not necessarily a matter of cowardice, Mr Hyatt; no: it's just that they can't find the switch when they need it – or maybe they can't reach it. Hm.'

This was of course very kind of J. F. Morgan. I wasn't a coward. No. I just wasn't prepared, competent, practically able, or trained, when it came down to it. As it wouldn't be cowardice for a man to . . . to hold back from entering a burning house in which a person was known to be trapped, if he weren't a trained fireman; not cowardice, but just being sensible. Though who ever attained glory, enhanced his reputation, picked up a lady, by being sensible? Being sensible isn't cool; there's no story in it. Are there films about sensible men – or novels? Granted, people might be grateful that someone behaved sensibly – afterwards, in a quiet word . . . *Thank goodness you were sensible! Let's put the kettle on.* But no glory, no story.

'So you should stay here,' Morgan was now saying.

'Where?'

'Here in the car, my friend. Us lot'll go in and sort this. No disgrace in it.'

Oh, very good. I wasn't an individual, and I wasn't a fighting man either. What the fuck was I, at the end of the day? A kid stuck in the back of the car while the adults went in the pub. Might be an idea to kill myself – in a sensible manner. All of them checking me out now. 'What about this lot?' I said shirtily.

'Well, young John's on his mettle, and we know what Turbo's capable of,' said Morgan. 'Fifth dan in karate, and he's boxed as well. Stir porridge,

Turbs!' With this, Morgan raised his left hand, then Turbo magicked a hook from where he sat and cracked the palm of his guvnor, who hissed.

Damn. Why had I never trained or sparred a little?

'What about Hanley?' He was certainly no fitter than me. He smoked a lot. He stuffed himself with pies. He wore glasses. How could he be a hardman?

'When Karen asked me if I got stick as a boy,' he said now, 'the night you asked me up to your flat . . .'

'They called you "Paki". You and other Latin kids.'

'Yes. Well remembered, *paisano*. It did get heavy. Take a night in autumn '78, when I went to the chip shop for my treat – my old lady used to give me fifty pence on a Friday. As I queued, some youths kicked off outside, two were from our school, the others were older, wearing crash helmets. They were banging on the window, making noises; it was me they had their eye on. Well out I went with my chips, sausage, curry sauce on a tray, and one of them says, "Why you eating English food, Hanley? Coon food you should be eating!" I tell them to fuck off. One of the others says, "He is eating coon food. He's got Paki gravy on there. Can't have Pakis telling you to fuck off, can you, Deano?" And Deano, a bastard with a big face and sideburns, he slaps the tray out my hands, and all the curry down my front. Then they start giggling: "Now he's shit his T-shirt! Look at him!" Giggling, and shoving me. It was the giggling got me. If they hadn't giggled, I'd have walked away. But the giggling was such a malevolent sound, I thought, If you do walk away from this, turn the other cheek, you've given up any right to respect till your dying day. Because if you ever have a great hour in your life, you'll hear that sound again, and it'll turn it over just like they flipped your tray; so you'll never achieve anything, or become a man. There was scaffolding round the flats above the bike shop next to Poseidon and the men had left some tools, podgers, spanners. I went over, and these four shouting, "He's gonna climb up there like monkey boy!" A heavy-duty wrench with a hex head, that's what I picked up, and they're going, "What's he doing now?" Well I came back, and Deano's got his helmet on, but it was open face and I got him clean on the nose with a swing, then I gave him a couple of belts in the heart.'

'What d'you do then?'

'I went home. My old lady cleaned me up, sang me a Spanish song.'

'They try and beef with you again, Mr Hanley?'

Hanley shook his head.

1978, eh? Hanley a coon all those years ago, and just the other week, Turbo called the same (source: Sibyl Grove) – and we knew what he was capable of. So both these warriors had smashed the nose of their tormentor. No reason to disbelieve Hanley either. Indeed, it struck me now that the disadvantage I had was being a white boy. No one had ever given me racial grief. Another disadvantage was being straight. No one had given me gay-hate, like my little gamecock here, whose violent prowess and criminal record had no doubt been picked up by J. F. Morgan's 'fight detector'. Even Morgan had had an eye bitten out, and he was white, and straight (I'd have thought), though maybe being Welsh had toughened him up. What chance did you have if you were like me? My parents hadn't helped. They weren't poor, abusive or alcoholic. No wonder I was soft. Weren't well off either. If I'd gone to a brutal public school, I could have learned to be vicious when it was called for. O all of you who've never done a violent thing, are you with me?

Then Morgan said the nicest thing I'd heard: 'You're our Harry Hopkins, Mr Hyatt. Too important to risk!' Pure bullshit, since nothing he'd said about that diplomat resembled me; simply no pattern there. But none of them laughed, or looked at each other, and now he was out, stamping like a troll. In gloves of black leather and sharp trilby, Turbo followed him, and he had that hard-shell briefcase, and Hanley in his fine-striped Hackett suit and Donna Juan with his golden satchel, and bringing up the rear, Hyatt, whose vanity turned bullshit to merit; we all stamped our feet and lowered our hips as we went forward, and Morgan signed to Turbo, who signed to us to slow it.

The White Cross wasn't flash hard. No one on the door; no stand-out musclemen with tans, lieutenants, babes, thick bling. There were middle-aged tradesmen in Timberland boots, black combat boots, tucked-in joggers, one of them cuffing Jonas; others held their pints at a 'Thursday' angle as they heard an Albanian scam. There were a couple who'd come in for a drink at lunch and stayed. The woman was a Celt, with a tough sandy face and hair in a bun, but her eyes were electric, and you couldn't get eyes like that no matter what you blew on cosmetic refurbs; she didn't live straight, but she wouldn't be going down. Her partner was mean, weak, good-looking, ready to do as he was told, if anyone pissed her off, or their money ran out. She gave us the once-over and her eyes marked DJ and Turbo, but she might have admired the one, and fancied the other, and when her partner was going to say something loud, she silenced him with two fingers across her throat. A few old boys who'd got away from their wives, or been sent out during the soaps, read the paper, glanced at rolling news. Through an arch, some youths played pool; they weren't tasty – in T-shirts, their arms were white and undefined. A pregnant woman drank O2 and tapped at her phone. On a blackboard was a notice for Quiz Night. An ordinary place in its way: so they relaxed after work, got leathered, got out the house, chatted, tweeted, looked forward to their quiz. The coloured chalk read *Don't let Danny's Mob clean up YET again!* Brainy Danny. Him and his team mugging up, one on rivers, one on sport/entertainment, Danny on history and current affairs. Maybe we could come back and challenge them, instead of fighting. Fair chance with our buffs. Down the end, white shirt, arms folded, the landlord was chatting to a regular, failing to acknowledge us without ignoring our presence. He had a fly-rink, narrow face, steel specs. He'd serve when he was ready, that was the idea, or if we made the effort to go down his way; but he didn't need our custom – didn't much want it. He knew the law on refusing to serve, and he wasn't going to resort, since it would cause a fuss and, glasses rising, catching light, pool cues clicking, Radiohead and Britney on the sound system, things were ticking over as he wanted. For when you've history like this place, you don't want it stirred.

And for a moment, like a superimposed painting, I see all five at the window table, leaning one way, George Arnold at the head, coaching them for interview (bloodied clothes now smouldering in Thamesmead). Then a notice thanks all our regular customers and friends for raising £386 earlier in the month (Jubilee Charity Barbecue).

Up the bar comes landlord. What Father Raymond said about publicans loving their customers, this one had certainly risen above, at least where we were concerned. On his right forearm was a faded tattoo, blue cross and curve. Behind the bar, a framed *Daily Mail* front page from 1994 that showed some old boys in berets; a photo of our landlord with big flares and hair and West Ham's 1980 squad. Right of refusal was his (Licensing Act 2003), and this gave him the power of serving unlovingly, provided his contempt was spread even, so he didn't change his face as he looked from one of us to the next, and considered the options.

This was a very white pub – that's something I've been trying to suggest about its character. Straight white gaff. The most multicultural thing was either us, or something on the lunch menu, if they had a kitchen – say a baked potato with Tikka or Chilli.

'What can I get you?' Wiping his hands on a little towel. Perhaps we'd already infected the place. His voice was a smoker's croak, deep Cockney. He'd have started out as a docker. Taken this place on redundancy.

'What's that then?' said Morgan, hand to ear. He took his time, this one. Wasn't just the stage act. The landlord must be clocking his false eye. Did he know something of that? Certain punters observing us more closely. DJ with hand on hip, satchel flashing, Turbo's ringed hand on the bar, hard-shell briefcase at his side. Where were their hardmen?

The landlord asked again.

'Can you turn that down, my man?' said Morgan, like we were waiting for a train. 'I don't like nineties pop.'

'You don't like the music, you can go back where you came from,' the landlord told him. Careful it wasn't all of us. 'You won't be missed.'

'Where's your top boy?' Morgan said. 'We've come to see him.'

'Don't know what you're talking about.' Under his chin the landlord had a wattle. He did know. Maybe knew as well this'd happen one day. What you get for serving the notorious, making them feel at home. Sightseers, crime buffs, toadies, campaigners; one day a motley crew with a heavy manner.

I checked Hanley. Hanley was at the theatre.

'Ah,' said Morgan, 'you don't know what I'm talking about. See no evil, hey? Disappointed in you, Jeff.'

'How d'you know my name?'

'I've seen it spelled in leaves,' said Morgan obscurely. 'Where they blow, they formed it: J-E-F-F-R-E-Y.'

'You what?'

'Know what that means? You shake your head, sirrah. You've neglected your ancient history, Jeffrey.' With ardent enjoyment, Hanley looked on. 'But ancient history hasn't neglected you. Nursed you through the cycles, on its bloody apron.' Hanley seemed to be pinching himself, in his good suit and golden glasses. 'De Lacey's a Frenchman, isn't he? Your top boy's a Norman, Jeffrey.'

'He ain't a Norman, he's local. Born and bred down this way. You're lucky he ain't here now. Don't like being talked about, Mick; and he don't like being looked at, and he don't like being looked for!' Jeffrey was building up a fair head of steam.

'So you concede he is your top boy,' Lawyer Hanley put it to him, 'which is to say, a particular favourite of yours?'

'I ain't got no favourites!' Jeffrey said in an ornery way that had Donna Juan giggling.

'Yet he is your top boy?'

Jeffrey sniffed, and I thought I saw a trace of something like a father's pride, and curse me if I didn't feel for him (a little) in this baiting. Shit-soft.

'I take it your silence indicates agreement?'

'You got him there, Mr Hanley,' said Morgan. 'His top boy is a naughty Norman.'

'I take him as he comes', the landlord said, trying to lose interest. 'Past's the past. Let bygones be bygones. A man can change.'

'You lack a sense of history, Jeffrey,' Morgan told him. 'The past is here. Always. That's one thing. Eleventh century, the Normans came. They left him here as a sleeper. Consider his surname, Jeffrey. That's not an honest English name, to my reckoning. The second is this. Your top boy hasn't changed, hasn't grown; all he's done is lose his hair. A dog doesn't change. Hasn't repented either. He hasn't acknowledged his crimes, young Micky.'

'Crimes! He deserves a fucking medal, that lad!' cried Jeffrey.

'Tell him to come here, then. Tell him we want to shake his hand. Tell him to come here now. We want to buy him a pint. Won't want people thinking he's scared, Micky the Norman. Won't want people tweeting that he's "yitten".' Along the bar, Morgan, Turbo, Hanley, Donna Juan, leaned like cowboys.

'He ain't no fucking Frenchman! And he don't drink with pooves –
or coons, or wops; and let me tell you, he wouldn't touch a one-eyed
Taff with a Dyno-rod,' crackled Jeffrey. Spittle flecked the corners of
his mouth; a vein stirred in his fly-rink like a snake beneath a sheet. So
the only one Mick de Lacey'd drink with was me? Some distinction!
You alone belong, son . . . Don't leave me, boys!

'What d'you know about my eye, Jeffrey?' Morgan was saying.
'Here we come close to the nub, isn't it?'

'He should have done 'em both!' snarled Jeff the Unkind.

'Who's *he*?'

'Whoever. Whoever done it.' Down the bar, punters had been
waiting for drinks. At first, they made signs and called Jeffrey. They
were silent now.

'Come on, Jeffers! You know very well who he is. Where can we
find him? You've suddenly gone quiet. Biting your tongue. Shouldn't
have said that, should you? After all, could have been an industrial accident that did for my eye, melanoma, car crash, overhanging branch. But
you knew it was a local face. You knew this very well, and what you
said before trying to cover up with a generality, suggested to me that
it's still remembered as a great sporting moment, not far from here.
But – silence, sirrah! When I talk I talk till I've finished, and I take a
long time about it, too, long as I fancy; and there's no power on earth
I've known that can prevent me either; I can talk men to death, and have
used the skill on two occasions, which is to say sparingly, seeing as
occasions grow to surfeit – but, this great sporting moment is only
referred to by a chosen few; and on pain of nasty treatment, you aren't
meant to blab about it in the presence of strangers. Which you just did.
You've blown it, my man. And when his uncle hears, you better head
for your retirement chalet in Thorpesby-under-Shit, lock the door, and
string yourself up. Make it easy on yourself, old-timer. It'll be less painful.'

'Who are you?' wheezed the landlord. 'Don't want no grief.'

'You've been visited by the Cunctator. I've put the slow sign on you, butty. The old man'll know where to find you.'

'Hoy, Jeff!' On came an English lion in overalls. 'You got problems, mate?' Chest out, he trash-talked Turbo, whose left hip swayed before the dull crack.

Jesus Christ . . .

'He reacted with reasonable force to a threat he couldn't safely ignore or walk away from, owing to severe provocation within a confined and notoriously hostile space, and other circumstances, such as the landlord's use of hate speech, Section 4, Public Order Act,' declared Hanley, as lion blew red bubbles. A mate crouched at his side.

Morgan hummed. 'At least friend on the floor's got more bottle than your top boy. Where the hell is he? He already ran away from us once this evening. When the white-bellied rat does turn up, tell him he forgot his catch.'

'What catch?'

'This fucking catch!' Morgan made a sign to Donna Juan, who unhitched his golden satchel, opened it, and spilled the tench one by one on the bar, where they lay in armoured row. Someone gagged.

As we left The White Cross, a red hatchback entered the car park from another entrance. Only I witnessed this and kept it to myself, jubilant with having gone in, and come out alive. We seemed to have made our point, if only symbolically. For a coward, that was cool, though I could barely reckon with everything we'd done. On the way back, we stopped at a churchyard, to look at Marlowe's grave. Next year was the four-hundredth anniversary of his murder, twentieth of Eldine Matthews. We'd have seen this through by then. So said Hanley. A late bird screamed in the trees. The air was still, dead still.

CHAPTER 31

BEFORE WE PARTED COMPANY, Morgan advised us this was just the phoney war. I found Karen sitting in the dark in her day clothes and could have wept with relief, but she was fierce and talking of going to stay with Lolly, if I didn't level with her. Never mind about Angie Pole. That was for another time. She wanted the whole truth about what I was up to and she wanted it now, no soft-soap, dodging, palaver.

But what had the dibble said?

Hadn't 'said' anything.

But she texted he'd been round to the flat.

She marched to the window. Standing over there looking up he was, like his eyes were painted on pole ends. An ancient fuzz.

I tried to hold her. Reminded her what she said in the Lebanese, about being unable to be myself by myself, needing others for my meaning, my sense of what I'm about, etc. Tactical error.

'You bloody well should be able to stand alone! What kind of a man are you, Carl? Tell me! When the kids say they did something because their mates led them on, even then it's no bloody go. That's crucial is that. I teach them Maths and Physics, and I do my bloody best to teach them to take responsibility for themselves. You must have been taught that as well; I know you were. With a thirteen-year-old, they have half an excuse. You haven't any! Hanging round with middle-aged fellas plotting – pathetic! Like bloody *Junior Police Five*. Don't grin! It's not bloody funny!' She was building up a green-eyed passion, hands on hips, nostrils double-barrelled. She'd kept her heels on (or put them on when she heard me at the door), for height and power; also, there was a dressing-for-the-lawyer quality to her presentation. Which sent my thoughts on a curious circuit . . .

'You're having a crisis, Carl. I should have expected this when I married you. As a matter of fact, everyone warned me: "He's ten year older than you, he'll do summat weird or go astray in his fifth decade. All blokes do." I told 'em you were special; Christ, you didn't deserve that! "He's down-babed once"– me they meant by that – "he'll do it again; or he'll go off it, or get some really naff clothes, or a hobby." And what have you done? You've gone for the hobby! At least we could have had a proper fight about it if you'd been shagging someone else.' Here was a thought. She'd have chopped my dick off. 'But you, oh you have to be crafty, bloody dodgy, so I can't pin you down, and you make promises – you made one about Mulhall – you did, that you were calling it a day, that time we were in the Japanese garden watching the fish – by the waterfall you hugged me and promised! But you haven't ended it. All you've done is gone sideways like a bloody crab. And I don't know what you're doing and I can't catch you, and I'm frightened and I hate you!' She stamped, heel thudding in the red rug, exited, marched back: 'And don't try touching me! I'll not go with a black-leg. You aren't you anymore. You're a stand-in for who I married!' She dry-spat. 'I'll not have a fucking scab coming on to me. Keep away! Don't come anywhere near our bed, you dirty lying bastard!' Exit.

She'd recovered from this morning. That's an individual.

A decision was called for.

Say you level with her. How, when nothing is concluded? . . . Nothing inconclusive about attempted murder, son. That, she'll have to take seriously (though being impressed is a different KOF). You weren't in the car, no idea of the plan – but she knows the meaning of joint enterprise . . . Of course, Mick de Lacey would hardly go running to the cops like any innocent fisherman; no, he'd just go to one cop. Would George Arnold (retired) bring it about that a complaint of attempted murder was investigated by the police? Would de Lacey have recognized anyone in the car? What if he memorized the plate? Surely Morgan and Turbo would be smart to that? You think of levelling, these questions catch you.

Well, Jeffrey would have made identifications to Arnold by now – of appearance at least. Furthermore, both sides had been shadowing each other. Surely we all knew who the hell we were? Arnold knew me and Karen. The Gonk knew where we lived. He'd have let Arnold know what Turbo did to him. Was Bowler retired or still serving? Hanley should know. (DS Chris Butler would know.) Mulhall knew of me. He'd know Donna J. The Gonk would know DJ, from his snitch trips to Van Spenser. As a lawyer, Hanley had to be uncountably known – to cops and shady folk. Which left J. Fabian Morgan.

Who'd been known from the beginning, as the man whose eye was bitten out by Mulhall's nephew – and that went back before the Matthews murder. The cops would have known all about him, Arnold and Bowler particularly, even as they tried to snuff the case. He was the original, Morgan . . .

In her dressing room, I heard Karen on the phone. Here she came again, in little furry slippers.

'I've given you five minutes to work out what you're going to tell me. I'm sorry about shouting in your face, Carl.' She'd put on her crucifix.

So I told her the lot. Maybe because she'd come in being nice. Maybe because I wanted to be taken seriously, or I felt inspired . . . Maybe you know why? I don't. There we sat together with a beaker of brandy and lovage, and she listened quietly, once or twice interjecting, or requesting clarity, to this barbarous tale. At times, she put her hands to her face; for William, she wept. At last, she said quietly, 'I never saw it coming to this.' Her eyes were like old water.

How had she seen it?

She'd been looking forward to being middle-class, me and her. We'd have good jobs and respect and no matter what I thought of the *Chronicle*, Andy thought the world of me and I was someone there – and that wasn't all, either . . .

'So I've let you down?' It was no time to scoff at the ambition.

'Maybe it was a false thing to want. D'you think it was?'

I wanted to say we could still make it all right. I hadn't been in the car. But the other side ran people down for far less. Where'd we go anyway? Emigrate? It had started; and would take its course, and end, as it had to. No known vaccination. In city, island, continent or country, no safe place. They always found you. We leave such trails nowadays.

'No. Nothing false about it. It's natural to want that. The only philosopher I remember from my degree said that all men (he meant women as well) want felicity, which is the assured enjoyment of happiness, continuous small success. That's what you're talking about. The job of the state is to arrange it so they don't fall out about it and start a war among themselves, since everyone's in competition for felicity.'

'So why can't we have it, you and me?'

'Because for some men, felicity is war, and violence – and trouble. That's how they get their glory. This philosopher was a very fearful man, "timorous" someone called him who'd met him once or twice. He admitted it too. Fancied it was because his mother heard the Spanish Armada was coming that she went into labour suddenly – from fright; so he was frightened when he appeared in the world, and he stayed frightened. The English Civil War gave him the fright of his life. His whole philosophy on the political side's the philosophy of a frightened man.'

Karen put her head on my shoulder. Her feet were eyeless creatures. 'Are you frightened, Carlo?'

Takes a man to admit fear, though admitting doesn't make the man. (One for the whiteboard.)

'I was before, because I wasn't being honest; didn't like the feeling of that, sweetheart. Dabbling with Mulhall when I promised you I'd cut it out. Then it got worse, by a long way, after Hanley showed up and started telling me all the other stuff, and I knew it was George Arnold we'd met on holiday. Everything I've heard these last six weeks, it's been a black surprise: the world's much worse than I thought; not just the places the news comes from – the whole thing. I've missed this entirely; all the time I wrote about crime, I never had the knowledge. Info, connections, sources, plenty of that. Curiosity too, about the difference between criminals and us, what it was like on their level, living their own rules, breathing a different air; what it meant, how it felt, to break the law, when most people keep it; how it set them apart, even placed them above us – some of us; and of course, I could have been accused of "glamorizing" the criminal, and was now and then; that's hypocrisy. The whole world's mad on crime, fascinated: just flip through the channels. To me, it was a challenge, that fascination; I really wanted to satisfy my curiosity. Then I got burned, and promised to back off; but curiosity doesn't keep promises. Which is why it causes such trouble. But it's only these last weeks I've got the knowledge. The two worlds aren't separate, the straight and the foul. They're demons, these people; they're always at the door and they don't knock and wait to be shown in; they're in already, among us; they're corruption itself, inescapable corruption. You can't escape them any more than you can gravity.

There's no rhyme or reason; they're just here. Why did we bump into George Arnold on holiday? We were drawn his way. He wasn't tracking us, or anticipating. Nothing to do with my past.'

How could I be so sure?

'Because of this. For him to be keeping an eye on me on account of a three-year-old libel, and to follow us on holiday, and know our café, and at the same time be familiar enough with the place to know the name of the old guy who showed us the path across the beach, and a pargeter in Calahonda – all that's incredible as a stake-out; I know how these things work when they're planned. I didn't merit that. The network'd have to be so big, efficient, it'd outdo any government agency.'

So what was it?

'It's like God's eye, that's what it is. But it's not God's.'

'So it's the Devil's. That's what you mean.'

Being a Catholic, she could hack this.

'We met a priest this afternoon – forgot to tell you. Me and DJ. And of course, he was connected with all this. He was there when Morgan was mutilated. He's a good man – an Anglican, mind. You could go and stay with him.'

'You what?' She lifted her head from my shoulder. 'Like sanctuary? Honestly, Carl! I'm staying put, me. With you. That's flat.'

'I don't understand. When I came in, you were seething. Now I've told you the lot, you're cool.'

'What's the mystery, Carlo?'

'Well, it has to be worse than you expected – a hell of a lot worse.'

'Yes. And that's what makes it all right. There's pissing about, and there's deep trouble. What you've told me makes all the difference. You're my hero now!' She kissed me, in a way I fancied soldiers leaving on troop trains were kissed, then held my head as if she would protect it with her life.

She should go to Lolly's anyway, till it was over (whatever that meant), but she'd become very kissy, murmuring about going down with me. I saw Barnfield's bloated head, monitors and drips. All he'd done was ask a question. We would get killed; only, that lot'd get killed superbly; they knew how to rumble; to me it'd happen without flair. Have you ever had to think of this? They'd text her: *Your old man died like a dog!*

She kept kissing, and telling me about cornea, so I thought she meant Morgan's eye, and she kissed me more till I got to thinking the sex-strike was arbitrated, then she mentioned a play, and it turned out she was saying 'Corneille', who wrote them about three hundred years ago, and I was instructed that *Corneille* was the last exponent of honour and glory in the theatre, also that *ressentiment* was Corneille's word for injured honour (which didn't mean much to me, but seemed significant to her, owing to that it had later acquired a reverse meaning – which she thought I should know, tongue in my ear), but delightful as all this instruction might be, I was wary of the words 'hero' and 'honour', which made me realize hard what I should have acknowledged long since, namely that the reason I scoffed at Thomas Hobbes as a student was because I resented the fact that the philosophy of that excellent coward was all about people like *me*. I could feel her imagination renouncing that sovereign desire of the middle classes, namely, the desire for security, and long life. And when a woman's coming on to you as she now was, lifting a bumper of brandy and lovage to your lips, such renunciation is seductive, wildly; but is it sensible to want a dose of it?

Yet is it glorious to be sensible? This again.

I expanded on the subject of Morgan. Like what had he been doing, these past twenty years? Well, he'd given an answer up on that balcony (the time she took Turbo for cordials). Waiting, delaying, 'cunctating'. Handling time like FDR, slow and sure (omitting 'lethal'). Yes. Slow, full-time revenger, that was Morgan, and he'd devised a new career as a diversion or disguise that also called attention exactly to what he was up to.

Like he'd made revenge his art?

Indeed. Then took his art to precisely the kind of places favoured by the young men who'd injured him so foully and murdered Eldine! What kind of man was this, living among enemies and their insolence? What nerve did that take? Did the offence he'd suffered give him immunity? Anthropologically, what did a deep offence confer upon its sufferer? Even Mulhall must know it was excessive, what happened in The Bosun and Monkey, Sophie B. Hawkins on the sound system. Like he was owed something back. Was that it? The crime world had sensibilities, even if they were often much diminished; a sense of measure, even if it was eccentric, unpredictable, alarming, to the civilized. Did it suppose there'd be no comeback from Morgan? Or was it bracing itself? Morgan seemed dreadfully confident; was he mad?

Maybe he was. Did it matter, though?

If only we hadn't mixed the levels.

Which levels?

The humour and the violence.

For a while, we pursued this line like a pair of wacky students. Who knows how flippantly people in danger have spoken, over centuries? But there was a point (and one favourable to my desire for safety). Morgan had made a strategic and professional error, with Hanley's backing, in plotting or entertaining the idea of violent revenge – hadn't he? As a stand-up comic, he knew the power of ridicule was total in itself. Between death, and shame or humiliation, what choice? He'd told Jeffrey he could talk men to death. We had Turbo's account of his blasting badmen with his act.

But they weren't these badmen. How did you get this lot together for some fatal ridicule? Was it possible?

And so we worked our way through the brandy and lovage, pulled this way and that between humour and violence, in Morgan-maddened speculation. And from time to time, I was her hero: was ever such promotion justified?

Dawn advancing. When the school office opened, she'd have to phone in sick. Today was meant to be her interview as well. As it found room, the thought troubled me. What was she going to do? All your fault.

Lifting her off me, I showed how we walked into The White Cross. Karen clasped her hands, so I did it again, with flourishes of my own. Then she must have a go. So both of us, up and down the room, to the alcove, round the fucking sofa, like Stig of the Dump and his babe. By God she was hot, even trundling like a troll. We ranted about Morgan going viral on YouTube with parodies of the murderers, surveillance film, stabbing demos, egg-throwing, TV interview . . . till I imagined the argument was carried.

It was nearly eight. 'Now what are you going to do about your interview, darling? Can't go into work like this.'

'You don't know me, Carlo!'

CHAPTER 32

I N THE MEWS, SIBYL tapped at an iPad.

'You look bleeding awful, son! What time did the party end?' She wore a dress of black linen and straw flip-flops. Could have used her feet to skin a lamb.

'Haven't been at a party.'

'Fucking smell like you have! Ain't going into work like that, are you? You'll get fired.'

'They won't fire me, Sibyl,' I told her. 'How long you had that?'

'It's my new friend. I can view porn with it!'

'What's this?' She was checking MSN news. There was a photo of Danny Flowers. So much for Fabian's 'phoney war'. He'd been found on Bostall Heath, naked in a pair of Ugg boots. They'd used the 'Murderers' mugshot. Always the one last mentioned, not the Sixth Man, but the weakest of L Troop. What did Father Raymond say? *Sullen . . . moist-eyed . . . out of his depth.* Naked, booted (what kind of insult was that?), hanging from a yew. Suicide, or murder, both possibilities. Investigating Officers energetically pursuing enquiries. Morgan and Hanley couldn't have been back east again last night? But their blood was up now. Turbo and DJ. Four pairs of hands. Not you.

'What's the matter, cupcake?'

So they dropped you home, 'calling it a day', then off for some real war. Not to be involved – now that should have been an immense relief; but when our advantages freeze in our hands, how can we count our blessings? Unmanned. The hours with my wife turn to chaff. Neither Hopkins, nor hero, but *husband* . . .

'Hey! What you looking at? Lady with three teats?'

'This.'

'What's your interest in him? To do with that trouble you had?'

'Trouble I've got.'

'All one, aren't they?'

'How does that help me?'

'No need to yell, dear!'

I was ready to weep. She made room for me on the lounger.

'Lie beside me, cupcake. Sibyl won't grab your polony. Tell your trouble.'

I closed my eyes. Goulash red filled the space behind them. 'They're making me kill. They're leaving me out. I don't know what's expected.'

'Hanley and those boys?'

'Yeah.' Looking out. Potted fern, patch of sun: if only we could lie and watch such things; forgo the bustle.

'Your wife went along there yesterday.' She pointed at the solid cinema. 'I know who she is. Seen her with you.'

'What of it?'

'Why should there be something?'

'Well, you mentioned it.' Feet like a condor.

'What if you never saw her again?'

'What? What d'you mean by that?' Another black bubble, was it? I could throttle the hag.

At the end of the mews, Earl Holmes practised golf swings with his stick.

'There's a carefree lad!' declared Sibyl Grove. 'Seventy-eight if he's a day. Proper rogue, is Earl. No more shame than a wasp, a cactus!'

'Where does that get me? What's he got to do with my wife? Was she talking to him?'

'How long you been married?'

'Ten years.'

'After ten years, most fellas'd like to see the back of the missus. They won't say it but they dream it!'

'Well I don't!'

'Pooh! Hanging round with that filly. What does that say to the world, Carl? Looks like your missus if you half close your eyes!'

'What the hell d'you mean by that?'

'Maybe it was him I saw yesterday. '

'You couldn't have. He was with me all day!'

'Bingo!'

'Working. We were working on something.'

'They all say that. "Late at the office again, dear? Put your bollocks on the scales. If they weigh less than this morning, they're fucking coming off!"'

Behind me, the old bitch hacked. As I turned off the mews, she was trying to shout, fiddling with her inhaler.

That Flowers'd topped himself was in fact quite possible. Pressure of the years; like a man with perma-dogshit on his shoes: sniffed wherever he went. Unemployable, bitter, watching his back. Maybe he'd heard Mick de Lacey was nearly taken out last night. Get it over before they do me. Don't give 'em the satisfaction. Like all of them, though, he drove a good car, changed it regularly. And they all had their women, kids by them. How did that come about? Must keep them going when they felt the rain . . . *Get outta bed, Danny! Past's the past. Put it behind you, babe. You ain't done nothing anyway. It was them others. Can you collect Jade? I got Zumba at four . . .* More than loyal, ultra-loyal, hard-line: *You're a hero, Mick. All my Facebook friends know who I'm with. This is England. You don't like the flag, we'll help you pack! Fifty-eight likes. Put it just the way you said, Mick! Me and the girls are gonna burn a burka! Unfortunately, there won't be no one in it – not this time anyways! Got that pike stuffed for your birthday, Mick, in a wall-case. No one best make an enemy of you, Mick. You're King of Shooter's Hill. Take me with you to The White Cross! Ain't you proud of me, Mick? Omigod can't believe I'm with you. You're the OG! . . .* Prospering too: *Pete, I spoke to the accountant. By autumn, we can float the company. New Merc for you, Scion for me, place in Barbate or Mallorca. You, me, the girls. Get out of this multicultural toilet. We've made it, Pete! You're a man of steel, babe. Moved on from all the shit and lies. Done what you said. You gone forward like a blade. Always. You could be a motivation guru, Pete. Your brother's like an old geezer. Fishing and beer. What else? Nothing! No ambition. Him and Lara shop at Tesco! What she ever done but temping? She can hardly spell. Know who I saw the other day? Danny. Forgot to tell you. He was like this – must have had his head in the fridge for a month! Spotted me, he did. Couldn't get in his jeep quick enough. He's one flake, that lad. He's done. Never had it. Born to follow. To him, you were a star, Pete. But to see stars, you need backbone; he ain't got one. Wanders round looking for himself like he's dropped a fiver. Check the spreadsheet! Luchini! Yo! Do me there, Pete, plunge me! Again! That's it, Pete! Johnny Depp ain't nothing on ya! . . .*

We weren't going to get them with comedy. Goodbye to all that.

*

THE *CHRONICLE* OFFICE WAS still there, Andy, Fabiana, acting calm; maybe they were calm. I said nothing about yesterday's edition. The phone seemed to be going a lot. I'd warned him, hadn't I? Inserting headphones in the 853, I began to play through. Storage on that thing was incredible. From DJ on shoplifting and his hawk 'Adbeel' to the long talk with Father Raymond, boat and car journeys, the torment of Jeffrey, ride home via Marlowe's grave, all there. How to edit the fucker? Twelve-hour play-through. At times, I heard murmuring, laughter, grunts, which I couldn't recall from the day itself; in the garden of The Jennings, for example, there seemed to be a low, insistent chattering, many-voiced. Did Father Raymond attract demons? If anyone, a priest would. Part of the job, if you believed. But I didn't. Yet here they were. He'd been witness to more of L Troop's antics, presence, than any of us. Did he carry it round like pestilence, in the folds of his being? Fabiana came over, squatted by my chair, considered me.

There's a world in those eyes. Everywhere, women look out at destroyers, developers, berks with ideas. This is what they have to put up with. They join them at it; then they've been corrupted; or they do their own thing, and that's equality, but still they join to us or we to them, and one way or the other the issue gets forced, so it doesn't end in equality, which is no realer than heaven. But some women fight men. I'd read an article about the PKK, and the women's regiments in Syria. There were photos of them in the field, bearing machine guns and ammo belts, in the distance smoke plumes. On patrol, they crouched under broken walls radioing in enemy positions. In barracks, they relaxed in battle fatigues and pink socks, smoking long white cigs, tapping at tablets and laptops; in many photos, they sat close, smiling, brown-eyed girls in headscarves; and their eyes showed exactly what they were about. Fabiana rose and plucked the headphones.

'Carl, I don't think you're well!'

'You don't understand the danger.'

'Yes we do. Of course we do! This is journalism!'

'They've started killing.'

'Who have?'

'All of them.'

'No one's dead round here, Carlo!' called brick-face. 'You're mis-counting. What you frightened of, mate?'

'You don't understand. You don't know what you're up against.'

'I'll tell you what I understand, Carlo.' He came over to stand by Fabiana, who watched me with steely affection. 'You are wacko where criminals are concerned. Think they're something special. You've built a religion of it. Now all you see is the Devil. What you were saying in here the other day, that it was going to get dark for me if I mixed it with Mulhall, not to take a fight where it can't be won – bollocks! What makes you so obedient, mate? Look! No dark! Light everywhere!' Andy began to prance –

'Bumpitty, bumpitty, bumpitty, bum,
I'm riding along on my charger!'

– while Fabiana clapped merrily. 'Cheer up, Carlo!' called Andy, cantering that way. 'I'll get a laugh out of you somehow!' How I loved this pair; they made me feel what an undeserving thing I was. Fabiana hugged me like teacher, smelling of Pomegranate Noir . . . *Carl sometimes feels quite frightened. His spelling is coming on nicely.*

'It's going to be all right, Carl! All going to be all right! We're your friends. We won't let them hurt you!' Mouth close to mine.

She didn't know what they could do, did she? But what good was the knowledge? It was killing me. I'd be finished before the devils got near.

'Have you spoken to your wife?'

'Yes. What does Karen say? She's a sensible lady.'

'I was trying to keep it all from her. Last night she made me tell her the truth. Everything. Now she's cool.'

'So why are you in such a state today?' Andy placed a broad hand on my desk, leaning while Fabiana crouched. Like one of those paintings Morgan was telling us about: *Two Angels and Coward*.

'Ah, like I'm trying to tell you, because the killing's started.'

'Which "killing"?'

I showed them the report on Danny Flowers.

'Who's behind this, then?' said Andy. 'Mulhall?'

'I dunno . . . for sure. I think Hanley could have something to do with it.'

'But Hanley and Mulhall aren't hand-in-glove.'

'I know that! I fucking know they aren't!'

'Stop screaming or I'll slap you!' cried Fabiana. 'Disgraceful behaviour!'

'You're imagining things.' Reasonable Ravage.

'I'm imagining nothing. Now for Christ's sake listen. I was with Hanley, a one-eyed comedian called John Fabian Morgan, Morgan's wingman Turbo, who's a very hard lad, and Donna Juan (the rent boy) – I was with them last night, in Deptford and Shooter's Hill. They tried to run down Mick de Lacey in a Ford Granada. They tried it and they meant it. Weren't frightening him. It was attempted murder. They're after all the men connected with the Eldine Matthews murder.'

'Christ! What d'you mean, you were with them?'

'I'd been with them for a couple of hours. When DJ and I got off the boat in Greenwich (it was part of the interview), they were waiting for us. We willingly went along.'

'So you were in on the plan?'

'Not explicitly. But a few nights ago, Morgan and Hanley laid it all before me, and I did nothing to discourage them. When they tried to ram de Lacey, I wasn't actually in the car – I was trying to call Karen. But I spent the rest of the evening with them. D'you understand now? Next up, we all went looking for de Lacey in his local in Shooter's Hill.

They wanted to do him there. Turbo had a briefcase with him, which I suspect might have contained a gun.'

'I take it you didn't find him?'

'No. There was a scene, though. Morgan gave the landlord some vicious verbals, I mean he broke him, and Turbo slugged a local who was getting fresh. This is what I'm saying. They're on search and destroy, these guys, it's started, it's happening.'

'So you're an accessory?'

'Technically. Not that the de Laceys have any pals in the law – except one; though we know what he can do. But they're more likely to come back at us themselves. That's the code, the way it works. But the point is, when I gave Karen the whole story, she started coming on like I was a hero.'

'What's the problem with that?'

'What every man wants from his wife, isn't it?' Fabiana grinning.

'But can't you see the pressure this puts me under? Jesus Christ, I'm supposed to be a journalist, not a bleeding hitman! I want out of this, totally.'

'You're scared of getting hurt?'

'Scared enough – though I've accepted the possibility. It's been there all along, since I started on Mulhall. I'm not sure it's that.'

'So you're scared of jail?'

'Well, as much as most straight folk. But . . . I dunno: I've not really entertained the idea; this whole thing's so wild, we're much more likely to get whacked than pinched.'

'Killed?'

'Yeah.'

'So you're scared of that?'

'Oh come on, both of you! We all are, aren't we?' They watched me, like they knew there was more, if I could find it. 'But I'm so fucked up now, I wouldn't mind it all ending anyway.' Fabiana put her hand on my thigh.

'So what is it?'

'It's me. I've been found wanting. I'd say I'd had my self sucked out of me, but I'm not sure I had one in the first place.'

'Mate, that is bollocks!' shouted Andy. 'That is not the Carl Hyatt Andy Ravage knows and respects. What's the matter with you?' He pinched my sleeve. 'They've slipped a sham in there. That's not Hyatt. He's out on the trail somewhere, doing what he does like no other man: genning up on what matters in our time – in our community. Pah! What we have in here's one of those misery-guts who sits on his arse at home and comfort-eats, comparing his problems with the losers on *Jeremy Kyle*. You'll be remembering you were sexually abused next. Your old man never hugged you . . .'

'Leave him alone! What's got into you?' Fabiana rose and pushed Andy, who stood off, calculating a way back round her. 'You're not helping by shouting.'

'He's right,' I told her. 'Only he's overestimating me. Lately I've been looking around me, at everyone, you two included. I don't seem to have the character, the will, you all have. I get pulled this way and that, I can't decide; it's others who do the deciding.'

'No, no, no!' Andy clenched his fist, Fabiana interrupting:

'You don't understand what other people think of you. You've got a rotten dose of self-pity and self-hate at the moment, Carlo. Your judgement on yourself isn't the key thing; that's just false honesty and it doesn't do you credit. You should have heard Victor Hanley talking about you yesterday!'

'What? Where were you speaking to Hanley?'

'In here!'

'What?'

'He dropped by,' grinned Andy, hands stuffed in pockets like a mighty scamp. 'We had a useful talk about the Mulhall piece. He can't see any possibility of libel.'

'Really? Well, Hanley doesn't know libel like I do. Hasn't had the experience. That wasn't the issue anyway. Mulhall wants this land.'

'Ah, well Hanley explained that the Land Charges indemnity is quite a binding thing.'

'Hanley's a lawyer,' I told them now. 'He makes speeches. Getting people to believe things that they may not be inclined to's his profession. He's been persuading me for weeks. He does voices, other people's; did he do that yesterday?'

Fabiana protested Lawyer Hanley's integrity.

'Maybe you're hearing things,' Andy suggested.

'Know what he said about you?' said Fabiana brightly, shoving Andy over the way.

'Jesus!' called Andy, now at his monitor checking feeds. 'They're going down like flies! Carlo, Fab, look at this!'

We went over. Vincent Drew, thirty-six today, had been attacked by a group of Islamic prisoners. They'd rushed his cell at Pentonville, stabbing him repeatedly with biros and toothbrushes, then given him birthday bumps, dropping him from a height. He was under guard in the prison hospital. His attackers had already tweeted it.

'Now I'd say that your team can't possibly be responsible for this, can they?' Andy Ravage put it to me.

His hair was the colour of cornflakes; I saw him overwhelmed, skull fractured, as I fiddled with the DJ profile.

Danny Flowers and Vincent Drew in twenty-four hours. Could Black Flag boys have stripped Danny and strung him up? Maybe another revenge outfit was operating. If they were, they'd save us work . . . so why did it feel like plagiarism?

CHAPTER 33

THE WARM-UP IS HELL — like *I just want to go home to Mummy.* Thirty of us, opposite walls. You have to run over there, dodge them coming, run back. You have to run over there, slap their shoulder while you pass, avoid *being* slapped, so do they. Fucking Norah! What shape am I in? Others blow a little; grinning and bonding when we pause for a sip, and find ourselves a partner . . .

Flushed with excitement, Lolly watched my face. Don't apologize, Lol, you're cool. She wore a black T-shirt with 'New York/New York' in gold letters. Along the wall were cannon-balls with hooped handles. There were racks of slim steel clubs, and parallel bars. I was enjoying myself too. So what if my teeth stung! The drill before was an elbow smash of which she must have underestimated the impact area, or speed, since the trailing edge caught me in the gnashers. Again I raised the rubber knife and brought it down in an overarm swing such as witnesses to the murder of Eldine Matthews had reported. This time, Lolly blocked my wrist with an outside defence, dropping a hammer punch on my nose that she pulled a split-sec from major vandalization. Never knew what you could do with a hammer punch. In boxing, you don't see them. Recommended for women, whose fingers are fragile, and anyone who wants to hurt someone else fast at close range. All you do is make a fist, then you strike with the bottom rather than the knuckles. Try it!

No good? That's because you haven't got the stance, bub. The first thing we learned was the stance. I got it quick because I'd watched how Turbo stood. You want to hurt someone good, you need the stance.

*

NOW, HOW THIS ALL came about was that as I considered how to finish the Donna Juan profile yesterday afternoon, something white and trailing came through the window with a clang, taking out the microwave. Followed by another that nearly did for Andy's chin as he approached the damage area . . . *Enemy fire incoming!* Out ran Fabiana, Andy following (Hyatt observing), too quick for two men who'd paused for a moment to check the effect of their missiles, and weren't expecting pursuit, so that as they turned to mount a pair of Viper 125s and make off on the flyover, Andy kicked high at the first, failing to connect. The men now came at Andy and Fabiana, and the first headbutted Andy – not without effect, since they were wearing helmets. Andy sat down and tried to grasp the legs of the man as he put the boot in, while Fabiana blocked a haymaker from the second man, flat-handed him on the helmet, sent in knee jabs to his groin, punched him low, and as he sagged, stepped back, made space and kicked. Then to Andy's aid, blocking blows, jabbing with her feet at his attacker's knees, driving him off with roundhouse kicks. Meanwhile, the fella she'd done staggered to the kerb, and the two men mounted their mopeds like a storm was blowing head-on. She gave chase a few yards as they exited westward on the pavement, picking up speed, then returned to Andy, whose nose streamed as she brought him in, raging, red, exultant. Was that the best Mulhall could do? Fucking pussy! Yes, yes, Fabiana said. Now let me see that. Broken. Tending to the nose with a napkin from her drawer. While Andy made energetic movements, refusing to sit still, I examined the missiles, which were half-bricks in carrier bags. One of them contained a note, written on a strip of till roll: *Sorry about this, but you ain't worth a libel suit! (Phase 1)*. I put it in my pocket. Behind me, Andy blustered and exulted. If that was the best, the *Chronicle* had won! Escaping from Fabiana, he ran out with his camera and took pictures of the broken windows for the next edition. As he came in, he winced and held his side. Probably had a rib or two broken by the driver's kicks. Without Fabiana there, he'd have come off a sight worse; so much for Tarzan stuff. But a fat lot of good I'd been. And they'd be back in force, since 'Phase 1' meant nothing on its own. Meanwhile, there was Fabiana's performance to marvel at; and it was here she revealed (to me, at least) she was an instructor in Krav Maga.

Hey?

Krav Maga. A form of self-defence devised by a Hungarian called Imi Lichtenfeld in the 1930s, to help his community defend themselves against anti-Semites, who definitely weren't confined to Germany in that decade. Lichtenfeld was a skilled boxer and wrestler, but he sussed that martial arts and what you needed in street fighting were quite different, and that's why he devised his system, which was fast and simple, since it was based on natural movements, reflexes and reactions (such as when you throw a hand up to block a blow). There wasn't time to teach his people ring skills, the way intimidation was going. How to put someone down, take them out, cripple them, if necessary, kill them, that's what they needed to learn fast. When the war started, Lichtenfeld escaped by boat, he fought under the British in North Africa, made it to Palestine. After the war, he trained Jewish paramilitaries against the Arabs; later in life, he trained the Israeli army, the IDF, in unarmed combat. Krav Maga was their system. What was up?

I was staring at her. The world was full of surprises, forces, people who were something other, extra, than you took them for.

'You seem surprised, Carl!'

'Did Andy know?' I was a journalist. Wasn't meant to be surprised. That was understood. When I went out to get the story, I knew what I was after. Wasn't depth, and it wasn't character.

'About this? Yes – didn't you? Of course he did!'

'Why didn't you tell me, though?' I asked stupidly, like I'd just found out that sexual intercourse was the efficient cause of all these people moving around and looking at their phones, queueing on computers for Olympic tickets, writing about criminals.

'You could have asked. You've never asked me about myself. All the time you've been here.' She moved on her chair in a slow arc. Andy's eyes were starting to blacken.

Why didn't you? She's a woman. Don't want to know what else they do. That it?

'You have to be careful who you tell about it, Carlo,' helping me now. 'People think Israeli tactics are fascist, lots of people do, all the intellectuals, and the socialists, and I thought you'd be like that, coming from *The G*******. That's so, isn't it, Carl?'

'It is so, but not with me. Especially now.' I thought of Eldine Matthews. Thought of Donna Juan, Lolly Morris. Hate flows and gathers, hate flows back, like a bore tide. I thought of Vincent Drew – and couldn't reckon it.

'Well, personally, I don't identify with groups or movements – and I don't invent enemies and monsters, when the problem's something you can settle on your doorstep, like just now. Sort it, forget it, move on. If it comes back, do the same; till it's tired of coming back and it leaves you alone.'

And that's an individual. Viva Fabiana! Proof against Mulhall, White Power, Black Flag!

*

SO SHE'D PERSUADED ME to come to an induction at a gym where she instructed (to be followed by personal training if I dug it). Which was how I came to be sparring with Lolly Morris. And it was good to feel her punch, and elbow-smash and hammer the long blue pad I held in an arm grip, imagining her tormentors. These drills were timed at one minute. You slacked off, Fabiana or Instructor Alex yelled at you, or they came right up and said something in your ear. Ah, you know the lung-scrape, heart-crack, of a minute's violence? The quicklime thirst? Helps to think of murder scenes. You mind your body less. And when the rubber knife comes down in that arc, pretend you're Eldine Matthews. This time you don't die, son. And when you punch, don't clump your fist from the off, like thugs and cowboys and hardmen in photographs with heavy rings; keep your hand quite loose till the impact; that way, you get more snap and speed in the punch. With a bunch of fives at shoulder height, like *I'll smash your fucking teeth down your throat*, what happens is the tension comes too soon, sapping force and elasticity; four-fifths of the way to the target, let the fist appear; strike with fist knuckles, not fingers. And don't forget the stance! Feet on the diagonal of a rectangle, left foot forward, right heel raised, keep your face covered, Lolly! I'm coming for you! Pad up, gal!

By the end of the session, I was buzzing, fronting Pete de Lacey in the corridor of The Old Placentia, as he gave me a dead arm, and Karen said she saw fate in me. They'd shown us a neck blow we should never use, but here was the way you did it . . .

PART III

Women and Armistice

CHAPTER 34

BUMPING INTO LOLLY IN the gym'd been a surprise, so either she hadn't mentioned the induction to Karen, or Karen'd forgotten, for Karen knew my destination that Saturday morning. At any rate, Lolly was meeting Karen now, so *I* went along as a surprise. On our way she told of Karen's fame among their colleagues, who were begging her to go home sick when she turned up yesterday morning. She refused, bit the nail, taught her classes. 4 p.m. she took the interview by storm.

'We celebrated again last night,' I told Lolly. 'Two bottles of Taittinger. I don't know how she does it.' On the low wall of The Horseshoe, we clinked glasses. Glowing from Krav Maga, Lolly drank a pint of Urquell. Beyond lay Town Hall. I watched for her shining hair. The pavement was narrow. From behind another stroller she'd bob out, all over Lolly. Didn't do to make a fuss of your man . . . *So what did you think, Lol, when you saw him in shorts? Did you have a fright? No idea you were up for this lark. Get us a drink, our Carl, don't just stand there gawping! . . .*

She made no such entrance.

Didn't answer her phone, and when we checked the flat, she wasn't home, and there was no message, no sign of struggle, nothing missing, nor sign of packing. Lolly took off her pumps and went about in pale footlets checking Karen's beauty stuff, and her dressing table and the bathroom, and told me everything was there, while I sat by the alcove like a pilot in a dive. When Lolly said we should call the police, I asked if Karen wasn't at her place, and she was puzzled at the question, so she couldn't have known Karen's plan when I came in on Thursday night. There hadn't been any problem between us, had there? Which got me in the heart, because it meant that Karen had kept all her worries about me and my 'work' to herself, without a word to her best mate. And it meant (though I knew this already) that whoever'd taken her would find she wouldn't snitch on me, not a thing; so they'd have to torture her; and still she wouldn't . . .

'Was there a problem?' Lolly said again. 'Please answer, Carl!'

'No,' I told her.

'She wouldn't ever not keep an arrangement, Carl. Never.' Lolly shook her head. For her height, she had long feet, twisting one behind the other ballerina fashion.

'I know.'

'We should call the police then.' She had her phone in her hand.

'We'd have to go to the station, Lol. For missing persons.'

'I'll come with you.'

This I didn't care for. Explaining to the duty sergeant or duty inspector why I thought my wife might have disappeared was going to require a lot of information, much of it incriminating. By the time I'd finished, he'd be applying for warrants for everyone on our team. Not only that. The whole Mulhall–Arnold business was a thing the police probably didn't want reminding of (outside investigations they may, or may not, be pursuing themselves), on some such principle as 'Keep it in the family' or 'Don't be stirring shit round this way, matey!' And where was my evidence? George Arnold spoke to my wife on holiday, and again at a mayoral function? . . . *Did he threaten to abduct her there and then, sir? He didn't? Was nasty language used? Not as such, sir? So was Mr Mulhall present during these meetings, sir? He wasn't? Is he in any way known to your wife, sir, or she to him? No? So on what do you base your suspicion, sir? Are you quite certain that she and yourself haven't had a tiff, sir? Mightn't the lady be upset at the company Sir's been keeping lately, and a certain incident at Walsingham Ponds where a defenceless fisherman was terrorized by a smoke-grey Granada Mk II? Oh, the lady applauded that particular action, did she, sir? Well we may be interested in speaking to the lady ourselves, when she elects to reappear, if Sir would be so good as to bring her along . . .* Yes, it was going to coil and recoil, involving the police. When once you've crossed over from the law as we had, the law can't help being more curious about you than any incident you report, or cause you maintain. Then the law turns philosophical: rising above practicality, life pressure, local circumstances, it thinks to itself, Now what is really going on here, in essence, under the aspect of eternity? What's he up to, this one? What's his game? Cross over from the law, you break a contract of understanding. Then your dedicated officer begins to scratch his chin, and speculate. Which isn't a way to get the wife back.

'Why are you looking like that, Carl?' Lolly standing back in 'ready' stance.

'OK. I've got an idea. Let's go, Lol.'

'There's something I have to tell you.' We were on the stairs now. 'I've been having trouble at work. You know about it, the boys with the project – which I've been logging on Tapestry.' And on to the street. 'Well, Karen took them aside in the corridor the other day, and told them to button their shirts so the T-shirts weren't showing. They did as they were told, grinning like they always are, then Karen asked one of them to read what it was he had written in marker on his rucksack. It was "Basil al-Kubaisi Commando: Che Guevara of Gaza Group". She told him that slogans weren't allowed in school and he had to clean it off, or buy a new rucksack, and he said his mum had just got him that one, and she couldn't afford a new one, so Karen said the choice was his and he wasn't to come in until he'd made it. Which it wasn't really in her initiative to do just like that, but you know how she likes to see to things herself – and she was thinking of me, of course.' Lolly's voice shook. 'I'd told her what it meant.'

The slogan rang a bell. Burning summer, long past; Minister for Drought; Close battered black and blue . . . 'What's it mean?'

'They hijacked a flight from Israel to Paris. They were German and Palestinian revolutionaries, Carl. When the plane landed in Uganda, where there was the stand-off, the Germans separated Jews from the other passengers. They let the others off the plane; the Jews, they kept on board.'

I remembered.

'It was a long time ago, but we haven't forgotten. One of the Jewish hostages, he showed the German leader his death-camp number. The German said they weren't Nazis, they were revolutionaries. Now these boys are researching the history – that, or someone's telling them all about it like it's a glorious matter – and putting it on their rucksacks like other boys put "Arsenal". We are going to the police, aren't we?'

'We are – now.'

'And the following day, when she was leaving, Karen told me two men were parked on the other side. One of them pointed, and he said something to the other. And the other one made a sign across his throat. He had a beard.'

In silence I walked on.

'I think they may have kidnapped her,' said Lolly at my side. 'Carl, that's what I'm scared of! We must go to the police.'

We could give them her version.

*

LATE EVENING, I PUT Lolly in a taxi. Then I went along to the passage between Frango Oporto and the charity shop, and upstairs to the flat where I'd talked with J. Fabian Morgan and Hanley. On the third knock, the door was opened. In joggers and a crimson vest, Turbo led me down the corridor and into the room with the L-shaped settee. So much for the training I'd done earlier; take years for arms like this fella's. Two holdalls on the floor, one of them zipped; so he'd been packing. I pictured him and Fabiana, one-on-one, square go. His hard-shell briefcase stood by an empty TV bench, where someone had made patterns in the dust.

Uninvited, I took the long settee: 'Are you leaving?'

Turbo sniffed. 'Ain't leaving.'

'Looks like it!'

'We ain't leaving cos we were never here, Mr Hyatt.'

I weighed this up, wishing he'd been gladder to see me. 'What was it then, this place?'

'Just a temp. We got others.'

'Really?'

'Yeah. We got others, that's how we roll.'

'Right. Where's Mr Morgan?'

Turbo watched me, flexing his lower leg. 'Fabian is doing fieldwork.' He shook his head as if I was terribly slow; a kick in the teeth might lively me up. 'He's gone to the beach.' Here, he bent to the other holdall, said something else about the beach, shook his head again.

'Which beach, Turbo?' Maybe the exasperation wasn't meant for me.

'When he says the beach, he means a lot of beaches, like all the way down the coast, man. Clifftops also.'

'Which coast?'

'The Peninsula of Gower.'

'And you're going down there with him?'

'That's my drill. Whatever way he winds about, I follow.'

I'd have liked to ask why this was, what'd brought these two together in the first place. No time for that. 'Why's he doing this, Turbo? Night before last, he was hot on revenge, following the plan like there was no time to lose. Now he's gone two hundred miles west, to the fucking seaside!'

Turbo looked at me sharply. Shouldn't have sworn. 'You must have gathered what's going down these last days, Mr Hyatt. We've got another party to contend with.'

'You mean it wasn't you, Morgan, Hanley, that did Danny Flowers?'

'There's that,' agreed Turbo with a nod. 'That is one consideration.'

Oh-ho! This didn't persuade me entirely. Indeed, if they were responsible for stringing Flowers up bollock-naked in Ugg boots, wouldn't they make themselves scarce exactly like this, packing up and quitting the scene?

'What you've got to understand, this is how Fabian Morgan regroups – you with me?'

'Right.'

'By looking for signs.'

'What?'

'There will be a sign,' recited Turbo, 'and when Mr Fabian checks it, we can recommence our operations.'

'What sort of sign? What d'you mean?' I could have screamed.

'A certain motion of birds, Mr Hyatt. Of the family of hawks.'

'Why's he had to go to Wales, for Christ's sake?'

'Cos the member of the family of hawks which is the kite, has returned to that area – which Mr Fabian happened to know.'

I held my head. 'You don't know what I'm up against. He's pissing about on the beach, and you're going down to join him! Where's Hanley? Is he regrouping too? You lot drag me into this mess, you follow me around, you jump out on the pavement, everywhere I go you fucking pop up, then when it gets bad, you're off bird-watching!'

'We were warned our strategy was too contemporary,' Turbo told me solemnly. 'That's the truth, Mr Hyatt. We ain't toying with you. We have to go back to advance.' Kneeling to speak, like to a child.

'Who warned you?'

'The lady.'

'Which lady?'

Saying something about a lady I knew as he uncoiled to answer his phone, Turbo left me chilling with the image of treachery . . .

Returning from the hall, he stared at his watch, like he wanted me out of there. I asked him when my wife warned them.

Warned them what?

That their strategy was too contemporary.

Wasn't my wife who warned them. It was the lady in the mews.

'The old lady? Sibyl Grove?' Immediate relief . . .

Wristwatch-fascinated, Turbo sniffed: 'Yeah.'

'When?'

'Within the last twenty-four.'

Since I spoke to her, Friday lunchtime. Black flash. *Your wife went along there yesterday . . . What if you never saw her again?*

'What did she tell you exactly?'

'Mr Fabian, she told him you was upset what she showed you on her tablet, about the dough boy that was lynched.'

'Right. And Mr Fabian, what did he say to that?'

'Mr Fabian said that was understandable, and he shook his head like this. Then, he said maybe this thing was getting out of hand and he shook his head for the second time, so.'

'And what happened then? Come on, Turbo – please. You don't know what I'm up against!'

'Sibyl Grove, she nodded her head.'

Christ. 'And what did she say?'

'She told Mr Fabian pell-mell antics ain't the only way. Ain't the right way either. Told him she seen it in the stones.'

'And?'

'You digested that already, Mr Hyatt?'

'Yeah – she told me the stones thing as well.'

'So why you asking?'

'Maybe she told you more.' Lame.

'Maybe so. You curious?'

This bastard had learned slow tricks from his guvnor. 'You know I am, Turbo.'

'So, she told him to watch where the hawks have returned. Count their numbers, and the way they fly.'

'What?'

'This being the science of augury. Which Mr Fabian happened to know.'

'What's this got to do with her stones?'

'A cobbled mews being a street of hawks, in ancient times, which Mr Fabian also happened to know.'

'So?'

'So this reminded him of his classical tradition, which he has almost forgot to observe –with our pell-mell antics.'

'Then?'

'The old lady goes to sleep in the sun.'

Jesus! 'Then?'

'Mr Fabian did one of his walks, the "Tarentum". Back and forth he goes like that dude from *Reservoir Dogs*, when he snipped the boydem's ear. This represents, one, Hannibal's taking of the city, two, Cunctator's retaking of the city. Like he's going forth, so, he's retreating to his lairs, supply dumps and strongpoints, so; then in final phase, he's going forth in triumph – also in patience.' Turbo attempted demonstration. 'Simple walk. In its simplicity, I ain't mastered it.'

I knew the feeling.

'Old lady was only shamming. I could see her peeping at Mr Fabian. She claps her hands, like, "That's the way, baby!"'

Yesterday, I could have enjoyed this. A patient, or indefinite, moratorium would have been welcome; or an alternative reality in which this lot (Donna Juan included) entertained themselves with fantasies of hawks. Instead of a 'pell-mell' revenge rush, a thickening, disintegrating, polymerizing, virtual plot. Then Sibyl Grove was a counsellor of violence evasion – wise woman! Yesterday . . .

'It's no good to me, Turbo, any of this. I can't find my wife.'

'Your wife, Mr Hyatt?'

'Yes, my wife. Karen. You know her.' The discipline of being patient with the young man, the gamut of aches from Krav Maga, were inducing a fever. Maybe this was the way. If I could actually die of chagrin, frustration, galloping vexation, before midnight, Karen'd reappear pronto to mourn. She'd be back and safe. Serve her right for worrying me. Let her organize the hearse, ride behind, fishnet veil over hazel eyes. I'd made my will. And if she didn't return, I'd be well out of this.

'I know her,' agreed Turbo, madding me further. 'We all went to the music hall together. She gave me hard times about Mr Fabian, and his powers of humour.'

'I'm sorry about that.'

'Bah!' said Turbo. 'She put me on my mettle. That's just drill. I'm cool with that, mate.'

'Listen, Turbo, that night I came up here with Mr Fabian and Hanley, you and Karen went off for a juice, or whatever.' Turbo watched me. Rather long teeth. In his arms, muscle drowsed. Here, I needed to go carefully. 'What did you talk about? I mean, did she say anything?' He watched me. 'Anything about why she's gone – or what's happened?'

'You think I ain't telling you something, Mr Hyatt, like I'm holding back?'

'Everyone else does,' I replied, not wanting him to take anything personal.

'Am I everyone?' Twice he curled and opened his fists.

'No. Of course not.'

'So we didn't talk about nothing.'

'What d'you mean? You just sat there?'

'Yeah. I just sat there. She – your wife – she did the talking.'

'So what did she talk about?'

'She talked about you. You've got a good woman there, man. You should quit this running around, acting like a pug.'

'Was she mad with me?'

'Now that – that ain't a man's question,' Turbo said severely. 'That you shouldn't need to ask. Your problem is you don't know if you're man or boy. Man, boy, soldier – you ain't sorted your status. Like you're shapeless.'

'Thanks.'

'Doing what you need to do, according to your status, you shouldn't give a damn if your lady's mad at you. That's not here or there. Once you've decided, you shouldn't mind. But you keep things from her like a little boy, then you go wiping your eyes in her skirt when she's caught you. Pah!'

He was calling me a pussy. Bang to rights. To him, her leaving must be quite in order. 'So she was complaining about me?'

'Never. Never once did she complain.' Turbo stared at his watch.

'What did she say then?'

'She said –' like a jet plane, Turbo's attention was leaving – 'said you was fatal. Said to keep it lope. Damn!' He left the room, returned in a leather hoodie, raised the holdalls: 'See you around, Mr Hyatt!'

CHAPTER 35

TURNING OVER TURBO'S LAST words, I sat alone on the sofa. The air was close, biscuity; tubes rumbled. Karen didn't come, no one came. Eleven. I could go to Father Raymond: that was giving up on her being alive, close to hand. There were texts from Lolly, Donna Juan. I could head for World's End: catch Hanley at home, or wait for him.

I was saved the journey. Exiting The Tavern by the side door, Hanley hastened down the lane past Van Spenser's old cabin. At his side was a blonde; they were talking hard, Hanley making with his hands. As I slowed down behind him, Paulie popped up to my right.

'Hoy, Hyatt! Where have you been? Hair looks like a fucking hedge!'

'What you up to at this time, Paulie?'

'We're watching Spain–France. Came out to smoke.'

'You and Tyrus?'

'There's a bunch of people downstairs. It's our Euro club. Fucking rabble.'

'What are you drinking?'

Paulie sucked on his roll-up, rooted in his trouser pockets: 'Aberlour 12, Double Black, Andalusian gin.'

'Andalusian gin?'

'A woman's drink.'

'You've got women down there?'

Paulie laughed. 'Course we got women. We're men, aren't we? Come down and join us, Hyatt, you don't look yourself.'

'I can't. I've got trouble.' I could open up with this fella; often enough he'd touched me; so we had our intimacy. I'd let him in on things; not deeply, but more freely than with other men.

'You have trouble, you should be home with your wife, Hyatt – not sneaking round the lane like a pimp. What you up to, anyway? Got a girlfriend waiting in The Hank? With a wife like yours, Hyatt, I wouldn't be sneaking round the lane at night. Wouldn't be in the cellar with Tyrus either. I'd be home with her on the settee, nice bottle of wine, hold her hand and watch the football, or a film – understand me? And don't look like you're going to argue! Paulie's been around.' He spat out his roll-up, rooted in his pockets, arched his back, stuck his silver face in mine.

'That is the trouble, Paulie,' I told him quietly. 'She's not at home. I don't know where she is.'

'What? You're kidding! The lady ran out on you?'

'If that's what it was, I'd be OK – at least I'd know. But I don't know what the hell's happened to her.'

'You called her?'

'Of course. No answer. No texts. No note in the house. I was meant to meet her with a pal of hers this afternoon. She never turned up at the pub.'

'Where was this?'

'The Horseshoe. By Town Hall.'

'Did you tell the cops?'

'Yeah.'

'For all the good the bastards do. More interested in complaints from people who've been called a name and they haven't got the guts to sort it out themselves. Which is when the bastards aren't sharing swag with crooks, and fitting up anyone who tells the truth about them. Understand me? Come in, Hyatt.' He took my arm. 'Drink with Paulie.'

Hoots rose from the cellar, a Slav or Spaniard rapping, so we stayed in the shop and I sat in his chair like I was there for a cut, while Paulie reviewed his fiery squads. We clinked glasses of Glen Garioch (48%).

'You know enough about cops.'

'Yeah.'

'More than me. Not that I haven't had the experience, you understand. As immigrants, we had enough trouble, me and my brother. They'd pick us up for sniffing, the bastards. Put us in a cell for thirty hours in '74, when we marched against the Turks.' Paulie Charalambous hawked. 'So when I see a cop, I'm on guard, you understand, Carl?' Sniffing richly. 'And when I come across a bad cop, I get a twinge in my bones, like fucking arthritis. You understand me?'

'Yeah.' The whisky had an extra burn. Was he going to add to what I knew?

'There's a fella comes here once a week: he wants a beard trim or a head shave, one week the beard, next the head.'

'Is he a regular?'

'He's no fucking regular. Last two, three months, maybe a little longer.'

'That he's been coming?'

'That's right. Yeah – you remember the time you came down the cellar, you and that wop lawyer?'

'Hanley's not a wop.'

'Don't split hairs now, Hyatt. I'm asking if you remember.'

'Yeah. You were watching Cahill tackle Van Persie.'

'That's right.' Paulie sniffed. 'Around that time it was, he first came in. Sat there in the corner waiting, pretending to read the paper, looking round, like this, all the time listening. When I get him in the chair, I get the twinge like I never had it. He didn't want to chat. One-word answers to everything. In the mirror, he was watching my eyes. I didn't like this bastard. Wouldn't surprise me he was a killer – not a murderer, a killer, professional.'

'What age, Paulie?'

'Late forties, older maybe. Fit though. Not gym fit like Tyrus and his pals. Different fit.'

'What was he after, Paulie? Any idea?'

'He was waiting for someone to come in. It so happened, whoever he was waiting for to come in, they never did at the time he was here. Lucky accident maybe, for whoever it was. You any ID on this bastard, Hyatt?'

'Yeah. He's called Bowler, he's ex-military. For twenty years or so, he's been a cop. You've got him sussed, but he's only wingman for someone worse.'

'Well if we're talking about the same person, he's made his appearance as well.' Paulie sniffed.

'A silver-haired fella?'

'Yeah. He's come in here with Bowler. Sat there in the corner while I did Bowler's beard, and he's the opposite. Chatting like he owns the place, calling over to Tyrus, all the time, looking round. More than once, he's been. Tries to get to know me like only a man who's trying to trip you does. I've been around. Friendliness, that's one thing; this fella, he's like my grandmother warned me. She stirred soup, she chopped salads, she prayed. That was her life. A village woman, understand me? Here's what she warned me: "Paulie, be careful day by day. Sooner or later, Satan pays a call. On everyone."' Paulie Charalambous sniffed for his grandmother. 'He came in here, Carl, just over there he sat . . . Pah! What the fuck is all this?' He poured us more whisky. We sat silent. I shivered. Paulie patted my shoulder.

'Who's he looking for, Paulie? Is it me?'

'You're known to him?'

'Karen and I bumped into him on holiday. It was an accident, had to be; but I've been feeling since that it was meant, like there was something behind it. His name's Arnold, George Arnold.'

'So he's on your tail?'

'I suppose this is what I'm frightened of.'

'Takes a man to say he's frightened.' Paulie hawked. 'That one-eyed Welshman, the comedian, you know him?'

'Fabian Morgan?'

'Whatever he calls himself. Changes his name like I change my vest. They're on his tail too.'

'How d'you know?'

'This fella Arnold, showed me his picture. Said he wanted to catch the guy's show, but he never advertised or put posters up, so did I know how to get in touch with him? I got the other photos up there.' He was proud of the celebrities and celebrity associates he'd shorn, was Paulie. Had them framed and signed on the wall, above his whisky bar. 'Like I'm born fucking yesterday. Never heard of him. Welsh comedian? Impossible. And this lying bastard, he laughed with me like we're hand-in-glove. So I watched him with the one you call Bowler, when they went outside.'

Confirming what I'd heard of Morgan's history, this also appealed to my instinct for preservation: they wanted Morgan more than me. But why would they come in here looking for him? This needed elucidation, even as it rang a bell. Paulie wasn't flamming. For a while, me and memory chased in the dark – tig! Downstairs with Hanley, that time . . .

'Tyrus knows Fabian Morgan, Paulie? How's that?'

Paulie looked drunk, clasping his forehead: 'I'm too fucking old for this, Carl!'

'Come on! You asked me in here. Tell me, Paulie! You don't know what I'm up against! Time's running out!'

Paulie looked at his hand. His hand was steady. He rubbed and pinched his shoulder. His shoulder was wrecked. So he told me . . .

Him and Tyrus used to pop in at The Tavern. Every Friday. Upstairs was their place. There they could talk about football, family, so forth, in peace. All sweet, till they started the Glee Club. Then you get these middle-class bastards, students with ponytails, freaks with beads, up at the mic, trying to make people laugh who just wanted to grumble about the wife, kids, girlfriend. Which was what the pub was invented for – Paulie'd read the history of these things. So him and Tyrus, they said to themselves, Why should these fucking nincompoops drive us from our bar? Paulie and Tyrus versus the Glee Club.

Paulie showed how they'd sat, arms folded, faces cold as seals. Thus they'd broken stand-ups' dreams. Word got round.

The pub put up a cash prize – not for a laugh, just a smile – they brought in a judge that was impartial. The judge watched Paulie and Tyrus. One night a glass-eye bastard turns up, dressed like Ben Hur, mumbling, walking this way and that, like he'd shat himself. Worst yet, so they're thinking.

Did he tell jokes?

Jokes? More like history lessons. Paulie knew history. Paulie didn't need lessons. Paulie and Tyrus sat firm. Glass-eye had nothing coming. Paulie'd seen the great acts. Tarby. Tommy Cooper. Frankie Carson. Hippodrome, Palladium. Clem Sandler got Paulie tickets. Cutting Clem's hair since '77. Never seen a thing like this one-eyed freak. Credit to him: Glass-Eye wasn't fazed. Wouldn't let up with Paulie and Tyrus. If he could break them, he had the room. They sat him out like men of stone. Bastard came back for more.

One Friday, Tyrus brought his nephew. Now this nephew, he was running wild, a box of trouble. Sixteen, seventeen, fucking delinquo. Tyrus bought him beer, packet of nuts. Starts flicking nuts at One-Eye. One-Eye tells him, Flick all you want, son. I'll still be doing this when you ain't got any nuts left to flick, including the pair you got stuffed down your trousers. And the nephew's wearing strides so tight, they look like they been fucking sprayed on. Which the nephew finds amusing, and the more Uncle Tyrus threatens not to let him and Paulie down, more the fool giggles, tee-hee-hee, then the whole fucking place cracks up and the judge – a councillor, Labour man – he scores it to One-Eye. Well, Ty and Paulie, they're men enough to know when they're licked. And end of the day, what's the fucking issue? Grown men trying not to laugh. A joke in itself. How are you going to sort the world out, making an issue of something like that? So they become friends with this comic, Fabian, Morgan, Cunctator, whatever he calls himself. And when he hears Tyrus's name, you know what? He says, No wonder it was so hard with you. It means 'rock', your name, sir, and you go back before the Romans to ancient Tyre! I'm Morgan, which means 'sea', and you are Tyrus the Rock! Now what about this young man?

Well, Tyrus tells him this kid, this *thing*, Turbo, he's allergic to ambition, and he ain't once done a hand's turn, except he worked in a pizza place for a night until the customers complained he dropped ash from his reefer on the food while he's coming through from the kitchen. Won't work, won't work out. Tyrus's taken him to the gym. In the gym he's an embarrassment, mooching, rapping, staring at ladies' arses. Mother's at the end of her tether with him. He's hanging out with rough boys, some of 'em already been in jail. Which is why she's sent him to Uncle Tyrus for a holiday, get him off his patch.

'Hold on, Paulie!' I'd been trying to keep up with this. 'You're saying Turbo is Tyrus's nephew?'

'Yeah. That's what I'm telling you.'

'How – Tyrus being Lebanese?'

'How? Tyrus's sister, Nancy, she married a Jamaican. When Turbo came along, he made himself scarce.'

My shallow reckoning of hates and sides was whirled by this genealogy, but the new shapes I couldn't make out under pressure, except as in a dream that there might have been no need – or Turbo could stick up for Lolly . . .

'So, Paulie, what happened with Turbo?'

'Well, Fabian Morgan, he says to Tyrus, "I'll take this lad on. What d'you say? I need a PA. I'll train him, pay him, make him into something." And Tyrus puts it to him, thinking the kid's going to turn his nose, but the kid, he's "*Aaaiiiight*, I go with this dude. If only cos he's funny. He snapped you, Uncle Ty. Wild style."'

So that was the story there. And he'd made Turbo into a regular soldier, had Morgan – good as his word. Seasoned in nephews: Turbo, Robbie Woods . . .

'Listen, Paulie, why was Arnold asking about Morgan – apart from the spiel about wanting to catch his act? What d'you know?'

'He said they want to do a deal with him.' Deep voice from the stairhead.

'Hey, Tyrus, what you doing there in the gloom?' called Paulie. 'Where's your pals?'

'Game's over. The Spanish are partying.'

'What happened?'

'Alonso scored twice.' Like a piece of nature, Tyrus approached our corner. 'Yeah, I heard the old cop outside, with the guy who drives him. Parked the other side.' Tyrus nodded where. On the pavement, he kept a Bonneville 800. Must have thought they were out of earshot . . .

I lived the scene for myself. Arnold leaning at his ease, buck jacket, Bowler hands in pockets, back to Tyrus. What d'you hear at that distance, two devils chatting in low-to-normal voices? Maybe you hear exactly what's said, though that may be what they want you to hear. And maybe you hear what confirms your general experience, supports your imagination, then you miss a word or stress, or you add them. They could have said, 'We need to deal with him,' nothing about *doing* a deal. Savvy? *We've got to deal with him.* Then all speculation about Mulhall, the criminal's sense of disproportionate violence between his nephew and Morgan – all that was vain. They wanted to do him again; not pay him off, or yield to some demand. He was getting out of hand was the implication – wasn't it? Treatment required. Supposing *him* was Morgan. Jesus. . .

'His wife's gone, Ty,' Paulie was saying. 'Doesn't know where to find her.'

Tyrus didn't laugh. 'That gin he brought you, what'd he say that time?'

'Dear God, Ty!' Paulie dry-wiped his silver face and sagged. 'Said he'd met Hyatt's wife on holiday, she dropped something, earring, necklace, he wanted to return it to her cos it looked like a valuable one. Wanted her address. Understood they lived round here, and the husband, he looked well groomed, so he was hoping to catch him in the shop, but him and you, Carl, you were like ships in the night. So he wondered if I knew where you lived, so he could take it up, or just post it through the door, cos a good turn never did anyone harm, in his experience.'

'Who said this?' I cried wildly. 'Arnold? What the fuck did you tell him, Paulie? Did you tell him anything?'

'Hey!' Tyrus crouched beside me. 'Paulie never turned a friend over in his life. You can trust me on that, Carl!'

'That's right, Carl,' Paulie told me. 'Ty put the fucking wind up me there cos I'd forgot something. But I kept it like this!' Across his lips he made a sign.

'But what about this gin?'

Paulie indicated his bar. 'Said he could see I was a connoisseur; thought I might like to try it. It was a nice bottle. Unusual gin. I said thanks, very kind. But I didn't tell him nothing.'

I believed him. Arnold would have meant it as an investment. They'd come again; sooner or later, Paulie'd say something, or not say something; they'd make use of it. You can't tell certain people nothing; they're already on the way to what they want; what you withhold is just extra juice. But I was certain now what had happened to Karen. Lolly's fears were groundless.

'We're with you, Carl,' said Tyrus. His big hand dropped on my shoulder.

'Yeah, Hyatt,' Paulie said. 'I'm old, but there's one fight left in me. Let it be this one. Consultant says I've got two, three years in the tank with this heart.'

I thanked them for their support and left. Lights were out in The Hank of Rope. I'd missed Hanley.

CHAPTER 36

HIS PHONE WAS ON voicemail. On the way to World's End, I stopped at the flat, hoping for a miracle . . . *Where the hell have you been, Carlo? It's bloody two o'clock in the morning!* A chair'd been budged in the alcove. She'd been back, and gone again. I hugged and kissed it. Dear chair! Don't be a twerp. Lolly sat there. Or someone's been in. Cunts fitting you up. Frenzied, I went through drawers; weary, I went through drawers. We had so many fucking drawers, so many places to hide something bad. We had a desktop, three laptops, tablet. Guess my password? They'd bring a spook to crack it; hide paedo matter on the drive. Again I tried Hanley. Where was the bastard when I needed him? His home address I didn't actually know; this I haven't let on, for reasons of morale — as a captain might pretend he knows the route, so the troops won't frag him. I called his name, I cursed his name. North and south, traffic moved. There was nothing.

Seconds later, here he was with the woman. He'd seen my lights on. Like he'd stepped out of winter sun, my eyes dazzled. He fussed about introductions, not disturbing Karen. I settled them in the living room, fetched booze, came back. Hanley, russet with drink, was at the window being funny. On the settee, Claire Sykes grinned. She was not at ease. Hanley asked behind his hand, 'Is Karen asleep?'

About to tell the truth, on instinct I held back. Say Hanley knew something, he'd show clearer signs if I pretended all was as usual where Karen was concerned. Wait and see. Such cunning might have been pointless, or worse still, time-wasting; but telling blokes she'd gone wasn't helping find her either. Time to keep something up my sleeve, till I could max it. I agreed she was asleep, and shut the door, so, and Hanley, glinting, lowered his voice: '*Paisano*, Claire is our woman!'

Claire Sykes rolled her eyes. She was squiffy as well. They'd had quite a night, the pair of them, but Claire took a bumper of Viña Sol, while Hanley rocked his brandy, wishing he could smoke.

'She knows them, knows everything about them!' Hanley whispered.

'Smoke if you want,' I told him, at normal volume. 'Just open the window.' From the way he'd shown up when called, I was surging.

'No, no! Karen won't want the place stinking!'

'It's cool. – So who's "them"?'

Hanley lit a roll-up, murmuring to Claire, who seemed to want one as well. I provided an ashtray. Claire's eyes caught me in the cross-hairs. She looked away. Blonde, strongly built, she had a dock-leaf scar on her left leg that rose above the tan. Was he having it off with her? Some contrast with pale Milly.

'The de Laceys. Isn't that so, Claire?' Claire shrugged. Hanley sat down by her, ventriloquially. Claire had been with Pete de Lacey. Claire nodded. Did he mean once, or today? Or she'd slept with him? Hanley and his doll weren't clarifying. I knew what I wanted it to mean (as a journalist I did); my curiosity repelled me. There she sat, blowing smoke, making eyes. Had he brought her for a three-way? Her nails were painted chocolate. That would be the end. The moral end. Yet the way she looked got me dead centre, that lustful sniper gaze. Where was Father Raymond when you needed him? Hanley actually winked at me. Did he mean we were getting somewhere? Or, *What say we move on her*, paisano*!* But where was the difference? For a moment, distinctions vanished. Maybe we were in hell.

I asked if I could get her water or a snack. She looked delighted, said she was OK; I was glad all it took was kindness. Then this pair began to set it out together. They had quite a tale.

———————

CLAIRE SYKES WAS ONCE a copper. The CID was her dream. Not long into her training, a DI came to the college, asking to see her and a couple of other young women on the development programme. They'd been noticed as three 'keen beans', there was nothing the service liked better than a keen bean, and it so happened a certain undercover op required one. It was important. It wasn't without risk, as these things went. Indeed, they were free to say no and get on with their training – totally free. But anyone who volunteered and came through, well she could expect to be rewarded with promotion (immediate effect) to Detective Sergeant. Naturally enough, one of the young women asked what manner of work it was, and the DI said, Ah, he was coming to that, they were entitled to a full briefing, but first they'd have to sign a J70 (basically, a secrecy doc), not to disclose anything – whether they volunteered or not. Of course, they were free to leave now, and not sign anything. The DI went to the door and he opened it, and one of the young women, she rose and walked away, blushing; which left Claire and the one who'd asked about the manner of work, a feisty person called Nora Field. So the DI had these two sign, then he explained the work, and the background – though he was sure they'd read about the case for themselves in the papers, and so forth, which was the murder of Eldine Matthews.

So the work was to get to know the gang responsible, or 'L Troop' as they were known, and become friendly with them. And by friendly was meant hanging out with them, meeting for drinks, and indeed whatever might develop from friendship – such as physical relationships. Because it was a fact that serious criminals uttered things at moments in a physical relationship that they kept shtum about at all other times, e.g. when being questioned by police officers, when being covertly filmed, when appearing at coroners' inquests, even when being asked by their mums if they done it or not, and cross my heart. Wasn't a nice fact, but the nettle had to be grasped: lying in the dark beside a lady, a criminal often forgot to keep quiet and dropped his guard. And as the psychologists explained, it wasn't surprising, since one of the trickiest things for criminals was beating the notorious human habit of talking about oneself sooner or later, which honest folk, like the DI, and no doubt the two young ladies before him, could indulge in whenever they pleased without fear of arrest. Any questions so far?

Nora Field had a question. How were they going to get to know the gang? The DI nodded. Very sensible. And of course, they weren't expected to infiltrate this mob under their own steam, who, as well as being pretty nasty, were inclined to be suspicious of strangers. No. Introductions would be made.

Made by who?

Why, by someone known to and trusted by the gang. This being an agent with the field names 'Blue Wolf' or '.303'.

So 'Blue Wolf' was a copper?

Here, the DI made a mouth-zipping sign and winked twice, at Claire, at Nora. Whereupon Nora Field stood up and said sorry, she couldn't be doing with this hush-hush stuff. If the service wanted her to put her fanny on the line, she deserved to know a bit more about who'd be organizing it, and for all she knew, Blue Wolf 303 might be a pimp, a perv or a hoover who'd manipulate their tits off and chain them both up in his garage; and the DI smiled and said he admired her frankness, and thanks for her attendance at the briefing. But when she'd walked out, he told Claire that Nora Field wouldn't have been fit for the job, since he'd been advised she had a tendency to lose her rag – as they'd just witnessed – in a way that would jeopardize the mission from the off. And she hadn't been listening either. Had Claire noticed how? He looked at Claire like a good teacher, but Claire didn't want to do her mate Nora down, yet his look was waiting on her kindly, so she said, off the top of her head, was it by saying 'Blue Wolf 303'?

When she should have said . . . ?

When she should have said 'Blue Wolf or .303' – was that it? And the DI, he clapped his hands, like 'Bingo!' That was it. He'd slipped the pair of them some info and what had TDC Field gone and done? She'd stuck two options together when the briefing clearly indicated they were alternatives, meaning, the one or the other – if you were listening, rather than dreaming or getting ahead of yourself. Now, if you made a mistake at that level, which was known to old-school cop-pers like himself as 'gumming', you were apt to do it all the way up, and this didn't only harm operations in the field, where you had to make split-second decisions and distinctions, and certainly not take it that one thing or person would do as well as another. No, it didn't just cock up fieldwork. It was also fatal for your reports, and the presentation of evidence. For if there was one thing defence lawyers were sharp on, it was gumming as a sign of confusion at every level, and many a case had gone west because of an honest copper (and unfortunately here and there, a dishonest copper) maintaining that *a* was *b*, when the jury could plainly see it wasn't; and then what happened? Our good name suffered, ugly phrases such as 'fitting up' were on people's lips, and the media started remembering Countryman; then your chatterers were wondering if things had actually improved one bit since nineteen-seventy-whatever, the service had to investigate itself all over again, and you could forget about bringing murderers to book. Lesson: the service had to be extremely shrewd, who it entrusted with deep missions.

Which was why the DI'd employed his 'filter' on this little briefing, which was to say, he'd made up both the names of the agent, 'Blue Wolf' and '.303', and Nora swallowed the pair of them so fast they ended up in one big lump in her gullet, like a fishbone that finishes you off, whereas Claire'd been a sight more canny, and said nothing straight off, which was a sure sign of good sense in his experience. And in confidence, the days of TDC Field in the CID were already numbered – she was strictly uniform, and her mum had better have kept it pressed for her as well! Whereas TDC Sykes had a future as bright as the afternoon (here, the DI got up and held the black blind aside for a mo, sunlight filling that part of the briefing room, before he let it fall back). Assuming she was up for it?

Yes, sir, she was up for it.

Attagirl!

Later that week, she was taken down to Greenwich and shown a flat. The flat was hers, for as long as the operation took. She was given a wire, a brooch recorder and a compact with a camera in it, as well as a mobile phone with a camera – which was a one-off at the time – and some other bits of James Bond-style kit; but the DI who was handling her, who she'd been getting to know since the briefing, he told her straight: there was no substitute for basic intelligence gathering. Ears and eyes! Ears, eyes, a cool head – and he wasn't kidding her, maybe a bit of courage as well; he couldn't promise that wouldn't be required of her. Was she still up for it?

Yes, sir!

Attagirl!

Quickly it got heavy. This was around four years after the murder, and the gang were larging it, running wild. They had a bad rep and they were at liberty. They could do what the hell they wanted. People were terrified of them. So they were fencing stolen goods, selling drugs, protecting turf, extorting money from Asian stores, takeaways, pubs, taxi-firms; they carried weapons with impunity – knives, sprays, oven-cleaner aerosols, truncheons, brass knuckles, coshes, screwdrivers, hammers, grenades. Wherever they went, people made way for them, parted to let them through, smiled and nodded, or avoided their eyes. They had flash cars, pockets full of notes, expensive clobber. And they seldom stood still for more than five minutes. Which made it difficult to track them down, but easy to run into them: from bar to bar, pub to pub, club to club, they moved like they were storm-driven.

Meanwhile, Claire'd been introduced to Kim. How the introduction came about was that the DI'd taken Claire for Sunday lunch at a carvery and a slim girl with a brush-cut carrying a short-haired cat came over and said hi, long time no see. The cat had a fawn-champagne coat and thrust its head eagerly at the DI, then escaped from Kim's arms and began to climb up the DI.

'Oh, Frankie!' called Kim. 'Naughty!'

'He's all right!' the DI said.

'He likes your jacket!' Kim explained. 'That's what it is.'

'Sit down and have a potato!' the DI told her as Frankie went at him in his rough pranking way. 'Or how about some crumble and custard?'

'I've had lunch, thanks,' said Kim.

'Bet you only ate soup, gel!'

'I didn't then! I had a roast and *all* the trimmings!'

Frankie was short for 'Frankenstein'. Claire asked why he was called that, and Kim said it was because no human could control him, but he did like human company – in fact, that was all he wanted. As long as he got company, he'd do no harm. If he didn't get company, he'd turn the house over, wreck the place. But it was only cos he was looking for friends. Which had Claire wondering if Kim was the agent, the way she came out with her lines like she'd practised, and appeared so prompt. The brush-cut, lack of make-up, and rather clear eyes, made her seem younger than she probably was. A good disguise, Claire was thinking, as Kim darted glances at her while telling Frankie off.

As to Claire's own cover, well it had fallen out this way. The DI asked her if she knew anyone in the area who ran a business; didn't matter how well – a vague connection was satisfactory, might even be securer. Well, she had a cousin she hadn't seen since a kid, but his fianceé, she was positive, ran a salon. Leave it to me, the DI told her, and the following day she had a chair at Gemma's, in Plumstead. It was all fixed. She wouldn't have to do ladies' hair; it was just non-official cover, to pinch a bit of jargon from the spies! Anyone asked, she could say she was training there; and if anyone came looking for her, she was at home with a stomach upset. With Gemma, it was all kosher.

At any rate, that Sunday afternoon, the DI found he had to move on pronto and he left Kim and Claire chatting, then Kim asked if she fancied taking Frankie for his stroll, so they came along the lane with Frankie on a slim leather lead, and into the woods, where Kim let him mess around and chase squirrels, and then down into Welling, where they saw two black guys get out of a car beside a shop with steel shutters with a lot of graffiti on them, and spit on the shutters and kick the door like they meant it, then get in the car and drive off again, which got Frankie excited and rearing on his lead. Claire asked what all that was about. It was the Nazi bookshop, that's what, Kim told her. Claire took that in. Hadn't been mentioned in her briefing. She should get back to the flat and make notes; but how to shake off Kim (who'd been kind to pal her around)? She said she was expecting a call from her mother, to see how she was getting on in the new place. Oh, said Kim, don't you have a mobile? Here was a problem. If she denied it, Kim might take that as a sign of distrust, since if she was the agent, she'd expect Claire to have the field kit mentioned earlier; also, Kim might have spotted it in her bag, which she'd opened a couple of times at lunch, and she didn't want to come across as a liar; so she said her mum was very old-school and would only phone her at home, and Kim laughed and asked where home was, and about that Claire had to tell the truth as well, since if Kim was the agent (and was checking her out this afternoon, as she suspected), she'd already have been given the address. So Claire looked at her watch and, oh dear, it was quite a way, she didn't realize how far they'd come (naming her road), but Kim kept looking at her smiling, then said she was going that way too, cos her boyfriend worked at The Black Gun, which was just round the corner, so they could get the bus together, and they jumped on a 96 with Frankie. By the time they'd got to Greenwich, Kim'd persuaded Claire to come for a drink later, since she'd sussed that Claire had no one at home, and didn't seem the type to be watching *Antiques Road Show*.

At The Black Gun, Kim's boyfriend made a fuss of Claire, which was just to be welcoming, and had Kim pretending to be jealous. The boyfriend was called Marcus. He bossed the bar well: punters he liked, he rewarded with his manner; when he did smile, he was your friend, and meant it. He had chocolatey eyes. On a wooden wall behind the bar were a couple of posters of young men barred from drinking in The Black Gun. Claire didn't recognize them, but when Marcus clocked her checking, he said they were just Charlton thugs, not consequential. Which got her thinking. And all the time, he was watching like he was waiting for someone in particular. So it wasn't a surprise that later that Sunday evening, Claire encountered one of the gang. By then, she'd had a few Pernods, and Kim'd got Marcus to make her a Red Witch. Getting tipsy was part of the cover. And when a young man in mirror shades appeared beside her at the bar (she hadn't noticed him come in), it all seemed worked out. The DI'd taken her to meet Kim, who'd introduced her to Marcus. They were both agents, and they'd made preliminary connections with L Troop – since Marcus was now greeting Pete de Lacey and introducing Claire. And it was her job to come on to him.

So she came on to him, kept touching his arm, and laughing when he said things. In The Black Gun he was the top boy, and he probably knew it; though he didn't seem to care all that much; it was like he was after something else, behind those mirror shades. For the time being, anyway, he went along with who he was: he took his money out to buy drinks for hangers-on and toadies who were hoping to treat him; he banged his bottle down and turned suddenly, and now and then he clenched his fist slowly, or made a throat-cutting sign, and either he laughed or shook his head when he did that. With racist remarks, he was sparing, limiting himself to throwaway comments on coons and Pakis; laughing once when someone said something in his ear about the taxi driver who got drowned in Victoria Dock, that that was the best you could expect from West Ham fans, who weren't even clever enough not to get banged up for it, seeing as they left enough evidence to fill a sixteen-yard skip, boasted what they'd done, then got turned in by their fucking step-mums. It was old hat anyway, done and dusted, boring, mate. Then someone said, 'Not like you, Pete,' and he turned to him and said, 'What did I tell you, Tony?', and pointed his bottle of Bud and made the throat-cutting sign with the bottle-neck, so Tony flushed and crept away down the bar – for all the good it'd do him, if Pete was annoyed. And at last orders, he turned suddenly to Claire: What we doing then?

She said they could go back to hers, she had beer in the fridge and a bottle of Smirnoff. That wasn't no good. He only drank Absolut. So she said she could get some Absolut, and he said where? Wasn't nowhere round here sold Absolut this time of night on a Sunday, and he stared at her like she might have blown it, but then he said, Come on, let's go down Robbie's – you come too (meaning Claire, along with the hanger-on who'd mildly disgraced himself with the talk of the Victoria Dock murder, but now seemed in favour again – assuming he had a choice whether or not he came along). So they got in a blue-black Cosworth that Pete de Lacey told Claire he kept for tearing up when he was half caned, and they went south through roads and woody lanes at high speed with the hanger-on whooping, Claire frightened for her life.

Robbie's was a big house, set back from the road down a dark drive with an electric gate that Pete de Lacey shouted something at, before they passed stone lions and eagles, Claire trying not to giggle in the back; but now they'd screeched to a halt where the drive curved on to gravel and the front door was open in a blaze of light, and in the door, a young man with a bird's face and fair hair was bouncing. As Pete de Lacey approached him, he shouted and bounced and leaped at him, and began to nuzzle at his face and make pecking gestures; so Pete, he wrestled him and put him in a headlock and pretended to duff him up. Then the young man bit Pete through the sleeve of his shirt, so Pete threw him with his left leg and went down with him and they scuffled and play-hit each other in the bright hall, while the hanger-on and Claire stood over them and the hanger-on shouted, 'Do him, Pete!'

After a while, Pete, now sitting astride the young man, said, 'You got guests, Robbie, you cunt!'

'I can't see no one,' said Robbie, and as Pete bent back to point at them, Robbie wriggled violently to the side and bit Pete's calf, whereupon they both rose, red, laughing, tucking in their shirts. Then they went through a big kitchen, and gathered by a black Smeg fridge that looked like a safe, and Pete de Lacey asked where Robbie's mum was, to which Robbie replied that he didn't have a fucking clue and scratched his fair hair, and began to stare at Claire as if he only now was noticing her. So Pete said she was a friend of his, and Robbie said, 'Yeah? You fucked her yet then?' And Pete laughed and said open the fridge and show his fucking wares.

Behind the black door, bottles glistened and ready meals were stacked. Pete told Robbie he was a greedy cunt with all that stashed in there, but Robbie scratched his head again as if he didn't care for his own flesh, and said his fucking mum left him that stuff when she went off, handing out bottles of Bud and Stella. Then he remembered where she was, and his face was all nose for a moment, like that's where he did his concentrating. She'd gone up the West End to see a show with her mates. Wouldn't see her again till next week. Pete de Lacey asked Robbie if he didn't have any vodka in there, and Robbie said come in the pool room, got some there. So they followed him in the pool room, which was a flash den, and when they saw how Claire shot pool, they thought she was all right, and Pete wanted to play doubles with her against the hanger-on and Robbie, as they chased the Stellas with big vodkas. And when she woke up, Pete de Lacey was beside her.

CHAPTER 37

FOR A LONG TIME after, he was beside her. She was his bitch —
that's what it came down to (though Pete would never use a word
like that). She was his, he wasn't hers. Understood. He was a player,
had to be, with his rep. He enjoyed collecting people; it was a power
thing. Or semi-enjoyed it, like it was a substitute for something bigger
he wanted. Sex itself, he didn't much enjoy; took too long. He wouldn't
let go; he was thinking of what he'd do next, hurrying there. He didn't
like her letting go (whether or not she was putting it on). No need for
that. He didn't do it, shutting his eyes and howling; why should she?
But what did he have against it? It was when you let yourself go that
you was vulnerable, weak, that was what. Anyway, it was just a plunge,
that's all, nothing more than a plunge. Why make a big show of it?
Claire told him you might if you loved someone, that's why. He shook
his head and laughed. As she watched him, she reckoned she'd found
a weak spot — but it would only have been the weak spot she needed if
she were genuinely interested, as opposed to working on him; in that
respect, he was giving away nothing. And this put her under a pressure
of a kind untouched on in her briefing — which went like this. Since he
was notoriously associated with a particular crime, any girlfriend was
likely to mention it, sooner rather than later. You couldn't not know
what Pete de Lacey was supposed to have got away with, could you?

Not if you were an English girl who purported to be from around these parts. Therefore, you'd be curious. You'd want to hear him deny it outright, wouldn't you? Unless you were a starfucker that got kicks from race crimes. And when he denied it, either you'd dig him the more for getting on with his life after the false accusations and bad publicity had made it impossible to find a job, and so forth; either that, or you'd push it under the carpet: you'd asked what had to be asked, and you'd heard denied what had to be denied; now you could help him 'move on'. But that Claire hadn't once mentioned it – well, that must seem odd, and as it got odder with time, it would begin to seem suspicious, like she was playing some game, and knew already. And this was one of the ways in which she began to lose control: she was meant to be investigating, or entrapping, him, but it felt like it was turning. She needed to act fast.

To encourage him to give himself away, she began dropping certain remarks herself (hoping he'd take her as a starfucker). But when she came out with stuff about immigrants taking our jobs, he said a lot of them weren't immigrants – they were born here. She asked him, What's the difference? He didn't answer; then he said they could have our jobs for all he cared; he just wasn't bothered; the jobs were basically shit anyway. He wouldn't be drawn on this. It was like he was a thought ahead of her. So that bookshop she'd passed with Kim and Frankie, she went down there and bought some papers and pamphlets, *Blood & Honour*, *British Nationalist*, *Redwatch*, *Totenkopf*. She came out with positions and slogans she'd picked up. He watched her and shook his head. Sounded like she'd been reading that stuff just to impress him; wasn't her. 'You don't really mean it,' he said. 'That ain't you, babe, ain't you one bit!' Did he want her to mean it? It wasn't possible he could want a racially tolerant girlfriend, was it? No. But he didn't want her putting him on; and he was too quick at sussing when she was. One time, she started about the Lübeck hostel fire, how the suspects got police alibis, even though they'd scorched their own faces. He asked her what was funny about that. He asked her again. Nothing really.

A thing that interested him was how she felt about the others (these being his other girls). Wasn't she up for cutting their throats? They were for hers! She was well alarmed, but he was like, 'Don't worry, babe. I ain't letting them at you!' They wanted to cut each other's throats too. When Claire heard that, she calmed down; though there was still the problem of her lack of jealousy. Could he see under that as well? She wasn't jealous because she was just doing her job? Fucking frightening! She told him she was above all that throat-cutting stuff. It had no class, being like that. This seemed to impress him. He stood with his hands in his pockets watching her, then he looked down at the floor. Thinking. To consolidate, Claire said, 'If you love someone, you've got to be ready to let them go. My mum taught me that.' He seemed to nod his head, and asked her where she fancied going. She said, Take me somewhere cool.

The night was a disaster. They went to the Rack Club in Greenwich, Pete was being nice, trying to make her laugh; then his brother Mick appeared with Robbie, and Pete suddenly turned. An Asian guy was dancing with a blonde girl, pulling some wild moves on the floor; so these three started hooting. At first, it was like they were admiring the Asian, but then their sounds became mocking; a few couples left the floor and went to lurk by the bar, looking on, but the Asian and the blonde kept dancing. The track was a metal cover of 'You Spin Me Round'. A bouncer appeared, but when he saw who it was kicking off, he shook his head, grinned, like *Boys will be boys!*, went away again. Then Pete put his fingers in her drink, pulled out two ice cubes and threw them; and when she put her hand over the glass to stop him taking another, he stared at her, and Mick said, 'Fuck me! You ain't letting her pussy-whip you, are you, Pete?' So Pete snatched her glass and threw the G&T over the couple, while Robbie and Mick grinned like they were coming, and that horrible beak of Robbie's – ah, he was an animal, that one! Well, the DJ stopped the music and the lights came on, and the blonde partner of the Asian, she comes running over to where they're all sitting, though the Asian guy's trying to hold her back, and she starts screaming at them, and the more she screams, the more Pete and Robbie and Mick laugh, and mock her voice. Then she turns on Claire, and says she should be ashamed, to be sitting with three toe-rags like this, and the three lads watch to see how Claire responds, and what she comes out with, it has them cheering. This is what she said: 'Ashamed? Well at least I ain't a fucking race traitor!'

She didn't mean it – couldn't have. But out it came. And it protected her cover. Yet she had no one there to tell she didn't mean it. And without anyone to tell what's behind them, your acts might be just what they seem. What was worse, the gang rated her for it. With them, she was almost a made woman. Pete put his arm round her: 'Didn't think you had it in you, babe. That's why we was testing you, like. Proud of you.' By that time, the blonde and the Asian guy were leaving, but at the exit, the blonde turned and stared at Claire, then shook her head; and it chilled Claire, what she seemed to mean by it.

SHE HAD A MEET with the DI at Carshalton Ponds. What happened at the Rack, her own part in it, she told him the lot. She was confused, this was all turning out the wrong way. They were standing by a little Venetian bridge. The water shone, taking colour from the trees, a great cool emerald bath. She'd have liked to fall in and sink. The DI shook his head and smiled. Darkest hour before dawn – that's what he told her. A sure sign she was getting somewhere, that she was feeling frightened, compromised. He'd seen it before. When you started reporting you were in too deep, why that was exactly the moment you were learning to swim. People were depending on her; he hadn't told her how much; perhaps he ought to have, but he didn't want her under too much pressure. Basically, Operation Medway, which was the name him and his boss had chosen for her op – Operation Medway was a solo jolly, her and her alone. So they'd considered three keen beans, and Claire'd seen for herself how she was the only bean who made the selection. And one thing she was proving, she was a tough bean too, a go-it-alone bean! The DI smiled at her and did a thing with his chin that she'd noticed before. So she said, What about Kim, Kim and Marcus – weren't they in on it as well? And the DI shook his head. Kim wasn't no part of it. So who was Kim then? Oh, Kim was just a family friend, snout, micro-grass.

Hey! Was he serious?

'Oh-ho!', said the DI, 'you look shocked, gel! How on earth d'you think we keep the wheels turning? Come to the Bakehouse. You need a pastry!'

At the Bakehouse, he explained about Kim and her family, and how her old man escaped jail for fraud on condition his daughter, who was herself mixing with the wrong people and dabbling with the possibility of a career in dishonesty – on condition she turned herself into a useful person to the service, performed errands and obliged the DI. Now what was up with Claire's custard slice? Wasn't off, was it?

So who was Blue Wolf or .303?

He laughed. Now Claire was forgetting. Those were just made-up names.

But he'd said someone would introduce her to the gang.

The DI nodded.

But who was it who'd introduced her?

The DI laughed again: 'Why, you introduced yourself, gel! That's the beauty of it!'

The beauty of what? What she'd half felt about him from the beginning was beginning to take shape. Underneath the heartiness swam something, like a big dark fish they'd seen from the bridge earlier. Sometimes it went slow, others it darted; took its time, as only the powerful really can. The coloured fish, silver, blue and orange patched, they caught the eye, while the dun fish went its way. Nobody'd caught it, they wouldn't even try: it was against the law to fish in those ponds.

He was pointing his pastry fork, telling Claire she was indispensable. The Inquiry was hard by. What she dug out down here could make all the difference. Think of that, gel! As for coming out with the sort of thing these thugs like to hear, like she'd been telling him, now that was a sign of a true professional: she'd been putting it on, that was all. She thought undercover people hadn't had to act ugly before now? Or say what they didn't believe in, just to gain credence? She had something to learn, let him tell her.

But then he started asking her about the salon, and Gemma and the other girl – Sally, was it? Anything to report there? Claire asked why there should be. It was just her cover. The DI shook his head, like No no no! Gemma Cook and Sally Roberts were known to the service. And they'd said nothing to Claire? Sure now? Thinking back? Ladies did talk, after all, and she'd spent a fair while in the salon with them. They must have asked what her real game was? Come on! He grinned and squashed crumbs with his fork and tidied them, like a line of coke. She certainly wasn't cutting or dyeing, was she? Hadn't blown her cover with Gemma and Sal, had she? Come on! He wagged his finger at her.

Well, what had she been supposed to do? It was obvious she wasn't a hairdresser. They were bound to ask, sooner or later. Well, hadn't she chosen that cover? True, she'd come up with it (after he'd asked if she knew anyone in business in the area), but it was him who'd sorted it for her, and told her Gemma was kosher with the story about her being in training. Well then, said the DI, why'd she opened her mouth? And the way he looked at her meant she had to tell the truth. You couldn't lie to your handler. It was a cherished principle, cornerstone of undercover work.

Well, one Friday they'd gone for a drink after work (Claire'd spent the afternoon sweeping hair and making coffee for customers). They were in a wine bar, and Gemma said, 'You ever been back in The Bosun, Sal?'

'I'll never set foot in there again,' said Sally.

So Claire asked what they meant, and they told her about The Bosun and Monkey on the Highway, and what happened there one night a few years ago (warning her she'd need a strong stomach). It was a horrible story all right, sickening, but when she asked how a teenager could do that to another man, Sally told her the teenager was only a human in disguise and really an animal – though that was unfair on animals. But anyway, he had a horrible nose like a beak, and then Claire guessed they were talking about Pete de Lacey's mate, Robbie. Gemma and Sally said sorry when they saw her face, the shock they'd given her, but they didn't know it was because she'd been in his kitchen, and shot pool in his den.

She told them not to apologize – she needed to know. So of course, they asked why that was, and she replied, Oh, it was useful to know places to avoid when you'd come to an area. But they sussed there was something else, and said come out with it, Claire. We're your mates. We know you've been holding back on us since you came to the salon. We've been cushty with you. Don't we deserve a bit of straight talk? What are you up to, lady? That 'mentor' who came in just before you started, who said he was from the Chamber of Commerce or Rotary or some such, is he a cop? Cos the cops have been keeping an eye on us since that incident at The Bosun (no pun intended – sorry, that was gross!). For why? Cos we were witnesses, that's why. They took a statement from both of us at the time, though we never heard no more of that, even though everyone knew the lad's name, Robbie Woods. Probs we never heard no more cos he had powerful family – everyone knew that as well. And that's the way things work round here. But there's one comes in now and then, with a little square beard, and he's always asking if we heard anything from Raymond recently.

So Claire asked who was Raymond, and Sally said, You tell her, Gem. Tell her about Raymond. Well, Raymond, he'd used to be the bar manager at The Bosun and Monkey. And he was a nice, sound fella – too good for a place like that; a sight too nice. The time they were telling Claire about, when Robbie Woods bit the Welshman's eye out, he'd been working there a year or two. And Sally and Raymond, they'd had a thing, hadn't they, a romance? The two women giggled, like you had to. Yeah, they were the good days, looking back, though it didn't seem so then. And for why it didn't was that Woods was a regular in The Bosun (though he was well underage), and the gang used to come over from their manor to visit him (and they were all underage too). Claire asked which gang, and the two women, they looked at her and said, Why, L Troop, as they call themselves, the lads who murdered the black teenager. So Claire, she put her hand to her mouth and said oh my God! But the two women, they shook their heads, and asked her not to take them for fools. Bit of respect please, lady! You know all about that gang! Oh, why do I? Because you bloody well hang about with them! Which took Claire by surprise. She felt sick with shame. How did they know? Well, ladies talked, didn't they? And in the salon, they talked a lot. And one thing they talked about was what they'd got up to the other night. Well, one lady who was in the other day, while Claire was out doing something else, this lady, who was called Julie (let's forget the surname for the time being, just in case), though it was odd how she was a ringer for Claire (as one of the other ladies noticed), she came in for a colour and trim, and she was talking about being at the Rack in Greenwich. Well she wouldn't be going there again, not on her life. Oh why not, Julie? Cos she'd thought she'd seen herself in there. That was one thing. What d'you mean, babe? You hadn't been having a toot had you – or some of those funny pills? On her mother's grave she hadn't! It was a girl, just like her – and who d'you fancy she was with? Who was she with, Jules? Those maniacs, the two brothers that murdered the black guy, them, and that psycho with the budgie's nose, the one with the attention disorder. What, Robbie Woods? Yeah, that was him. The de Lacey brothers and Robbie Woods. So the other reason she wouldn't be going in there again was that lot started kicking off, and it was her they were picking on – her and Bobby Singh. Obviously cos Bobby was Asian. So what were they doing, babe? Ah, they were hooting, mocking, throwing ice. Of course, the bouncers were like pussies when that lot was around, standing like this, counting clouds. So she went up and gave them some verbal, told them they were scum and they shouldn't be out of their kennel. And of course they started giggling like five-year-olds, which is what they were, infant psychopaths (Julie was a nurse on a secure unit); but the blonde girl who reminded her of herself, she just sat there (Julie thought she'd been trying to control them at first), and d'you know what she said? What'd she say, babe?

'Well at least I ain't a race traitor!' – that's what she said!

Oh, what a horrible thing to say, Jules!

That is – it's truly disgusting.

So Claire, sitting there with Sally and Gemma, she had to put her hand up and say, 'Yes, that was me, ladies. But you have to understand,

I didn't mean it. On my mother's grave I didn't! It was just something I had to say.'

Why? Why'd she have to say something like that, to a girl who had the courage to be hanging out with an Asian guy – which took something round these parts. As everyone knew. Wasn't like the rest of London, round here.

So she asked them to swear not to tell anyone, so they swore, and she swore she trusted them – as she had to, cos if this got out, it was funeral bells for her. Like, literally. She'd get the treatment. So she was a police officer . . .

You what?

Yeah. An undercover cop, that's what she was. Investigating the gang.

So, like, she had to pretend to be like them?

Exactly!

Like in *Donnie Brasco*, where he insults the Japanese guy, Johnny Depp?

Like that, yeah. More or less. That's how it was. But seeing as she'd levelled with them, they could answer something for her. Why was it the copper with the beard came in to ask them about Raymond, every so often. What was all that about?

Probably it was cos of this. Just after the night when the Welshman lost his eye, a fella came into The Bosun and tried to bung Raymond, so he'd withdraw his statement.

His witness statement?

Yeah. His witness statement.

And Raymond, he wouldn't do that?

No. Raymond wouldn't. He might have been a bit weak when it came to dealing with the gang – God knows, Sally'd given him a hard time about that often enough. And she'd regretted it after. Like, who wouldn't have been weak when it came to dealing with them? Way they acted when they came in a place together, they was like a horrible team, like Siamese quins with a psycho streak. No one person could tell them where to get off or cool it, let alone take 'em on. Which was somehow what she'd been expecting of him.

'You wasn't to know, Sal,' Gemma said. 'We all want our men to be men. But sometimes, it's not manageable – not in life; in films, yes, but films ain't what our lives are like, are they? Most you can hope for is decency. And Raymond, one thing you couldn't take from him, he was a decent bloke.'

Sally agreed. He might have been weak, like in his personality, certainly when it came to that lot he was; but he was a decent bloke. Matter of fact, he had character – more and more she'd come to see this. And how that went with the weak or weakish personality, she couldn't work out. Beyond her. Anyways, he'd refused the bung and off the fella went, Raymond thinking he was a villain and some family friend of Robbie Woods. Well, the next night, the fella turns up again at The Bosun, with a bigger envelope, see if he can't bribe Raymond this time. But he's also got a younger bearded fella with him, and between them, they're doing the double act on Raymond where one's kind and the other's downright unpleasant, so you're either beaten down by the nasty one and you do what they want, or you're so grateful to the nice one for saving you from the other, you still do what they bloody want. So they're on at Raymond, older fella's chatting to him while the beard prowls round the place and says is this where it happened, boss, or here – or over there? Like he can't see no trace of the incident (which shouldn't be surprising, seeing as the forensic team was in on the night and measured the stains and photo'd them and whatnot, and then Raymond was up till two hours before opening cleaning them off with 1001). But it's making like it never happened. And the worst of that is

Raymond's now seeing that these two aren't villains, oh no: they're plain-clothes fuzz, the pair of them. Rotten fuzz. The sort who make things happen against the proper rules of policing, when folk know they didn't – and the sort who make things not have happened as well, when every honest person knows they damn well did. Which is like saying his witness statement, it's going to seem moody, or he makes things up, or he's a bit of a loony – whatever, it's going to be the worst for him. And then, if that wasn't bad enough, this bearded berk, he's turning the whole thing right over from how it was, like totally. Suggesting the fella who lost his eye and the two others he was with were perverts, you know, like paedophiles, and they've come in The Bosun hunting underage boys, which is why they got attacked, and serve 'em right! And then from that – oh, this made her so mad – from that, he's making out that Raymond knew as much, like he's actually welcoming paedos, cos he is one himself. And what's more, he's knowingly serving underage boys (as young as fifteen) to cater for the paedophiles, letting them drink alcohol so they're vulnerable to older men. Meaning that from now on, the service are going to be keeping an eye on The Bosun and Monkey – and maybe performing a few little tests.

But within days, Raymond'd been given his notice. Sally told him he should fight it, but he didn't have the stomach. They told him he wasn't serving the reputation of the brewery properly. In the history of the chain, there'd never been an incident such as that allegedly witnessed in The Bosun and Monkey on the evening of 25 February 1992. Add to that the information that the bar manager'd regularly been serving youths below the age of eighteen, and his position wasn't tenable. He got two-and-a-half grand as a gesture of regret (without prejudice), and the brewery wished him luck in his future.

So where did he go, what happened to him, Claire wanted to know? Oh, he came to Sally's one morning (they'd never got as far as moving in together). He had a rucksack, and two cases. All his things were in there. It was cloudy, had been for days, not a hint of sun – she remembered that. He was wearing a woolly hat. He'd come to say goodbye. She should have held on to him, totally refused to let him go. If only we knew what to do before it's too late! But all she could think of then was his cowardice, and she knew that wasn't really fair, but it was easier to blame him than understand. So she acted tough. Told him to keep in touch, not to be a stranger.

Yet the bearded copper, he kept asking after him?

Yes. It was maybe – no, probably – because Raymond'd never withdrawn his statement. So they were worried about him. That, or someone close to Woods who was paying them didn't like it that he was still at large – quiet enough, but not like he'd been silenced.

Now all this, more or less, Claire told the DI in the Bakehouse, while he smiled, shook his head, and did that thing with his chin. Then he said, 'Well, well, Claire. What have you done? Oh what have you done, gel? Here's a to-do.' And he couldn't well see how he was going to be able to save her, after all she'd just told him. So she asked why, like really panicking. Well, had she forgotten the J70? The what? The secrecy form, that's what. But . . . But what? That form was binding, as he'd explained at the briefing. He put down his fork and held his head. He wasn't smiling. Jesus Christ, Claire, but this was heavy. Bloody heavy. Where to start?

OK. Let's take Raymond first. Was she aware, for example, that he'd actually been offered a new life? No. Course she wasn't. All this fa-la-la about envelopes one size one night, half-inch thicker the next, that these girls were telling her was bribes – did she seriously suppose the service operated like that? Seriously? Cos if she did, there was no place for her in it! Where was the trust, if she believed that guff? A copper who didn't trust was a cynical copper, and a cynical copper, well, she was on the way to becoming a rotten copper. That was a black-and-tan fact, and old dogs like himself had seen it happen, and though it was rare, there was nothing worse – if you cared for the service like he did. What was in those envelopes, if he dared tell her (and here he looked around the Bakehouse and used his hand as a baffle for his voice) – what was in the envelopes was indeed money, but it wasn't no bung. No. It was money to set Raymond up in a new place, new career. Let him retrain, that was the idea, somewhere else, well away from here. His statement was on file. The service were gathering evidence on Robert Woods in an op like hers: Operation Dex. They were well aware the youth was protected. It was worth a copper's punt to keep him at large a while. And for why? Cos that was how you got his protector to show himself, risk his own security every time his psychopathic nephew kicked off. Sooner or later, the protector gets caught or trips himself, paying off or nobbling Tom, Dick or Harry who's got a complaint against the nephew. No matter how careful he is in his own lines of business (on which evidence is steadily gathering), he's prone to cut corners or overlook something when it comes to his sister's kid. Maybe he's not seeing eye to eye with the sister, on that particular occasion. Or he's hungover. Or he's got trouble of his own. So he delegates some violent Noddy with a big mouth to go and sort the problem. Noddy drinks a bottle of voddy on the way over, forgets what he was meant to say, slashes the face of the witness to Robert's latest escapade when he was meant to offer them a grand, has a rummage, then falls over the garden wall into the minnehaha while making his exit. Along comes Ploddy. Ha ha! What you doing down there in the minnehaha? Got yourself all muddy! You're nicked, Noddy! Now who put you up to this nastiness? Wasn't Uncle Michael, was it? We seen you eating pie and peas with him often-a-times. If you remember properly, you might get lenience. Otherwise it's GBH with Intent plus

Aggravated Burglary. OK, says Noddy. I tell you, boss. Now, no less than everything, Noderick. Remember good and do yourself a favour. This can't be the first job you done Uncle Michael, can it now? Considering how many pie-and-pea feasts you've consumed alongside him, not to mention leftovers at his barbecue. So Noddy tells all.

Then we go in and the house falls down, whole rotten castle. Uncle Michael, nephew Robbie, and a god-almighty bunch of hangers-on, journeymen, hitmen, accountants, bobbins and blondes who ain't never worked a day in their life or claimed any benefits who can't explain the mortgage on that eight-bedroom brewer's cottage in Bickley. Jail for all the fellas, and Mareva injunctions for the ladies! Justice done! Raymond gets his chance to testify. Gladly he appears in court. Thanks to the service, he's been safely out of the way, no one threatening him, till the day of reckoning. This we call patient, dedicated policing. But Operation Dex, it has now been severely hazardized by the fact that a female copper working undercover has gone and blabbed over drinks that she's involved in the op against the killers of the Matthews boy.

What harm there, you may wonder? Well, here's a thing. Just as the fella we refer to as Raymond was the key witness in the Bosun and Monkey incident, so an extremely valuable witness in the Matthews murder just so happens to be a relative of the owner of the salon, one Gemma Cook. Now this witness goes by the name of William Cook, and he ain't too steady as a character. Indeed, he's what you might call a loony, albeit a loony who's the only witness to what happened to the blood-stained clothing, where it was taken for disposal and so forth, the night of the murder. But he's such a loony, no one listens to him, locals take the mick, his family – with one exception – they can't bear the sight or sound of him, what with his antics, his shouting, his veganism and so forth. So that when he does a bunk from Tavy Bridge (Thamesmead South) the night of the murder, cos he's frightened the gang are going to top him, no one reports him missing, no one even goes down the road to the park to see if he's sitting on the swings howling and chattering to himself, as per – with one exception. And who would that be? His half-sister Gemma, that's who. She cares about William. Their dad went through several wives; none of 'em stayed around long; Gemma and William, they had different mums, and, sad to say, the same dad; but whereas he went for William like a tartar, he was sweet to Gemma (which he had his reasons for). However, Gemma's looked out for her brother all their lives. And if anyone knows where he went after the murder, or where he happens to be now, well it's Sister Gemma.

But if anyone knows where he is now, the last person she will let on to is the service. And for why? Because Brother William, if there's one thing he detests as much as racist killers, it's the police. Oh yes. And that shouldn't surprise us, seeing as he's filled his head with nonsense about police oppression from his records and CDs, and anarchist leaflets, and also some meetings he's been to, where for once in his life he's fallen in with some folk who've made him feel welcome – Workers' Revolutionary types this being, who want to smash the state, and would as well, if the police weren't there to protect shops, factories, stations, houses, democratically elected members of Parliament, and so forth. Point here being that if William should catch on that his sister is hand-in-glove with an undercover cop, going as far as offering her a chair in the salon for hokey's sake, then he ain't ever going to be in contact again, not with her, not with no one. Indeed, he's likely to go to ground terminally, which isn't unheard of with strays like him.

Now Claire'll be asking, but who's going to tell him his sister's employing a copper anyway? What's the chance of that? Well, if you were a betting man, you'd favour the chances as being very tidy, and for this reason. There are people that are well in favour of William going to ground and never coming up again. These being (1) the de

Lacey brothers, who clocked him flapping around in The Lunar Five that night they came to burn their clobber; (2) the Tavy Bridge boys, aka the 'Young SS', who helped them out that night, brought them up there in their sky-blue Astra, then dropped 'em back again. They wouldn't mind at all if William went to ground terminalio. Not that any of them'd drop him themselves – they know they're being watched, they know he's too hot. Indeed, you could say William Cook's been the hottest witness, or *potential* witness, in England, these last five years. But if they could get word to him, wheresoever he might be, that the cops are interested in talking to him, so interested they've moved in with his sister, like literally, then you won't see the boy for dust. Which is why the race is on. The service has *got* to find William, jolly him up, persuade him all's kosher, and above all, that justice demands he appear at the Inquiry – all that, before these young men have their way and persuade him to bury himself. And how they wish they'd topped him that night in Thamesmead five years ago! Could have been done. Wouldn't have been no hue and cry like with the Matthews boy. But it's too late now. He who hesitates is lost. Go fishing, instead of just a-wishing, hey, Claire! But they can still get to him, and within the law. Takes no more than a word from some newbie in a hostel he's known to be dossing at who's been planted by the boys, like, *Here's a ton to tell that loob from Tavy the fuzz wanna chat to him about The Lunar Five. Hang around till he's got the message and slung his hook. Take another coupla sheets to get your threads dry-cleaned from the roaches and that. Cushty, son, cushty!*

Now TDC Sykes'd no doubt be thinking, but Gemma and Sally, they're sound, they won't tell no one about me. Well that was as maybe. But maybe wouldn't answer. And for why? Here were reasons why. Round these parts, people didn't have book learning, university diplomas, and whatnot. Time had been, if you was a bright kid, you put away your books, poetry, geography, Roman history, so forth, the day you left school, and you took your chances with the world. And in those days, the world did you fair if you were shrewd, talented, or ambitious, or if you were prepared to graft. You could work in a bank, as a clerk or technician; you could become an accountant without any of this degree palaver – you just learned on your feet, and you learned by listening. You just 'picked it up', as people used to say. And if you weren't a swotty type, there was the docks, the rubber plant, bakers, coal shops, garages, scrapyards, haulage companies. Take your pick. You could stuff ships, like the DI's old man (Royal Vic was his dock). Make tyres, and hoses. Bake cobs and tin loaves. Supply the fuel to keep folk warm. Calder's Coal Yard, marvellous; smell it now! Went down there one November with his mother to order a hundredweight. They sat in the front shop while the lady did the books. She gave him a baked potato from a furnace in the passage. Big blonde beehive she had, and this little flat bit at the end of her nose. You could mend cars; sort copper, iron, chrome, lead, aluminium; you could drive a truck. Or you could join the service. That'd been his choice. And he hadn't regretted it either. Wasn't like that now. But people were as shrewd as ever. Maybe they was even shrewder than they had been. Cos whereas in the sixties and seventies, people had their jobs to occupy them and the ambition to get on, nowadays the world didn't do 'em fair. Anyone could see that. As a working area, this part of old Kent had flatlined. In common with a great deal of England. So people was up against the world; and when you are up against the world, why, you improve your weapons, your defences, don't you? That, or you throw in the towel. And round these parts, they would never ever do that. But a funny thing was, the world showed them how to improve their defences, like it was looking after them even as it took the work and money away. And one of their defences was they became watchful, they noticed more. Like idle people – or, fairer to say, people with nothing to do – since the beginning of time, like shepherds on a hillside, or sailors that have lost their ship, they sat and watched, and they noticed. And like people who've sat and looked at the same thing for a long time, like a hillside or the empty sea, when something different appears on the horizon, well, they clock it and they become hyper-alert. And they start wondering, Now what's that doing there, who sent it, why's it suddenly showed up at this time, when there was nothing there before? If she knew what he meant. And so, when a new girl appears at Gemma's salon, people say to each other, Funny, that, she's in and out the place, but I ain't never seen her doing someone's hair. Nor me neither. Or me. This is how they are. And because they're savvy, they know the new girl's up to something. And maybe they let it rest at that, and maybe not. But even if they did let it rest, they couldn't keep it quiet.

And that's how it was, round these parts.

So Claire obviously asked why on earth he'd permitted the salon cover in the first place, if what he'd just said was true.

She had a point there. He did the tightening thing with his chin. He'd foreseen all this. On that, she had to trust him. But Op Medway was his responsibility on the ground, and there only. From above, it was being supervised by his boss, and his bosses, and they was being shunted by the Home Office (here using his hand as a baffle again). And the Home Office, they was insisting on results pronto. And for why? Because the Inquiry into the Eldine Matthews murder wasn't no more than six weeks off now. So when he advised his boss there was a particular risk in running an undercover op in the area, such as he'd just been explaining to her, his boss called him in to his bosses, who made their position clear. The service'd have to take the risk. That's how it was. Sorry, John. This one's got to run, and it's got to score. So get your best woman detective constable in there, and get her signalling. We ain't got no choice.

So Claire's like, You knew it wasn't going to work, sir. But still you put me in there. And her world's falling apart. From age fifteen, a detective was what she wanted to be. Set her heart on it, all her ambition. Dad said he and Mum'd back her all the way. She got into her studies, abandoned the company of yobs, achieved her grades. Left school, did voluntary work in a kids' hospital, and care home; learned martial arts (ju-jitsu, tae kwon do); went interrailing. She was one keen bean. The day of her eighteenth, she entered the police college at Sunbury. Her mum and dad were proud, so proud; but also they were grateful that she'd come right. And now, sitting with the DI in the Bakehouse, the dream was over. She'd messed up totally. And what's more, become a racist in the process.

Ah, the DI said, you ain't done that right either, Claire. You was too half-hearted, gel. One sure way you could have passed for kosher among these people (and I regret to tell you this) is you could have turned it on so's you was more like them than they are themselves, if you see what I mean. Then they'd have respected you, taken you to their hearts. As it is, they'll know you are just acting. That was your one chance. I was banking on it.

But Pete de Lacey, he was – there was something between them. From the way he talked, the conversations they had, she knew this. That was something to work on.

The DI shook his head. He'd read her reports, listened to the recordings. There was nothing there to go on. He's been playing you, gel, he told her now, de Lacey has. Must have sussed you from the start. He could tell there were things you wanted to hear. He ain't dropped a stitch. He's kept his cards to his chest. That's one thing. Next is this. He's waiting, they all are, for you to give yourself away. Then they'll see you get the treatment, Claire. She begged the DI for a last chance. She knew, *knew*, she was nearly there. It was her instinct. She'd get evidence before the month was out. For once, the DI showed some temper, made a hammer with his fist; his voice changed. No. She was coming out now. Medway was terminated. He couldn't risk her being down here any longer. An unmarked car pulled up outside the Bakehouse. He paid the bill and took her to it. The driver was a man with a short dark beard. He told her to get in: 'Take us home, Bowls!'

How could she redeem herself? They watched her in the mirror. At her flat in Greenwich, they stopped to pick up her things. The DI and Sergeant Bowler started checking drawers, lifting rugs; Bowler felt under the settee, all the way along the bottom. What was this in aid of? What it was in aid of was the uncle – Robbie Woods's uncle. He'd naughtied three or four coppers from 5 SERCS, who called themselves 'The Bushwhackers'. They were bugging folk left, right and centre that were involved with the Eldine Matthews case, folk on the right side that was, to intimidate witnesses and stymie the Inquiry. There was a chance they'd been in here. Claire asked how they'd know to break into her flat. Sergeant Bowler shook his head, like she hadn't learned nothing. Cos Pete de Lacey would have told Uncle Michael he reckoned she was moody, that was why. The DI closed his eyes, tautened his chin. He was well let down by all this. God, how could she make it all right with him, after he'd trusted her? They took out her bags, her boxes of things and some little ornaments she'd brought to make the place seem comfy. Then they drove her away. She'd wanted to be a Detective Sergeant, more than anything; but she'd never have the close manner, the control, of the Sergeant at the wheel.

It was evening when they stopped to drop her off. There was something she could do that might save the operation – or if not save it, compensate. Had Gemma Cook never spoken to Claire about her brother? Say if she scratched her pretty head and thought deep, wasn't there anything? Nothing about William Cook, whereabouts, address?

Surely must have been something dropped among ladies. Hadn't ever been known for a lady to keep a secret, had it now? But as she sat there with them watching her in the mirror, she couldn't recall a thing.

At her mum and dad's she went straight to her room and bolted the door. On her old bed she lay and wept. She wept to the deeps, till she felt she'd burst, like a diver whose tank has bust, or been tampered with. Pete de Lacey, in his mirror shades, she hated. When she thought how he'd been inside her, she wanted to burn herself out with a red knife. Robbie Woods she hated, with his brute nose and black Smeg, his stupid animal bouncing. The Bushwhackers, who'd been through her flat, searching and sniffing, she hated with a passion. Nothing worse than a rotten copper. That really was the pits. How could she turn it round? God, how could she? She actually tried to pray. At her door her mum called; her mum got her dad, and her dad called. She screamed at them to leave her alone. Beyond the door they muttered. She prayed again and something came to her, sambuca-flavoured.

So they'd finished off the night in the wine bar with some slams — she, Gemma, Sally. Sally said, 'I couldn't have married him anyway, if he's a priest.' But, Gemma told her, he wasn't a Catholic priest but C of E. Raymond this was, who they were talking about. And Sally said, Well, you know more than I do, Gem, by the sound of it. Like she was a bit miffed, like, My ex, but you got all the information on him now-adays. Then Gemma, she said — no, muttered — Well, that was only because Raymond'd been looking after William, who was dossing round that way, and William'd been more grateful to him than . . . But here, they'd all left the wine bar and got on to something else as they tried to find a taxi.

Lying on her bed, Claire wept for joy; and thanked God.

CHAPTER 38

AT UPPER NORWOOD LIBRARY, they sent her to *Crockford's Clerical Directory*, which was where you could look up the parishes, addresses and so forth of all the priests in England. She found a Father Raymond Vernon of St Aubrey's, West London. His biog was short and modest. Before taking orders, he'd worked in hospitality. Now he tried to offer a more loving kind of hospitality. Claire made a journey to his parish.

The door of St Aubrey's was open. She sat alone in the smell of old leather. At the front, a reading stand in the shape of an eagle. Would the priest turn up? She had an address for him close to the church; but it was peaceful being here. She played with her fingers; then ceased, and bowed her head. For what she'd done, she said sorry. She began by saying it to herself. When she looked up, the eagle had her in its gaze. Someone behind her said, 'Mind if I join you?' It was a broad-faced man, who didn't quite look the sort to wear a dog-collar, and knew it, so he carried himself apologetically, as if to say, *I know! Best I can do!* The black trousers and brown sports jacket reminded her of a liquorice allsort. He took his place some way from her on the pew, because he was a man and she a woman, even if it was the house of God, and he probably thought he looked a bit of an impostor, though it made you trust him all the more somehow.

337

They introduced themselves, Claire Sykes and Father Raymond, and though ninety-nine men out of a hundred would have asked what she was giggling about, he didn't, maybe because he knew how odd he looked; or maybe because he was more bothered about other people, and giggling doesn't necessarily mean you're happy. So she told him she was a copper. He deserved to know; but when he heard, he looked unhappy. She had to speak to him. Like it had to come sooner or later, he waited. She knew he was a protected witness. He laced his fingers and watched her. She mentioned Operation Dex; his filed statement. He kept watching, eyebrows raised. Anyway, her business was a bit different. There was a young man called William, William Cook. She had to find him. She thought Father Raymond could help her. In her CID training, she'd attended a seminar by a police psychologist who told them the ways to spot a liar. The look he gave her was hard to take. Like the eagle over there was coming for her.

William was a very vulnerable young man, he told her now. He'd promised him not to snitch if anyone came asking for him. Couldn't betray him. Getting William's trust had been such a task, it had to be protected at all costs. Well could she ask about it? He watched her, and smiled. Of course.

One day, he'd been walking in the gardens. There was a public toilet underneath. As he went down the steps to wash his hands, two youths passed him giggling and, at the top, paused and tried to outdo each other in crazy voices. The toilet was empty, but he could hear a hoarse murmuring, which got louder as he turned to check the cubicles. All were empty, except for one whose door was locked. The voice seemed to be in conversation – and of course, he supposed the obvious (that there were two male lovers in there), which was none of his business. But as he listened, the voice or voices became quite unworldly, speaking of Baal, burned clothes, Kentish devils. Strange place for a prayer meeting! But God watches over strange places. He was intrigued, and though it wasn't right to intrude on the spiritual progress of others, he had to admit, he used the hand-dryer, which was particularly noisy and vibrated because it had worked loose from its wall bracket, as a way of signalling his own presence. Whereupon the cubicle door burst open and wild eyes stared out. A lanky young man it was, with a twitchy, quick-carved face. At Father Raymond he yelled, 'I wasn't saying nothing!' and began to fidget. Father Raymond assured the young man he had nothing to fear from him, and began to mount the steps. The young man hurried behind, wanting to know what he'd heard, where he was off to. So Raymond suggested they walk in the gardens, and the young man came along in a pouncing manner. At last, they sat on a bench by the Long Walk, and Raymond told the young man that no one should have no one at all to talk to, or feel he had to keep everything to himself, especially when his heart was as full as this fellow's seemed to be. Then he offered his hand and his name. The young man grinned hard. So he'd got Raymond's name! Wasn't no way he was giving his, though! Done ya there, he cried. Done ya like a kipper! He had plenty people to talk to anyway. Where, asked Raymond? At the hostel. That was where. And where was the hostel? Ain't telling you that, the young man murmured. No way, Ray! So Raymond tried to engage him in conversation on other matters, but the young man was suspicious about traps, and wanted to know why Raymond asked whatever he asked, or mentioned whatever he mentioned, then he wanted to know why Raymond was being patient. What was that all about? Another ambush? 'All vicars are scum!' he yelled, and ran away across the grass. As he receded, his pouncing bony figure became smoother in its stride, like a distance runner's. Until he disappeared among the trees, Raymond watched him, then rose and departed. But at the West Gates, he heard a hoarse cry and turned. The young man was just behind him, flushed and panting, wanting to know where he was off to. He came back to St Aubrey's for his dinner. His name was William.

This was a year ago. William'd been in the area close to five now. Father Raymond kept his secret. Life wasn't at all easy for William, but he'd actually achieved a degree of stability – as people will in the most dreadful circumstances: something to thank God for. He had a community of sorts, folk from the hostels, rough sleepers, and others who were running from their fears, or from abuse, selling sex, drugs, used travelcards. His real vocation was making speeches, about injustice. Father Raymond'd heard several of these, and sometimes wished he could introduce as much passion and fire into his own sermons. He'd ventured to suggest that William himself took orders, which provoked a tirade against religious oppression through the ages, the Crusades, witch-burning, missionaries and empire. At the time, William was consuming tart and custard in the church hall and Raymond's helper Bobby had to perform the Heimlich manoeuvre. As William tried to flee, choking badly, Bobby clung on (he was a rugby player) and brought William down at the door. Out came the plum stone and William was off, Raymond much concerned that he'd really put his foot in it. But a couple of days later, he was back for his dinner.

So Claire asks if William still comes to the church for his meals, and the priest, he looked down, for he couldn't lie, and he'd already said too much. Claire touched his arm, and said, 'I've met Sally you know, Ray.' The priest looked across at her but was seeing something else. He asked what Sally said, and she told him that he was Sally's hero. He held his forehead in his palm; after a while, he looked at her again. He wished her gone, she knew, but she was a copper, she was on the case, had to stick with it. Last chance. Yes, now and then he came. And at what times did the church hold its homeless dinners? Mondays and Wednesdays, Tuesdays and Fridays, alternate weeks. And she could come along? He told her she was welcome, of course. Which wasn't so welcoming. And she saw now that she'd not got that far with this priest, for time was of the essence and she couldn't spend the next month turning up at the church hall looking for William. Canny Raymond.

But she'd located William's patch. She thanked Raymond and went through a garden square to the main road, then back to the Tube, where she'd noticed homeless folk singing, dealing, touting travelcards; none of them resembled William. She asked an older man with a grey face if William was around. He watched her, scratched his ear. Whae? William? Shook his head. William wasnae around. Did he know when he might be? No he didnae. He said something about bolting her rocket, then turned away. Smelled the cop in her. She had the obvious idea. Down the road to the local police station. Here she identified herself and spoke to the sergeant. The sergeant acted tight with her, but she made him feel good about himself, and when she described William Cook from the DI's account and Father Raymond's, he shook his head and laughed: for Christ's sake, don't bring him in here if you want to book him! So she asked if William'd been in the station before, and the sergeant said indeed he had, and everyone had a fucking headache for a week afterwards as well, the fuss he kicked up. Was he violent? Only verbally. He made threats? Not as such. So she asked if she could maybe see the charge sheet, and the sergeant said there wasn't one. For why? Because William and a twenty-stone halfwit known as Beefburger Mike had been in the gardens last year when Diana died, and William was howling about racist murders while Mike kicked flowers and bears. They got brought in under Section 4 (partly to save them from the crowd, who were nasty with grief). When the legal aid fella turned up, he established they hadn't drunk a thing, and that William was Mike's voluntary carer (the mong actually had his name and address stitched on his collar). Then William, he goes off on one about police

341

harassment, royalist sycophancy, and a bunch of other stuff, and the sergeant suggested they leave the station peacefully (and maybe find a carer for William as well, while they were about it). She asked who the legal aid fella was. It was a lawyer called Hanley, who had a high opinion of himself, went around like he had something up his sleeve, and knew a lot of law – or spoke like he did anyway. In the courts, he was known as 'Zipmouth'. He'd do well one day, Mr Hanley – that, or he'd crash and burn. She could check his firm, if she needed to get in touch with him. But there wouldn't be an address for William? There wouldn't. Since he hadn't been charged. But the lawyer'd seemed to be acquainted already with him.

Not wanting to speak to a lawyer, who'd no doubt take a professional attitude to enquiries from a police officer, and certainly want to know what her interest was, she recced the area on her own. Down a side street, she came upon a sort of little Hansel and Gretel house all made of wood with a gable roof. It was called 'Kut-Lunch Kabin', and a sign said *Back in 10*. The street forked, and from the doorway of a pub, a man in a black denim jacket called hi, and strode over. Did she want something to eat? He had hair like Terence Stamp, and a noble face – or would have, if his eyes weren't so quick. She hadn't eaten all day, so she could maybe do with something, but the matter was settled anyway, since he'd unlocked the Kabin and pulled up the shutter and was now busy opening tubs of fillings. The man had a South African accent and chatted about her choice and this and that, and how he hadn't seen her round before. He could be useful. She ordered a tuna mayonnaise and he began to spoon the filling (without washing his hands) into a baguette. The beige filling squeezed out at the side, so he wiped it neat with a J-cloth before slipping it into a paper and cellophane bag and handing it to her. She asked how much and he winked. On the house. She thanked him but insisted on paying, since there was a bigger favour she wanted.

But he was now asking if she needed work. Oh, what sort? Well, here in the Kabin, for instance. Or there were other kinds, for young ladies who looked like her and wanted to make good bucks. His eyes went quickly over her. She grinned back at him. Maybe they could have a drink and a talk. She put the baguette in her handbag and they went along to The Hank, where he bought her a half of lager and said just call me Van, Van the Man. So she said just call me Claire, Claire the Scare, and he laughed. They were sitting in a window seat, and his thigh pressed hers. You aren't scary, darling, he told her. You are sweet. Oh, you should see me when I get going, she said. Not so sweet then! And Van the Man raised his eyes to the ceiling and out came a laugh; he slapped his thigh; his hand felt for hers, but she'd moved it. So they had some more banter, then Van bought her another half, and when he returned from the bar his eyes were saying this is the next stage; let's get to business. But she got in first, and asked if he was the main man round here, like she was only interested in top boys and players. So Van tells her, Baby, I'm the lick. I got more connections than a feeder box. Ask anyone. They haven't heard of Van, they aren't at the party. Name anyone. If Van hasn't heard of 'em, they aren't even on the shelf. So she named a few people, but the names were either made up or they were celebrity names or personal to her, which made Van the Man grin and not like her at all, as she came out with more and more of them, and he didn't know any of them except the celebrities, but he wasn't connected to them either, of course. So she said, Well this isn't getting us anywhere, let's try something else. You tell me some names, and I'll see if I haven't heard of them. Then Van said, Why not come with me now, and I'll introduce you in person? And she's, like, Oh, that'd be fun, but it's nice sitting here with you too, so why don't you tell me all the people at your party, then I'll pick the ones I want to be introduced to! Making eyes at him, and he at her; and of course he'd sussed that

343

she was playing him, but for why he hadn't yet sussed. Yet as he processed that she didn't want him as a pimp, and nor did she want him as a lover or pal, Van the Man was cutting his losses, reshuffling. He had something, and that something was what she wanted. Well, she could pay for it. People don't come free, names don't either – though none of them are priceless. But now she was asking about William, William Cook, and Van was like, 'William?!' What in God's name could anyone want with a *boemelaar* like William? Of all the dunders, William was the lowest. Man, that fella was fit for the shredder. Wasn't a single useful thing about William. And that might not have mattered if he just kept quiet; but the *deugniet* was forever howling, putting off tourists and visitors. For business, he was a disaster. Pooh! Van the Man was on the verge of becoming bored with Claire, looking around, eyes settling on a blonde traveller at the bar who was sticking her arse out and counting her money. Claire needed to come up with something, so she necked her lager, rose and said, 'I've got to dip, Van. You've disappointed me! Babe over there needs you more than I do.' On her way out, she patted his shoulder. What d'you know? As she reached the main road, Van was striding behind her, something like love in his eyes, and calling hey, hey, hey! It was no trouble for him to take her to William.

They crossed over to the Tube. At the entrance to the foyer, the grey Scotchman was chewing a pasty from the bag. Van the Man reintroduced him to Claire as Al, and said they called him the 'A-No. 1' round this way. Scotch Al spat some pasty the other way, and said how're you doing to Van, and nothing to Claire. Van said they were looking for William, and Al said he hadn't seen the boy, so Van grinned and said since when, and Al sniffed and told him he hadn't seen William since a long time ago, watching Claire, and Van said she's a friend, Al, but Al said if she was a friend, his heid was buttoned up the back. A polis is what she was. So Van said if Al wasn't going to help, he might start remembering something he'd forgotten about the A-No. 1, and Al stepped back and raised his grey chin, and said, You may be a bigger man than me, Van Spenser, but I'll drop ye! Anytime ye want a square go, ye fucking know where I am! And Van Spenser shook his head as if this was the silliest thing, and said it was William he wanted, so why didn't Al go and take a cold bath – and a couple of his heart pills while he was about it? In another corner of the foyer, a big black man with a bald head chanted, and glared and sucked his teeth.

They came back out and they took a left, along a road of hotels, Claire wondering what sort of kickback Van Spenser was after. He was clearly a pimp of some sort, though not a particularly elite one, a grubbing hustler and blackmailer, with his finger in several pies. In her handbag, she still had her tuna-mayonnaise baguette. Soon as she was shot of him, it was going in the bin. Well at least he wasn't scary like Pete de Lacey. Besides that Greenwich bunch, he was a pussy. And he was going to give her the goods. She'd leave it to the DI to square him up.

On another main road where traffic roared one way in three lanes, they stopped at a mansion block called Cumberbatch House; the windows needed cleaning and the sills were cracked. A large greasy man in racing-flag sneakers was outside attending to bins, and Van Spenser called to him if William was in. The man didn't have a clue, got on with his bins. So Van Spenser went along the little path and kicked the black bag the man was tying. Tins, cigarette packets, plastic bottles, and takeaway trays soiled the ground. Clubbing his hands, the man looked with hate at Van Spenser; he couldn't hold it. William'd gone out ten minutes ago. Where? Which way? He'd gone with the lawyer he hung around with. Van Spenser said damn, and said something in Afrikaans. But later that night, they caught up with William . . .

CHAPTER 39

I KNEW WHERE THIS WAS going, and didn't have all fucking day.
'We're *still* in 1998, aren't we?'

Hanley waved his hands.

'Between you, you did for William, didn't you? Didn't you!'

I stood. Hanley stood; Claire Sykes stood – and fell over with a cry.
Hanley swooped to her aid, while she watched me on all fours, hair
hanging like old corn.

'We'll go, *paisano*,' Hanley was saying. 'Overstayed our welcome,
I fear!'

Regaining the settee, Claire sat well back.

'Hold on! You two've had your shot. I haven't even started.'

Hanley wiped his glasses like a badly treated devil, summoned,
scolded, now enjoined to hang around.

'How did you get William onside?' This directed at Claire Sykes.
'From what I've heard of him, he'd have been off like Usain Bolt if he
got the faintest impression you were a cop. I don't think Van Spenser
could have persuaded him. He sounds like his own man in a way none
of the rest of us gets even close to, William. And I bet you did it independent of Hanley here, since you didn't want him advising him of his
rights, which were considerable, with regard to appearing as a witness.
(How you and Hanley hooked up's another question – and we'll come

to it as well.) No. What I reckon is you were introduced to him, and you mentioned his sister, Gemma. That's how you got him.' Claire Sykes beginning to sniff, Hanley produced a pale-blue hankie. 'You told him that, for Gemma's sake, he had to appear at the Inquiry. That got him in the heart. She'd have been the only person he missed after running away from Thamesmead South. You had him in your hand then. No doubt you added that the lads from L Troop had been hanging round the salon, they weren't amiable, and they'd harass Gemma Cook till she gave him away (which she wouldn't, and couldn't). By testifying, he could right a horrible crime, and do right by his sister. He'd have agreed to play the game. Back to work you went next day. You called DI George Arnold. "Boss, I've got your boy!" And along came your handler, took you for another plate of buns, and told you what a good girl you were, "Sergeant Sykes".

'Then the precision engineering started. DI Arnold and Bowler, they had to know William's movements, not so he could testify, but the opposite; so he couldn't. Because he'd been taken out by an untraceable car in a narrow road that runs under a viaduct. So what you did (and let's not go into how just here) was get Van Spenser to keep close tabs on William, his every move, and stated intention (which wouldn't have been hard, given his volume issues). The day he went to testify at Sidon House, shouting his mouth off to the foyer because he thought he was doing a big, important thing, Van Spenser rang you pronto, and you rang DI Arnold. Half an hour later, William had been mashed; he never shouted again; within the week, he'd passed away.' I was talking well, yet found myself weeping. 'And then –' Hanley'd come up and put his arm about me as I gulped – 'then . . . these bastards could make it known to the Inquiry that the Met had done its damned best to produce a key witness, even subjecting a young woman detective constable to grievous danger, only to have that witness whacked by the other side. Well at least they tried their best, say the Home Office. Talk of police corruption quite unjustified, with the isolated case of Five SERCS, who have now been permanently quarantined.

'Yeah, that's your side of the story, Claire. But it's only a side. Because what you didn't know then, though you must have gathered it since, was that Victor here was trying to make exactly the same thing happen. You know that, don't you? He –' I tapped Hanley's face – 'he wanted William to testify at the Inquiry, not to save his career, but because he was a campaigning anti-racist, that's why. And he thought he could make a name for himself – didn't you, old pal? So although you thought you'd worked it with William single-handed, Victor'd already been persuading him. They went down to a little shed by the tracks and that's where it was decided that William'd testify, and that's where his fate was decided too – though in fairness to Victor, at least he was willing to go with him and hold his hand. And if only he hadn't been lying in with a hangover owing to a patriotic footballing disappointment, William might have survived. But as it was, he had to go on his own, in new trousers that were too short and a jacket that made him look like a bullfighter. So that was his life.

'And at least Hanley had the shame to visit him in hospital, Claire. Did you ever visit? Or did you go and speak to Sister Gemma, tell her the truth?' Why was I giving her a hard time? Say I was full of the fire of justice. Say there was something sly about her. Say I wanted Hanley to fuck off so I could move on her, which he no doubt would not. Or she was sitting where Karen should have been. And everything was my fault. Yeah, that was probably it. 'Why don't you say something?' Hanley tried to shake his head at me.

'OK, Claire. So maybe it didn't go well for you after DI Arnold ditched you. You were noticing his methods. There was something straight about you that he wouldn't have cared for, middle- or long-term. Maybe he told you the NCA'd taken over the case, seeing as a substantial gangster was involved. Their brief now. The service was finished with Eldine. Or he called you and said well done, gel. Now he was retiring. He'd have been elegible by that time. You and him was through. Nice to have done business. And good luck!'

I felt the grip of a gentler ventriloquist.

'I'd fancy you had anything but, Claire. I fancy Pete de Lacey came after you. You were his until he said different. Now you had no handler, just a lover, with a heart as black as his shades. What were you to do? You had no one. You got depressed, you started drinking. You took sick leave. You tried therapy. What sort of therapist could understand what you'd been through? You'd got a young man killed, giving your all to get justice for a young man who'd been killed. And you were still going through it. The killer of the second young man was sleeping with you when he felt like it. It was rape now, wasn't it? You cracked up more, you took what you could for it: white wine, lager, gin, skunk, Valium, Xanax, horse tranq. You were never going back to the service in this state. And all the time, you had to hide from Pete de Lacey that you were a cop. Ah, the pressure of that! You went travelling. You thought you could find yourself, God, peace of mind, some righteous state. All round the world, you dragged these horrors like you dragged your rucksack.

'Something bad happened then, too, really bad. You went to a jungle where travellers like yourself lived in huts at the tops of trees. There you overdid it on Thai rum, knocked over a rice-bowl candle. A copy of the *Mail* you carried with you everywhere, that caught light. The faces on the front flared yellow and blackened. Then the whole fucking place was on fire, and when your buddy came over to help you, the roof fell in. You escaped down a creeper rope; above you, your buddy was a fireball, screaming. That's how you got that bad burn on your leg; maybe you needed work on your face too, Claire. The years went by. Time's meant to be the great healer. How could it heal you, kiddo? You must have felt like the Angel of Death. You loved your mum and dad – I know that. It would have broken them up, what you'd come to, the trouble you'd had, and brought with you. And no one to look after you – even though you'd have been known about, among cops and lawyers. Your DI wouldn't have been scrupulous, once he'd quit the service. Maybe never was. Rumours would have spread. Sooner or later, Victor Hanley would catch on. A great one for hobnobbing with detectives is old Vic. Oh-ho, thinks he. She sounds right up my street. Could do with talking to this lady. But Victor is nothing if not a gentleman. He'd have listened, but he wouldn't have joined in, finding the tone of these rumours ungallant. So he wouldn't have asked DS Chris Butler, in The Lord Clyde or friendly room of this or that court, where he might find DI Arnold's protégée, since DS Butler would have been unable to answer without detraction. No. What our Victor would have undertaken is a quest to find that lady, all by himself, guided by his heart, and native resources. And he might even have not altogether hurried about it, seeing as, (a) he's not much more than average brave (which is way more than some of us), and may have been frightened of what he'd hear from her; (b) he is very patient and would have been taking the long view with this project – his life's work you might call it. Furthermore, there's an old Hindu proverb, revenge is a dish best served cold – that's of the essence in this business. So he set about his quest, but made sure he was usually looking the other way. In fact, my guess is that he took around thirteen years to hook up with her, and then it was by coincidence, or serendipity. This takes us to the time of the trial of Drew and Roche, when it's probable that her name and information about her began to be passed round with some animation in the circles in which he moved. Like, "Hey! That bird who got planted in L Troop, know what she's

350

doing now?" "What? The constable that went in and laid one of the boys?" "That's the one! She's got a new cover now, bucko!" "What as?" "A Ukrainian cleaner." "You what?" "Trust me, bucko!" "Did the service sort her with it?" "Did they fuck! Sorted it herself – that or she's got some very peculiar accomplices. All the service gave was disability pension. She ekes it out with the cleaning, over West London. She had some accident, the face needed treatment. Which changed her voice so she could pass as a Slav. Which was helped by the fact that post-op (the undercover one), she was so fucked up she never talked much again anyway." "You're joking, son!" "Straight eight, me bucko!" "Ha ha!" And up prick Victor's ears, because what d'you know, a client of his has just such a cleaner. Introductions are made, stories swapped, oaths offered, "To William!" and so forth. And so the pair of you sit before me now.'

'How d'you know, *paisano*?' Hanley glinted. 'How d'you know that was how?'

'How else could it have been, Vic?' Claire Sykes had me in the cross-hairs.

'But how d'you know? Come on!'

'Something tells me.'

'Used to read your stuff in *The G*******,' declared Hanley. 'Nothing came close to that. The real deal, *amigo*! Marvellous – hey, Claire?'

Claire Sykes should have hated us both, in different ways perhaps; but she'd lost the will – or outgrown it.

Her in The Jennings's garden. Wearing shades. Ray Vernon with his back to her. Another wrecked soul. Too many already. God, let it end! No more of this.

But Hanley wasn't finished, leaning forward now on the settee, Claire with him, as if they'd braked suddenly. 'She knows where they go!'

'Who?'

'Pete and Mick.'

'We already know where Mick goes, don't we? That being why we brought a sack of tench to The White Cross in Shooter's Hill, after trying to run him down at his fishing ground.'

'Claire knows where else!' glinted Hanley.

'OK, where else?'

'They go to Mulhall's grove!'

'What? You what?'

'They go dogging there, the pair of them!'

As when your jacket's no good on a real winter day, north or north-easterly lancing, so my core responded, panicking from contact. Sibyl's warning joined the weather, Hanley waiting . . . *You'll listen to him.*

'Mulhall's grove . . . evil thing for me. Where my problems began.'

'I know! Thing is, *amigo*, we can take them there. Hold on!' He seemed to have developed a nosebleed. 'They turn up in animal masks, the de Laceys, Mick as an eagle, Pete as white tiger, or polar bear. Sometimes they go solo, other times, with their girlfriends. It's a real scene.'

'Yeah?' Trying to picture it. 'So how would we take them?'

'We go along ourselves – in masks. When they're on the job, we can finish them.'

Was this more ridiculous than terrifying? Dabbing at his nose, handkerchief a fine mess, Hanley radiated looks of deep encouragement mixed with rascally grins, as if this were a heck of a stunt he was pro-posing – as opposed to a diabolically stupid mission into the darkest place of sex and death. What was the general idea? White arses going in, out, at the rear of a hatchback, while a lady who doesn't really want to be there waves her heels – like they'd be more vulnerable, trousers down? They could just pull 'em up and stab us. Their blood'd be high. Was Claire going to come with? We'd need a pathfinder. Maybe she was going to turn up with Pete de Lacey, blow him and give a signal, whereupon Hanley and I'd appear from a thicket like Bill Badger and Algy Pug and seem to be joining the queue; but when he'd come, we'd do him. How the hell would we? Get our dicks out and give him a fatal fright? This ought to be sheer fantasy, this latest kill plan, but it was somehow in keeping with the tale of cruelty imparted to me in recent times, its devils of corruption and ineffective angels.

'How do we get in? Mulhall has the whole area guarded, patrolled.'

'Claire knows a track,' Hanley told me. Claire made a face. 'The security's not what it was. Whole place is crawling with open-air shaggers and voyeurs.'

'So what are we going to get them with?'

'Milly,' said Hanley from the side of his mouth.

So she was coming too? In the circs, it made sense, dogging being a couples thing. You were less obvious assassins, with a lady along. Maybe that was the draw, the bait. Hanley and pale wife by tree trunk. In the dark wood, figures gather, our side, others. Here come Eagle and White Tiger, fancying a bit of that. When they're on the job, we whop them with cudgels, string 'em up on the lower bough of a great oak. Damn! Must have been how Danny Flowers met his end. Obvious. Out dogging and this lot caught up with him. Found dangling naked in a pair of Uggs. Turbo prevaricating when asked. Who was the bait that time? Milly again? More to that pale lady than met the eye – as we guessed. Oh, thus an answer to their animal cruelty: lynch 'em while they're hot! Coffin lids a-tilt for twenty days . . .

'Karen won't be coming though,' I told Hanley.

'Coming where?'

'Mulhall's grove.'

'Of course not,' Hanley said. 'I wasn't suggesting . . .'

'But you're bringing Milly.'

'What? My wife? Are you serious?'

No. I wasn't serious. What the hell was I these days? Claire Sykes watched me like a curious show, a TV trial that won't run. Wasn't kind to be having this talk in front of her, was it?

'You said "Milly"!' I screamed at Hanley. 'Why don't you make yourself clear? Make your fucking mind up, for Christ's sake!'

'I meant a handgun, *paisano*,' Hanley said. You had to admire his even temper. 'A "milly".'

'Fucking hell. I didn't realize.'

'No. You didn't. Well, Turbo has one – or can get.'

'They're coming to the grove as well?'

'Of course. We're in this together, aren't we?'

'You know where Turbo is?'

'No. Where?'

'He's gone away with Fabian.'

'They've both gone?'

'Yeah. Gone. I spoke to Turbo last night. They've cleared out. Gone to South Wales to look at birds.'

Claire Sykes just sat there giggling.

'Why've they done that? Why didn't they tell me?' For the first time, Hanley looked shot, miserable, utterly let down; balling his bloody handkerchief. This was his life's work, not some fancy, and he'd pursued it with dedication, given it his all, for a decade and a half. The glint had vanished; his face was a piece of stale fruit. Oh, Hanley, you poor bastard!

'They got a heads-up from Sibyl Grove.'

'Who?'

'That old dame who lies out in the mews.'

'What did she tell 'em, Carl? Hey?'

'She told them our strategy was pell-mell. Which isn't far from the truth. The Shooter's Hill trip, for example, that wasn't a tactical success, was it? And this dogging wheeze – it's all over the place!'

'What's that got to do with bird-watching?'

'She reminded Morgan of augury. He has to watch for a certain kind of hawk – then take counsel from that. I've heard her come out with this kind of thing before. To Morgan, with his classical routine, it signified. – She sees it all in the cobbles.'

Hoarse laughter from Claire Sykes.

Hanley blew smoke: 'This hocus-pocus plays right into their hands, doesn't it? Divided, we're no good. How d'you know Mulhall hasn't suborned Sibyl Grove? She'll have us all separated before we know it, then they'll pick us off, one by one.'

'She isn't corruptible. Sibyl Grove's got too much of her own venom for anyone to corrupt her, whoever they are. Besides, if it's just hocuspocus, you're the one who believes in magic.'

'Am I?'

'Yes, all that *Faustus* stuff.'

Hanley said something that sounded like 'OK'.

'I've had a prediction from her myself,' I told him now.

'What did she tell you?'

'She said she'd seen Karen going down the road, then she said, What if I never saw her again?'

'Karen?' Hanley flushed.

'Come with me a minute.' I took him to the bedroom, Claire seeming to follow. The quilt was thrown back, as Karen would have left it Saturday morning. Crimson nightie folded on the wicker basket.

'When did she go out?' Hanley asked. 'I didn't hear her go.'

'She went out yesterday. Never came back.'

'What?' Hanley tugged my arm. 'What are you saying?'

'Karen's gone. She's disappeared.'

'Why didn't you say anything?' cried Hanley. 'Christ! Why didn't you say?' On his moustache, blood hardened into beads.

CHAPTER 40

L IKE IT WAS ALL his fault. That I'd been to the cops, Lolly and the Black Flag theory, everything from the talk with Paulie, dropped necklace included, back to first encounter with Arnold, I let him know. He seemed to rally: couldn't be responsible – we'd rekindled our association only when I returned . . .

Claire Sykes exited, Hanley held his head, recalling Karen's text at Walsingham Ponds. And this visiting of Tyrus's place, ominous, *amigo*. Jesus. But how could I have sat and listened to him and Claire, just saying nothing?

Well, first, with an abduction, there'd be a message. If they were going to kill her, they'd do it quick. Otherwise, keep her alive – and make contact. So why not wait?

Hanley looked on. Was I testing him? Did he know I called in hope; that when he came, I was desperate? Did he think I didn't care?

Giggling in excelsis, Claire Sykes returned. Crossed to that plane where endeavour seems ridiculous. Oh, the voices of men! Hanley leading her round like a prodigy; end of her tether. Holding her sides now. I wished they'd go away, but he was rock bottom. Feeling for his phone, he whipped it out and winked. Message from Fabian Morgan. There were photos. Hanley showed me. Morgan watching sky, Turbo with binoculars. Morgan making like Max Wall, banks of pebbles, sea behind. Jesus Christ! Were they serious? Hanley glum again, moustache pepper-corned. Where was this going to get us? Claire Sykes had never seen the like of it. Let him take her home.

What was I going to do?

*

PURPLE VOLUNTEERS HUNG ABOUT, sweating in their anoraks. The foyer was vivid with ghosts. I'd waited here for Karen at day's end. When her dark head appeared from the lift, it was an event.

Outside Paddy Power Earl Holmes leaned on his stick. He wore a fedora, black dinner jacket, white scarf, cricket trousers. 'Where you going in the sun, boy?'

'I'm going to church, pal.'

He laughed. 'You getting rid of devils, boy? Devil's bigger than the church round this way.' He laughed again and glowered. 'Bigger army. You ain't figured that, you no better than a baby!'

'What d'you know about devils, pal?'

Earl Holmes raised his stick. The scarf and trousers matched his eyebrows. Time passed; traffic passed, people passed, watching as they went. 'I strike you down, boy! Trust me!'

'Come ahead!' I told him, fighting stance. From traffic, guys looked on, hating that they'd miss it.

In time, Earl lowered his stick and spat. 'In my day, boy, I'd have licked you. Hear me?'

I grinned in his face.

'Old now,' said Earl, with an ancient's serenity, and serenely spat. 'Lef mi to me horses, me chicken an' yard.'

'Where's your yard, Earl?'

With his stick, he pointed westwards.

'Cumberbatch House?'

Earl stuck his thumb at his heart. King of Cumberbatch House.

'Did you know William?'

'William who?'

'William Cook.'

Earl Holmes shook his head.

'You were touting in the foyer, in William's time.'

Earl Holmes loomed over me, leaped away and cackled. That was William's move.

'Did he talk much to you, Earl?'

'Pickney never shut his mouth. Drat the boy! Snitched on himself, minute he got up to lights out.'

'You know what happened to him?'

'Yah. Wiped him out.'

'Who did?'

'The force.'

'The cops?'

'Hell boys!' Earl was amused. 'Take who they fancy.'

'Listen, Earl, I think they took my wife.'

'You may be right, junior. Know why?'

'Why?'

'Cos you ask too many damn questions!'

I had others for the priest, but waiting for a gap in the traffic, saw Hanley pass on the other side. By the time I'd crossed, he had the lead on me. When I called his name, he vanished. Past the office, I hurried up the flyover, watched him run along the tracks below, then fall. He stayed down, rose and stumbled, till he came to a shed, trying the door, slapping the door, kicking the fucker till he sagged. I turned away, eyes burning.

At the office, they were in, with another man and woman, clustered at Andy's desk. Before they clocked me at the window (mended now), I made off. Then Karen called.

To the bells of St Aubrey's, I hastened home.

CHAPTER 41

SHE WAS MAKING A fuss about the stink of cigs and had other bones to pick.

I sat me over there. 'And where have you been, miss?'

Know what she told me? This you might have guessed, though I wouldn't bank on it. It took some time to come out. All she said at first was she'd been with a friend.

Which friend?

A friend of ours.

OK, why?

Because she was scared.

Scared?

Yes. After all I'd told her on Thursday night.

I pointed out that she'd got less and less scared, and more and more excited, during that long talk, if memory served.

She lifted the vase from the alcove, threw the flowers away in the kitchen.

And what about Friday night? Didn't seem so scared then, did we?

Well that was a party, wasn't it – returning to living room. To cele- brate *her* success, 'if memory served'. And Saturday when I went off to my lesson (which she'd googled, incidentally, and what she'd seen online hadn't done anything to *un*scare her), she'd taken stock, which was something she should have done long since, if only I hadn't been so untruthful with her – which I had to admit, hadn't I? Hadn't I been untruthful, after promising I was done with all that gangster stuff?

All right, but that didn't decide anything at all, since my untruthfulness was hardly a shock, and it wasn't straight of her to present it as one either. We'd been managing it together for some time, and I'd levelled with her totally when I got back from the Shooter's Hill expedition, had I not?

Oh yes, I'd levelled all right. But I'd dumped so much on her in one go (the night before she was preparing for her critical interview) that she'd behaved the way she had then so as to protect herself, and give herself time to clear her head and ears and eyes and, yes, her heart. And on Saturday that's just what she did. And then she started thinking clearly.

What about?

Why, about our future together. Since it was obviously impossible for her to build her career the way she'd set her heart on if her husband insisted on hanging about with the most sly and disgraceful ne'er-do-wells who were leading him into God knows what trouble, including murder, and he didn't have the strength to tell them where to get off – not to mention taking male tarts for a super-luxurious day out on the pretence it was part of his 'job'. How did I think that made her feel? And if I wanted the truth, the only reason she'd gone slightly wild on our Friday night party was to try and remind me, without the greatest success considering how long it took me to get the job done (so much for the art of seduction!), who my actual wife was.

So where had she been herself?

She'd been taking stock.

Yes, we knew that, but she'd been with a friend, hadn't she – a friend of 'ours' to be precise? (Here was a shot in my locker. If she named

Lolly Morris, the game was up, wasn't it? Since I'd spent Saturday night with Lolly looking for her. She had plenty of other pals, but Lolly was her best girl, the one she'd have gone to.)

When she said she'd been with Craig Norman, I was taken aback. I don't mean astonished, for the surprises life prepares for us are there to see all along, long enough anyway, if we bother to look around; they creep up the league like a team we should have noticed, then suddenly, *Have you seen how they're doing!* I was taken aback because I hadn't reckoned with this.

So Craig (first names now) had called her again Saturday morning after I left for my lesson and asked if he could talk.

Who with?

With both of us, obviously. He'd tried me several times, but my phone was always off these days – wasn't it? And I wasn't there because I'd gone off learning how to kill or maim other people if they came at me with knives, or handguns – or *grenades*. Which she could hardly tell Craig about, since it would confirm the rumour that Carl Hyatt had terminally lost it, and that was one thing Craig was rather concerned about. She'd had to say I was away for the day visiting my mum (which I'd barely done all year, of course), so Craig asked if he could talk with her in confidence. He wanted to know exactly how I was, that was one thing.

Hold on a minute. She'd just said 'called her again'. When was *before*?

If I wanted to know, it was Thursday night while we were arguing.

(D'you remember anything of this? I don't. Let it lie a minute.) So what did she tell him?

She told him I was not good, and I ought to know that she got really choked up saying that, which had worried Craig even more. He'd spotted us at the Imperial, in the bar at the interval, but hadn't wanted to intrude, since he thought I'd noticed him, and given him a look, which he'd been worrying about.

(This you may remember.)

Not that she'd gone into any detail – not immediately – since (a) she was embarrassed, and (b) Craig was a busy man, and it wouldn't have been appropriate, just when he had something important to tell her. They wanted me back – no probation, carte blanche.

Meaning?

Meaning, a pretty free hand, provided what I wanted to write about accorded with editorial principle. Was I listening?

(She did take a call after Shooter's Hill. Heard her on the phone in the bedroom. Leaves room in fury, comes back and you're her hero. What was this about? Woman's caprice, or some fucking deep skulduggery? Let us see.)

Yeah, I told Karen, who'd been going on for a bit about 'carte blanche'. I was listening. But what Craig meant by editorial principle was ideology; i.e., I could write about what I liked, provided it didn't upset their poster mentality.

OK. Well, why couldn't I?

Why couldn't I what?

Write for the paper without upsetting their principle?

Oh surely she knew my latest interest. It was her who'd introduced me to it after all. In part it was. She went quiet, and I felt for her, then she asked what it was, and I had to go on. Telling me about Lolly and her problems with the Black Flag students and their Imad Mughniyah project, that's what, which had got me thinking about what had happened to Donna Juan, aka 'Golden Satchel', when he was at university, and then I'd got to thinking about a new form of racism whose target was the white Kuffar, which was the flip of what Hanley'd spent his working life tracking.

So what was I going to do? Become the paper's reactionary liberal?

No. I wasn't. Since I'd been keeping an eye on Alexander Brons lately, who was now in charge of even more of the paper than he used to be; and he'd raised the red flag over Farringdon, had Bronsovich, which meant that Western foreign policy was the cause of all evils, Black Flag extremism most definitely included. Therefore, I wouldn't be given a free hand, or any kind of hand, to write about what currently interested me.

There must be other things?

Not really. As we knew, I had a one-track mind, and my old employers wouldn't be indulging it (particularly when it came to a certain convert from Combat 18 to Islam I'd been checking out).

So I wouldn't go back?

Couldn't.

God, what was wrong with me? She swore I was getting worse. Though this was exactly what Craig had said he was worried about, that I'd react pig-headedly to the offer. Exactly this. Which was why he'd asked Karen if she could possibly meet him for lunch, to see if they couldn't maybe plot a little, so of course off she went.

(*Of course* . . . All for duty, what, our Karen!)

Craig had suggested The Tiresias, which was a confidential place to talk, and quite symbolic in a way, considering how things had begun between us.

I'd been thinking the same thing myself lately.

Had I? Well, Craig went into all that, and what sort of person I'd been in those days, ambitious, idealistic, committed, with a bit of an edge, not to mention all these wonderful contacts and sources. An inspiration to young people like Justin Fox . . .

Lord, what bullshit!

No it wasn't! This was the problem with me. I'd no trust in others, their memories and good opinions – and how important they were. All I believed in was nastiness. That was my problem. If anything was nasty it was true; if it was nice or valuable or positive, I had an issue with it. Basically, I was too stupid to see how deep this went with me (which was why she'd told me about Corneille and *ressentiment*) – not that she'd put it like that to Craig, who actually hero-worshipped me (God knows why). Well, she was no cynic. Let Craig keep his illusion! Maybe he could convince her. She was willing. God, she wanted to still believe in me!

(Stupid as I might be, I foresaw which way this may be heading. These exclamations were a sight too passionate for her conscience to be clear.)

By this time, Craig was on his second bottle of wine. Gina came to join them. She was all over Karen, it had been ten years after all. Buried Karen's head in her tits and darlinged her. She'd become rather tweedy, had Gina, like a disgraceful marchioness. Apparently she'd had cancer – she was extremely blasé about it – and Archy was long dead. She kept a pug called Mehitabel who had something about Craig's trousers – as if he cared; he was positively diking the wine, on the third bottle now.

(Fucking hell! All this for my benefit?)

So Gina asked if Karen had become respectable since the old times. Well, what was she to say to that? Not that Gina was taking the piss, though she did ask if a deputy headmistress was compromising herself by entering the shabby heart of The Tiresias, which had Craig guffawing like no one's business – he was easily amused, that one. On the surface, she seemed to have, become respectable that is, and she didn't mind giving the impression; if only it wasn't so hard, and actually bloody dishonest, when her husband was up to his neck in foul business, not to mention working for a paper they gave away free in the Co-op.

Thanks.

Well it was true, wasn't it? And of course, Gina must get on to the subject of who she'd wed in the end before she disappeared from their lives, and she remembered the way I turned up alone looking for Karen and announced on the street buzzer that I was the god-daughter of the Prince of Wales. Which did get me in. She remembered as well the way I watched everyone else in there – like they wouldn't do for me, or they were just poseurs, and I wanted to take Karen away from them. So she asked Karen where I had taken her.

And what did she say?

Well if I wanted to know, she'd become upset at this point; they were making her feel at home, sort of, Gina and Craig, though this wasn't her home now; but she wondered why she'd left it, seeing as her man had simply led her up a gum tree, when all was said and done. She reminded them, and she was frank, that even then, I'd had a bee in my bonnet about criminals, deluding myself that they were the only genuine people, when anyone with a couple of grams of common sense, native wit, or life experience, knew that criminals were the most dishonest folk that ever drew breath, which was a matter of definition – if I'd ever bothered to look up 'criminal' in the dictionary – not to mention being so bleeding stupid for the most part that they spent three-quarters of their lives in jail or living with their mam without a pot to piss in. And whether they were stupid or smart, the one thing they weren't was genuine, though the tricks of the smart ones were ultra-toxic. Which had caused me no end of trouble in my career – and Craig shook his head here, not in disagreement but sadly – and patted her hand, and pressed it a bit (yes, she knew his game, before I started on that); and Gina gave her a look that said she wasn't going to say anything (and I probably remembered how Gina could blaze away, so that look was bloody heavy – quite beautiful, actually, tragic even). Then Craig filled her glass, and began to refer to lunch.

(Oh-ho! Some aperitif. Three bottles between them already. Must have sunk at least one herself.)

But she went off on one – she had to get it out of her system, after months, no, years, of holding it down, banging her head against a brick wall, pleading (which I no doubt thought of as nagging) – and told them how I'd caught dishonesty from my work (like Nellie Kershaw got asbestosis from roving yarn). By now I couldn't breathe without lying – or if not lying, concealing, pretending not, dissembling (Gina's word), dissimulating. Day in, day out, she had to endure the feeling that I was up to something. It had got so she couldn't trust my face anymore, eyes, nose, teeth, or a way I had of smiling with my mouth only so I looked like a wolf, no, fox, and twisting my wedding ring at the same time.

(At least she didn't mention my dick – though that might be to come in these reckonings with deceit.)

And it wasn't helped by the fact that the company I kept nowadays was – though here Craig came in, because of course he'd spotted us at the Imperial, with Turbo, Hanley and Milly, and did she mean those people? The two guys, yes. So Craig said they looked like smart dudes, and Karen told him that was all very well, but since when did a flash appearance give you trust in a man? As a matter of fact, Turbo, the black guy, sometimes carried a Springfield 9mm – he'd told Karen so one night when he was meant to be chaperoning her. Gina said wow and flared her nostrils at the Turbo effect (which made Karen all the prouder about her own immunity to the 'charms' of that young hero), though Craig went a bit pale. Indeed, he'd boasted he could get Karen a 'compact' if she fancied, as a lady's protector – though it wasn't really boasting, since the fella was hardly a bullshitter, and indeed acted as a sort of minder to the person we'd all seen on stage that night, if Craig remembered, the so-called 'Cunctator'.

Well of course, Gina had to hear all about J. Fabian Morgan, and his strange eye, though when it came to how he'd acquired it, Craig lost interest in lunch, again, and said oh my God a couple of times, while Gina turned white and witchy and pinched Mehitabel. And this Morgan was another of my new friends. Indeed, it was he, along with Hanley — the lawyer Craig'd seen us with in the swank suit and chocolate trilby — who were involving me in a plot to kill. Yes, she had told them. Everything. Why should she keep it back? Did I expect her to deal with this all on her own?

Now hold on! Hadn't she forced me to tell her everything Thursday last — that, or she'd leave — when I came in from Shooter's Hill?

Yes. She had. But telling her didn't excuse me. Since when was owning up the same as being innocent?

But hadn't she called me 'hero'?

Ignored. — So Craig kept saying right, right, we've got to do something, and drank some mineral water. He'd actually got wind of some of this. Shouldn't reveal his source, but his wife's cousin Jonas worked at the court in Redbridge, and when he came to dinner mentioned to Craig an odd conversation he'd had with a lawyer who sounded like Hanley, the conversation being about an ex-*G******** man who was me. This was serious. As Craig repeated several times, Gina sat there stroking Mehitabel like Blofeld, when who should appear with a curious perfume and melodious twang, but Larry!

Shyly, sideways, making choo-choo with his hands, he approached them; in his eyes was wonder. Again, she had to wonder why she'd left the place. But enough of that! She'd made her decision, thrown in her lot with me. Larry ordered champagne, beer for himself, and a bottle of Pouilly-Fumé as table tiff, which Craig fell upon gladly. Now in proportion as Gina'd become aristocratic in her deportment (she'd taken to keeping bees, by the way), Lord Larry had down-styled, and was wearing sneakers, a hoodie and scrubby blond beard.

(How I loved to hear this stuff – even, truth be told, the obloquy directed at my wretched self! Damn me if the little witch wasn't enchanting me with her words, all over again – though why should she want to? Listen on, son!)

After Larry'd fussed her, scratching her face with his scrub, they had more talk of olden time. Blonde Cassie, often part of the company in those days, and there indeed that fatal night I came through the door with Craig and the others – Cassie Evans had gone away to Spain to be a fisherwoman. If she failed, she planned to be a whore instead. And if she couldn't cut it at that, she was going to paint, or play piano in a bar. Then Larry asked Karen if she was still writing, and they reminisced about *The Dedicated Vagrant*, which had gone the way of all such squibs – here Larry toasted Craig Norman of the enduring *G********, and Craig choked on wine which spurted from his nose. And the question saddened her, because of course she had no time to write nowadays, and Larry said what a pity, Gina assenting, for she'd absolutely had a gift; so she had to tell them she felt she was doing something really worthwhile now, though it saddened her a little that she had gone for the bourgeois option when it had turned so sour and foul, not to mention fatally dangerous. Well, hadn't it? Oh she hated me!

Hated me for making her be there on a Saturday afternoon when she was meant to be meeting her best mate, and when she tried to ring her, Lolly wasn't answering, so must be mardy with her.

But why didn't she leave her a message?

Because she had to speak to her. She didn't want to text or leave a message. That was right low, that was, standing your best mate up and then texting. Ugh! Typical!

(I could have tested her honesty here, since the only time when Lolly wouldn't have answered was when she was whacking that padded black shield behind which I happened to be hiding, which Karen wouldn't have known about there and then – though of course, there'd have been time since for them to collaborate on an account. I let her run on.)

And then they'd had to go upstairs and do some coke, since Craig was exhibiting a tendency to put his head on the table, or Mehitabel, or the floor, whereupon Craig sharpened up marvellously (Lord Larry's coke being rather pure and choice). For what was the point of this business lunch at all, if Craig was going to fall asleep like Rip Van Winkle? And of course, with three lines of cha-cha up her snitch, she couldn't try Lolly again because Lolly would know. This was how I'd affected their friendship.

But hadn't Lolly tried to call Karen?

Of course she had!

As I knew, while we sat together at The Horseshoe.

And by then, she daren't answer. But I hadn't, had I?

No I hadn't. Not in the afternoon. Because I wanted to surprise her by being with her best mate, when she arrived. But I'd tried her half a dozen times over the evening. So why hadn't she answered me?

Because it was too bloody late then. And did I know what? The fact was she actually wanted to worry me, like existentially. I'd put her through enough. So there! She *chose* not to answer my calls. Did I hear that?

Yes, I heard it.

And did I know another thing? They got no further with the planned conversation, the one about *me*, that afternoon.

So when did they get further with it?

Here, the intercom buzzed, Karen went to the hall, Turbo and Morgan entered beaming.

They were supposed to be in Wales.

'We was, Mr Hyatt, now we ain't,' Turbo told me. Behind him, Karen made faces, like we could be pals.

'Dring-drang, Turbs!' cried Morgan. Frivolous, for once, the young man set up a guitar sound, while Morgan did the duckwalk and sang 'Baby, Come Back' (The Equals). 'So here she is!' Morgan informed an audience. 'We've been wan with worry about you, my dear!'

Karen made more faces at me. I asked Morgan how they were here so quick. They'd sent Hanley beach photos only hours ago.

'From Pwll Du Bay, Turbo cranked it home.' Morgan made signs of joy at Karen, then at me, then Karen again, and Turbo, who was tic-tacking.

'I went to see Turbo to help me find you,' I told Karen. 'Last night.'

'Oh aye. Well he didn't, did he? You didn't either! Were you as worried as they were? Were you "wan with worry", our Carl?'

Morgan and Turbo watched me like rum uncles. I wished to God the pair of them'd fuck off, so I could have it out to the end with my wife. If she was wanting me to worry she'd done the deed with Craig Norman, I wasn't taking the lug. Just beefing on DJ and me there, wasn't she? It was the other hours . . .

'Of course I was, sweetheart.'

'I'll make some tea then,' Karen said: we were all in disgrace, she wanted to be on her own, but at a sign from Morgan, Turbo followed her to the kitchen, while Morgan took a pew beaming hard.

'She's back!'

'That's right.'

'Large as life, Mr Hyatt! Thank God – a miracle!' Morgan stood, and sagged against the alcove wall. 'Remember this one?'

'Kind of.'

'Laudable Conditions of the Blessed Virgin Number One: *Conturbatio*, or Disquiet.'

'Oh yeah. You were a scholar in the history of movement.'

'And this?' Left foot forward, Morgan stared down on me.

I didn't remember.

'Why should you either?' Morgan hummed, held the pose. 'Number Three: *Interrogatio*, or Inquiry.'

I didn't like the way Turbo'd trailed after her and closed the door, didn't like the way Morgan stared, with that dead eye. Had she been sporting with these bastards? 'Pwll Du Bay' my arse. Photos could be any time.

'Large as life, butty,' said Morgan, sitting down. 'Where have she been?'

'I dunno – altogether.'

'You oughts to know, bach. In times like these.'

I could have told him it was none of his fucking business, coming round here beaming, giving me the hard eye, talking to me like a Valley boy; but I didn't know – not enough to tell him Karen was just trying to worry me the way I'd worried her. Did he understand marriage, this one-eyed humorist? Was it in his range?

'What if they're trying to turn her, Calderoni? Think that's never happened before?'

'I'll tell you something, Morgan. There's no way that woman can be turned. She's tougher than the fucking lot of us!'

'You may speak for yourself, Mr Hyatt.'

I regretted 'us', that hard eye on me. 'Her own person, I meant.'

'Well, the end will prove that – one way or the other. Recall what your pitbull poppet told us in the car the other night: we judge the individual by the fate he, or she, creates for herself. Has she done that yet, in the last issue? You say nothing. Since you don't know what she's been doing. And the last issue's yet to come.'

'She was trying to get me my old job back.'

'She was trying to get your old job back? So you've made amends? Who with? Mulhall?'

371

'I'm not going back there. Told her.'

'But she's trying to turn you, Mr Hyatt. Isn't that the crux?'

'It's got nothing to do with *turning*, Morgan. It's just what wives do.'

Morgan pressed on the arms of the chair, like he was stuck in it, or he'd fly over and do me. For a second, his false eye was dull. 'She put you in a panic at Walsingham Ponds. Turbo tells me you were in a panic when you went up last night.'

'Wouldn't you have been?'

'Did Pheidippides meet the god Pan on his way back to Athens – 490 BC?'

'What?'

'As he ran from Athens to Sparta for aid at Marathon, and back to Athens, did Pheidippides meet the god Pan with his hooves, his horns, his cubital cock, smiling in the shade of a grove? Say he did. What reason have we to doubt, Mr Hyatt? It was long thought he did. Herodotus says so (6.105). It's fashionable to think so again. I'm at home with the old thought; the present catches up with me. So, did Pheidippides panic? You shake your head. Why should he? Pan caused groundless fear. The strong, the single, weren't affected. Pheidippides pauses, Pan promises victory. Had Pheidippides fled screaming, fallen in a ditch and smashed his head, Athens falls to Darius. For the Spartans wouldn't help before the new moon, owing to *religious* scruples. At even pace, without a backward look, Pheidippides runs on, bearing the promise. You're familiar with the story?'

'Twenty-six miles. – That's what he ran.'

'Bollocks, Mr Hyatt. The organizers of our first modern Olympics were sham classicists, twenty-six miles being the distance from Athens to Marathon. The legend that he ran that distance to join the battle, fought the Persians, ran back to Athens, cried, "Greetings, we win!"

and dropped dead, is without authority. He ran 125 miles, in two days, met Pan, didn't panic. Unlike you.'

'But it wasn't your wife, Morgan!'

'We're in community aren't we, *mwn*?'

Could I deny this?

'You, me, Turbo, Hanley, young John (he's got some fire in his belly, that one) – and Karen. That's community, or what does it mean? Which is why Turbs and I made haste from Pwll Du, where we'd planned to take our time in augury. I don't like haste, Mr Hyatt, and I don't like panic. A pair of red kites was circling, I wished to see their prey; but Turbo, who'd driven through the night, would press your case. We've come out of our way to help you, and conferred with Paulie Charalambous (that's an old boy with fire in his belly) and Tyrus, who are now preparing to mobilize; so when your wife admits us to your hall, I fear we've been made to look a pair of berks. But what you tell me suggests we are just in time.'

'For what?'

'To nip this in the bud.'

'She was trying to win me with words, like you do, Morgan – when you walked in.' As if from a long time off, he stared. 'She was reminding me of the past like you do, Morgan. What's the difference?'

'You're afraid of her; she makes you panic.'

'I've fucking had it with this!' I told him. 'You're under my roof. Get up!' As Morgan rose and took off his jacket, shaking his head like I didn't know what the fuck I was in for, Karen entered with the teapot on a tray, Turbo bearing biscuits.

'What on earth are you two up to?'

'Dancing!' Morgan told her.

'Don't you need some music? Me and Turbo've been trying to meditate, and all we can hear is you cracking on.'

'Lady's a guru, boss,' Turbo said. 'Showed me "4-7-8".'

'What's that then, Turbs?'

'Breathing drill.'

As we drank our tea and nattered, I caught Morgan observing us differently, and he winked. On their way out, he turned to me: 'Nor did Harry Hopkins panic, when he left his meds in Moscow.'

'Was that a code?' Karen asked me.

'Never mind codes, madam. What about this conversation with Craig Norman?'

Well, he'd invited her back to his work flat in Clerkenwell, where he had folders of my articles he wanted to show her.

And had she gone back to his work flat in Clerkenwell?

No. Done that years ago.

With him?

Ah, hadn't I realized! Could have had Craig for keeps – he'd have left his wife for her. Chose me instead.

But she'd told me she saw nothing in me, that afternoon on the *Marco*.

Served me right for asking, didn't it? That's the treatment you got in the North, fishing for compliments.

We were merry for a minute. The picture of her sitting on Craig's middle-class mush I'd entertain later.

Seconds out.

CHAPTER 42

SO WHERE THE HELL was she the rest of Saturday?

Been truly, madly worried, had I?

Yes I bloody well had. She should ask Lolly Morris.

Oh, she'd spoken to Lolly. Lolly said I wasn't particularly keen to visit the police station to report a missing person.

So when had she spoken to Lolly?

Never mind when. Why hadn't I wanted to tell the cops?

Because (careful here) I wasn't sure she was missing, strictly – as opposed to winding me up.

But Lolly'd wanted to go to the cops immediately. And I'd put her off, hadn't I?

Yes, for the reason I just gave (and another one, which you may remember).

After Lolly'd told me about the bearded man in the car outside the school?

Well, that had come to nothing, hadn't it? And two could play at changing the subject. Where had she been after not going back to Craig's 'work flat'? That was still to be answered. And I would put my cards on the table. After Lolly and I'd parted company, I'd been to see Turbo to help me find her.

We'd heard about that.

375

And after I'd visited Turbo, I'd been to see Paulie the barber, to ask for advice. That was how anxious I was. And then I came home, longing to find her there.

Yes, and been so anxious, I'd had a party to cheer myself up. The place smelled atrocious.

It wasn't a party. As a matter of fact, it was one of the grimmest nights of my life.

So was that why I'd had a woman up here? She'd found blonde hairs aplenty. Did she make it grimmer?

Yes she did, as it happens. Her name was Claire Sykes, by the way.

Oh, she knew all about Claire Sykes.

Did she now? And how was that?

Because she'd had a phone call, late afternoon.

Who from?

Why, from that diffident lady, Milly Hanley. They'd exchanged numbers when we were at the Imperial, had Karen and Milly, as a gesture of sisterhood, on the sisterly intuition that at some point, they'd probably need to have an emergency chat about their husbands.

(These bloody women! Was there ever a fella with their craft?)

So Milly'd called her and said Hanley was cruising the district with a blonde tart called Claire, no doubt hoping to bump into me in that 'accidental' way he'd been practising for a while now. He'd been meant to go to Westfield with Milly to look for a new dining table, and take them to see *Django Unchained*, then this piece had turned up at the front door – that was manners for you, on a Saturday afternoon – 'Víctor' coming on like he has a mega-professional emergency on his hands, dashing out with the tart, back for his hat, Milly and Esme utterly let down. And it was more than Karen could bear, after everything, to walk into another bloody murder session with me, Hanley and a hooker – in her own house.

But how did she know they'd be at home with me?

Well they had been, hadn't they?

Not that afternoon.

Oh, she knew they'd turn up, all right.

But Claire Sykes wasn't a hooker.

Oh, wasn't she? Well, according to Milly Hanley, she was an out-and-out bloody fantasist who had Hanley round her little finger. Telling him she went undercover in the Eldine Matthews investigation, and all kinds of baloney, about being connected with the gang, and left in the lurch by her handler when she was a detective, and how her life had been destroyed with no compensation.

Hold on! Hanley'd told Milly all this?

Of course Hanley bloody hadn't – wouldn't favour his wife with any secrets, that one. Oh no!

Well how did Milly know then?

Because she'd had a call.

Oh she had, had she? And had the caller identified himself? Because we could nip this all in the bud pronto. No doubt she'd been called by George Arnold, or his sergeant, to queer the issue.

Well, Milly'd said it was a woman called her, not the dibble.

OK. Well, Arnold must have put someone up to it. I wasn't having this. Either Arnold'd persuaded a girl to call Milly (like 'Kim', for example, who'd been in his power), or it was one of the de Laceys' current girlfriends, who'd got the hump about a copper who'd been sleeping with her man all those years ago, and was now out for revenge because it had become known that the lady policeman had surfaced again, and was chatting to a concerned lawyer about her experiences.

So 'Claire' had told us about sleeping with one of the murderers, had she?

Yes, she had. In detail.

Well, that was quite the thing, wasn't it? Having a blonde tart – sorry, ex-police officer – round for drinks and telling me and buddy Hanley till all hours about her sex life! We hadn't paid her to talk dirty, had we? Cos there were plenty of fellas who did pay hookers just to do that, sit on the settee with their legs far enough apart to demonstrate they'd forgotten their knickers, spinning yarns of fucky-fucky. Till the fellas heard so much they were close to bursting, when the hooker was bid adieu and tripped off down the stairs, leaving our connoisseurs to clean their rifles; or perhaps she hung around to help with a finely phrased peroration, before leaving with an even fuller purse.

Well this was different.

Of course it was! But how long had we listened to her talk about having sex with murderers?

Well, we weren't just listening. It was her and Hanley together, telling the tale, filling in. And there was no way she had him round her little finger. You could tell how they trusted each other, those two – desperately. They'd had the experience they were telling, each with their own share of it, and their two parts bore each other out. There was no fantasy, no flamming – no fucking deception.

So it'd been just me listening to this horrorshow?

Now what was she getting at? Well I could put her right on that, as well. And here was for why. Because I had done some telling as well.

So what had I had to contribute?

Well as a matter of fact, it was me who'd told Claire a lot of her own life, the consequences of going undercover and so forth, how rotten it had turned, the damage she'd incurred.

And how did I know all this to tell her?

Oh, it had just come to me, through me – like ventriloquism, or power to know without information – a voice I didn't know I had.

Well, hark at Dr Diabolo! Telling people their lives backwards! And was 'Claire' pleased by what I told her, as a just representation of her general past, so to say?

Well, Hanley said I had it exactly right.

And what did Claire say?

Very little, which was no surprise considering the truths I'd told were pretty sordid, but she accepted that was pretty much how it'd gone with her.

Oh, compliments to Carl! They hadn't by any chance been buttering me up, the pair of them, had they? An ancient trick, was that. Classic cunning. You let someone think they've got you down to a T, till their sense of their own wisdom goes to their head – and that's exactly when you take them. Was I born yesterday? And what was it this pair were proposing as a course of action, since they surely had not come round just to reminisce, or listen to Oracular Hyatt? Come on! What was it?

With tactical haste, I told her that Hanley'd brought Claire not just as a witness to the past, but because she had information about where the murderers could be taken.

Where?

At a dogging spot, that was where, OK?

Silence. Laughter, brief, harsh. So they wanted to take me dogging? That was what they'd come for? Oh God, this was all so bloody corrupt, the whole bloody shooting match! All this fanfaronade about revenge, what was it but a big disguise for lust? Oh, she was done with me, disgusted! She was leaving for good! Did I hear her?

And I'd forgotten, hadn't I, while I was partying, and contemplating group sex with these pigs and God knew who else in a lay-by or thicket, or wherever the hell these things went on, that my wife was missing. I'd forgotten that, had I not?

Well that was exactly where she was wrong! And if she hadn't been harassing me with an interpretation of what I was up to in the flat on Saturday night that was in fact the exact opposite of how it had been, then I could have told her that I took Hanley into the bedroom to show him that she wasn't there, and that I was worried. Frantic.

Hold on. I'd taken Hanley into our bedroom?

Yes. And we'd seen that the bed was empty, and her nightie was on the basket, the crimson one.

But why'd I taken Hanley in there?

To prove she was gone, obviously.

So Hanley'd been thinking, all the time he was there with this bint, that she was asleep? Was that what I was telling her? Christ, this beggared belief! I'd taken Hanley in our bedroom! And 'Claire', was she invited along to see the empty bed, and sniff the laundry? For God's sake, what need of woods or lay-bys, when there was a perfectly useable empty bed just along the hall?

No. Claire didn't come in the bedroom.

Oh, I'd just remembered that, had I? So where was 'Claire' when this particular pilgrimage was being made?

Well, as I remembered, she was in the bathroom.

And what the hell was she doing in there? Freshening her cooch with the flannel, squirting aftershave on her feet? Did I not possess a single particle of knowledge of the protocol, in the pack of marrowfat peas that passed for my understanding, that you never took a strange woman in another woman's bedroom? Even when you were worried, or frantic – and she'd never heard of anyone being frantic as slowly as I seemed to have been on Saturday night.

Well, I hadn't taken her in the bedroom. In fact, I'd asked Hanley to take her home.

When we'd both been efficiently de-spunked, was it? Or had Hanley and I diddled each other while she whacked her twat sitting on Karen's pillows? She'd seen the way he looked at me. With that rum, bum and puncheon glint of his.

Here, I advised her to cool it. I'd been making the best efforts to find her, and if she was intent on stitching me up with a bunch of things, and an attitude as well, that never happened, and that I didn't have, then she could sling her fucking hook. Or, she could cut the bluster, and have the manners to tell me what *she'd* been doing in the many hours of Saturday yet unaccounted for, a matter that continued to outpace the argument – or lag behind in the hope of getting lost.

CHAPTER 43

'So I WILL TELL you.'

'Good!'

'You better wait till I've finished before you decide, Carlo.' She came to the settee, beside me. Her voice was quiet now, and resolute.

So she'd been on her way home from The Tiresias after lunch with Craig, she'd spoken to Milly Hanley, she was passing Frango Oporto. A red car pulled up beside her, the bearded guy was at the wheel. The silver-haired dibble was in the passenger seat, and he dropped the window and called to her if she'd lost something. She was going to tell him to fucking do one and leave her alone if he'd be so kind, when he said he had something for her from her husband. So obviously she stopped and went back, and he was holding the opal necklace I'd bought her on his finger. The one I'd got her in Narixa at the stall. She must have dropped it when we met him at Abril's, and he picked it up after we left.

(Somehow, this cast a haze on Lolly's account. To be examined . . .) So why hadn't she told me she'd lost it?

Because she was ashamed, seeing as I'd bought her it only two days before. When she was throwing up, the chain was stretched and it must have weakened the clasp – that was the only way it could have dropped from her throat. Then George Arnold, he must have noticed it on the

382

floor and decided to keep it in case he ran into us again. Well, she was so grateful for him finding it, and having the heart to return it to her – whatever I'd said about the fella, and she herself, for that matter – that she had to give him the time of day when he began to tell her something. We all had to agree to an armistice.

Ah-ha! An armistice. Did we now?

Then he asked her in the back, since they were in traffic.

What on earth made her go in the back, with George Arnold? She knew the danger, for Christ's sake!

He gave his guarantee. They were police officers, him and Bowler, his sergeant.

But Arnold was retired.

No, he was a consultant to the Met now. Showed her his privilege card.

But she knew what I'd told her about these two!

Well she was still alive, wasn't she?

That wasn't the issue.

So that didn't matter, then!

Of course it mattered.

What was it, then?

Never mind. We'd come to that. So where'd they gone?

They'd driven down to the river. Bowler'd parked up behind the Tate while she and George Arnold crossed Millbank.

So Bowler'd not come with them?

Not at first; then she saw he was behind them, or along the railing when they stopped to look at things on the river. It was getting dark, but there he was.

Look at things? This was meant to be a crisis talk! They had time for sightseeing? (I liked this less and less; though a sort of comfort was growing.)

Not exactly. George Arnold kept looking at the boats, like he wished he was on one. Then he asked her if she didn't wish she was. A pleasure launch was passing and she thought of me, and the day when I asked her to marry me.

Hadn't blabbed to him about that, had she?

No. That was our secret. Then he said we were all on a boat, the lot of us, him and his sarge back there, she and her husband, all these lads who'd gone wrong so many years ago, badly wrong, to be frank, as wrong as you could go, and now your fellas who couldn't let it go, and were going badly wrong as well, on the evidence of certain recent incidents, and were destined to end up no different from the lads who'd kicked the whole thing off, that were now grown men themselves, and maybe wishing things could all have been different, though it was too late for that, since what was done was done, and once blood was spilled, you could never get it back into whoever it was spilled from; but was that a reason to cover the world with it? When he looked at the river now, he saw red, like a great tide of blood budging eastward, and we were all in the same boat; but we could turn off the engine, put down an anchor, make her fast in the mud, start a different conversation; have a sing-song even, as we was all Londoners, at the end of the day, and that's what Londoners did; or we could go to the stern and look west, see if we could catch the last of the sun. We had options, in other words. Didn't have to be the way it seemed to be going. Nothing was inevitable, no matter what people were planning, saying; if the wind turned, so could people. Didn't she agree?

Yeah, she supposed so – she knew what he might be up to (I shouldn't get her wrong), but he ought to be heard out.

Why ought he to? Never mind the wind. This was exactly how George Arnold turned people. This was his way.

And how did I know?

I knew because people'd told me.

Which people?

Father Raymond, Hanley, Fabian Morgan . . .

And who knew *they* weren't trying to turn me?

I knew (curse her!).

But how did I know?

Because in this world there was a basic distinction between people, which she might have come across herself. Which was that some people could be trusted, and others could not.

And what about the people in between?

Like who?

Like me, for instance. What if more people were like me than my 'basic distinction'? What if there wasn't a basic distinction? And people like me only went on about one when they'd decided what they wanted, and didn't want to have to think about it anymore? Stopped you from having to scruple, weigh things up carefully, imagine consequences, did a black-and-white distinction based on trust and distrust. Which was stupid. As most women knew. That was a woman's politics. And if more of these things were left to women, there wouldn't be rivers of blood.

So what would there be?

There'd be talking, and listening, that's what.

Yeah. Plenty of talking – and no action!

Well, wasn't talking an action? And listening, for that matter. Why did men have to equate action with kicking someone's head in, hanging them from a tree, or driving a car into them?

So she'd heard about Danny Flowers?

Yes. George Arnold'd been very sad that it had been found necessary to string him up, and make it look like suicide. Gutted, in fact, if he was honest. The lad had been trying to lead a normal life, which wasn't easy, considering how often he was turned away, spat on, cold-shouldered. How long was that going to go on? Till he was seventy, eighty? We let the Germans prosper, and the Japs, after all they done. Why not a lad with learning difficulties, who'd run with a gang cos he didn't know much better? Cos we wanted blood as much as they did, was that it? Wouldn't be satisfied till his life was out, strung up naked on the heath. Well at least his mum and dad knew he wouldn't be spat on no more. They had that consolation. As for his kid, all they could hope was she never got wind of what happened to her father, but people being what they were, that was highly unlikely. So it went on. Cross the generations. How much longer, hey? How much bloody longer, for pity's sake?

Couldn't she see how she was being turned? For Christ's sake, if there was one thing I respected, honoured, above all in her – and there were plenty – it was that she was her own woman. She could spot a fake at one hundred yards; no one had ever told her what to think; to think for herself, and be herself, for those things she had the courage, which was more than you could say for most people – and I included myself in that. The courage, and the wit. She'd come from a background that gave her no advantages in life, and she'd made her way – and she'd glowed while she'd done it too. Which was what had attracted me to her in a way I certainly couldn't resist, and probably stronger men than me couldn't either. And now . . . now she was falling for this drek. Swallowing it like a baby at a poisoned tit.

She wasn't falling! She was listening. And I needn't bloody soft-soap her either. Too late for that. Did I think she wasn't master, mistress, of a bobbin like George Arnold? And most men, for that matter. There were things Mother Jago'd taught her I didn't know a tittle about. Of that, let her assure me.

(I let her. Not unaffected by her performance, I was listening for the undertone. I wasn't born yesterday either. But my secret was I made less noise about it. She was being turned, all right, suborned. You can hear it, can't you, how the voice had taken in her? Against my own wife, I was on guard. And when it comes down to it, any of youse left listening, you better be on guard against those you love best as well. For I will tell you this. That is how you save them. Throw in your lot, and you're both going down. Distance necessary. She was talking to the fucking Devil, after all.)

So what else did he tell her?

He said an armistice ought to be manageable. No doubt there was plenty of heat on our side, and a sense of justice, which was sometimes the most dangerous thing in the world, especially if people weren't thinking clearly, drinking too much, plotting, bucking each other up, losing sleep, drawing the line, acting as a crowd, or mob, which was well known to be a thing with a lot of damage potential, and for why? Because it had stopped being sensible at exactly the moment it noticed it had twenty pairs of feet, or two hundred, rather than two. Then it got it into its twenty heads, or two hundred, that it barely needed no head at all, seeing as single folk with their heads still fixed in place tended to get out of its way pronto, and didn't try to argue or make their point. Yeah, a mob with a sense of justice was a danger to law-abiding people who got caught in the slipstream, or otherwise tangled up, on account of this or that kind of loyalty to certain members of the mob that'd been at one time functioning individuals, and a danger to innocent people who were often mistaken for something else in the heat of the moment – not to mention to itself. Which was the very reason an armistice was required as a matter of urgency. For everyone knew that life-long criminals tended to go under as a result of the path they'd chosen. You removed yourself from civilized society, you went to the wolves. No sirens among the wolves, just their howling. Well, that was what you chose, as a career criminal. But for civilized men, and women, that wasn't tolerable; you couldn't last out there, biting and bleeding. The wolves'd always survive you, just because they weren't used to nothing else; and as you were carried off to the ITU, or crem, they'd still be howling. But as a righteous mob, you might lose judgement, overlook the difference between yourself and the gangsters, think you could play their game when you never really had the training, which wasn't training anyway because that was a word used only by the civilized. Gangsters didn't train; that was the principle. Police officers trained, as did the army, professional footballers, athletes. Look at Team GB. See any gangsters among the sprinters, cyclists, rowers? No. You saw people who might have turned gangster, or had a dabble, but they decided to train instead. Which saved 'em from a life of crime. Now you might object, it's well known that some of the top crime fellas are handy with the fist or boot, therefore they must have trained, at boxing, mixed martial arts, what have you, not to mention the use of the long dagger. But as a broad rule, they all gave up the training once they got into the career violence, for several reasons. One being that the career violence kept them quite fit and that fitness shouldn't be underestimated; even a plump, wheezy gangster could generally find the bounce for a bit of extreme physical nastiness, should the need arise. Another being that as they got established, they could usually tell someone else to give so-and-so a hiding he wouldn't forget, or remove his ring-finger with a pair of secateurs. You didn't keep a wolf and howl yourself, so to speak. The point being, criminals didn't train; they lived it; and because a righteous mob had never lived it, but in the heat of the moment, or season, they might fancy they had, that was a fancy likely to prove expensive to themselves, and their loved ones. Then they'd go under, as the criminals did; but it'd happen to them a lot quicker. Indeed, they might not even last the summer, if they didn't draw their horns in before it got too late. Which was why an armistice was crucial, for everyone's sake. Forgiveness for the original offenders, a safe way out and back for a group of men who were getting well out of their depth, and who had their ladies, families, professions to consider. But an armistice required a meet. And where on earth was that to take place, things having reached the pass they had?

So did he mention anywhere for the 'meet'?

He'd been considering The White Cross.

Oh, that was a surprise. Did he really think we'd buy that? It was his fucking headquarters. He'd have the lot of us whacked. Never get out alive.

Well, it hadn't been the lot of us he had in mind.

So who did he have in mind?

Karen indicated who.

Just me?

Yes. And he explained why. Incidentally, this was why he'd asked her specifically to talk to him. Because her husband was the only reasonable one on our side. As the last visit to The White Cross had proved. That being the occasion a regular customer'd had his jaw broken in two places by the Welshman's minder. Poor fella'd had to sign off work, and all he was doing was trying to protect Jeff Gidney, the landlord, from the most violent harassment anyone in the place could remember, in a manner liable to harm his trade drastically, from what the Welshman and the lawyer were coming out with, while the tranny tyke was threatening law-abiding customers with a lager bottle like a professional hooligan. Jeffrey himself was in counselling, he had the shakes so bad every time he tried to stand behind his own bar. He'd been trying to tar him with association with some dreadful stuff, the Welsh fella, and the lawyer's there backing him up with all the jargon that impresses the layman and makes him feel he's done something bad, when he knows he's innocent. Severely frightening. The witnesses were terrified themselves, and wasn't even them being shouted at. The place still stunk of the fish that had been spilled on the counter, incidentally. They'd been shut till evening on the Friday, with the cleaners trying to get the mess off the counter and carpet, and deodorize the place. A number of punters had come down with a stomach bug, Thursday night and into the weekend, which suggested the fish was tainted – either that or it was sheer psychological fright from the performance of our side. Yes, we'd certainly left our mark there. Yet during all this, one person had tried to moderate things, pour oil on troubled waters, that person being her husband – which made you wonder what exactly he was doing with this mob. Incidentally, a theory, pretty silly to his mind, was now circulating that her husband was the main man, and he'd set this mob to terrorize The White Cross while he stood back like a puppet master. At any rate, the only man Jeffrey'd countenance coming to his premises for a meet was me, and me alone.

Well, that wasn't happening. No way. Did she want me clipped? I could scarcely believe she'd listened to any of this!

Oh, Geordie A. knew I'd react like that; and wouldn't blame me when I did either. What he was driving at was that I was the man to negotiate with, if we were going to be spared, the whole lot of us, from more of this trouble that was now spreading like wildfire. But was I up for it? That was the thing. Now, he had some intelligence that a certain clergyman I was acquainted with was after the same sort of armistice terms as himself, and if this clergyman could be tracked down, or approached, then we might just start getting somewhere, since a church would be the place that no one could object to, and in which – you'd hope – everyone'd be on their best behaviour for the house of God. And it was his guess – he might be wrong, but let him put it to her – that with the clergyman, whose name was in fact Raymond Vernon, onside, I might be willing to come to terms. Which of course depended on my persuading my side that the time had come to bury the hatchet. And he thought if anyone could do it, I was the man. So she asked how he was so sure; and this is what he told her. About a little thing he'd noticed, which went like this . . .

That time we were sitting at Abril's, well he'd been the fella who got chatting with us. Big deal, she told him. She knew very well he was. He'd already 'reminded' her at the Mayor's do. Why make a mystery of it? And George Arnold, he made a funny face, like he was touched in some way. The fact of the matter was, he'd been more than half hoping she hadn't remembered him at all, after the way she took the hump with him out in the sun. She had some fire in her, he could see that. And only trying to help her about her tummy ache, that's all he'd been doing. And no doubt, he'd seemed to be interfering, which was exactly what a person with a stomach virus didn't want, everyone noshing around her, parasol not functioning ever so well, and the mercury rising steadily. But anyway, to come to the point, he couldn't help noticing even then, if she didn't mind him saying so, what a calming influence her husband had when she was just about to tell him to stick his opinion up his arse. Oh-ho! He'd known what she was thinking, all right – tell him if that wasn't so! Well she had to admire his nous, though obviously it made it easier for 'mind readers' that she never hid her feelings, particularly if someone was pecking her head; but it had been something exactly like that when he told her he hadn't heard of any virus. And it was only cos I was giving her a look that she didn't come out with it too, she was feeling that rotten. But she didn't have time to think through this little mystery, because George Arnold was back to the idea of me being Mr Armistice, and what I managed that lunchtime in the sun, well that was just a token of what I was capable of.

I didn't believe a word of this. So what if he spotted I was trying to calm my wife down? Didn't turn me into Gandhi. As to the scene at

The White Cross, it was rank flattery to make out I'd been active in defusing that. Truth was, I'd been scared; I'd also been extremely envious that the rest of our team were gung-ho and up for it. Which was why I'd started the Krav lessons two days later. So I could mix it like the rest of them. What was more, Father Raymond, the clergyman – and surely I'd told her this? – Father Raymond was a witness Arnold had lost track of; which was hard to account for, active priests being easily located. Twenty years ago, he'd tried to bribe him not to testify against Mulhall's nephew, when that animal bit Morgan's eye out. Following which, Raymond left the catering trade and entered the church. With his army of spies and narks, it was astonishing he'd never hunted Raymond down (Claire Sykes managed easy enough); and it wasn't plausible he'd lost interest either, since the nephew'd persistently been whispered about as the Sixth Man, which made Arnold's protection vital, long-term.

So what then?

So he was up to something, obviously.

Such as?

Such as trying to get me to lead the priest to the slaughter, that's what.

Well how stupid could I be? This really got her, did this – this mushy-headedness. Hadn't I just said Arnold could have found Father Raymond any time this twenty year as easy as owt? So if he could, why should he need my help? Cut out the middleman and go straight to the rectory and top the fella. That would have been Mr Arnold's method, if he'd decided it was necessary, or got the word from his gangster pal. Therefore – was I listening? – therefore, Arnold was either not particularly mithered about this priest in a 'professional' sense, and I'd been fed some dodgy info to the contrary, and it'd be interesting to discuss who that might have come from, when we had five minutes for supplementary issues; either he was not mithered, or, he actually had some respect for this priest, and that wouldn't be easy for me to entertain in my cynical heart, but what if there was a part of George Arnold that wasn't snide?

What, after he'd tried to corrupt him, not once but twice, and not just with envelopes but with threats that he was running a paedo hub in his bar? Which, incidentally, I'd heard about from an excellent source, namely, Father Raymond himself.

(My wife had been turned. Hadn't she? Yet there was a lump of something hard, clear, persuasive in all this. Father Raymond had been left alone, even after Claire Sykes blabbed about talking to him; he'd been allowed to thrive. She must have blabbed, mustn't she? When she shopped William, Raymond would have been a bonus offering from good girl to her boss, to show her diligence, make amends for blabbing to Gemma Cook. All this blabbing, counter-blabbing – how it drove us humans! Unless – and here heart rose to throat – Claire Sykes had kept faith with the priest, told Arnold nothing when she was debriefed, so the priest was protected; tout William eliminated . . . Or unless she had told Arnold all about Raymond and St Aubrey's, and he'd never acted on it – until now. Which suggested an undevilish sense of sacrilege; and in this I wished to believe, for I wanted nothing less than that my wife'd been turned.)

So say I agreed to this meet, and persuaded Father Raymond to be present, which might take any amount of doing, since he was so uneasy about Mr Arnold's intentions that he'd wet himself while he was talking about him and Mulhall's nephew – I'd smelled it for myself, by the way, seen the stain, so this wasn't from one of the suspect sources she'd built up a fair head of paranoia about; say I agreed, what instructions had Arnold left her with? Was there a number?

No. He'd just asked her to put the proposition to me. Fancied I might not be willing, since I'd no doubt heard a lot to his disadvantage recently. What was more, he advised her not to go home immediately – Bowler was driving them back now – since he had intelligence that a psychotic fantasist who'd persuaded a number of people that she'd once been a detective constable was making a beeline for me. And this lady, who'd more than once come close to prosecution for wasting police time, and perversion (a certain op having been severely hazardized by the lady's antics, in the days before she'd changed her name to Sveta Sekshenko) – this lady would make special efforts to get Karen onside with tales of what certain coppers and gangsters had put her through. Which wouldn't necessarily be easy to resist, even for a lady of Karen's savvy, since this fantasy undercover copperette could spin a web like very few villains he'd ever come across and get honest folk up such a gum tree they'd never see ground again. Better for her not to tangle with her with things in the balance as they were – he'd experienced for himself how she could turn the cat in the pan; not to mention her trick of getting two people together to believe the same thing quicker than you could get one, on the mob principle – which was why he and his solid sergeant had made it a rule never to speak to her together, but one of them always stayed at a distance, preferably in fresh air, so's he could decontaminate his partner of her fantasies, which were as wicked as they came, when the partner'd left her company. And this was why she should keep away from home until this particular trickster had visited her husband and gone away again. At which point, let her return pronto, decontaminate him if necessary (though from what he'd seen, I might not be as easy to bamboozle as many others had proved), and put the proposition, using wifely skills of persuasion.

That was it?

Then they dropped her off.

Whereupon?

She went to Lolly's.

Of course.

They sat up and talked.

What about?

Everything. And the caves. Because that was the first thing Mr Arnold said to us, wasn't it?

What was?

'You should take the lady to the caves.' If she hadn't been sick and we'd gone that day, we wouldn't have run into him. We'd have gone for lunch at the caves, rather than to Abril's for a mineral, and never have known him.

(I wouldn't have gone to Bales alone either. Something took possession there: a tabloid headline, and twelve pages of 'analysis', that made me susceptible to Hanley, and all that followed.)

But hadn't she just been sticking up for Arnold, regarding the armistice?

That was just making the best of a bad job. There was that other thing Arnold said. Remember?

Which one?

When we were talking about poetry, and she told him what Lolly said about the caves. They were full of monsters and weird shapes.

Coming back now. What was it?

'The caves are OK, babe. All the monsters are in the sun. It's the world we know that's full of weird shapes.' When he said that, it was like he let the monsters out.

And she'd called him a poet.

The monsters were his making. He might wish they weren't.

So we should take the proposition seriously?

Well, what else was there to do? Carry on with the violence? Because whatever I thought of Mr Arnold, it was true what he'd said about the tide of blood, wasn't it? Had to be. We'd all end up dead, or in jail. That was the truth; getting away with it was sheer fantasy. And wasn't there some honour in an armistice?

Maybe.

Wasn't Arnold meeting us more than halfway? And in doing that, he was conceding something about his side, an evil past, even if he did have a twisted way of doing it, wasn't he?

Perhaps.

And it was going to be all right? Between us. Forever. Like we'd planned?

(So our life together would proceed with all legality into a prosperous future, we'd die holding hands in bed – and that image of felicity was no more to be ruffled. For the misgivings that fluttered about me were themselves devil-sent, fire thoughts that didn't suit my personality, which we might as well acknowledge as conservative.)

Yeah. Like we'd planned.

And did I promise? Say it, darling.

I said I did. In my gullet something burned, as she kissed me.

CHAPTER 44

Smoking with Sibyl in the mews, Donna Juan trilled, 'Hiya, darling!' He had a little dog on a lead, gladiator sandals, lime-green shorts, matching sun visor. Looked like a bleeding tree frog.

'Where you off to?'

'Work.'

'I'll come with, mardy-pants!'

'Why don't you meet me at the rectory?'

'When?'

'Later.'

'When's me profile out?'

'I'm just going in to finish it.'

''Kay.' He came my way, past the garden square. So he'd left Lords. The Russian had given him money for a pet. He'd loads of free time now. Him and Hanley'd been talking.

Where'd he seen Hanley?

On a bench by the Westway, while he was taking 'Freckle' for a dump. Yesterday afternoon. Suit all messed.

Must have been after I saw him, banging on that shed.

'He were almost skriking.'

'What?'

'Crying.'

'What about?'

'William.' Donna Juan waved. 'See you at rectory.'

*

MONTY HAD THEIR BACK on the Mulhall campaign. That was the first surprise. Saturday afternoon, post-Krav Maga, Fabiana found him with Andy, taping the windows. They'd been online to search the application to run a Sexual Encounter Establishment at Lords. Monty, who actually thought it was just a chess club with a bar when the licence was granted, had 'expedited' a visit from the Premises Licensing Inspectors. Guess who else was helping them!

Dunno.

Steve Barnfield and Marcia Jones!

Had they come up with anything?

'They will!' cried Fabiana. 'No one stands in Barnfield's way, now he's on crutches. He's like the Terminator!'

Things had changed, what? At the Levee, Andy wouldn't give the councillor the time of day. Remember? And Mayor Montgomery lost his cool at Barnfield's question. But the Mayor was an honourable man, and though the awkward squad on the council gave him the pip, he wouldn't truckle to gangsters on his patch. He was old-school in that way. Andy's Mulhall feature of last Thursday (which seemed a long time ago now) would have appealed to his Churchillism, or whichever of those historic grandees he took after. As for the issue of whether Tory councillors were in the habit of using Lords – well, if Monty really thought they'd been up there playing chess, innocence still had its . . .

'And this is your doing, Carl!' Andy called to me now. 'You are squarely behind this, my man. Years ago, you lifted the lid. You've taken the flak. Now you lead us to victory!' Andy began to march, singing

398

what he knew of 'The British Grenadiers' while I spoke to them through the din . . . 'What?'

'He said "armistice".'

'Forget about victory, Andy. What we need is an armistice. To stop the violence. It's out of hand. We're all of us running wild. You know everything that's happened. I told you both last Friday. Just before the office was attacked. It will get worse. That's what happens with feuds, vendettas. A stain's a stain. Can't be removed, but it stays where it was, till a group of people decide that whoever it was made it should be called to account; then the stain liquefies, starts to flow, and you have a little stream, but it's rapid; and that stream widens, still rapid, and it widens again; till it's become a feature of the territory, so you build your house beside it; and it grows still wider, and it winds about, and as it winds, it encloses more people, till it meets the sea. By then, the whole world's red, since the river's prone to flood.'

'Well that's mighty poetic, Carlo, but it's just words. Not action.'

'We've had enough action, Fab.'

'So what are you after, chum?'

'Peace, that's what. All I want now.'

'All you want?'

'Yeah. All *you* want?'

'Or you and your other half? She – Karen – has been on the phone to me this morning.'

Didn't waste time, did she? Well, I'd made a promise: 'Yes. Me and my other half. All we want.'

'Who came up with the word, Carlo? You or her?'

'Or was it when she was out to lunch on Saturday?'

'How d'you know about that?'

They came at me with phones.

'Craig Norman tweeted.'

399

'What d'you follow him for?'

'Makes sense! All one community, aren't we, Carlo?'

There was a photo of him, Karen, others: *As it was/always will be!* The cha-cha must have set him on. Fucking ponce.

'She wasn't lobbying for you, was she? She was, then! I can see from your face! Oh, we always knew this would happen one day, me and Andy. Well, Andy thought so, but I told him you were a straight-up guy. You wouldn't rat on your pals. And maybe you wouldn't, Carlo! But you aren't strong enough to stop other people working on you!'

'I'm not going back there. I told her.'

'Was it Norman came up with that word?'

'Which one?'

'*Armistice?*'

'Why on earth would he?'

'Cos he doesn't want the *Chronicle* succeeding where his newspaper got pissed all over by a gangster.'

'This is nothing to do with Craig Norman. Sit down both of you, for Christ's sake! George Arnold took her for a ride. Down to the Embankment. He had her necklace. She agreed to go – wasn't coerced.'

'So she willingly got in a car with Arnold?' Fabiana stood again, knowing about women, as men never can. 'For a necklace?'

'It was one I bought her – he'd found it. It was him who brought it up.'

'What up?'

'An armistice.'

Fabiana gripped my wrist: 'Why d'you think he wants an armistice, now of all times?'

'He's seen sense. Maybe he's seen the light – you've got to give people the chance to improve, Fab, redeem themselves.'

'Is that you, Carlo, or are you just telling me what your wife reported? D'you believe what you just said?'

'I'm ready to.'

'Well, I'll unready you, mister! Listen up. Monty sent the Licensing Inspectors in on Saturday night. Conor Gard and Meredith Jhaliwal. Con's a rugby player, and I happen to know that Meredith does Punjabi martial arts. What d'you think they found?'

I didn't want to speculate.

'Here's the first thing (there's loads!). The application is a joke – if it wasn't a scandal, it would be. They lied about their heights for a start.'

'What?'

'Their heights. The applicants for a Sex Establishment Licence have to state their height.'

'What the hell for?'

'It's the law. So Mulhall's lied about his height! He's tall, isn't he? That's well known. Andy and I got pictures of him leaving court after the libel case. He's got heavies with him, and he makes them look like Pipkins. He's six-five if he's a day.'

'So Mulhall's an applicant?'

'He's a Director. They have to give their heights too. You may think it's silly, but wait till you hear. It's like Al Capone. They pinched him for unpaid tax, then they took his empire apart!'

'What height did Mulhall declare?' You couldn't not ask.

'Five foot three. Even smaller than Tom Cruise. Imagine! And that's only the beginning. Van Spenser's given a moody address for his place of residence before he became an applicant. He's put that sandwich cabin he used to run, which Conor and Meredith have now reported to the Immigration people because it looks like Van Spenser's got a fake-residence trail. They're examining his passport photos, which may not even be of him. And a stall address – which his cabin technically was – can't count as an address for residence. You know how it is now with illegals. They'll have the bastard on the boat home before the summer's out. And guess what! He actually put in previously for a sex licence for a stall – that would have been his cabin – which wasn't granted. That's why he ended up selling sandwiches all those years ago. Ugh! Imagine!'

I imagined.

'If you look at Sections 39 and 42, you can see all this. Section 6 is the height bit. Between them they took the piss utterly. Every bit of the application's either piss-taking or totally dishonest. Steve Barnfield was here by then. Marcia Jones brought him. What a mess they made of the guy. The consultant blew his top when Steve discharged himself, but he was like, I'm out of here, pal. Work to do. Free up a bed for you. Never know who'll turn up next in ITU. Long live the NHS! Marcia told us that. She's so proud of him. Now *there's* a fella with guts! How dare they ask for an "armistice", after what they did to Steve? Tell me! Anyway, Steve's positivo that the application was expedited –' Fabiana watched me – 'by Zac Cumberbatch. His uncle's the one who set up the hostels. The uncle was a benefactor, but Zac's a slime. Steve says he's waved a lot of dodgy stuff through in the past. He introduced a small-business steering group on the council, just so he could do his pals favours without ratification or checks – or auditing. And he's also a member of Lodge 97. Does that mean anything to you, Carlo? I know it does! I can see it! We can absolutely have Mulhall, and Van Spenser, busted for tax, and any number of false declarations and infringements. And Monty and Steve – you know they haven't seen eye to eye in the past. Andy told me all about the row at the Levee (oh, I so wish I'd been there too, Carlo!). So Monty takes his Stetson off: "Mr Barnfield, I fear there has been difference between us in the past, sir, but I offer you my hand now in recognition of your courage, and in hope that we may work together towards a common enemy that is poisoning our patch." And Steve, he's like, "Let the past drop, Monty. What say we turn these bastards over and kick their arses!"

'That's only Saturday!' Andy rubbed his hands as Fabiana handed round a bag of sherbet lemons. 'Hit him with it, Fab!'

'So, Sunday morning, we all gathered here. Me, Andy, Conor, Meredith. They hadn't slept. I hardly had either. You could have been here too, Carlo . . . And what d'you think Con showed us?'

'What did he show you?'

'Well, he'd gone beyond his remit a bit, but he said if we really wanted to give this bunch a shoeing, we might find this useful. And what d'you think he had? Can you guess? Well wait till you hear! So Van Spenser's trying to bargain with Meredith – you wouldn't imagine the bribes he came out with, he's unreal, that fella, inviting her in his VIP Lounge for a glass of something fizzy, and licking his lips. Ugh! Anyway, Meredith calls Con and asks if he's checked the VIP Lounge. Van Spenser tells them it's locked, like he's really proud of it, so they ask him to open up. Well, he's still coming on to Meredith – he actually brushed her with his pee-pee while they were in the lobby and told her mixed-race babes were the lick – so she goes up the other end to put some space between them, Van Spenser's following her like a dirty dog, and while Conor's in the VIP Lounge, which isn't even tat it's so shabby, like it's got a big screen, cocktail bar, cabinet of toys and butt plugs, red rug that's covered in stains and aftershave – while Con's in there, one of the boys comes up to him: "Hey, boss, you take that thing away with you!" He's pointing to a rat-repeller, you know, one of those plug-in things with a signal, in the corner. So Con's like, Ah-ha! Health and Safety! cos the switch at the socket's stuck at OFF. But the boy – he's Italian – what d'you think?'

Oh God. Here it comes. Forgive me.

'He says to Conor, "There's a recorder in there, boss. Justin left it." So Con asks about Justin, and the Italian boy – he won't give his name – he says Justin was a totty who came down here three or four years ago, but really was no whore. He was a spy, a mole, and his *capo* from a big newspaper sent him up to gather shit on Mulhall. So Conor, he puts it in his bag, and he asks the boy about Justin and this *capo*, and who he was. And the boy says, Well, Justin, he was always talking about a guy called Carl, who was his Numero Uno, his hero, he'd do anything for him. Why are you crying, Carlo?'

Because here was a kind of miracle. And what can we do with miracles, but weep? Impossible, but there it is. So we recognize a miracle. The few of us they happen to. Justin kept faith with me. Went away broken, muddy-eyed, and all the time, he'd been working for me – if this thing was still operating. 'Have you played it?' Fabiana was hugging me. 'Must have run out of space long before now.'

'Carlo –' Fabiana stepped back – 'your boy Justin had a 512GB card in there. Like, MI5-standard. Lasts for yonks! The beauty of it was he snuck it in the VIP Lounge, which Van Spenser let hardly anyone use except the cream of the scum, Mulhall for example, Zac Cumberbatch, and Lodge members. It's voice-activated, so it doesn't run while it's quiet in there. We've been playing it all night. Some of it's him talking to boys.'

'Mulhall, you mean?' Asking Justin what kind of man he was. Did he have a better idea than God? If so, what? Asking what he was frightened of, fucking his soul . . . Had they heard all that?

'Yes, Mulhall. But that's only a fraction of it, with the boys. We've got him chatting to the coppers. Andy says they're the ones from the Levee, the silver-haired fella and his sidekick.'

So Arnold and Bowler went with boys as well? No. It was a place they wouldn't expect to be bugged; they'd have taken pleasure in meeting Mulhall there; we can overestimate men's pursuit of the carnal, when they enjoy darker powers.

'Hear this, Carlo! File One.'

CHAPTER 45

'WHAT'S HAPPENING WITH THE priest, George?'

'Don't be going there, Mickey. The hairdressers will kick off, I warrant you. The bird Sally, she lit a candle for him because she didn't back him when your nephew done the Welsh fella's eye. She's had twenty years' grief over that, and this ain't the first time I've had to mention it. The other one, Gemma Cook, she's the sister of the shouting boy we flattened. She ain't satisfied with the justice system, not one bit, and this tally-ho lawyer that's traced Sykes, he'll be stirring them up.'

'Thought you had the woman copper under control, George. What's happening there? Robbie's mother, she's at my fucking ear about this priest. It's her who wants him drilled.'

'Why you letting her drive you, fella? Just tell her where the fuck to get off. Man of your calibre, Mickey.'

'Easier said than done. She's seen the details.'

'You what? Who the hell showed her, Mickey?'

'No one showed her. While I'm away, she's stayed a couple of nights cos her kitchen's flooded. Bitch must have popped the safe. She's had a good look, and made a photocopy. Now she's wanting the priest sorted.'

'What's it to her?'

'With Vince Drew and Andy Roche gone down, it's live again, there's curiosity about the "Sixth Man" and his ID, people's "coming forward" whose memories have improved – and the priest's still at large. Not that she's prejudiced against priests; but if it's between her Robbie and a vicar, that's a no-brainer. The vicar goes down, or the details goes to *The S***** T****.*'

'Well that can't be, Mickey. No way. I've drawn the line there. That priest's so much as lightly bruised, these hairdressing bints'll go to certain straight coppers – the lawyer'll see to that – and they will offer information about two witnesses that said straights will be mighty eager to hear, these being Ray Vernon and William Cook. And when your straight coppers ask around about William Cook, and learn how he ended his days, and where, and *when*, the shit's gonna hit the fan good and proper. Then we'll all be making for the caves. Lucky you got hold of that land, Mickey, that's where we'll be, anything happens to the priest. We'll be lodged in them caves like World War Three. Nuclear winter. Living on tins . . .

'And I'll tell you another thing. The woman copper ain't under my control nowadays. She's fucking running wild. Apart from the lawyer's turned her, Hanley's his name, she makes it her business to keep an eye on the priest. Follows him round like a fucking angel. I tell you, these bastards are gathering force. She's changed her name and her mush as well, which don't make it easy to keep tabs. No way we can take anyone out just like that, without it looks like a Dirty War. That's your issue, Mickey. We done William Cook to help your nephew and his pals. We done our best to bung the priest, scare him off. We marmelized Nulty. We're tracking Barnfield, that's the councillor who's been making a fuss about the land you want over this way. He best remember his Green Cross Code, that fella. But the long and short of it is we can't be hitting people to order. That's your issue. Make some fucking hits yourself. Don't just be bribing, blackmailing, giving the word. Use it, or lose it. When's the last time you gave out a hiding, Mickey? Talking ain't enough. You're getting lofty, fella. The journo that libelled you, behaved like a fucking peer of the realm with him, didn't you? Like the Right Hon. Princess Michael. "Master's Bench Injunction"? What the fucking hell's all that about? You'll be painting your coat of arms on your Merc next. Shoulda popped him yourself. You won the case, but you lost face. He won't be finished with you, that one. Bowls has done research on him. He resigned from *The G********. You think with his tail between his legs? Bollocks! He's gonna track you hill and dale now, through the fucking jungle. He won't let up till he's snagged you. And what you gonna to do? Put out an instruction on him? It's a matter of time, I'm telling you, before the lawyer gets to him. Then it's gonna be the biggest fucking free-for-all since *Gladiator*. Like fucking village primitive football when there weren't no rules, cops, manners. And it ain't just the lawyer and the journo. There's the one-eyed Taff playing the long game, and they're going to hook up with him too. He wants your nephew, and he won't be leaving this earthly scene till he's got him. They want the whole pack.'

'You're pissing up the wrong tree, George. Two of them's put away, rest are at hazard – all of 'em except Robbie, that is. Why should this lot be after doing it themselves?'

'Cos they have seen how long it fucking takes, cos they know what we done to the law, Mickey, cos they know the door's now open, cos their blood's up. Just think about that, big man. And what's more, cos they know we'll be mobilizing to the max. That's why as well. So they got to get their revenge in prontissimo, before we start putting up a firewall that no one's gonna cross. That's why.'

[*Silence.*]

'ARE THESE FILES DATED?' I asked Fabiana.

'That one's late March.'

So the caves that Arnold mentioned, they must have been a/the motive for Mulhall's purchase of the woodland in Greenwich. Right? So what the fuck was he doing with caves? This was something I should have sussed at the time. The land abutted on caves, or lay over caves, or whatever the fuck land did. Jesus, but here was a blind spot! For a mountain-top gangster, a king of crime, caves were a swank addition to the Kentish manor. So much you could hide or bury down there – swag, bodies, imports. Yet was it just the practical benefits that had stimulated Mulhall's imperial adventures in Bostall Woods? What if a crime king wanted a deep, dark, winding fantasy court to prowl in? So he could be away from a world he was tiring of, losing his grip on. From the recording, it seemed this was the way it was going with Mulhall. My heart surged when I thought of Arnold's tribute to my stamina, will for the hunt. As this pair must have known it would . . .

Something else. The 'marmelization' of Nulty. This bore out my allegation about the accountant who'd disappointed Mulhall, discovered hanging in a hotel room in Orpington, head in a bag of Liquid Gold, naked from the waist down, March 2002. The inquest found that Nathaniel Nulty had succumbed to an auto-erotic accident, and recorded a verdict of accidental death. But I knew that three glasses had been found on the desk in the room with traces of whisky in them. Coroner McQuaid, noting the glasses, suggested that Mr Nulty'd had company before the accident, and observed that as a man of some professional distinction, it was likely that he'd concealed his homosexuality from family and close acquaintances, indeed from everyone except the sort of associates who'd be rather likely to come and go in a shadowy fashion, to whom no blame could be clearly imputed in this unfortunate case – unless anyone present had information for the court? So it was Arnold and

Bowler who'd sat drinking whisky with Nulty. And they'd left the glasses as a taunt (since they knew well enough to clear props like that from the scene), as if to say, *Only us! What you gonna do about it?* Or, *Of course it wasn't an accident!*

Such actions referred to as the 'details'.

But those jaunty killing days were over too. It sounded as if Arnold was tiring as well.

'Give him File Two, Fab!'

'Over the top!'

CHAPTER 46

'SAY I RAN INTO him lately in the sun. [*He means you, Carlo.*]
Let's call it coincidence. Such things happen.'

'What would you have been doing down there, George?'

'Our place in Calahonda. Say Janet wanted it hacienda'd. I'd been looking out for a pargeter. You can't find a decent pargeter nowadays. I was occupied over here, so I put an advert in *Sur*. No response. Another ad. Long last, I get a call from Rico Flores. His girlfriend's Luna. She gives soothing prostatic massages. The bums had stuck my advert in the "Adult Relaxation" columns. Dungeons, domination, squirting, fanny licking. What is this world but a whorehouse? They thought a pargeter was a sex worker, which was why my ad went where it did. Anyways, Luna's pointed it out to Rico, who happens to be a decent *yesero*. Which would be why I went out there at this particular time.

'Then I ran up to Narixa for lunch. Say I'd been thinking about our problem with this hack Hyatt. Thinking hard. You with me? I'd have maybe known him and his wife had flown out this way for a break cos I've got a postilion at City – in the Costa by Departures. On that infor-mation, I could maybe have asked around, shown his photo. There's a place called Lola's. I go there now and then. They do meat on the stone. Now Lola, she's a wily piece. She don't much like me, that I can tell.

Which of course I take as a challenge. She's got me sussed, I fancy, though she won't say as much. Well, thinks I to myself, you can't expect everyone in this world to like you – ain't that true, Mickey my son? And no hard feelings. Might as well have a bit of fun with her. As a matter of fact, how about coming close, confirming what she thinks, so to say – but just like in play? Perhaps I showed her Hyatt's photo. Like, had she seen him round these parts? The look she gave me, Mickey! People don't realize how they snitch whatever they do, they just don't realize: *I ain't telling you nothing, you English berk! Pay your bill and fuck off out of here!* Now what does that tell me? It's all in the manner. Of course Lola's seen him round these parts, in here in fact, and recen-timo. I tipped her good. Watched her through the window as I went on my way; she's looking at the tip like I shat on the salver. Then I go down the front to digest things.

'There's a bum round those parts called Joe Pordio. He'd be a fair snout, he wasn't perma-sozzled. But he does have a knack. As a matter of fact, he's canny. Cos what d'you know but I'm standing by this old cannon, watching the water, and a young lady over on a flat rock in her communion dress looking really pretty, like girls don't tend to look nowadays, when up the steps from the beach comes Pordio, and who d'you think might be with him?'

'Tell me, Geordie.'

'These steps, they save you going round by the road, so Joey P. has brought the pair of 'em to me, Hyatt and the missus. About five-two she is, younger than him, nice yabbos, all this mascara running down her mush like a Hammer film. She's a fiery gel all right – but I'm jumping the gun now, Mickey, because it wasn't then I got chatting with them. That was the next day. They went on up the hill – Hyatt's checked me out, but he ain't sure. Meanwhile, I whistled Joey back, to keep an eye where they went, which he didn't need persuading about, seeing as

Hyatt didn't tip him for showing them the way, whereas I lined his palm. And back to Calahonda to take stock.

'Well it's a small world, Mickey, small, small world. All gummed to each other, ain't we, knuckle? Cos that evening, Rico introduced me to an interesting lady called Cassie who plays piano (so she says) in Bar Alta, though I didn't fancy that was her only game. And would you believe it, after a few sherries, she lets on she's just been up in Narixa with a client, like leaving his place, and who should she see coming along the *calle* in a big fancy sun hat and celebrity shades but an old pal of hers, Karen Tynan? Who's that then, Cassie? says I (not letting on I know that to be the maiden name of Hyatt's missus).

'Oh, years ago, like, these two was regulars at Tiresias, which was a West End joint for book-writers and hacks. They had a mag coming out of there that they wrote all the tricks they got up to in. The hostess of the place, and a lord who put up the money for the mag, they both had a soft spot for Miss Tynan. And I'm nodding like this and treating for a big jug of sangria – they got a boss recipe in Alta – so's to keep Cassie going, and see what else I can't absorb that might come in handy. At any rate, Cassie's bumped into her old pal in Narixa looking flash (which wasn't how she looked to me when she come up off the beach, but that's another matter) – or to be precise, she hasn't bumped into her exactly, because she's got a feeling that one of them dodged or blanked the other, and maybe it was her, and maybe it was the other, like it can be when you bump into someone from long ago, cos you're so surprised, by the time you've put a name to the face, you've missed the chance and they're too far down the road for you to run after them without causing a scene, or you're too far up the way to go back without looking like you've thought it through – which ain't exactly friendly. But she goes along behind them keeping an eye on them, Karen nagging Hyatt about when they'll see the caves, and she sees where they sit down for lunch, which is a joint called Abril's, so she's going to go and say, Cooee, hallo darling! to her old pal, but she gets a call from another client. Ho-hum.

'Well, Cassie, says I, that is a small world, gel! What's he like then, the husband? Nice fella? Oh, says she, he used to come to The Tiresias. I do remember him, not that he fit in especially well. Wasn't the type somehow. Like he wasn't comfortable there, didn't talk the way everyone else did. Didn't seem to know anything about writers either, which was surprising, given he was a big journalist – or maybe it wasn't. Do they read books? Search me, Cassie, says I, I wouldn't know, my dear. Never had any truck with journalists. And Rico's there, laughing his head off for some reason, so I give him a dig. But what was his game as a journalist – sport, politics, some such? Oh no, says she, he used to go on to K.T. about gangsters, how crime was his thing, and the only thing, cos everything else in the world was settled really; it was only the crime folk that had anything about them anymore – like a kind of nobility really, not that most people would share the opinion, but everyone else had lost their nerve more or less in the modern world, and themselves with it. Men weren't men, and women were jugglers. The main things in life were to avoid standing out, and giving offence; for the straight world, nothing else counted. Everyone was on the level now, the flat; except the crime boys. They was still some way up the mountain, some of them was even hanging out by the summit. So if you wanted to get a sense of how life used to be before the levelling set in, you had to approach these fellas.

'This was how he used to come on to Karen; Cassie overheard, or Karen told her the score in private, and he once said there was a particular criminal by the name of Mulhall that no one had got near his peak yet cos it was a hell of a long way up there, and bleeding slippery as well, but he was going to find his way to that peak, was Hyatt, and when he got there, it'd likely be the case that Mulhall said, "Ain't no room up here for two, fella! So what you going to do about it?" You hear that, Mickey? We never knew it went back that far, did we now? Ten years, this is. And d'you know what he said, Hyatt, when he was giving it to young Karen with this mountain scenario? Tell you what he said, Mickey: "Well you better make way, pal, cos I'm here now. Down you fucking go! Ain't the boss anymore!" Which might have been the charlie speaking – the drug was used liberally and openly, according to Cassie, on those particular premises – or the liquor. At any rate, the trash talk turned her mate's head, Mickey. So Cassie reckons. Next thing they know, she's going to marry Hyatt.'

'I can't be allowing that, George. I thought he was just an overexcited hack got out of his depth, like they do, fancying a big paper's like an army that'll cover you, advance or retreat. Thought my beef was with the paper, not the cunt himself. Now this is different.'

'Right you are, Mickey. Well that night, I got to thinking. Got to thinking what we was on about last time we were up here. And I regretted what I said about you losing your bottle, which was just a way of saying I might be losing it myself . . .'

'You always had bottle, Geordie.'

'I've been busy, Mickey.'

'Attaboy, Geordie!'

'Needs must, Mickey. For instance, that night down in Calahonda, I got to thinking, We best nip this in the bud. Bowls here, he's of the same opinion. Except it ain't a bud anymore, it's a fucking big root we're dealing with, when you take into the reckoning all these other bastards that's now talking to Hyatt, the lawyer, the one-eye, his minder – who's already given the mother of all fucking hidings to a snout I keep in the area, and in broad daylight, on the public highway, which I take as a declaration of open war. And that root, it goes deep,

Mickey. For one thing, Hyatt's had a second on these premises. That's how close the bastard's coming. Didn't I tell you he was a tracker, wouldn't let up?'

'Thought we'd done with his plant, Geordie. The kid Justin. Blocked his transmission. Sent him away.'

'Not him, Mickey. That's well finito. There's another one. My good snout put me on to it. Saw him coming down the mews with this boy, just the other day.'

'Which boy is it, Geordie?'

'Small dark-haired lad, slim.'

'One of them Romans it'll be. Van Spenser should have been on to that. What's with that Cape cunt?'

'More fucking trouble than he's worth.'

'Should have clipped him long since. Took this place over myself.'

'He's had his bounty. From us both.'

'We've got to arrange for this boy, Geordie.'

'We have done, Mickey. Me and Bowls took him into rehab. He's saying he's never set eyes on Hyatt. Can't persuade him. And I'll tell you another root Hyatt's put down. He's been on to Barnfield since the Mayor's do.'

'Thought the bastard had an accident?'

'Don't stop Hyatt. He's been at his bedside in ITU, discussing land licences in these parts.'

'Couldn't you have finished him in the sun, Geordie?'

'Don't think I didn't try and make it happen, Mickey. That night after we left Bar Alta, I remembered Cassie saying about the wife wanting to visit the caves. They was discussing it the pair of them as they passed her. Well, Bowls'd hacked the BA manifests, and we knew they was due back eighth of the month. Sixth it was I saw 'em coming up from the beach, and Cassie'd encountered 'em that lunchtime, so they hadn't been to the caves that day, being as it's a substantial outing, and the lady'd wanted to make a day of it. Then I had a dream. Hallelujah! And in my dream, I saw this pair wandering through the caves hand in hand, looking at all the shapes in the rocks. Oh, there's some strange shapes down there, Mickey, very strange. You was an imaginative person, you might fancy they had faces too, and they was watching you back. And in my dream, there's Hyatt and the lady, and he's in his element and she's clutching his arm pretending to be frightened like ladies do, though it was her idea, this particular excursion, and what d'you know but something comes out from behind one of the rocks with a grey face that's not identifiable, but his face ain't rocky, it's just a stocking he's got over it, and he's got a big knife. Now that woke me, Mickey, and I had a look at my phone and there's a message from Pete de Lacey. This is two a.m. He's just been with Danny Flowers and he's worried the lad's showing the strain. Not but that he wasn't always a dipstick, Flowers, but since the convictions, Pete fancies he's been acting very odd. So I called him: What's he been up to then, Pete?

'"Oh, he's got fucking fat, for one thing, Mr Arnold. I said to Julie, why've you let him get like that? She's like, Oh he's comfort-eating. He has a Full English, then he's out to Costas for a bag of brownies for his elevenses. Half the time, he sicks the lot up as well, like he's got an eating disorder. I told her, she should see to it he goes to the gym, takes some pride in himself. Oh, he's stopped his membership. Why's that then, Julie? Cos a black guy down there, he come up to Danny and he said, Seen your picture in the paper, bruv, with them lads who went down. Best make yourself scarce, droog. You ain't wanted in here. And next time Danny went in, the black guy's got his mate with him and they give Danny a slap in the changing room. He had a weal the size of a sausage from his cheekbone to his jaw after, and bad vision. So I'm like, What's this, Jules? He's taking orders from coons? What's fucking happening to him? Where's his fight? Who are these dogs? And she's like, It ain't the way it was, Pete. You might call 'em dogs, but the blacks are top dogs now. And not just them. He was at the Peshawar, which is his favourite kebab house, getting himself a snack, and three Asians on bikes, they was making faces and knocking on the window, and when he went out, they're like, Hoy, where you be going with that tiffin, butters? This is Paki territory! And they slapped his food all over the pavement, threw him in the gutter and then they rode round in circles, pulling wheelies, shouting slogans, spitting on him. So I says, Well, well, Danny, what you got to say for yourself? This all true what Julie's saying? Don't sound like the Danny Flowers that used to roll with L Troop. What's eating ya, son? And he's just sat there twitching, Mr Arnold, and fucking fat as shit as well, like a fucking fat titless mong. And Julie's like, He's been putting stuff on Facebook, Pete, and this priest, he's friended Danny, and asked him to come to his drop-in sessions over West London. And I'm, How now, Jules! Priests? What's this about priests, Danny boy? You don't wanna be hobnobbing with priests, mate! They're all fucking child molesters, for one thing. Ain't you read the papers? Another thing, priests get people telling stuff they swore never to mention, stuff they done so long ago that it don't matter no more, except when a priest starts working on ya. Then you blow the whole fucking can, and you drop your mates in it that's trying to lead normal lives. And just by the way, you wasn't speaking to the service before Vinny and Alan went down, was you? Look at me, Danny, look me in the eyes! And Julie, she's, Oh he had nothing to do with that, Pete. I swear to ya. It's since then he's been shaky, I promise. Danny ain't no grass, Pete. All right, Jules, I told her, I believe ya. You hear that, Danny boy? I believe her. But I'd be happier if you could fucking stand up like a man and speak for yourself! And he got up from the chair, Mr Arnold, and he said, I ain't no grass,

Pete. I'd die first. And he's sweating like he's in the steam room. And I'm like, Who's talking about dying, Danny? What's the matter with ya? That ain't on the agenda! – And that's how I left it, Mr A. I didn't believe him, either. But if he figured that, who knows what he might do?"

'Yeah, you did right, Pete, I told him. You're best keeping away from him, cos if anything does happen to the lad, the service are going to be on to you pronto. You've probably been observed visiting him as it is. In fact, what I'd suggest is you come over here for a while. I mean first thing this morning. Don't be coming private. Get a commercial flight. That gives you an alibi. Cos I fancy something could happen to Flowers, might be next week, might be next month, might not be till midsummer. That's my prediction, if you know what I mean. Meanwhile, you can do me a favour.

'So Pete arrives here just before lunch, Mickey. I've picked him up, and I give it him straight. Told him there was things I didn't want to say over the phone. Told him he had to steel himself, cos this whole affair was going nuclear. And I told him, if there was anyone who did have steel in his heart, and ice in his veins, it was Pete de Lacey. That he's proved before, when there's others would have cracked. Well, now's the real test. And he has had a training like few men. He's had his freedom too, Mickey, I had him remember that. Twenty years. And it's you and me he owes it – him and his brother. They know that. Well now, Pete, says I. Are you up for it? It's going to be naughty this, Mr Arnold, ain't it? That's how he replied. Yeah, very naughty, Pete. But you owe me a life, and you owe Robbie's uncle a life. That's two lives. So I want you to deal with a couple of people. There's a journalist that's been trying to destroy Uncle Mulhall; and this journalist, he'll be coming after you lot as well – that's my hunch. As you know, Pete, you and the boys have never had a single friend in the press, not one.

You ain't had no more chance than a Berlin Jew in Hitler's time, any of you. That's how it's been for you all. They're competing with themselves to take you down. We got to strike like lightning. So I want you to go down to some caves (I'm taking you there now), and I'll provide you with a photo of this journalist and his wife. I want you to take them both out in the caves. Make the old knife sing again, Pete! You're the man for it, the only man. Meanwhile, I'll be back in town making sure they come where you're going. What's more, I'll sort it so they don't arrive in time for one of the official tours (they're every two hours). You can't do the job with a bunch of pax gawping and waving cameras. You strike fast and decisive, carotid, heart, or femoral, you leave the knife (I got one for you), you wear two pairs of grey examination gloves on each hand, you wear a grey stocking over your head, grey jeans, T-shirt; you can change in the back of the car. Leave the shades with me. Don't listen to anything the woman might say to you. Do him first; don't want him wilding on you. Then do her. Don't forget, she's put him up to a lot of this. She's a violent, ambitious slag herself. Don't forget how dishonest women can be; as a matter of fact, Pete, they're the original traitors. From Eve to Claire Sykes, that's how it is, son! Pure poison, chronic trouble. That clear? If you're still up for it, nod once. In that rig, they'll think you're a man of stone, like you just stepped out of the rock itself.

'Now when you done the job, you'll be covered. Can't be leaving by the exit. Here's what you do. Observe this postcard now: "Hall of the Cataclysm". Up there on the right, just under where you got that stalactite like a corn-cob – nod if you follow – you got a passage; it goes uphill – it's steep, it'll make you sweat; it's narrow too, but you'll get through. Go up that passage and you'll come out on the hillside, other side of the caves. There's a track there, which you follow down-hill past a couple of farmhouses. You won't see no one but hikers, that time of afternoon. You come across any hikers, take your T-shirt off. Understand? You'll pass a little meadow on the right with goats in it. There's a sort of lay-by there, and in the lay-by you'll see a rust-red Nissan van. The back'll be open. Get in the back and someone will bring you to my place in Calahonda. Savvy?

'So I drop him off at the caves, drive back to Narixa to snag this pair. Along they come – I ain't been there at Abril's more than quarter of an hour – they sit at the table beside me, she's already talking about the caves. Except there's one fucking problem. All of a sudden, she's come down with some stomach bug, and she ain't feeling fit enough for the excursion, yapping to Hyatt, and she can't eat or drink, and him all lovey-dovey, noncing about with the parasol in case the sun's a bit much for his darling. I get talking to them anyhow, and I tell you, Mickey, she's got some will, gastroenteritis or no. I'm on my mettle with her. She'd do all right under caution, this one. Anyway, I suggest she picked up the bug from Lola's, the raw meat and that, but is she having any? Oh no, not she! It's a virus, it's going round, the waitress told her, etc., etc. Well, says I, ain't heard anything of that, and she comes back at me like my knowledge ain't worth a scratch. So I play it kokum – get her agreeing to one thing, she'll agree to a second. Now I'd seen them coming up from the long beach, so I put it to her she might have caught the sickness from the sea, being as there's an outfall to the west, and no treatment plant, and believe it or not, she comes round to the suggestion she might have swallowed a mouthful of effluent, when the water down there looks so pure, just like a stain-glass window. Now I take my chance. She wants it pure, there is no better place than the caves: no germs in the air down there. And she says something back, and I tell her she's poetic, just to flatter the green-eyed bint, so she turns that back on me. Jesus, she's a handful, this one. You know, I could have sworn she's a mind-reader, Mickey, cos she then says a mate of hers called Lolly has told her the caves are full of monsters, monsters and frightening shapes – just when I'm trying to get her down there, for Christ's sake. So I give it some about all the monsters being out here, and now I'm a poet – first I ever fucking heard of it. Meanwhile Hyatt's sitting there giving her looks. They're off the caves for today. He'll take her next time, or whenever. So I give him a tip about somewhere to go later, place called Bales, with a view to an ambush after dark; but by the time I rendezvous with Pete back in Calahonda, he's in no mood for more instructions after waiting for two hours with a pair of tights on his crust, and a tear-up with Rico about sitting in the back of his van. So I fucking take Rico's van there myself and wait for him to leave, Bales being on the Calle Carreta, which happens to be extremely narrow. But he never comes back down.'

'You had a square go, George. Can't say fairer than that.'

'Square go ain't enough, Mickey. I won't let them slip again. The wife, she dropped a necklace at Abril's. I picked it up; it'll come in handy. She's the one to work on. She takes the lug. Unlike Hyatt. He's slippery, but he'll come her way. You know for why, Mickey?'

'For why, Geordie?'

'Cos he's in love with her.'

CHAPTER 47

WHEN WAS THAT?
    'File Two's last week, Carlo – Tuesday.'

Another miracle: Karen's stomach bug saved our lives. Then saved mine. When she called for frozen yoghurt and I took a taxi, he was waiting in a van on the narrow *calle*. Jesus! On my sleeve, I dried my eyes.

And they'd taken Pep by mistake – DJ intended.

'Give him F-Three now, Fab!'

'Put the kettle on, Andy!' Fabiana handed round more sweets, and wrapped complimentary biscuits. 'Tighten your seat belt, Carlo! When we heard this, we were flying!'

'When's it from?'

'Late Friday, into Saturday, begorra! It's mainly the other one.'

'What d'you mean?'

'Mulhall.'

'WE NEED TO CALM the whole thing, Geordie.'

'You what, knuckle?'

'We need to cool it, time being at least. These tactics ain't suitable.'

'What you telling me, Mickey? You now got this rag Hyatt works for on your tail. I told you he wouldn't stop. Wants to stiff your portfolio good and proper. The P-PGS app – he knows all about that. Zac Cumberbatch told me this fella Ravage never lets up pestering the Mayor about the Land Indemnity, and Barnfield's got Hyatt's ear – the site's his pet subject. I had a plant on the ward Barnfield went to – Kim Perry temps as a nurse nowadays. She passed that on. They're hand-in-glove on this. Now Hyatt's wound him up, Ravage this is, to start this campaign against you, Mickey. You ain't gonna let that go, are you?'

'Hear me, Geordie.'

'Tell me something, Mickey.'

'I sent a squad to alpha Ravage and his crew.'

'When would this be then, Mickey?'

'Yesterday this would be, Geordie. I had a walk in the woods with Tony Friend, asked him to recruit it. Didn't want to know names. Half now, half on delivery. That's the deal. I put up 3K there and then, assuming he still knew where a Tec-9 or suchlike could be quickly sourced, and he was yeah yeah yeah . . .'

'You should've asked me about Anthony Friend, Mickey. He's got very silly, has Anthony.'

'Yeah. He offered to do it himself, but I told him again I didn't want to know names, so he better delegate, and the operative would need someone to help dispose of the SAP so there'd better be a driver. Well he's gone and muffed the whole fucking show. Starting with he only asks Noderick if he's game.'

'You're fucking joking!'

'Noderick, he fucking leaps at it. Fucking clown. More likely to shoot his own dick off than drop the hacks. So he takes Noderick with him to get the SAP, which shows how bad Friend's cracking up, cos when his man sets eyes on that fucking loon, he suddenly remembers he ain't got a single piece handy just at the moment. Oh not to worry,

Tone, says Noderick, more ways to kill a cat than a fucking plastic tommy gun anyway. We can use axes, like *Donnie Brasco*. So Friend tells him, it ain't going to be them two, by the way, seeing as he's marked; Noddy'll have to sort a wingman. And it's yeah yeah, leave it to Noddy. All cushty. Friend phones me Friday lunchtime, to update me with all this, and I said, I thought I told you not to name names. Sorry, Mickey, says he, I forgot. Well maybe that's as well, cos you're a dumb berk, recruiting Noderick. What the hell you playing at? Call the cunt and cancel the commission! Cancel the fucking mission! And he's, Too late, Mickey. They've gone west now. Noddy's turned his phone off so's he won't leave a call trail while they're engaged in business. So I asked who he'd taken with him, and he goes, I thought I wasn't meant to name names. Jesus, Geordie! And I'm just, Fucking tell me who he's taken, Tony, just tell me! Who is it? Oh no way, I ain't telling you, boss. Friend, you tell me now, or I'll come down to fucking Carshalton and I'll staple your dick to your garden fence. And you know what he says, Geordie? Oh, I ain't falling for that, Mickey! You might just be trying to test me! If I name another name, you won't pay me the other half. Taking the piss. So I tell him, Right, Friend, you better leave for a foreign land cos I am now coming down to torture you. So he's, OK, I'll tell you, Mickey, who Noderick's taken with him. He's taken your nephew. Mickey? Mickey? Why you gone quiet, Mickey? So I tell him, I think I'm going to torture you anyway, Tony, cos that is the most unwelcome thing you could possibly tell me. Why in fuck's name did you let him take Robbie? Oh, they was having a drink, Noderick and Robbie, and Robbie's mum seen this thing about you, front page of a free paper cos she was up shopping in Harvey Nicks Thursday, and the cab driver'd been reading it, so she asked if she could have his copy. Then she went home and showed it to Robbie, and she's like, Look what they're doing, son! They're libelling your Uncle Michael again, the fucking scum. We can't have it, can we? Robbie meets Noddy in their pub, and Robbie's going mental. So, when Friend mentions the commission to Noddy, the first person Noddy thinks of as a driver is Robbie – chance to revenge his uncle. He's gagging for it, that one.

'So I said, Well I'll tell you one thing, Anthony, anything happens to Robbie, he gets pinched or identified, I am going to torture you with your family watching, then when I've maimed you, I am going to torture the rest of your family one by one, while you watch. I am then going to burn your house down with the whole fucking lot of you inside. It'll be a fucking favour to humanity. Cos if anything does happen, his mother is going to make things hard for me, and if you think I'm tasty, you should meet her. Then you'd know what terror is, you cunt. And he goes, Sure they'll be OK, Mickey, I swear it. Then I said, Robbie's lost his licence anyway for drunk driving – how's he going to get Noddy over there? Oh don't worry, Mr Mulhall, that's all sorted. Sorted? How's it sorted, Tony? Well they're going on mopeds, the pair of them. Mopeds? So they got no gun, no car, and they're going over West London on mopeds with fucking axes over their shoulders? This what you're telling me? You sent a couple of fucking woodcutters on the job? Hold on! I coming down to see you now. Don't try and leave the house, Anthony. It'll only make it worse for you.'

'Jesus, Mickey, but this is messy.'

'You haven't heard the fucking half of it, Geordie. Cos by the time I get down to this ponce's place, Noddy and Robbie are on their way back. Noddy's switched his phone on and given Anthony the signal. So we stand at the window waiting. Friend's wanting to take a slash, but I tell him he ain't going anywhere till these two've appeared, and he'll have to piss his trousers. Nothing else for it. Don't want him slipping out the back and over the fence. Wet yourself, you wanker. And here they come, down the drive. I said to him, You told me they

425

took two mopeds. Why's Robbie on the back with Noddy? Why's he sitting side saddle? Where's the axes? Why's Noddy helping him walk? Let us go to the front door, Anthony, and let 'em in.

'Well they're in a state. Robbie's took a real hiding. He's on all fours, retching. But first things first. I ask Noddy if they've done them, taken out these hacks. Well they've done the windows! The windows? What's he mean? They've smashed all the windows in the newspaper office. Ah, this cunt's looking so pleased with himself, Geordie, and with Robbie down there spitting his ring on the rug, and Friend trying to clean it, I'm – I dunno, I'm having trouble reckoning with this, know what I mean?'

'Carry on, Mickey, carry on.'

'So I say to him, Is that all? You did the windows? You were meant to be finishing these hacks. What you do the windows with? With axes? Oh, we done 'em with half-bricks, boss. In carrier bags. Jesus Christ. I wanted these people eliminated, you've gone there with Robbie like a pair of fucking chavs and thrown stones at the windows. That all you've got to tell me? Oh no, Mickey. We had a rumble with them as well. A rumble? What sort of rumble? Well, I've given the bloke a battering. Which bloke? Hyatt? The big red-faced bloke. Well, that ain't Hyatt. How bad did you hurt him? Oh, he was on the floor, broken nose. Yeah yeah. So he was on the floor. But did he get up again? Oh, I didn't notice. I was helping Robbie. So what happened to Robbie? Oh, this bird came running out after we done the windows and she give Robbie a real shoeing. You what? A woman? A woman done this to him? Yeah, boss, she kept kicking him. Well why didn't he fucking give her a slap? Ah, he tried to drop her, boss, but she was well handy. Done him half a dozen times in the bollocks, and hard. Landed one on me as well. She had a fucking iron punch, boss. So you broke a couple of windows, then you both got your heads kicked in. That what you're telling me? Ah, we didn't think they'd be as game, boss. Thought they were just straights, that's what Anthony told us. We put a note with one of the bricks. A note? Saying what? Did you happen to sign the fucking thing? Dunno, boss. Robbie wrote it. And what happened to the other moped? We had to dump it. Robbie wasn't fit to ride. Where you dump it, Noddy? Oh, we just left it. What, at the office where you was meant to clip these fucking donkeys? Near – we had no choice, boss. You've left a fucking lump of evidence then, haven't you, you ponce? Where d'you get the mopeds? The one you dumped, where d'you get that? Place in Bow, boss. So what security d'you leave? Anthony took us, boss, He sorted it. Ask him. All right, Anthony, what security d'you leave? Look at me, Anthony! Not at the window. You're not going through there unless I fucking throw you. What d'you leave? He left his passport, boss. You what? Can I believe this! Your passport? What in fuck's name were you up to? You what? You dunno? That all you've got to tell me? The shop's got your passport, and come six p.m. they'll be missing a moped. When you go along to collect your passport, all fucking three of you on the other one like the Flying Wallendas, they're gonna be unhappy. Since the moped was involved in a violent attack on professional property, and persons, the police will already have removed it to smell whose arse has been on the seat. They will trace it back to the shop cos it'll have an anti-theft tag. The shop will eagerly assist them with their enquiries, and they will show them the passport log. Oh-ho! says solid fuzz. Tony Friend up to his tricks again. Let's pay him a visit! Which makes me wonder who you are working for nowadays, Friend? You're fucking fitting us all up.

'Meanwhile, Geordie, I got Robbie down on the floor and he ain't looking at all clever. What this fucking bird's done to him – well I thought he'd be on his feet in ten minutes, but he's mullered, face all clammy. And his fucking mother's on the phone. She must have got wind he was involved in something naughty – she's a sniffer, Mandy, nose like that. Have I seen him, or heard from him, blah blah. I tell you something, Geordie, the kid's had it easy. Thirty-six years old now, but he ain't a man. And is that his fault? Whatever he's wanted, he's had. Pool room. Zanotti trainers. Quad bike. And he fucking wrecked that in an afternoon, like the JCB – sole time he tried working for a living. So he wants to bite a man's eye out, he fancies he's entitled to that as well, Geordie. Thinking on it, I dunno if a lot of problems don't go back to that incident.'

'That's past, Mickey.'

'Was he trying to impress me?'

'Long gone, pal. Forget about it.'

'And the other lads – were they trying to impress him when they done Matthews? Or me? Was it me they done it for?'

'The past's a fucking junk shop, knuckle. For tramps and toe-rags. Forget about it.'

'But he's down here now, he's in serious pain, his mother's calling. That ain't past, Geordie – it's fucking happening. And that gets me thinking of other mothers that's been calling, waiting for their sons to come home. And maybe they never made it. And when I see him down there moaning and retching, it occurs to me, we're gummed to each other, like you said, Geordie, but in ways we ignore or don't wanna see. I done that to people, I made people puke and sweat so they'll never stand straight again; now someone's gone and done it to my kin, and I'm not handling it. And it's a woman that's done it, fuck's sake. They're having their comeback now, and it ain't going to stop. We ain't any of us grown up properly. We're fucking out of date by centuries. And Anthony and Noderick, this pair of berks, both of 'em watching me like two postmen with a dog they're shit-scared of – well how is it, Geordie, when you see you're no more than a dog to your fellow man?

428

How is it? Tell me? – I begin to tire of the whole fucking show.'

'Come on, Mickey, hold the line, boy! You telling me, you're so worried what Robbie's mum's gonna make of the fact he's had a hiding, you're turning over a new leaf? How's that gonna save you from her?'

'Geordie, I ain't getting through. If you'd seen her in ITU with him – this paper bitch has virtually torn his bollocks from their mountings, not to mention what she done to his kidney – if you'd seen Mandy with him this evening, you would get the measure of what I'm saying. She's broken, Geordie. Not like when she says she's *in bits*. Broken. Won't be herself again. It's over. With her, with the lot of us.'

'Ain't over, Mickey – never. Life is war, my son – ain't it, Bowls? While you got breath, it ain't over – not unless you want to lose your privileges. Hyatt put you up on a mountain, right at the top, Mickey. Now look at you! Down among the civilians!'

'Leave it, Geordie.'

'You may be licked, Mickey. But I ain't. What about you, Bowls, what d'you make of this?'

'Got to finish what we started, Cap. Long way in now.'

'That's right, Bowls. We got to finish it. Take pride in the job. Besides, it's like crossing a river on foot. Of going back, there certainly ain't no possibility. It's gone on too long. You can't reverse twenty years, Mickey, not when there's bodies all along the line. And if we stay where we are, we drown. Hyatt and this crew, they've gone into fucking overdrive.'

'Yeah, and that's why we need an armistice.'

'You what?'

'An armistice.'

'What you need is a holiday, Mickey.'

[*Silence*.]

'That's it,' Fabiana said. 'There's no more.'

'Where does it get us?'

'Sorry?'

In this circus of violence, where did it get us? If it got us out, then that was no further than I'd been with Karen last night. Both phases ended with the armistice. Had progress been made?

'You're the hero, Fab!'

'Silly!'

'Of course you are. It's you who's turned it. You've got Mulhall's respect. You know what that takes?'

'Who says it's turned, Carlo?'

'Mulhall's persuaded Arnold on the armistice.'

'Evidence?'

'Arnold discussed it with Karen, seriously. And since File Three – the night after, in fact.'

'If you want to be persuaded.'

'Yeah,' Andy told me. 'Maybe you want to be persuaded more than Arnold did!'

'Why would I want that?'

Fab and Andy stood together saying nothing, their meaning plain.

'Well, what is wrong with it – if it's true?'

'For one thing, it aligns you with Mulhall!'

'Is that healthy, Carlo, or goodly?'

'Maybe not. But we've worn them out – thanks to you, Fabiana. And an end to violence, to come back to the point, what is wrong with wanting that?'

Then I rehearsed, tried to, all that Karen had told me of the conversation by the river, her and Mr Arnold; but as I tuned in, lost, recovered, what she'd said, heard his voice in hers, and tried to sift their motives, I stalled. If she wanted an end to it – and no 'if' here – then she'd editorialize, obviously she would. So she was influenced, turned, corrupted, but not to any advantage; just to make it easier for him to kill us both, which F2 had revealed to be a policy of which Karen's report knew nothing – though she might have *suspected*, for Christ's sake, if she hadn't been so set on a peaceful future! But that was supposing that Arnold himself hadn't been influenced by Mulhall in F3. What if he, too, was weary of it all?

'The point is, we didn't hear any more.'

'They didn't say any more.'

'What if Arnold is at cracking point? What if they said no more because he'd been persuaded?'

'What we know, Carlo, is he can't be trusted.'

'That's the broad point, Carlo. And there's a mountain of evidence for it!'

'Yes, of course there is! But should we refuse to trust, when a man finally wants to be trusted? Regardless – listen to me! – of how much he's lied and corrupted.'

'Of course we bloody should, unless we were only born yesterday!'

'But assuming he isn't to be trusted, he's still got the word "armistice" from Mulhall, who surely is licked? That's what F3 is telling us, OK? And if he is using Mulhall's new word, whatever the motive, who's to say that he hasn't already been won over, *to some extent*, by Mulhall?'

'Just saying the word doesn't convert you!'

'Come on, Carlo! How can an old hand like you be so gullible?'

'But we can't spend our lives never trusting. That's cynicism, that is – it's a kind of corruption in itself!'

'Cynicism's an excuse for doing nothing,' Fabiana explained. 'Which isn't where we're at at all, Carlo!'

'Tell him, Fab! Who the hell's George Arnold now?'

'Don't you see, Carlo? Without Mulhall on his wing, Arnold's zilch.'

'Meaning?'

'Meaning we can easily crush Arnold now!'

'By physical means?'

'That's *my* m.o. of choice, Carlo. Andy, Vernon, Meredith, and Barnfield and Marcia Jones, they all reckon there's enough on those files to lock up Arnold, Mulhall and Bowler forever – once the CID's informed.'

'Listen! You're forgetting certain issues – both of you. For one thing, physical means is going to get us all into law trouble – you must know that. Self-defence may be legit; hunting bad people down's a different kettle of fish. Don't make faces – listen! What's more, George Arnold still has two capital villains on his side, fighting fit, and spoiling for it, i.e. Pete and Mick de Lacey – they owe him plenty more than they owe Uncle Mulhall – not to mention Bowler. Chas Bowler's an ex-services assassin, for fuck's sake! Listen to me, not each other! When it comes down to it, so much of Mulhall's violence has been outsourced to George Arnold – I'm thinking William, Nate Nulty, Steve Barnfield, not to mention abductions, threats, bribes – so much of it, you wonder what Mulhall's ever done for himself, at least since he became a bigshot. You are up against a proper concentration of force, if we take on Mr Arnold. Look what he did to Danny Flowers!'

'Yay! Death or glory!'

'Christ, Fab! Death, severe injury, or jail, these are the options, if we take them on. I'm appealing to you as a woman!'

'As what?'

'As a woman! Andy, it's not fucking funny! End this nonsense! It's a woman's power to end violence.'

'Since when, Carlo? Mulhall said we're up with the blokes now in dishing it out!' Fabiana did some terrifying things with her fists and elbows. Andy stood well back.

'I know! And he was right. But, do you just want to take the place of the blokes, become as bad as we've always been? Or—'

'Or turn the other cheek, Carlo? That what you're asking?'

'Even when Arnold planned to murder you and Karen in a cave?'

'After pretending to make friends with you at a café?'

'After all that, you are prepared to meet him halfway, in this "armistice"?'

'What sort of man are you?'

They watched me.

'I don't know. – But I believe in the rule of law.'

'So we pass the files to the CID?' Eager again.

'This is the other thing you're forgetting. George Arnold's been corrupting and turning people for a long time. The service has been penetrated by his influence. If the files are presented to straight cops, there's an excellent chance that something will happen to them in the process of preparing reports for internal investigation. And that's only the beginning of the problem with the files.'

Unmatily, they watched me.

'Only the beginning. The rules about secret recordings are tight as hell, when their use in a criminal court's proposed. More likely than not, the use of these files as evidence would be ruled inadmissible by a judge. That's the law.'

'And you like it like that, Carlo!'

'He's glad we can't do anything!'

From me, and my stupid armistice, Fabiana turned away. Hot-faced, I fiddled with the DJ profile. It was out of date now anyway. They couldn't wait to see the back of me.

CHAPTER 48

REASONS FOR VISITING RAY Vernon had changed again: it was miracles I now wanted to talk over with him – hoping DJ wouldn't appear. But on the way to the rectory, I had a call from Laura, who was with Edward at the Premier Inn on Duns Road. They were up for the Olympics – she'd got tickets for his birthday (which I hadn't forgotten). But they'd come to London a bit earlier than planned.

Did they want me to come over?

That was up to me – wasn't why they'd come earlier.

So I asked why they had, as she meant me to, and she said there'd been something worrying them in Devon. Knowing Laura's habit of understatement, I didn't like this at all, and when she said she thought their house was being staked out, I got the flash-freeze round the heart. There'd been a shaven-headed man parked across the road, and she saw him speak on his phone when she left or came home, though when she looked from upstairs, he was just sitting in his car. Sometimes he walked as far as the park, smoking; soon came back. She'd seen him eat a takeaway, resting the tray on the car roof, like he'd never leave the spot. Did I know anything about this?

I told her I'd sort it.

What did I mean?

Look, did she want me to come round to the hotel?

There was silence while she consulted with our son. It was OK. They were just going out for a pizza now. Maybe later, if I wasn't busy?

I told her to let me know; in the meantime, I'd sort it.

Just like that?

No, it'd take some effort – but I would.

She thanked me, and I was ashamed.

At home, I found Karen packing. She'd bought tickets for Narixa. Our flight was from City, 7 a.m. She moved about quickly, white and silent.

I tried to reckon with the Laura situation. Coming out of the blue, it made settlement critical. Was there nowhere the intimidation didn't reach? I couldn't run now; couldn't mention Laura either, not at this point. Yet if their power was everywhere, what difference where we went?

'What about the armistice?'

'Leave it to me, Carlo.'

'But I promised.'

'You promised we'd go back.'

I mailed a leave form to Andy, and went out for a walk.

*

HE KEPT A SPY at City, so he'd know. Fuck him. Karen wore a straw hat, like that afternoon on the *Marco*. We had a drink in the bar, a couple on the plane. 8 a.m. I wanted to tell her of certain miracles, how she'd saved our lives, then mine, but rehearsing F2, I couldn't. They depended on his wickedness.

Could I take her to the caves, tomorrow or Thursday – like I'd promised?

Of course, sweetheart.

We clinked our plastic glasses.

I asked her again about the armistice.

What about it?

Wouldn't all of us have to be there?

Looking out at bright clouds, she touched my hand.

*

OUR ROOM WASN'T MADE up, so we sat in the garden. The trees were bulbous, stony. Their boughs spread like fighting fingers, and we thought the ends had faces: crowned devil, baby devil, horseshoe bat.

How'd she managed to get flights, and book the Parador, at such short notice?

Oh, her and Lolly'd put a shift in, Saturday night.

I loved her.

We unpacked and lay down, got up and changed. Outside, the mountains shimmered like tarmac. 37 °C. Around two o'clock, we had lunch at Abril's. Karen's appetite didn't seem much better than last time, though she put some wine away. There was the table where George Arnold had sat. I tried not to think of Laura and Edward. After, we went to the terrace where Joe Pordio led us, where I promised we'd come back. An old man fastened mesh on a wooden frame; sun flashed on the waves below. We sat by the black-and-tan cannon. From a shelter open on both sides, two men watched us. One wore a cavalry hat, and necklace with ornamental fangs, the other a yellow vest. I told them to fuck off. Showing their teeth, they came on in vagrant ballet. Karen held my arm. They passed away.

She held my arm on the way down to the long beach. No thought of swimming. We came right to the platform rock where the girl had posed in white, and as the beach swerved, saw a concrete block eaten away, large-bore pipe running into the sea, which must be the outfall. Families lolled, kids shrieked and ran. Over rocks, we came to a deep cove, where Rhinemaidens glided with long oars. In the shade of a blue yacht, a long man lay in a dinghy of steel. From a forty-foot drop, boys jumped into the sea. Quietly, we watched them. Emerging from a V at the water's edge, they climbed back shining to the jump point; most of them Edward's age. A podgy lad hung back, checking his phone. Leaping again, they egged him on. When he checked the drop, I prayed for him.

In the hard heat, we sat back like lubbers. Karen's lime-green parasol matched her nails. Bright deposits of salt lay in dips in the rock. From the cliff behind, a rattling shower, grey thing thudding between us. Karen screamed. What might have been a bird, was a rat. We sprang up as it ran, and the long man looked my way. That was Mulhall.

I took her for sangria at Charo's. The *camarera* didn't remember us, the bearded barman looked like he could. On the rolling news, the International Red Cross declared a civil war in Syria. Scene of shelling, hospital . . . *They sat here one night drinking beer and Bushwackers. Señora showing her leg (she wore a Chinese dress).* Guasónos los dos. *On the TV, Lazio–Tottenham, anti-Jew Palestine banners* . . . Fighting continued in Damascus. Broken wall, machine-gun post. Who the hell was fighting who? The barman shook his head and mentioned Islamists. They'd grow from this. Rebels, beards, bullet-belts; coast road to Aleppo, jeep evading check-points.

Passing Lola's, I saw her stub a cig out quick and make to enter, so I called her name, and she turned to us: '*Qué tal? Aquí otra vez?*'

I nodded.

'*Todo bien?*' Knowing it wasn't. 'Is very busy just now.' She wiped her forehead. 'By nine, I have you a table.'

'That's OK, Lola. Karen's not feeling so good.'

'*Ay, chica!*' Cuddling Karen.

I couldn't see the main restaurant, but there were plenty of tables on the terrace, as I'd noted as we came up the hill. She was saving us from someone. '*Hasta luego*, Lola!'

We wandered. At eight, we found a *plaza* as the mountains grew pink. There was a church, upper section like a giant ivory comb, though the teeth were set in a ridge, forming nine arches, which I counted and counted. The air moved with bats and swallows. At our wedding, Karen wore a comb like that. I reminded her. Guts burning, she kissed my ear. I left her on a little wall, and went to the *farmacia*, looking back to check her in her green summer dress. As I returned with omeprazole, she was crossing herself. I fancied Bowler passed behind her in the twilight.

We moved over to a café. For her sake, I had to settle this. How, I didn't know. Were we dealing with crime, or metaphysics? This whole business was subject to weird arrangement, principals pulled this way and that by something darker than gravity. The town itself appeared to have grown. We shared a long, dripping class of Cruzcampo; and another. The grave-eyed *camareras* were heavily tattooed. I ate a dish of spaghetti, with raw garlic sauce, watching the *plaza*, where kids of tourists played chase around a fountain. Karen stiffened, clutched my arm: 'They're here!'

White suit glowing in the dusk, Morgan was among the kids, amusing them with walks. I felt a light hand on my shoulder: there was Turbo in a Saint Laurent shirt of pale-blue palms, regarding us courteously.

Calling something in Latin, Morgan came over. We made space.

CHAPTER 49

FOR A WHILE, HE confounded the *camareras* with requests for Pramnian wine. Fingers interlaced, Turbo slowly made churches. 'Either our appearance is ordained by augury,' declared Morgan at last, 'or we had a heads-up.'

'You're here now, our Fabian,' Karen said.

'That's right, my dear. For the last issue, or *outrance*. With you both, and at your side.'

I told them I'd sighted Mulhall.

'Your business is unfinished, Mr Hyatt. Mine as well. And the business of others. Remember Harry Hopkins. He saw it through to the end, with no stomach to speak of.' Morgan's dead eye lay kind upon me.

We came out of the *plaza* and on to the Calle Carreta, Morgan and Turbo beside us. Did they know I should have died here? On the narrow pavement, Karen held my arm between the tiled house-fronts. Turbo and Morgan marched in the road. At the Parador, they took their leave.

In our room, we shared a beaker of Torres 10, from a bottle we'd picked up at Málaga, and had some talk of the armistice – like it was still on the table. We stood on the balcony, heard the sea beyond the garden. Yeah. Could go either way. All gathering here. The trees were demonic, pathetic. I told her of the raid on the office, Fabiana's treatment of Robbie Woods. Knowing, would Morgan still want eye for eye? Atop the bed, we lay in the heat.

If nothing had to finish, Karen heaped beside me would be our eternity, doors locked against the forces. But we'd need to let Laura in the ark, and my son; then Hanley, Donna Juan, Sibyl Grove, and so our whole community, since not to was betrayal, desertion; so conflict would return, for associations are no more easily satisfied than the natural man, their potential force many times stronger, and more restless. Unless we could all of us open our hearts to Father Raymond; but the lawyer, the historian, the philosopher, would argue with the priest . . .

Around 5 a.m., I heard shouts from the garden. Karen's dreams stunk of garlic.

We had breakfast on a terrace. In checked dress and flip-flops, Karen tried to eat a persimmon, yellow fragments piling on her plate. She wore the necklace I'd bought her.

Let's go, darling.

There was a market in the *plaza*. Like a body, cheese and ham soiled the air. Karen held a hankie to her mouth. Among stalls of soaps, pebble ornaments and baskets, Morgan and Turbo lifted up carved birds. By the church, a drum-and-pipe band played; and listening, I felt brave, as if the world were cinema. A tram jangled past, I took Karen's hand, we ran and made the footplate, Turbo and Morgan following. So we were all aboard, and as we passed the final stalls, we checked a shaven-headed peasant, squat, bulked out, beside a man on crutches.

Horn blowing as locals waved from gardens, past fields where donkeys rummaged, and a horse drank from a long box, we rolled down to the sea. Tourists crammed the carriages, stood like bandits on the footplates. A derelict building was graffitied '*España es ruina*', storeys pockmarked.

At the long beach, a party was kicking off, big screens for the Olympics. As we sat on the wall with cans, the crowd spat forth a *chica* in checked dress and flip-flops. Fucking hell . . .

'Hiya, Carl!' trilled Donna Juan. 'Wheear 'ast tha bin? Finished t'profile?'

'He never finishes owt, this one,' Karen told her.

They had some trans-Pennine banter. I kept my eyes on the crowd, heard DJ say, 'He were allus good as gold, like totally,' and Karen leaned against me. It wouldn't go off; we'd left that behind. I asked DJ why he'd come. Same reason we all had, and he looked down the way; by a drinks stall, Morgan and Turbo were now with Hanley. I made to get down off the wall, but Donna Juan and Karen asked me to stay with them a while, making eyes and pouting; when I checked, Hanley had his back to me. Then the party was starting.

Over the opening ceremony, an MC and sound system played. People were dancing on the sand now, Morgan joining in, Turbo as well, and Donna Juan, who threw his dress away to reveal shorts that were glued to his arse, and a blood-red vest. I sat holding Karen's hand. Morgan was causing a stir with his moves, younger people walking behind him trying to do the same. I recognized the music: 'Forever' by John B (Hard Mix) – synth generator, silvery female vocal: 'Forever, when I'm close to you . . . Show me the way.' Now Morgan and Turbo were speed-sparring, Turbo blocking blows from the Welshman, so everyone tried that as well. Then it was Taffy, 'I Love My Radio', Donna Juan in charge, and they followed him.

Standing apart, Hanley smoked and watched dancing doctors and Victorians, on one of the big screens. 'Put me in a taxi, darling,' Karen said. 'Go and talk to Victor. Go on! I fancy a lie-down.' I told her no way, but she smiled like that time in The Old Placentia, and took my hand. There was a rank across the road behind the wall. We had some sweet talk, made plans for tomorrow. She'd be safer away from what was brewing.

Hanley hugged me and hung on, in his white shirt and cravat, calling me *paisano* like old times. Claire Sykes had gone to the rectory when they'd left on Sunday. Ray Vernon was looking after her. Meanwhile he'd been reading George Michael on neo-Nazis and militant Islam. I'd put him on to this axis. Remember? Daniel Craig and Elizabeth II descended from a helicopter on wires. The Chinese had grown: blazered giants. By the wall, commotion.

A silver-haired figure sat on the sand, hands behind like a baby. People stood or crouched about him, paramedics worked their way through. We went over, and George Arnold shook his head: 'Where's the missus? Can't settle it without her.' Parameds trying to silence him; applying a defibrillator. 'Three-way bypass and I'll deal with you.' As they bore him to the ambulance, he tautened his chin, signalling left-handed. When I followed the sign, I saw a bearded figure. DJ smashed a bottle on the wall, and the figure slipped into darkness. Hanley spat. Before the ambulance made off, we'd returned to the party.

*

AT DAYLIGHT, WE SHAMBLED across the port, calling, singing, cracking jokes. A rag-tag bunch, but there was something to be done. That called us on; and Turbo as always was springy, straight-backed. We passed the tram-head where carriages stood empty, silent restaurants, white-walled houses. At a tiny play park, steps led to a wood of anti-septic pines. We began to move with purpose, among shaded paths, till two birds broke from the trees and soared. Turbo called to Morgan. In a clearing below, as if the mews had been brought and rolled, was a circular pebbly hut, with slits for windows.

'On the one, Turbs! Let's go!' So we flew down to the entrance.

'*Ecce* pilgarlicks!' shouted Morgan. Within was crouched Mick de Lacey, wearing shorts and the sandals of an Englishman on holiday. A finch-nosed figure stood over him, and his jeans were undone so de Lacey could attend to a dressing he wore. They'd been sleeping rough. De Lacey's feet were filthy; cans, milk cartons and a doughnut tray littered the floor.

'What shall we do, Mr Hyatt? Your call!'

Mick de Lacey looked at Robbie Woods and shrugged. His peasant eyes were stupid; where was their violence now? I remembered the thriller Frankie Sly once showed me. 'We've run them down,' I told my side. 'L Troop are finished.'

Morgan grinned.

'A woman got there before you. Let 'em be.'

CHAPTER 50

BEHIND ME, I HEARD laughter. That was all. Then a taxi back to the Parador. With a lightness of heart that was unfamiliar, I thought to find Karen on the terrace, eating breakfast with more appetite, or lying in bed reading, or waiting for me on the balcony. As I passed, the receptionist called, '*La señora ha salido!*'

'She's left?'

'She has gone, *señor.*'

'Checked out?'

'She has gone out, *señor!*'

'Where has she?' When panic's genuine, justified, what the fuck do you call it?

'*No sé, señor.*'

'What?' Her phone went straight to voicemail.

His colleague turned from a fax machine: 'The *señora* has gone to the caves.'

The driver who brought me from the wood was smoking in the sun. We were out of there. On his radio, 'Thank You for Being a Friend'. Phone to voicemail.

I stood below terraces and pines. A coach was departing. Tried to call her. No signal. Outside a restaurant with big windows, a *camarero* lounged in shade. I looked back at the coach. Let her be on it! We could row about missing each other. From the office, a man kept an eye on me; behind him, a woman moved around.

Next Tour 12 p.m.: four languages. Through the glass, the man ducked his hand like a leg-spinner. I didn't want a tour. Couldn't ask if he'd seen my wife. The woman came over. I showed my press card: '*Por* UNESCO!' They waved me over to another building, where men with ID ribbons showed me down.

A bare-rock passage had me bent like a miner, but the air was cool. Coming now to a walkway with a handrail beneath which – Jesus Christ! – was the Devil's own cathedral. Like the organ pipes had melted, petrified and bulged . . . Lord, such heights, and shapes and falls! On along the top, and here a chamber gaped, then down to a place where a cascade hung, white-whiskered. And up into mountains solo, indoor peaks beneath a fungal vault; past a mighty court, where faces showed from frozen-spilling rock: Assyrian kings in gashed-thumb hats, Malay goddesses, temple demons, buzzards, something like an ancient rocket. Stalactites lettuce green, like the stony trees of the Parador. Above, a giant's spear, racked for eternity; then I was upside down, a ceiling fly, and might drop and be run through, before it ever fell. Hurrying on, I turned to look again.

Darling, where are you?

A chopped-cone chamber like the Wall of Death, *La Sala de los Fantasmas*: here the limestone was numerously haunted, watchers on grey banks, patriarchs, goblins, those you've heard named, couched among them an old woman: so the game should never end, till these figures outsat the player of flesh.

I called Karen's name. At the echo, I saw movement, grey form crawling, down, across; watched, and watched it roll, and drop. I heard its end.

She'd made it to a ramp.

'I did the bastard first, Carlo!'

I told her hush, and held her.

'You always take so long, Carlo!'

'We'll get you out, baby!' The flip-flop fell from her little foot. I began to howl.

'Be peaceful now. Stop skriking . . .'

REFLECTING ON ALL THIS strained my powers; like it had no home in thought. In Hobbes, I found the Seventh Law of Nature: when revenge is the issue, men shouldn't be troubling themselves with past evil, only with the good to follow. Revenge without good intent is vainglory and cruelty.

Had our team been up to something good – or cruel and vain-glorious? Did we break a law of nature? Did we get that far?

What d'you think?

The Eighth Law of Nature prohibits men from showing hatred or contempt for another, since this *will* lead other men to risk their lives for revenge.

So L Troop – and Woods – broke the Eighth Law . . . Should the Eighth not come before the Seventh?

Another thing he says is that 'timely resolution', or determination, of what a man is to do, is honourable, because it shows contempt of small difficulties or dangers; but when a man weighs up an act, then decides not to do it, because of small difficulties, etc., he is dishonour-able, and pusillanimous.

Nasty words – hard words.

Were we in the end pusillanimous, because we decided not to kill? My call. They laughed when I made it.

Yet he talks always of *men*.

And like I told Morgan by that hut of stone, and witnessed in the caves of Narixa, Fabiana and my wife showed timely resolution; so they were honourable, weren't they – not cruel or vainglorious?

But was revenge the issue, when they maimed the Sixth Man, broke Mulhall's will, took care of Pete de Lacey?

What do you make of it?

Late November I saw Hanley in The Tavern. He talked about *The Spanish Tragedy*, he talked about *Hamlet*, he talked about a play where the women kill in secret. Your old plays made revenge a better home.

*

AT THE SOLSTICE CAME a postcard from McMurdo Sound, 1,200 mile south of Punta Arenas. Donna Juan had made the Dry Valleys . . . Six point five below, no snowflakes . . . Harder than gods, the ventifacts . . . Pond named for him, second saltiest on earth – like the council flytipped spoogee from all the boogs of London . . . Bleeding Norah!

We laughed ourselves daft for our geographer, his katabatic winds and dagger light. It's a fierce world, wherever you tread, though who's to say it's worse than it has been? You may as well laugh, as brood or weep, or fiddle on your phones for a better one.

AUTHOR'S NOTE

THE CHARACTERS AND EVENTS presented in this book are imaginary. What is their source? Here is one answer. In the British 70s, 80s, 90s, race aggro of every degree was more common than now. The character we've named Víctor Hanley is expert in this; he has experienced it himself, the treatment. The treatment can, as they say, 'define' you; Hanley tries to overcome this by talking and dressing finely, by style.

You can also overcome the treatment by writing about it, with style – and energy. That is, perhaps, the essence of this book. Style is not disguise, it is imaginative transformation, even sorcery. It turns people, actions, into other forms, even calls them into being; then the reader is interested neither in what was there before, nor whether anything was there at all, only in what she/he is seeing, hearing, feeling now.

At its energetic optimum, style works like the katabatic winds that fascinate the rent-boy Donna Juan; he too experienced a version of the treatment when told that he and his kind should be gassed. Blasted by such winds, the fact-world that is the profession of our narrator, Hyatt, turns into unfamiliar, alarming, sometimes humorous shapes: the assorted devils, heroes and in-between folk of the present work. They do not occupy a newspaper-world.

To employ a temperate image, the identifying of characters with actual people is like picking flowers from a bank or patch that is planted to grow wild. The same goes for their actions. What you have in your hand, you have torn from its world.

The treatment is also a programme of revenge. I hope the book persuades you that revenge is a bad option. Self-defence is another matter. The women of the book show how this is so.

ACKNOWLEDGEMENTS

My special thanks to Anne Witchard, Paul French, and Jon Riley. And to: Nick de Somogyi; Georgina Difford; Jasmine Palmer; Milly Reid; Simon Heilbron; Ben McKay; Seki P. Lynch; Min Wild; Paul Bernhardt; Jim Webb; Sarah Brendlor; Dave Nath; Azra Nath; Paul Nath; Tony Nayager; Roy Harper; all my pals at the University of Westminster; Jack Sims; Francesca Bonafede; Gwen Davies; Paul Simon; Eric Akoto; Ian Daley and Isabel Galán; Lorna Tracy; Nick Groom; Paul Hendon; and Mark E. Smith (1957–2018).